The Prelude to

C000240866

Reimar Breaking

Jonathan Rivalland

Elsewhen Press

Reimar Breaking
First published in Great Britain by Elsewhen Press, 2016
An imprint of Alnpete Limited

Elsewhen Press, PO Box 757, Dartford, Kent DA2 7TQ
www.elsewhen.co.uk

British Library Cataloguing in Publication Data.
A catalogue record for this book is available from the British Library.
ISBN 978-1-911409-00-7 Print edition
ISBN 978-1-911409-10-6 eBook edition

Printed and bound by CPI Group (UK) Ltd, Croydon, CR0 4YY

Reimar Breaking

For Emily

Table of contents

Dramatis personae

The Reimaran Royal Family

Abarron du Tealdan (His Noble Majesty Abarron du Tealdan, King of Reimar, Marshall of the Royal Guard) [Aba-rron doo Teel-dan]
Fede du Tealdan (Her Noble Majesty Fede du Tealdan, Queen of Reimar) [Feh-deh doo Teel-dan]
Ramiros du Tealdan (His Highness Ramiros du Tealdan, Prince of Reimar), son of King Abarron and Queen Fede [Ram-ear-os doo Teel-dan]
Siera du Tealdan (Her Highness, Captain Siera du Tealdan, Princess of Reimar, defender of the realm), daughter of King Abarron and Queen Fede [See-era doo Teel-dan]

The Royal Councillors

Modesto du Greco, Duke of Felde
Gaspar du Covas, Duke of Espinoza
Andrayzn du Tilmost, Duke of Gerva
Silvio du Firenze, Duke of Sapara
Nicodemo du Singara, Duke of Guerda
Silvio du Donati, Duke of San Seras
Zaballa du Arista, Duke of Gavar
Federica du Lucan, Duke of Calinia
Andrea du Tealdan, Duke of Fide
Lycea du Tilmost, Court Mage
Gustavo Espinoza, Luminary Academy Headmaster
Balendin Serrano, Coach and Stevedore Guild representative
Berezi De Alencar, Merchants and Lenders Guild representative

The Reimaran Suranic Church:

Livio du Nascimbeni, Grand Warden of the Reimaran Suranic Church

Reimaran Judges:

Elisa Baglio, Andoni Ybarra, Oihana Zuñiga, Baltasar Noguerra, Chiara Stabile

The Reimaran Royal Guard: Fourth Regiment

Siera du Tealdan, Captain [See-era doo Teel-dan]
Tomasso Rossi, Staff Sergeant [Toe-mass-oh Ro-sea]

Whitecaps

Bernat du Rodruigez, protecting King Abarron and Queen Fede
Agurtzane du Firenze, protecting King Abarron and Queen Fede
Hirune Faenius, protecting Prince Ramiros
Maria Ibarra, protecting Prince Ramiros
Viscount Clara Mercer, protecting Princess Siera
Quintus Castell, protecting Princess Siera

1st Company

Ermanno Gartzia, Lieutenant [Err-man-no Ga't-zee-ya]
Silvio du Cipriani, Staff Sergeant
Field Sergeants:
Giovanni Marino, Carmine Brunetti, Pacifica Sastre,
Vincenzo di Vitis, Feliciano Airaldi, Nico Labriola,
Eugenio Passerini.

2nd Company

Adalberto du Gallo, Lieutenant [Adal-bert-oh doo Gah-low]
Cecilia Perez, Staff Sergeant
Field Sergeants:
Cristóbal du Alescio, Pepito Casales, Kemen Elizondo,
Primo Vivas, Jessenia Cabrera, Ramiro Santos, Silvia Abana.

3rd Company

Gretchen Ailbhe, Lieutenant [Gret-chin Al-va]
Domenico Arnoni, Staff Sergeant
Field Sergeants:
Giacinta Caivano, Celio Espinoza, Paz Santiago, Mario Corvi, Erasmo
Marino.

Sky's Wrath

Terciero du Valtiera, Commodore [Terr-Sea-Erro doo Val-tea-erra]
Assistants:
Igon Tapia, Pepita Aldana, Eneko Abaroa, Carmina Muraro.

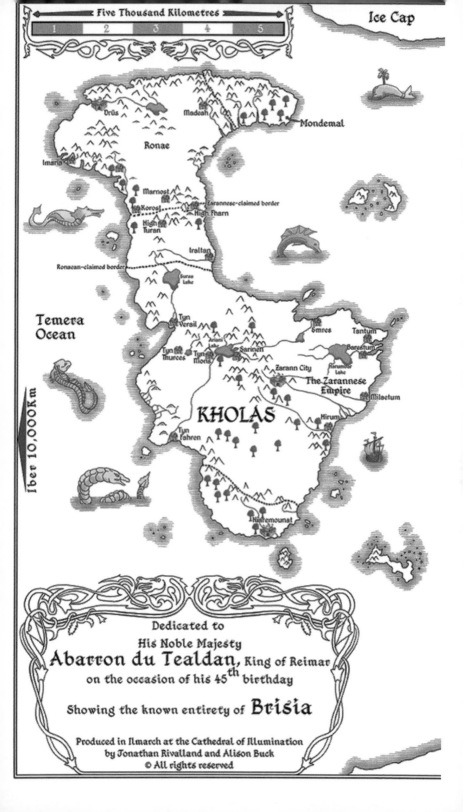

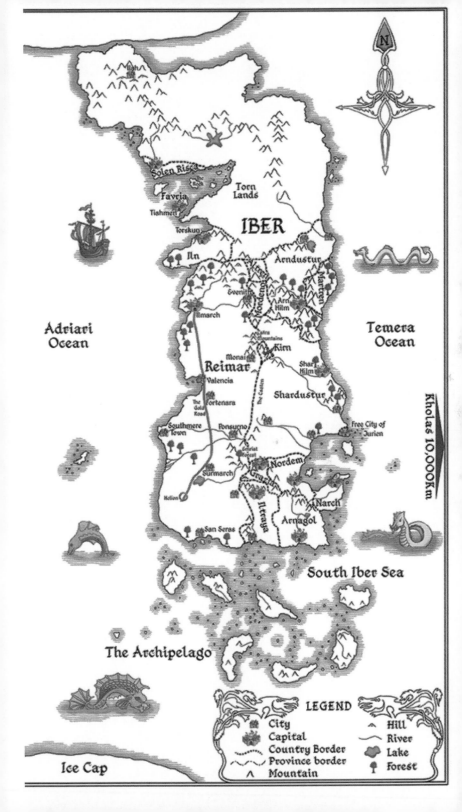

Prologue: The Proving Sea

6th Teurnot, 1279 CE, 708 RG

The sea swelled and the rain drove on, with that rich salt-spray smell that only the deep ocean brings. Among this vast expanse of blue, the real storm came not from the heavens, but from the two ships currently drawing alongside one another in the Iberan Archipelago Sea.

Commodore Paulo de Luca stood firm on the aftcastle of the *Reimar's Vigilance*, as the waves rocked the ship against its attacker, the Archipelagan pirate vessel *Soaring Dragon*. He raised his hands to keep the rain out of his eyes, and cried out:

"Archers on the quarterdeck, kill them as they cross! For Reimar, for the honour of the Third, the *Vigilance* cannot fall into Archipelagan hands!"

The rain made bowstrings less reliable, so as the *Dragon* closed with his ship and the first boarding lines were thrown, Paulo counted on short-range shots picking off attackers.

"Here they come! Loose!" he shouted.

The first pirate to dare the narrow gap between the ships was a lanky Archipelagan who was cut down as soon as he leapt from his ship, falling between the *Vigilance* and the *Dragon*, either to drown or be crushed as the two ships groaned and slammed against each other in the heaving waves. Soldiers and pirates alike roared and blood spattered across the deck. Although the Reimarans tried to cut the boarding lines, more came rapidly across from the *Dragon*, and pirates came after them.

Paulo cursed as he watched his men try to fend off the pirates. His marines were at two-thirds their normal troop complement due to ridiculous paperwork errors, and this attack came at an ill time. Without aid, he feared, they would eventually be overwhelmed. He gripped the binnacle and looked to see his first mate muttering through clenched teeth as he spun the wheel back and forth, to make it harder for the pirates to cross.

Around Paulo, archers kept putting arrows to strings. Irena Silvio, his second lieutenant, called out orders: "Volley, loose! Notch arrows again! Volley, loose!" Arrows streaked towards the swarms of pirates on the *Dragon* – but the driving rain made shots hard and even waxed bowstrings were unreliable. Few pirates fell to arrows, but at least the pirates' archers – who apparently had no formation – fared even worse, and never loosed a whole volley.

Paulo turned to his left, where the ship's sorcerer stood fiddling with some arcane trinket.

"Imanol, what word from the Admiralty?" said Paulo.

Imanol squinted and massaged his temples.

"Just a moment, Sir... I've got their message now – oh, Sir! It's Captain Siera's skyship!"

Paulo grinned, his eyes brightening. "You mean with those new drop-lines! We'll have this one yet, Imanol! No need for messages now, make sure we don't get some little shit trying to set us on fire."

"Impossible, Sir, there's no way the Archipelagans have a sorcerer who can manipulate fire in this rain."

"Well, as it works for us, so it works against us. I'd be a happier man if I could see pirates leaping into the sea to save their hides from being cooked alive!" said Paulo with a chuckle.

Paulo's grin faded when he was sure his subordinates weren't looking. He'd heard about Siera's new drop-lines, but had no idea if they actually worked. He tried not to think of soldiers dropping onto his deck like pats of butter, rather than coming to his ship's rescue.

On the gangway, the situation remained grim. The Reimaran soldiers had been forced to give ground towards the quarterdeck and forecastle before a mob of blond Archipelagan heads, and already a few enterprising pirates had tried the main hatch, only to find it barred.

Paulo leaned in towards Irena. "Silvio, drop bows and draw your blades. It's face to face now!"

"Archers, drop bows! Draw blades! Give them Reimaran

steel!" Irena shouted.

The last of Paulo's troops retreated up to the quarterdeck, or were cut down trying desperately to reach it, and Paulo drew his own blade as the Archipelagans swarmed towards them. As the first pirate placed a foot on the stairs to the quarterdeck a rope fell behind him, seemingly from thin air, and one of his fellows glanced at it in surprise. An instant later, a tall woman in the blue and black uniform of the Fourth Regiment slammed onto the deck, and as she stood up she smashed her buckler into the gawking face of a nearby pirate.

"Every blondie but me dies!" she roared, and with a short-bearded axe laid into the pirates around her, the wide claymore on her back impractical for the crowded deck. More ropes and more boots followed and, in mere seconds, fresh Reimaran troops were dropping down right amongst the shocked pirates. Yells and war cries from the forecastle followed, and Paulo felt his despair completely fade. He'd not suffer the indignity of losing his ship today, and he'd be seeing a great number of pirates die.

He grinned again.

The Archipelagans had neither seen nor heard of anyone simply dropping down from a skyship before, and having sighted only the *Vigilance* they had committed all of their number to boarding. When the Fourth Regiment's troops came down among them, the boarding turned into a quick and ugly slaughter for the Archipelagans. Even those who tried to flee back to the *Soaring Dragon* found that troops had dropped down there as well. Some simply jumped into the sea to escape the noose that they faced if captured alive.

There were few prisoners.

A surly rain still fell as Paulo laughed wearily, wiping at his forehead. "Imanol, send a message to the Admiralty thanking them for their assistance in co-ordinating this. Blondies might have had our guts if not for those reinforcements."

Imanol nodded. "I'll let them know, Sir, except for the part about the guts."

Paulo smirked. "You're a funny man, Imanol. Funny man. Silvio, have a runner fetch the Cantor and get the dead properly sea-buried."

Irena saluted, fist over her heart. "All the dead, Sir?"

Paulo squinted. "Eh, what? Of course not, only ours. Throw the Archipelagans to the fish."

"Yes Sir," said Silvio as she walked away, already calling out orders.

"Message delivered, Sir," said Imanol, pinching the bridge of his nose. "Also…" he gestured to the main deck.

"Hmm? Oh, I almost forgot – of course she'd come down. Pity I'm not in my dress uniform, eh?" said Paulo over his shoulder as he quickly walked down the steps onto the deck and towards the brown-haired woman in the uniform of the Reimaran Royal Guard. Paulo noted the two silver bars on her shoulder denoting her captain's rank: the leader of the Fourth Regiment, Siera du Tealdan. He slowed as she turned to speak with one of her soldiers – no, officer; single silver bar on the shoulders. It was the blonde woman who had dropped down from the skyship first. Paulo mentally blanched at the idea of leading an attack from the front, but he wouldn't be caught telling another officer how to command their subordinates so he put it out of his mind.

"Captain Siera! I wish I could welcome you more warmly, but we suffered a minor incident, as you can see." Paulo saluted as Siera du Tealdan turned to look at him, her stern brown eyes changing brightly to match her smile. "Commodore de Luca! Glad we could arrive in time."

Siera turned back to the lieutenant she had been talking to before Paulo arrived.

"As you were, Lieutenant Ailbhe."

Siera turned back to Paulo. "How have your crew fared?"

"We've normally a complement of fifty marines, but sailed with thirty-six, lost eighteen in this battle… but with a skeleton crew on both ships, we can get both the *Reimar's Vigilance* and the *Soaring Dragon* back to port in Surmarch." Paulo rubbed his hands together. "And, well, I imagine the Admiralty will put the *Dragon* to good use, after a new coat of paint and a change of name." Paulo looked around the deck, biting his lip. "And it could have been worse, it could have been Old Salt-Sword himself come to kill us all, if he is still alive. And I see that your new drop-lines work! A marvel of enchanting, however it's done."

Siera smiled. "The mages assured me that the work was very simple, but it took months to test and ensure they all worked properly."

Paulo nodded firmly. "Of course you had them rigorously tested before using them. Hah, they'd be too risky otherwise, wouldn't they?"

Siera nodded. "They were tested repeatedly. Still, this was their first field trial. I consider it an excellent success."

Paulo's expression momentarily froze. "Well then... it is... is excellent that they worked just as planned, and your reinforcements were deployed perfectly."

Siera nodded. "All is well at the quit of the matter." Siera turned and nodded to a staff sergeant who walked up next to her, saluted in response and walked back to the nearest drop-line. "We will have to head back ourselves after this, although we can certainly escort you back to the harbour."

"Greatly appreciated, especially after this attack. Did you take any losses, Captain?" said Paulo.

"No dead, seven injured, but we'd had to offload some sailors to get the *Black Witch* back to port; a pirate vessel which we raided earlier after it had attacked a small town... hrm... I've forgotten the name."

"Richeiu? Or La Chayne?"

"La Chayne, yes. Either way, we only caught up with them because they were weighed down with stolen goods, and they had managed to overcome the garrison since many of the soldiers had gone down with food poisoning. And now, here you are, having been attacked when your troop complement is low..."

Paulo's brows furrowed. "Well, there's no way that pirates could know our patrol routes, or have a spy in the garrison. The Admiralty changes the patrol routes for that exact reason, and I've heard nothing of any orders being intercepted or stolen. And certainly, no Reimaran would ever stoop to treachery."

"I've no doubt as to the Admiralty's competency, but these attacks are too well timed to be a coincidence. I suspect that, somehow, they have a well-placed informant."

"Well, that's easily remedied." Paulo smirked. "Arrest every blondie or any other foreigner we can find. No true Reimaran would ever sell secrets to the Archipelagans."

Siera shook her head. "It is not so simple; one of my Lieutenants is Archipelagan. More and more these days, you find them abroad, wanting a world beyond the isles. And sooner or later, some people of any nation can be swayed with money and soothing lies… either way, I'll have this brought up with the Admiralty."

Paulo scratched his beard. "Yes, well… while I agree, Captain… the admirals will not take well to anyone from the army suggesting that their patrol routes have been leaked, or that they have a spy among them."

"This is true… I will try to raise it indirectly, it will rankle less if it comes from General du Tilmost instead. And if they've infiltrated a garrison, then it is probably not just the Admiralty, either." Siera sighed. "Either way, you should stay on your guard. We cannot expect the Archipelagans to attack largely merchant shipping as they have before, I fear."

"Oh, I won't. Next time we'll have a full complement of welcoming steel for any scum that tries to board us." Paulo grinned.

Siera gave a quick smile to that. "And to speak of further practicalities, even if macabre, we might also be able to have the dead taken onboard the *Wrath*. Your marines can get a proper funereal pyre in San Seras."

Paulo thought for a moment, then shook his head. "I'd rather not have any… hoisting going on." Paulo leaned in towards Siera. "And the bodies will stink up all too soon. Looks bad before the common soldiery, and marines and sailors both know they might find their rest in the deep. Besides, the church's final word is that Riest judges us all, pyre or not."

Siera nodded. "I felt it best to offer. A good spread to you, Commodore. Signal if you need any assistance, else we will fly a quiet escort until you are in sight of San Seras' harbour."

Paulo saluted, and Siera turned away to have the drop-line hoist her back to the *Sky's Wrath*.

Chapter 1: The Glory of the Kingdom

8th Teurnot

Five hundred metres in the air, the *Sky's Wrath* sailed on, two days after escorting the *Reimar's Vigilance* back to San Seras. Its next destination was Ilmarch, the capital of Reimar. As the ship soared through the air, its deck gently creaking, a brown-haired and brown-eyed woman stood at the prow: Her Highness, Captain Siera du Tealdan, watching as the land rolled out beneath her.

Only a few months of being on the Wrath, Siera thought to herself, *and already the extraordinary views have become boring.*

From sailing ship to skyship, the basic design had not changed vastly even through decades of work. The *Sky's Wrath*, though, was the pinnacle of modern skyship design. Boasting four masts yet eight sails, as below the main deck a horizontal yard-mast ran through the ship, adding a sail to either side, and aiding *Wrath* to build up a respectable speed of 40 kilometres an hour. Recently-developed enchantments allowed the ship to accelerate to even higher speeds for a short time, although this would only last for less than a minute. The hull was built of oak, the keel being the sum of three trees magically fused into one huge piece, giving the ship a total length of 153 metres – roughly eighty-five people's height together. Siera had watched at intervals as the *Wrath* was built over fourteen months at Ilmarch's skyship yard, from the base hull, to the golden sun emblem that served as the figurehead, to its maiden launch. All the while, she had pointedly ignored the gossip that circulated around it. A Reimaran king financing an entire ship, solely for his daughter's regiment to use? The idea had seemed the height of excess, its execution as profligate as it was arrogant. Those rumours had only fuelled the gossip that the du Tealdan line was wastefully decadent, its second child playing at soldiers and burning through money to get an entire skyship at her disposal.

Siera grinned. Those whispers had stopped after she had proven her point: that skyships were as good for military endeavours as they were for trade and logistics. With drop-lines, skyships could be used for more than just moving troops and supplies around. Now, Reimar could drop onto its enemies' heads, on land or at sea.

This was in addition to the *Wrath's* complement of ballistae, eight on the crenelated aftcastle and eight on the forecastle. The *Wrath* would not yield quickly if it came across another ship, at sea or in the air.

Siera heard footsteps behind her, coming closer, then stopping. She waited, but no one addressed her.

"Come to enjoy the view?" she called out without turning around.

Staff Sergeant Tomasso Rossi cleared his throat as he saluted at Siera's back, right fist over his heart. "No, Captain, uh… you mentioned that you'd be able to speak with me once you had more free time… and…"

Siera turned to face her new aide, her expression flat. Tomasso was the same height she was, around one hundred and seventy centimetres. Black hair, brown eyes; nothing gave him away as not being born in Reimar. "Ah, Sergeant Rossi. So, you thought because I was idly staring at the scenery, I had free time?"

Rossi's mouth fell slightly opened as his panicking mind quickly tried to find an excuse.

Siera grinned. "Gracious Sura, Rossi, close your mouth before a bird flies in, I am only joking. Of course I have free time, come and admire the view as we talk."

"Yes, Sir." Rossi walked to stand next to Siera at the prow.

"It is unfortunate that I've not had enough time to properly speak with you about your duties, so do not worry if you feel you are not performing up to standard."

Rossi shifted from one foot to the other.

"So… you have a Reimaran name, but you are not originally from Reimar, are you?" Siera asked.

"No Sir, I was born in Mordeno. My parents moved to Reimar when I was six years old, so I don't have many memories of Mordeno. And they had been planning to move for years, so they gave me a Reimaran name when I was born."

Siera nodded. "So, you joined the army to secure citizenship for your parents?"

"Yes Sir. I'm uh… surprised you guessed that, most people assume I'm after citizenship for myself."

"But your parents moved when you were young, so you came of age in Reimar, which would make you a citizen. And you can't pay for a commission to staff sergeant, so you worked your way up, in all likelihood to gain citizenship for your parents."

Rossi's brows rose. "Ah… I should have realised you'd work that out, Sir. But it's not just for my parents, I've always liked the idea of serving Reimar in the army."

Siera shrugged. "Well, I would embarrass my father if I did not know my own country's laws. And that is an attitude I cannot expect from all too many these days, so I am pleased that you hold it regardless of where you were born."

Rossi rubbed his hands together. "Aah… thank you, Sir. Sometimes, though, I forget that your father is the king… is there some other form of address you might prefer?"

Siera rubbed her index finger and thumb together to be sure of his attention. "Most people do forget, and I prefer that they do so. In the army my rank is Captain, not Princess. Remember that I never expect bows from any subordinate, only salutes."

Tomasso saluted to that.

Siera smirked. "You are a funny man, Tomasso. I should mention that your file includes all relevant details about your time in training with the First Regiment, and although I chose you as an aide specifically because I prefer someone with at least some sense of humour, anything like that fiasco with the pickled eggs will not be tolerated here in the Fourth."

Tomasso gave a nervous smile. "Yes Sir, it won't happen again Sir. Just a prank gone wrong, Sir."

Siera frowned, then shrugged. "Excellent. Now, where to begin… well, what better way than the view?"

Tomasso stared at the land far below them. He spotted a small village, and a few surrounding farms. "I don't understand, captain... Ah! You mean that even this simple land beneath us is what we strive to defend?"

Siera raised an eyebrow. "No. We can only have such a nice view because we're five hundred metres in the air on a skyship."

Tomasso forced a laugh, his cheeks reddening slightly.

Siera spread her stance as she continued, arms crossed behind her back. "Reimar has struggled for decades with a great deal of money sunk into research and testing to achieve magical flight. Somehow, the wretched Ilnians have enchanted suits of armour to allow the wearer to fly, and no one has been able to replicate their success." Siera sniffed. "However, skyships are far superior. We can move more troops with them, as well as use them for merchant trade transport. And trade, more than anything else, is Reimar's lifeblood."

Tomasso nodded. "Yes Sir, my parents left Mordeno to pursue their trades in Reimar."

Siera turned to her subordinate. "What do your parents do, Tomasso?"

"My mother's an accountant, she works with the Guild of Merchants and Lenders. My father traded in textiles, but the market is too difficult in Mordeno, so he wanted to move here."

"Not enough dyes, too many sheep." Siera muttered as she looked down.

"Sir?"

Siera looked back up at Tomasso. "Nothing, just wondering. To continue, without trade Reimar is a shadow of its current self. And there – there is one of our most important national treasures."

Siera pointed to a distant yet imposing structure off the starboard side of the *Wrath*: a vast freestanding white circle, partway buried in the earth, reaching almost halfway to the skyship's current cruising height.

"Utterly beyond our ability to understand, let alone reconstruct. My father, as well as Reimaran rulers before him, and foreign rulers besides, have cast away a fortune in money and favours in trying to understand it or build another one."

Tomasso gazed off at the distant structure, eyes wide. "The Helion... the gate between worlds. I've... never actually seen it before."

Siera shrugged. "Well, we did have poorer weather on the way to San Seras, but now you can look all you want. We have no idea who built it, and to be honest most people truly do not care. We can reach the other worlds with this, simply set it and walk through – no more effort required. With this, our trade capacities are increased a hundredfold, and our revenues with them."

Tomasso nodded. "So... you're saying that our duty is to protect trade, and the Helion?"

Siera stared at Tomasso.

"No, our duty is to protect the people and interests of Reimar both. What I am saying is that in this modern age we can no longer rely on mere human power for Reimar to prosper and to be protected. Without magic, we would not be enjoying this view, or that bizarre edifice that transports us to other worlds. Nor would we have been able to reach Commodore de Luca in time today, and no disrespect to him or his crew, but that would have been the end of them."

Tomasso nodded. "I see... to be honest, it's something similar to that which attracted me to apply to the Fourth Regiment in the first place. It seemed that you, out of all the regiment's captains, were set on betting on the future. Er, not that I–"

Siera smiled suddenly, her eyes bright. "People never want to say that to me, Tomasso, they never admit that they think I am betting. They assume I will be offended; after all, gambling is uncouth, especially for someone of my station. Yes, I know you meant it as a figure of speech, but after all it is true: I am risking all of this. I am betting that before long all the nations of Iber, and the world, and all the worlds in total will have the means of flight. Whether it be skyships or flying armour... everyone will take to the skies somehow. That old dream of people soaring through the skies like birds will come to life..."

Siera clenched her fists.

"And those nations that do not have that power will fall, for to travel by air is far faster than any other means. And travel and even trade besides, those nations that have not mastered flight will fall to those who have." Siera stroked her thumb on her chin. "Well, apparently some mages have mastered the art of moving instantly, but my father's court mage and the Luminary Academy both say it is too unreliable and expensive to do on a large scale. Thus I am certain air power will come to prevail above all else, and I intend for Reimar to have its place in the skies."

Siera turned to face Tomasso, her arms crossed, her eyes meeting his. "So ultimately I ask of you what I ask of all my troops: bet on me being right. I had to convince many people that an entire skyship for a regiment was a good idea, I had to convince General du Tilmost that drop-lines would work, I had to convince my father and the General both that my expenses are worth it. And today, after months of some... terse conversations, I've proved that I was right. Unless we had come to Commodore de Luca's aid, both he and his ship would have been overwhelmed: there is the proof. So you will find that I run things differently in the Fourth Regiment than what you experienced in the First, and as my aide I expect you to understand my thoughts more closely than any but my lieutenants."

Tomasso saluted. "You'll find your trust in me well placed, Sir."

"That's a fancy salute, Tomasso, did you practice it in front of a mirror?" said a male voice from behind the pair.

Siera turned to see Ermanno, the First Battalion's lieutenant, walking towards her. He was lighting a cigarette, out on the deck where he had told her he was sure that he could get away with it.

Siera was often irritated that Ermanno was just ever so slightly taller than her. His grey eyes gave away little, but his grey hair confirmed his fifty two years.

"If you haven't yet met Lieutenant Ermanno Gartzia, Tomasso, this is about as typical as he gets. He heads the First Battalion."

Tomasso saluted. Gartzia nodded in reply.

Siera crossed her arms in front of her. "Ermanno, if Commodore Terciero sees you smoking on his ship again he will probably throw you off it."

Ermanno shrugged, practiced fingers flipping his nita case closed and slipping it back into his trouser pocket. "He won't throw me over the side if you're around, Captain, he's too big a fan of yours."

Siera shrugged. "He gets to fly my skyship, so I can understand it. But the man knows his job, and like it or not he is the captain of this vessel."

"But, you're the captain of this vessel," said Tomasso, frowning.

Ermanno waved his hand at Tomasso. "Common mistake there. Siera's in charge of Terciero, but Terciero is in charge of the skyship," said Ermanno. "Besides, while the ship flies, Terciero has to be there to oversee everything. He can't come out and shout at me for a bit, I think."

Siera smiled, waving a finger at Ermanno. "Hold there, Ermanno, have you been analysing when he can and cannot afford to leave the bridge?" she said.

Ermanno smiled slowly, and nodded. "Largely. I think I've got his pattern down, but who knows what mages are really thinking about or doing? For all I know, the army pays him to stand there and wave his hands around, pretending he's a chicken."

Tomasso stared at the deck to conceal a smirk.

"Regardless of your lack of appreciation for Commodore Terciero's abilities, your smoke break is convenient. As staff sergeant Georgino has retired, staff sergeant Tomasso Rossi here is his replacement."

Ermanno took a deep pull on his cigarette, a contented smile on his face. "So, you're the new officer of the biscuits?"

"The what?" said Tomasso.

Siera rolled her eyes. "Lieutenant Gartzia is implying that you're in charge of fetching my biscuits. And he is joking, as that is up to the regiment's cooks. Although you do also need to know that, in case they forget, as I will have to send you to remind them." Siera turned to Ermanno, her arms folded. "And as much as you scoff, Gartzia, I'll remind you that you are allowed your quirks due to your extensive service in the regiment. If Tomasso brings you an order from me and you ignore him, I will have your hide." Siera's gaze met Ermanno's for a moment, and he looked away first.

Ermanno waved his hand at Siera. "I never ignore or forget orders, you know that. Tomasso doesn't need to worry that I'll bite his head off either."

Siera rubbed her index finger and thumb together. "Speaking of convenient moments, let's make one. Tomasso, find Lieutenants Gretchen and Gallo, and tell them I request their presence at the prow for a few minutes. They will likely be in their quarters."

Tomasso stared at Siera, his eyes widening. "Who?"

Ermanno snorted. "Find two other people with a solid silver bar on their shoulders. One's a tall blonde woman, the other is almost your height and has black hair."

Tomasso saluted, then walked back across the deck.

"Admiring the view, captain?" said Ermanno.

"Actually, yes." Siera turned to face the Helion in the distance as the skyship slowly sailed past it.

Ermanno turned to see what Siera was looking at. "Oh?"

"I was talking to Tomasso about the Helion, and the wealth it brings Reimar," said Siera.

Ermanno dragged at his cigarette again.

"It's kind of ugly, I've always thought," he said as he squinted at the Helion.

Siera frowned and turned back to Ermanno. "Ugly? What? Who cares about its looks?"

Ermanno shrugged. "Well, I've always thought... why make it so big? Whoever made it, you know – were they sending a dozen wagons at a time, or were they also sending skyships through it? Heh, it always looks to me like it'll just fall over."

Siera scowled at Ermanno. "Who cares what was originally intended? It is convenient for us, that is what matters most. And you can even send a skyship through, if done slowly."

Ermanno cackled. "Yet we keep building bigger skyships..."

Siera rolled her eyes. "And if we could have a bigger Helion, we would build one. As we cannot, we will make do.

Oh, Rossi's back. That was quite quick of him."

Ermanno turned around to see his fellow lieutenants walking towards him, with Tomasso coming up behind them.

As they came to a halt, both saluted Siera, who nodded in return.

"Well, you both got here quickly. I have called you all here to introduce you to staff sergeant Tomasso Rossi, whom you have met just now. He will be my new aide; give him what advice you can. And as for introductions," Siera gestured to the lanky, dark-haired man who had just arrived. "Lieutenant Adalberto du Gallo, leading the Second Battalion."

"Good to meet you, Sergeant Rossi," said Adalberto with a smile that didn't quite reach his eyes. Rossi idly wondered what exactly Lieutenant du Gallo was trying to groom his somewhat patchy moustache into.

Siera turned slightly, towards the tall blonde woman. "And Lieutenant Gretchen Ailbhe, leading the Third Battalion."

Gretchen brushed a few errant strands of her long blonde hair out of her eyes. "Rossi? Sounds Valencian," she said.

"I was born in Mordeno, actually. I might have a Valencian ancestor somewhere, though."

Gretchen smiled softly. "Another foreigner in the Fourth, captain? People will think you're turning us into the Seventh," said Gretchen with a grin.

"Hah. Sergeant Rossi lived in Reimar before coming of age, and so is as much a citizen as I am. And you have earned your citizenship, Gretchen, so we are all equal in that regard. That said, I believe our introductions are over. Any questions, or anything to report?"

Ermanno looked over to Adalberto. "I see Cecilia has a new fancy-looking necklace. Nice stone too."

Gretchen stared, but then grinned. "I hadn't realised... are congratulations in order?"

Adalberto smirked and held his hands up, palms out. "It's not hanging from around her wrist, so have patience yet. And... nothing is official, family-wise."

Siera was impassive. "I noticed it was a garnet set in the necklace... well, it's not my business."

Tomasso blinked. "Cecilia?"

"He means Staff Sergeant Perez," said Siera.

Tomasso furrowed his brows. "Why would it hang off her wrist?"

Siera stared at him. "Oh? After twelve years…"

Tomasso looked around, realising that everyone was looking at him. "Well – I mean I've seen people wearing chains with gemstones around their wrists, but I never actually knew why. Isn't it just some fashion thing?"

"…Really?" said Adalberto, his mouth shifting into a faint sneer.

Tomasso's face was etched with confusion. "Uh…"

Gretchen leaned over and patted Tomasso on the back. "Reimaran tradition, bethrothed couples wear their wedding rings or stones on a chain around their wrists to announce their impending marriage."

Ermanno snorted. "Even Gretchen knows. How long have you lived in Reimar, again?"

"It is… a very prominent tradition," said Siera. "Did you just never think about it?"

"Oh, I see." Tomasso said, his eyes slowly widening. "Oh… so that's why!"

Everyone else stared at him.

Tomasso cleared his throat. "I have a… uh, friend… she had a new necklace that her father gave her a few months ago. I was asking her about it and she said it would look better around her wrist, so I said she could just wear it there if she wanted. She uh… glared at me."

Gretchen and Ermanno laughed. Even Adalberto cracked a smirk.

Siera sighed. "All of this aside, is there anything else appetising at the moment?"

Ermanno shrugged, and reached into his pocket to roll another cigarette. Adalberto suddenly looked over at Ermanno. Gretchen smirked, her eyes shifting to look at Ermanno also.

Siera raised a brow at Gretchen. "Is something amusing you, Lieutenant Ailbhe?"

Gretchen winked at Siera as Ermanno raised his cigarette to his lips. Gretchen eyed him eagerly.

Ermanno caught her staring at him, and paused.

"Something on my face?" he said, smoke drifting out of his mouth.

Gretchen shrugged. "No, just..."

Ermanno shrugged and took another drag, and his cigarette promptly ignited with a burst of flame and a loud crack. Ermanno let out a yell and stumbled backwards, his cigarette falling to the deck. Siera and Adalberto both yelled and leapt to stamp it out as Gretchen howled with laughter.

Siera looked up to see Commodore Terciero du Valtiera glaring balefully through the bridge windows at Ermanno, who stood up quickly and dusted himself off, looking around wildly.

Gretchen spoke haltingly through her laughter. "Sorry, but... I couldn't help it... I... I overheard Terciero, grumbling to one of his bunch... about you smoking out here, saying... saying that he'd cure you... cure you for good, hah, of the habit, the next time you tried." Gretchen sighed as she composed herself. "Honestly, I should have been out here waiting for him to do it as soon as I heard."

Siera's face was stony. "So that is why both of you were quick to get here, you were waiting nearby," she said, her eyes flitting between Ermanno and Terciero.

Ermanno coughed, his eyes wide, as he felt at his face and his hair. "No warning? You're a true comrade, Gretchen..." he muttered, as he looked back at Terciero on the other side of the deck, who was still glaring at him. Terciero raised his left hand and wiggled his little finger at Ermanno.

"Now he's just being rude." Ermanno raised his own left hand.

"Lieutenant Gartzia, if I see you make that gesture I will have that finger alongside my sausages for dinner!" barked Siera.

Ermanno jumped. "Fine, fine," he said as he turned back to Siera, scowling. "The Commodore gets away with it, but poor old Gartzia has to just take it."

Siera's face remained stony. "Horsepep– ah, nonsense, I have similar words for the commodore. Back to whatever you were busy with before I called for you, I have a new appointment on the bridge. Sergeant Rossi... tell Quintus Castell to meet me on the bridge." Sergeant Rossi saluted, and left.

"I was busy having a smoke," muttered Ermanno.

Siera did not look at Ermanno as she slowly walked next to him. "Now you can be busy doing something else. I think next time he might set you on fire entirely."

"At least demote him if he does," muttered Ermanno as he walked away, and before he took the stairs down to the lower deck he paused to glare one more time at Terciero, who was himself watching as Siera strode towards him, a flat expression on his face.

The *Sky's Wrath* bridge, as is common for skyships, is its own enclosed room with doors leading to the open deck as well as stairs leading into the interior of the vessel from the bridge.

Siera didn't bother knocking as she pushed the door open. "Commodore, I assume you have some explanation to offer?"

Terciero du Valtiera stood with his right side to her, eyes closed, arms outstretched and slowly moving up and down, a rough stone in each hand. Each of the stones appeared to be some form of metal entwined around a chunk of obsidian. In front of him was a large curved desk, with a variety of odd tools: rune-etched obsidian chunks, bits of metal, blank paper, scrawled-on paper, and a half-eaten pastry. Siera noted with distaste that it was a strawberry jam pastry.

Siera repressed a desire to ask if he was imitating a chicken, irked that Ermanno had made that comparison out loud.

One of Terciero's assistants half-stepped towards Siera, palms held outward, motioning for her to wait. She glared at him. One particular drawback and irritation which Siera usually kept to herself was that skyships required mages – usually sorcerers – in order to actually fly. Something about the enchantments required constant adjustment in order for the ship to change its movements, or such. When Siera had asked why skyships couldn't simply have a destination given to them as a command, she got a particularly blank stare in response. It was, even more irritatingly, the same blank stare that Gretchen gave her when Siera asked why she insisted in taking part in the frontline of many attacks.

Siera looked around the bridge cabin, packed as it was. Cabinets holding maps and a variety of navigational equipment – not all of it recognisable to her – predominated. A large cabinet in the rear corner held a variety of glass vials with strangely coloured liquids in them, each vial secured with straps.

In front of Terciero's desk was the ship's wheel, completely ornamental as the ship didn't turn by rudder. A brass plate on the wheel was inscribed with the regimental motto, 'Righteousness Never Falters'.

Terciero opened his eyes and took a deep breath, then placed both stones into small receptacles on the desk in front of him.

"I know, Captain, I know. But at the same time, I can't watch that damn idiot go smoking on my ship."

Siera glared at him, and folded her arms. "It is only 'your' ship as long as I require you to fly it, and if you attempt to do anything of the sort again you can look forward to a short career of flying towards the ground by yourself."

Terciero pursed his lips. "Understood, well enough. But if he smokes again…"

"Then you will do nothing without informing me, Commodore. I will speak to Lieutenant Gartzia about his smoking again, this time with a less patient tone. If the matter is so serious, then better you express your concerns to me directly."

Terciero flung his arms wide. "I did!"

Siera massaged her temples. "You said it would be unfortunate if he were to keep smoking. Just… unfortunate. What is 'unfortunate', Terciero? 'Unfortunate' to me means you lost at the horses, or slipped and fell on your backside. It does not mean burning an officer's property."

Terciero huffed. "Well it would be unfortunate if a largely wooden ship were to catch ablaze!"

Siera shook her head. "Fires don't spread quite so quickly, and you'd be amazed, truly amazed, at how quickly my troops would sprint to put out any fires, especially ones that would result in their deaths by meeting the ground at a very quick pace."

Terciero threw up his hands. "Just… just please make him

stop smoking."

Siera sighed. "I will see to it. In the meantime, I imagine you have your own duties to attend to."

Terciero blinked at Siera. "Oh, actually, it's time for one of my understudies to take the helm, so all I'm doing is making sure they don't make a mess while I eat the rest of my tart."

"In that case, explain to me again how all this–" Siera waved at the desk in front of Terciero "–has anything to do with a skyship."

Terciero moved out of the way as another sorcerer stepped in front of the desk and took hold of the stones Terciero had just been using.

Terciero thought for a moment, then shrugged. "I've said it before Captain; I mean no offence when I say that it's a confusing matter for most non-sorcerers. I don't think I can really explain it to you in a way that you can understand." Terciero saluted. "Leave it in my hands, Captain. I won't let you down."

Siera nodded. "I do not imagine you will. As I said yesterday, your manoeuvring of the ship over the *Reimar's Vigilance* was flawless."

Terciero smiled widely. Siera wished she could pop Quintus out of her pocket at times like these, he was immensely useful at looming over people.

Siera resisted a smirk as she had an idea.

"Oh, one more thing, Commodore... sorcerers manipulate the elements, don't they?"

Terciero nodded, leaning to grab his half-eaten pastry off the desk. "Correct, Captain. All sorcery is based on the six elements. Earth air, water, fire, –"

"Yes, yes, right. Fire. And if any fire broke out, would you not be able to just snuff it out? It is just an element, is it not?"

Terciero gave Siera a blank stare.

A short moment passed, Siera looking at Terciero, Terciero staring blankly back at her. "Well... what if I was asleep?" he replied eventually with a slight shrug.

Siera waved the tip of her forefinger in a circle at Terciero. "The irony of you objecting to lit cigarettes by causing one to explode violently is not lost on me; it just causes me to doubt your sanity. Ensure this incident is never repeated, Commodore."

Terciero saluted, the beginnings of a scowl on his face. "Yes Sir."

Walking down the stairs into the skyship, Siera saw Quintus Castell coming up the stairs towards her, all two hundred centimetres of him.

"Ah, Quintus. Did Sergeant Rossi find you?"

Quintus threw a sharp salute, his dark eyes meeting hers. "Yes, Sir."

"Excellent, I just… wanted to be sure he knew who you were. I will have him introduced to Clara when we return to Ilmarch."

Quintus grinned suddenly. "I think he was intimidated by me. I want to see his face when he meets Clara."

Siera nodded slowly. "Most living things are intimidated by you, Quintus," said Siera as she continued down the stairs. Quintus matched her pace alongside her.

"It's the face. Still, some women love a man with scars."

Of a similar height as Gretchen but sporting a variety of facial scars, one of which left him unable to smile in a straight line, Quintus was, to put it bluntly, built like a brick outhouse. His other distinction was a plain white beret, one of the highest marks of achievement for a soldier. Only those deemed loyal and capable enough to guard the Reimaran royal family were permitted to wear them.

All in all, Quintus Castell both looked like and was the kind of man who could snap someone in half and have them for breakfast afterwards.

"Which women would those be, Quintus?" said Siera, managing not to smile.

Quintus seemed surprised. Siera realised she'd never seen him make such a face before, and his left eyebrow, having been divided neatly in half at some point, made it seem as though he had three eyebrows to raise. "Uh… just… women. I mean, not all women. Just some women. No woman in particular."

Siera nodded. "Very well."

Quintus rubbed his fingers along his jaw. "So, Pri– ah, Captain, what did you need me for?"

Siera gave no notice that she'd heard his tongue slip. "I was hoping you would get here quick enough to help intimidate Commodore Terciero into behaving, but it seems fine. I still do not know where I stand with that one... or most mages, to be honest." Siera shook her head

Quintus rubbed his hands together. "Sorry I was late, then. And he also loves strawberry pies and tarts, I mean, isn't that a little odd? All the time, too. Strawberries. He's definitely odd."

Siera nodded. "Well, I doubt he means anything rude by it, but still..."

Quintus made as if to salute. "Well, if you've no need of me, Captain..."

Siera looked at her bodyguard out the corner of her eye. "Of course, you're free to go as you wish. But when you go past my room, make sure Rossi isn't standing around outside uselessly – I told him to get in there and understand how I prefer my records filed."

Quintus frowned. "I... was going back to the crew quarters, captain, but I'll tell Sergeant Rossi anyway..."

Siera avoided smiling. "Lieutenant Gretchen's quarters are right next to my own; you should not be going too far out of your way," Siera said.

Quintus frowned. "I, ah... yes Sir..."

Siera fought to repress a grin. She'd never seen Quintus caught this much off guard, not in the four years she'd known him; only variations of his stern solemn self. She nodded to him, and he completed his salute as he walked off. When Siera was sure he had passed around the corner, she permitted herself a quiet chuckle.

Four days later, the *Sky's Wrath* had come in sight of Ilmarch, the capital of Reimar.

Chapter 2: Home Again

The deck was crowded with soldiers and sailors as the *Sky's Wrath* approached Ilmarch. Most of the sailors had work to do, but even those off-duty wanted to see the city as the skyship slowly cruised in.

Ilmarch was positioned south-east of large limestone cliffs – which meant that almost all buildings were made from the white stone, and successive kings had pursued policies of keeping Ilmarch's self-appointed title of The Pale City by mandating that all buildings had to have at least an outer casing of limestone or be painted white. There were, though, some notable exceptions – the first being the royal palace, and the second being the cathedral of the Reimaran Suranic Church. Even without the various banners and pennants that hung from walls and stands alike all about the royal palace, the most recent addition to the palace was the Rock of Azure, a large domed roof of a deep blue colour, built over the various offices, halls, and private rooms of the Royal Embassy. Although over two hundred years old and now just another part of the city skyline to Ilmarch's inhabitants, it made for an impressive sight from the air. The Reimaran Suranic Church's Cathedral of Illumination, although made of the same limestone as most buildings in the city, had long been granted the right to build and decorate as the church saw fit. The cathedral was immediately noticeable by being an ornate, multi-levelled structure with yellow banners and solar iconography everywhere. Large golden discs stood at the roof corners, and lower on the walls were dozens of bas-reliefs, mainly depicting a multitude of humans worshipping the sun, the incarnation of Sura.

Although various churches and cults had risen up around the worship of Sura, the creator of humanity, the Suranic Church remained the oldest and most prominent among them.

Siera loved to watch Ilmarch unfold beneath her, the slow transition from the distant skyline to her being able to pick out individual details. As the *Sky's Wrath* closed in on the north part of the city where the skyship docks were situated, she sighed and pulled away from the railing. The soldiers of the Fourth Regiment were due for two weeks of general leave, but she knew there would be a cheerless variety of paperwork awaiting her in her study at the regimental barracks.

Siera was overseeing her lieutenants as they readied the troops for disembarkation on the deck, but they all felt the lack of movement that signalled that they had landed. A common landing for a skyship involved at least some banging and scraping as the ship was guided the final few metres into its moorings, but to Commodore Terciero's credit Siera only knew that the skyship had landed because the usual soft swaying back and forth of the ship had simply stopped.

"Single file down the boards, if I see you pushing and shoving you'll be right back on the ship scrubbing the toilets!" cried Ermanno. "Private Domenica if I see you try to jump down I'll break your legs myself, you can damn well wait until the ramps are in place. Private Plinion I hope your ankles still pain you from when you tried that, and don't look at me with that sheep's grin either!"

The ramps were pulled into place level with the deck, and slowly but surely the soldiers disembarked, the chatter picking up as soon as they left the deck. Siera knew that just beyond the dock's outer gates there'd be friends and family waiting to welcome her soldiers home; no civilians were allowed into the docks unless they worked there, worked on a skyship, or had a pass to board a skyship as a passenger.

As the last of the privates disembarked, Siera watched as her corporals turned to the sergeants, each saluting in turn, then the corporals disembarked. Next, the sergeants saluted the lieutenants, and then her lieutenants turned to her.

"You have two weeks general leave, I do not want to see a single one of you around the barracks, not even once.

Dismissed!" Siera said. Ermanno, Gretchen, and Adalberto saluted, and Siera returned their salute as they turned to leave.

"Captain, Commodore Terciero said to let you know that the ship has come completely to rest," said Tomasso from behind Siera. She turned, and he saluted.

"A bit late for that, Rossi, but I assume you got stuck behind everyone else after they were assembled on the deck. Do not worry, you learn in time. You have nothing more to do for now, but you should know already that the work of the army is never truly done. If you happen to come by the barracks and I am not there, I will have left a note for you. And if you have forgotten, you can always contact me by asking at the palace for my head maid, Rafaela Accai. She will know how to reach me, given some odd emergency. And if you can't find Quintus Castell, ask for Viscount Clara Mercer. You should meet her soon enough, anyway."

Tomasso smiled briefly. "I'll be there, captain. It's why I get paid extra, after all."

"Good man. Oh, and give your parents my regards."

Tomasso's brows rose. "I will, Sir."

Siera walked down the gangplank, turning back to look at the *Sky's Wrath* once she reached the cold concrete floor of the dock. The ship's flat base quickly rose into a curved hull that flowed up to the main deck, and for all its size the ship always impressed Siera with its grace. Already, a variety of crafters and mages were moving onto the ship, performing both material and magical maintenance. No skyship could maintain its ability to fly and manoeuvre without regular work on its enchantments, and for all that Siera did not understand why exactly magical enchantments tended to fade away, she understood that maintenance was a necessity.

She was about to walk around to inspect the front of the ship and the elegant work on the figurehead when a cough came from behind her.

Siera turned to see a stranger holding a bouquet of flowers – her favourite, lilac pansies.

"Excuse me, Your Highness, I have a message for you." The stranger said with a small bow.

"Very well, but you must excuse me, I do not believe we have made acquaintance," replied Siera, extending her right hand palm up. The stranger quickly extended his right hand to grasp her fingers.

"Of course, Your Highness. I am but a humble courtier before your father and an irrelevant acquaintance of your brother, Count Primo du Aquino."

Siera laughed out loud. "You are a blatant liar, Count du Aquino. I imagine you know your way around these docks better than I do, and not just because your family is responsible for building a fair portion of them. My brother has been regaling me with his and your exploits and troublemaking for years now, and yet I've only ever seen you from a distance at a few parties. You can hardly be too modest to introduce yourself, by all accounts."

Primo's genteel smile was instantly replaced by a fat toothy grin. "You have me there, Your Highness. It is true, your brother and I have sponsored half the bawdy songs from here to San Seras by both our purses and our deeds. But today your brother has sent me to deliver these flowers and his apologies, a minor court incident has kept him too busy to welcome you home from your duties." Primo extended the bouquet, and Siera took it with both hands.

"It is a rather weak excuse, but as long as he remembers my favourites I cannot hold it against him. I will be at the palace shortly enough."

"Well, if it pleases my lady, I have a carriage waiting to return myself. We could…"

"It does please, and indeed we could. Lead on, Count du Aquino."

The carriage arrived at the palace gates, and for a moment Siera felt smug as she simply drove past the line of petitioners waiting for an audience – anyone could petition the monarch for an audience, but they had to convince the bailiffs at the gate that they had a valid cause, or have a courtier try to get them in. Especially effective if said courtier was on good terms with Modesto du Greco, the mayor of the palace, who directed the gate bailiffs.

She then felt slightly guilty – after all, she could go where she wanted, along with the few others who had permanent residence at the palace. The rest had to line up in Ilmarch's midday heat. Primo, of course, got a free pass as he was with Siera, and she then realised that this was probably the main reason that he had wanted to ride back with her. Looking over at her companion, Siera realised she'd been thinking of the newly trained recruits the Fourth would be receiving, instead of keeping up a polite conversation.

"Here I am, idly thinking of administrative matters. How is your parents' health?"

Primo glanced up from staring at his palm.

"Ah, my parents remain well. My father still hates court, still prefers me to remain here and 'handle' things for him, just in case the king takes some offence. Not that I... well."

Siera shrugged. "Oh, I understand, these things must be considered. And now it is my turn to say 'no offence', but... I doubt my father notices."

Primo grinned. "I much prefer it that way, Your Highness. That way, I get to have my fun, and my father is assured in equal measure that the family interests are not being neglected."

"What is that in your palm, that's kept your attention?" asked Siera.

Primo smiled and closed his eyes. "A mere cameo of my lady Federica du Firenze, Sura watch over her."

"Is she... a friend?" said Siera.

Primo looked at Siera, his mouth half open. She wasn't sure if he was surprised or trying to laugh.

"I... Federica du Firenze, third daughter of His Grace Silvio du Firenze, is my fiancée... I had assumed the news had spread by now, Your Highness... we..."

Siera stared at Primo. "Wait... what? Little Federica? I thought – isn't she thirteen? She's getting fully married already? When?" said Siera.

"Err, my lady is nineteen, Your Highness. And we are to marry on the last day of Teurnot. And we have been engaged for these past three years..."

Siera blinked. "Well, it's the tenth today, so, twenty one days from now... Congratulations! Much belated congratulations, but still. My apologies, of course, if I had not been on deployment I would have certainly heard the news."

Primo looked askance at Siera. "Well, we made sure to send out invitations six months ago, before you left…"

Siera made a nervous laugh. "Haha… I see, my mistake. Uh, I did not even realise, you have your ring on your wrist and everything. Oh, well, look, we've arrived at last. How time flies!" Siera pointed out of the window as the carriage halted at the end of the road which led to the inner palace gates. "Well, I wish you and Federica all the best. I will certainly be at the wedding if I can make it. Must be away, talk soon!" Siera said as she opened the carriage door.

"Good day to you too, Your Highness, but…" said Primo as he waited for Siera to exit. As he himself got out of the carriage, he saw Siera walking briskly into the palace's entry hall.

Siera had gone no more than a dozen metres into the hall when a maid rushed up to her and clasped her hands together politely.

"Princess du Tealdan, welcome back. Your father has left word that he eagerly awaits you in the Pearl Study."

Siera slowed, and turned to look behind her. Primo was attempting to catch up to her, probably to try and get her to confirm her attendance at his wedding.

"Do me a favour – keep the good count busy for a moment or more." Siera had ten silver teals in the maid's hands in a second, and immediately strode off to find her father. Her father made knowing every servant's name his business, but Siera had never bothered. After all, a good tip made everyone just as happy. Smiling as behind her she heard the maid accosting Count du Acquino with some item of gossip, Siera quickly made her way to her father's favourite study.

King Abarron du Tealdan turned on hearing a knock at the door of his study.

"Who – oh," said Abarron as Duke Nicodemo du Singara entered without announcing himself.

"Afternoon, your Noble Majesty," said Nicodemo.

Abarron turned to glare at him. "If you can't announce

yourself, why go through the formality of titles?"

Nicodemo shrugged. "Too lazy to announce myself, really. And the page would have done it, but I glared at him." Without being prompted, Nicodemo pulled up a chair.

Abarron shook his head. "They're not going to listen at the keyhole, Nico."

"I have, in my employ – well, your employ, but you see my point – hundreds of people whose sole job is some form of listening at keyholes."

"Well, have you learned anything interesting of late from all these keyholes?"

"Certainly. For starters, I continue to be suspicious about Southmere Town and San Seras. Five more of my contacts have not sent me any form of message, and I assume they've been discovered. For all I know, they might be dead."

Abarron made a moue of distaste. "And you suspect this... conspiracy, that's working with those Archipelagan robber barons?"

"Meetings between emissaries of certain Archipelagan petty dukes and a few minor Reimaran nobles, yes. I have an updated list here – you should probably burn this after reading it, just to be safe."

Abarron snorted. "I hardly suspect spies here in my study... but you never know," said Abarron as he took the list from Nicodemo. "And you can't enjoy a pastry with your eyes alone, so stop your forlorn gazes and just have one."

Nicodemo made as though to bow, and took one of the chocolate pastries from a tray that Abarron hadn't even touched.

"I don't understand how those could have lasted more than five minutes. You have no taste," said Nicodemo as he stuffed a hand-sized pastry into his mouth.

"Or you're just addicted to them, bizarre as they are. I find it unseemly that something so... coarse and brown can be in any way delicious," said Abarron as he held Nicodemo's list next to one of his own, squinting from one to the other.

"Why whatever are you saying, 'Barron? Chocolate is a true nobleman's delicacy, a delicious and expensive package to both enjoy and show off to others."

"Half of its appeal seems to derive from its expensive

nature. Its taste hardly merits the congratulations I hear people give it year in and year out." Abarron muttered.

Nicodemo managed to speak and chew at almost the same time. "Mph, speaking of year in and year out, I tire of Berezi's excuses and tears as to why our poor, stupid farmers cannot grow whatever plant that makes chocolate."

Abarron held both notes with his right hand as his left fumbled for his quill. "That would be the cocoa plant, and neither our soil nor our weather appears to convince the damn thing to grow. We certainly would make a gross profit if we could, but no use crying about it." Abarron dipped his quill in the inkpot, and underlined four matching names on each list.

"At least if we could grow enough for me," said Nicodemo as he reached for another pastry.

"Look, here." Abarron pointed at the two lists in turn. "This newest report from you and this one of my own. And I'm certain they're on a previous report as well. Especially Enio du Donati, isn't that one of Silvio's nephews?"

"Mmm, that's him. It does seem that Enio has grown up and yet remained as stubborn and stupid as he always was. He's been a busy one."

"Stubborn yes, stupid... I always wondered. I want your opinion on this, Nicodemo. What do you think they're up to?"

Nicodemo gave Abarron a level gaze. "Well, judging by who they've met with and where they come from, I'd say rebellion."

Abarron's brows rose. Nicodemo continued.

"I realise you see it as being strictly related to our suspicion of certain military patrol routes being leaked and some shady profit being made, but – but I'm certain that it goes far beyond that. I think we have here just the right people in just the right places to try and pull off some form of minor rebellion, especially possible in San Seras. And there's no chance they're meeting for tea and cakes with those Shardustans I've listed – I'll bet they're all too happy to fund this. If they were just traitors out for money, they'd sell patrol routes to the Archies, so why involve Shardustur? And it's all second, third, or fourth children – the ones who won't be inheriting anything and have to make their careers elsewhere."

Abarron nodded. "And most of them from Surmarch, Ponsurno, Southmere, San Seras... all the old baronies, from before Reimar incorporated the region. Still... we have no proof. And from what you've found so far, they don't have the funds or the arms to pull this off."

Nicodemo swallowed the last of the pastries. "I assume they need time, but I swear to you I won't give them any. I'll have all the proof you need."

"Hmm. Good, because I cannot afford to let this continue. I'll not have secession bring strife to Reimar. Even if it means confronting those involved directly, I will not have it come to that. And are you certain that Silvio du Donati isn't involved?"

Nicodemo hesitated, wetting his lips with his tongue before speaking.

"I can't be certain, after all his sympathies seem to lie in that direction... but I have no indication yet that he's involved. He's spouted ten shades of jabber about his fief deserving more independence, but he seems unconnected, at least for now. And you know how much he likes to talk... the others might consider him too likely to let secrets loose, or he might be a hidden partner so far. I'll let you know as soon as I find anything out."

Abarron nodded. "At least we can have all of this attended to without the council hovering over our shoulders."

Nicodemo grinned. "I still can hardly believe that you got away with it."

Abarron smiled. "What, the funding for the irregular intelligence service?"

Nicodemo smirked. "No, making them believe that ridiculous story, that somehow you'd spent it all for naught, never a good idea in the first place, no more questions required." Nicodemo shrugged. "Sometimes I wonder if we'd do better without a council at all, but I'll wonder that in private. Or just to you. Meantime we have our plotters to deal with, again, I'll let you know as soon as I find anything out."

Abarron nodded. "Good. A few minor nobles plotting is

one thing… a Duke backing them is another. I don't like that, as soon as you start digging, your informants disappear – but you must dig harder and faster. We need to know nigh on immediately."

Nicodemo stood, bowed, and left.

No sooner had Abarron turned back to his notes then he heard a murmuring outside. He sighed and turned back to the door, but broke into a smile as his daughter entered.

"Siera! I've been waiting for you all day, come, sit and tell me everything. Or refreshments first, whichever you please."

Abarron stood and embraced his daughter, and Siera realised she was famished.

"Actually, I think I forgot to have lunch."

Abarron rolled his eyes. "I'll have the page fetch the usual, with extra slices of apple pie and cream." Abarron opened the door and directed the page waiting outside to get a plate of refreshments from the kitchen.

"Don't tell me you had the cooks whip up an apple pie just for me?" said Siera with a smile as she and her father sat down.

Abarron sighed. "Well, I told them it was for a friend. I doubt they believed me, but the day I think too hard about what my own cooks think of me is the day I foreswear eating altogether."

Siera smiled. "You care about what everyone thinks, father. It's what makes you a good ruler."

Abarron gave a half-smile to that. "Well, you have your awfully provincial apple pie, and nice cup of tea with some fruit coming your way. Until then, well, I've heard the news of the *Sky's Wrath* performing to expectations, but I'm curious as to any details you can provide about how it all went."

Siera smiled slowly as she leaned back in her chair. "I'll not let you off the hook, father. Let us cast our minds back a year, this same study, this same topic of conversation."

Abarron sighed and took off his reading glasses to polish them on his shirt sleeve. "Yes, here we go, here we go," he muttered.

"'Too expensive, will never work, will get people killed,

embarrass yourself'... was there anything else?"

Abarron gave his daughter a level look. "I am still amazed it worked at all. At all! It has no right to work, I still say – but – but –" Abarron continued over his daughter's objections. "It has worked, and for that I must salute your determination in seeing the project through." Abarron gave his daughter a slow salute, his fist clenched over his heart. Siera's cheeks reddened slightly.

"Thank you, father. We've argued over it, but in the end I'm grateful that you believed in me enough to fund it."

Abarron made a wide shrug. "Well, I had you on one hand insisting it would work, I had Andrayzn on the other hand telling me we need more skyships for the guard anyway, and then I had Lycea telling me that it actually could work and the enchantments could be done, but I had Gustavo telling me that your specific enchantments were all very unproven and unreliable... so, you're sure no one was killed trying to drop down from the skyship?"

Siera shook her head. "Not even an injury, father. Not one. I myself have used it, it's perfectly safe."

Abarron shook his head. "Your mother would not let me hear the end of it, either."

"Has she heard the news too?"

"Oh yes, and she has been crowing about it to everyone. Her daughter, leading valiant soldiers, putting Archipelagans to the sword, covering herself with honour, et cetera."

"I half expect her to announce one day that Archipelagans are not even properly human," said Siera with a soft laugh.

"Come now, she has never gone so far. She... has just stated that there can be no moral offence before God in killing them, as they are almost always guilty of some or another crime."

"Not certain which I dislike more, that her attitude is popular, or that she is all too often correct."

"Well, most people have spent somewhere between zero and no time with foreigners of any kind, Archipelagan or otherwise. For all that we are a wealthy and urbane nation, most people still live largely simplistic lives."

Siera shrugged. "Most people are poor and stupid, you mean."

Abarron waved his hands at Siera. "Poor does not mean foolish, you should know that."

"I know, I know. Still, sometimes…" Siera was interrupted by a knock at the door. "Hopefully that heralds pie." Siera said as she quickly stood. However, she opened the door to Nicodemo du Singara, not a page bearing food.

"Oh, Duke du Singara, a pleasant surprise," said Siera

Nicodemo nodded absently. "My apologies for the interruption, Your Highness, I just stopped by to deliver a letter to your father. Abarron, it's something that just came in."

Abarron leaned past Siera to take the proffered papers from Nicodemo.

"Good day, Your Highness, Your Noble Majesty," said Nicodemo as he walked off.

"I have often wondered why he's always at court," said Siera as she closed the door.

"He's an old friend, you know. And I value his advice."

"Well, you have said that you two were as thick as thieves when you were children, so–" Siera stood suddenly as another knock came at the door. "Excellent, at last–"

Siera opened the door to find General Andrayzn du Tilmost with his hand up, mid-knock.

"Ah good, I was hoping to find you here, Captain du Tealdan," said Andrayzn, general of the Reimaran Royal Guard. A tall, imposing man of fifty-two years who had somehow kept the majority of his thick black hair, Siera swore that Andrayzn's default state of being was 'looming'.

Siera saluted smartly as her father stood.

"Don't just stand there, Andrayzn, do come in. I have the whole world knocking at the door today, one more cannot arrest my concentration any further."

"I would, Your Noble Highness, but I have a few clerical matters to take care of. I simply wanted to stop by and congratulate Captain du Tealdan on her recent success."

"Thank you, Sir," said Siera, saluting again. "Oh, Sir, there is one matter I need to discuss with you."

Andrayzn nodded curtly. "Very well, but let us take that up tomorrow. Carry on Captain. Good day, your Noble Highness," said Andrayzn as he turned to leave.

"Maybe I should just leave the door open," said Siera as she sat back down.

"And have my study open to every passer-by in the corridors? No thank you."

"Very well, Father," Siera closed the door and sat down, but immediately stood up again as another knock came at the door. She opened the door to find Modesto du Greco, her father's steward, idly flipping through the dozen or so papers he had in his left hand.

"Good that you're still here, 'Barron – oh, Princess Siera, truly a pleasure. We so rarely get to see you around here anymore, how is your regiment going these days? No, wait, is it a Battalion? I can never remember these things, my apologies," he said, frowning.

"A regiment, and things go well as always, Duke du Greco." Siera turned to her father. "Actually, I think I'll just find the page in the kitchens."

"Very well, but don't eat too much, your mother and I have a small party in your honour this evening."

"Oh! Well, I will be sure to stop by and see mother, after a light snack, and thank her. And thanks again to you too, father."

Chapter 3: A Small Party

12th Teurnot

Siera and her attendants, Rafaela Accai and Catarina de Vives, walked towards the large double doors of the Opaque Ballroom. In the palace, this was the standard location for any party, ball, or gala: stately in its opulence and large enough for almost any gathering. Siera herself came in her dress uniform: a crimson long-sleeved shirt, as it is the fourth regiment's colour, with black trousers and boots. A white greatcloak, complemented with cloth epaulettes – the left bore the crest of Reimar, being a marble throne over a silver-tipped spear, surrounded by five Teals; the right bore the crest of the Fourth Regiment – as the Royal Guard's crest, but with the Fourth's regimental colour and motto, a silver spear crossed over a black bow with three Teals below. A silver chain connected the two.

Siera could hear quite a hubbub from inside as Catarina de Vives, her page, trotted ahead to open the doors for her. As they opened, the hubbub blew into a loud clamour of voices and music, easily two hundred people in attendance.

When her father had mentioned a small party, this was not what she had imagined.

As was the current fashion, dozens of tables dotted the room, rather than a few larger tables set in rows. The band, composed of violinists and flautists, was playing something new and energetic that Siera didn't recognise; '*Mother will probably know*', she thought, looking around for her parents and quickly spotting them at a horseshoe-shaped main table.

For most of recent history, the dukes of Reimar have preferred to spend the majority of their time at court, jockeying for position and keeping an eye on each other's successes and failures. With Ilmarch's rise to prominence as Reimar's trading hub and the booming skyship industry, now more than ever having the right place at court meant everything. This evening was no exception, with all of Reimar's dukes and their entourages seated around the outer arc of the table, the inner arc clear for servants to bring whatever dishes were requested. One of King Abarron's many ideas to impress foreign guests was to have the cooking staff provide both a set meal for occasions like this, as well as almost any other dish on request. Not that the planned fare was lacking – Siera saw whole roast swan, sautéed vegetables, dove pie, pickled fish, and an excessive selection of cheeses. Cuts of spiced meats, from beef to jackalope, were arranged on smaller dishes around the table.

As Siera walked in, maids at her side, her arrival was noticed. A loud cheer went up from the assembled guests, and she saw her father stand up from his seat and beckon to her. Paying no mind to the party guests who tried to catch her eye, she made her way to her parents' table.

"Good to see you've finally arrived, Sia," said Abarron with a smile.

Ramiros du Tealdan, her brother, pulled out a chair next to him for Siera.

"You are late, sister. What kept you?"

"What kept *you*, Rami, more like it," said Siera, faking a pout. "You were not there to meet me at the docks."

Ramiros gave a slow shrug. "Well, you know… my mistake, I realised too late that I was going to miss your arrival. I was in the middle of a fitting, so I couldn't rush off. Besides, Primo was there, wasn't he?"

"Yes, and apparently he is getting married?" said Siera as she took her seat.

"Yes, to Federica du Firenze," said Fede du Tealdan, Siera's mother. "And for the last two months, arriving early has been becoming increasingly popular."

"Wish someone had told me that," muttered Siera.

"If they had, would you care?" asked Abarron.

"Well… probably," said Siera with a grin.

"Oh, Sia, I had the servants open a few bottles of Jaurerriko du Alescio," said Fede.

Siera's grin widened. "Is that so? We cannot leave open bottles sitting around…"

Abarron nodded. "And the roast boar should be coming out soon. Everyone has already started eating, so there is no need to wait, of course. Mingle as you desire, it is your party after all."

Siera nodded. "Well, I will not stand on formality then, and I had been meaning to talk to Duke du Tilmost," said Siera as she got up to see her commanding officer.

There was an empty seat next to Andrayzn du Tilmost, most likely reserved for his wife. As she had not yet arrived, Siera walked towards it.

Before she had even sat down, Andrayzn had signalled a servant.

"Yes, Your Grace?"

"Do you have any Villa du Cipriani?" he asked, absently nodding to Siera, and indicating for her to sit next to him.

"We do, Your Grace, from the years 1268 and 1270."

Andrayzn made a moue of distaste. "No, those were terrible years. Do you have any Señorío Rama Frágil?"

"Yes Sir, a 1261 vintage."

"Perfect, I'll have a glass."

The servant turned to Siera. "And for you, Your Highness?"

"I will have a glass of the Jaurerriko du Alescio," said Siera.

The servant bowed, and left.

Andrayzn leaned towards Siera. "Before you say anything, never mind the sirs – it's a party, and ostensibly one for you at that."

Siera shrugged, half-smiling. "Can't go wrong with politeness. And only ostensibly?"

Andrayzn shrugged. "True. Proper manners are the mark of civilisation, I've always said. Even though I often fail to uphold them. And I suspect that your father wants another opportunity to show off to Henk van Rooijen, so this occasion suits many purposes."

Siera shrugged. "I can't blame him, 'two birds with one stone' is a favourite of his. Or three, if he can manage it. And even if you speak of manners, Andrayzn, all too many people have heard of your temper above anything else."

Andrayzn's smile came and went almost before Siera realised it was there. "Oh, just call me Dray. I know you don't mean it as an insult, and we can hardly claim to be still in formal relations anymore."

Siera nodded. "True. Ultimately, I'm to end up in your position anyhow... if you don't mind me saying so."

Andrayzn shook his head. "Not at all. I have to retire eventually, and there's no one better suited to take my place. You were a quick learner as my page, and you've done well as my subordinate."

Siera snorted. "Captain du Ochoa of the Second never thought so."

"Never has greed so thoroughly blinded a mind," muttered Andrayzn. "Good families can certainly sire half-assed progeny. Sura's breath, I still cannot understand how she managed to behave so lazily as to get demoted in the first place, for all that she worked her way back up afterwards. Can't abide working with her, I always imagine her reports as being spoken in her whinger's tone. Aah good, here's our wine."

Siera took a long sip from her glass before continuing. "I don't miss her sniping behind my back," she said, "but I tell you – I do miss Captain du Vives. I keep meaning to pay him a visit, I haven't heard what he thinks about the *Wrath*," said Siera.

Andrayzn frowned. "Du Vives, indeed. Huh, sometimes I still expect to look over and see him instead of you. Can't believe he retired after the riots in San Seras, I thought he'd be around for ever. How's ah... how's Catarina doing as your page?"

Siera rubbed her chin with her thumb. "She does well, I think she still holds out hope that her father will recognise her. An... unfortunate business."

Andrayzn grimaced. "An unfortunate business, San Seras. And I know from a personal conversation that Captain du Vives hadn't planned to retire for years yet." Andrayzn shook his head. "I still think he could have stayed on despite losing the eye, but the choice was his."

Siera sighed, then took another long sip of her wine. "Losing his eye was the excuse he used. The whole business had depressed him. He spoke once to me about it, afterwards, very intensely. He was immensely distressed, he felt that the guard could have handled San Seras better. He... hmm."

Andrayzn's face was stony. "If they wanted better treatment, they should have stayed away from rioting. A criminal has no place complaining about the law being enforced, by the sword or otherwise. The du Vives... they're under the du Aristas, aren't they? They're too principled, as a rule, especially seeing as their immediate lords are – well, the goddamned du Aristas."

Siera nodded slowly. "I can admire Dantes du Vives' stern virtue, but the Guard does what the Guard must. Still, a bleak topic." Siera looked around. "Well, ah... oh, your wife, is she in attendance?"

Andrayzn rolled his eyes. "She's damn well supposed to be, but she's hideously late. Again. I'd worry about how rude it appears, and I keep telling her so, but she seems to get off every time. I'd almost swear she had something on your father, that he never complains."

Siera smirked. "I used to wonder why he had both Gustavo and Lycea as advisors, but after hearing Gustavo drone on... I think it's more that he finds dealing with Gustavo to be an unending pain." Siera laughed. "He sounds like a slowly dying cow."

"A dying cow offends the dear Princess's ears? Such an uncouth individual should be challenged before both the law and my blade!"

Siera turned and recognised Agapito du Morandi, and despite his relatively handsome face and his reasonably sincere efforts to gain her favour over the last year, Siera felt nothing for him but a mix of pity and irritation.

Before Siera could speak up, Andrayzn turned around and glared at Agapito.

"Does this look like the local doghouse to you, young du Morandi?"

Agapito blinked. "Well – no, Your Grace, and also I am no–"

Andrayzn snorted. "Then you can wander off somewhere else."

Agapito gave a short laugh, biting his lip and looking around the room. "Come now, I'm here to speak to Princess Siera, Dray! Why, I–"

If Andrayzn had glared before, now his gaze bored into Agapito. "Do you mistake me for a common labour horse? My name is not 'Dray', and if you ever address me as such again, I will wear your guts for garters, boy."

Agapito's eyes flickered from Siera to Andrayzn. "W – well, if it's a challenge you want, then–"

Andrayzn's face remained stony. "When last did dukes duel? Or have you forgotten who you're talking to? And you can thank Sura that my wife is late. If she heard you say that, she'd work something foul on you, boy."

Agapito licked his lips, his eyes again flitting from Siera to Andrayzn and back. "Very well, Your Grace, if you have to feign disinterest due to your wife's waspishness, I'll take my leave." He bowed to Siera, then left.

Andrayzn sneered. "Good riddance. Fool."

Siera sighed. "It's not his fault, it's his father. His, and another dozen eager parents all pushing their otherwise inoffensive children to court me at any point, and in any way they can. I'd complain more, but Rami has it far worse."

Andrayzn shrugged. "Your brother doesn't seem to mind. Well, sometimes. And I heard that last year that uh... one of the du Lucan's, uh... whatever the really old one's name is..."

Siera rolled her eyes. "Oh him."

"Yes, he was pushing his grandson to excessive lengths. Practically forced him to embarrass himself in front of everyone, in open court, as well. Idiot," muttered Andrayzn.

Siera scowled. "I can't blame him, but I can and did blame his grandfather. My father was mortified – there's ambition, and then there's just blatant ill grace and stupidity. And he can't abide either. And du Lucan's excuses were ill-received."

Andrayzn smirked. "You're telling me. Oh, that reminds me, if your father's still on the throne by the time you lead the Guard – and he might well be – don't make my mistake and come to the council sessions in uniform. I didn't hear the end of it for months."

Siera gave a wide shrug. "I know he's never cared for the military... I know he makes an exception for me as his daughter."

Andrayzn shrugged. "He does, but don't think he fails to recognise you for your skill. And note that no parent is quick to realise that their children have become their own people, become adults. Abarron knows better."

Siera looked into her glass for a moment, then spoke up.

"Have you ever regretted not having children, Dray?"

Andrayzn glanced off towards the band, still valiantly playing after two hours.

"My wife and I have never managed to have any children. I prefer to leave the matter at that."

Siera nodded. "Of course. I hate to pry. Oh, I was going to come and see you tomorrow about this, but now's as much a good time as any. I have a –" Siera cast a quick glance around her before continuing, then spoke more softly. "I have a suspicion that somehow, our patrol routes are being leaked."

Andrayzn looked at Siera, confused. "What? Why would you think that?"

"Well, more and more naval patrols have reported being just too late to catch raiders. Specifically, although the Fourth was slated to patrol past La Chayne and then by San Seras, we would never have caught up to the pirates that raided it without the *Sky's Wrath* – had we come by land, we would have been far too late. And there have been more and more raids in the past few months... added to that, Commodore Paulo de Luca's ship was attacked when it was short of its full troop complement. It's too suspicious."

Andrayzn stroked his chin with his thumb. Siera made as if to continue.

"No, no, I hear what you're saying," said Andrayzn. "But there's no hard proof... that said, it wouldn't be hard to look for proof, and perhaps to find it." Andrayzn shook his head. "You're not just telling me this as a report of your suspicions, you're trying to sell me this idea, Siera. Why?... Ah, you don't want to go and accuse the Admiralty directly, and risk offending anyone. There's more of your father in you than you realise... I'll put these concerns across diplomatically. It might not be quick, but if there's any leak of patrols or such, it will be ended at the hangman's noose," Andrayzn said, baring his teeth.

Siera nodded, and leaned back in her chair. "I don't mean to play the paranoid, but... if there is some treasonous cur in the Navy or Guard..."

Andrayzn nodded. "Best to deal with matters quietly, if possible."

Siera thought for a moment. "Oh, there was one other thing that sprang to mind. While I was speaking to Commodore de Luca, he mentioned 'Old Salt-Sword'. That would be Heinrich Ailbhe, wouldn't it? I've heard all kinds of stories – half of them seem like deranged fairy tales – but why did they call him Salt-Sword?"

Andrayzn grimaced. "More than enough reports from the few captives who survived, or were ransomed. He would coat his blade in some glue-like mix and dip it in salt."

Siera baulked. "To... help him in battle?"

Andrayzn shook his head. "For torture. The man loved nothing more than to hack up his prisoners, then salt their wounds, or poison them, anything."

Siera shuddered. "And here I thought he was just a notorious pirate, that the stories about him were exaggerated."

Andrayzn scowled. "Well, Gretchen herself said that although some of those stories are exaggerated, the truth at the core of the matter is that he was an unrepentant, wretched beast of a man." Andrayzn shook his head, then laughed softly. "Here I am, supposed to be at a party, but I'm already dealing with work. Can't complain, this is the life I chose. Still, Lycea would be tutting at me for this. Hm, and speaking of her..." Andrayzn gestured, and Siera turned to see Lycea du Tilmost walk into the room.

"Considering she can actually move herself from place to place at will, I'm never sure why she's late..." Andrayzn muttered to Siera. "We'll talk again soon."

"Of course, Dray," said Siera as she stood, and offered a small bow to Lycea.

Siera was happy to leave Andrayzn if his wife was in attendance. Lycea was always polite, but she was a true oddity at court. No one knew her past or lineage, and Lycea always redirected the conversation away from any discussion about her background. She didn't seem to be Reimaran by birth. And Siera had noticed two things about Lycea that she disliked: that despite Abarron having Gustavo Espinoza as an advisor on magical matters Lycea had also been appointed a council advisor for a similar reason; and that whenever Lycea thought no one else was looking, her normally pleasant expression and demeanour dropped away to reveal a stark, frigid gaze.

Siera meandered around the party, making sure to speak to the right people and smile at the right times. Even if she wasn't taking the throne, appearances had to be maintained. After a few polite conversations with some minor Reimaran nobles, she found herself back near her father's table.

Fede caught her daughter's eye. "Sia, come sit with us."

Siera smiled and obliged.

"You've been away so long, Sia."

Siera smiled. "Mother, I saw you this afternoon. And not an hour ago, this evening."

Fede shook her head. "That doesn't count, you've been away for months."

Siera shrugged. "Patrols sound short and simple, but they're lengthy and boring. Still, there's no avoiding them."

"It's good to have you back regardless," said Fede with a smile. "I'm proud to have you do what you do, Sia. Even if it's sad to have you away so often."

Siera smiled. "But what if I have to marry some faraway foreign noble? I could be away for years then."

Fede rolled her eyes. "No prince or princess has left Reimar for generations now. If any ally wants such a strong marriage, then they come to us, not us to them. To do otherwise is preposterous, Sia. Reimar does not go with its cap in hand to other countries."

Siera smiled. "Rather the reverse, true. Still, you–"

Siera started as someone behind her kissed her head. "Oh, who–" Siera looked up, startled, as her father sat down next to her.

"Father, really. I'm not a girl anymore," said Siera, the

beginnings of a blush on her cheeks.

Abarron du Tealdan smiled, giving the slow, wide shrug he was known for. "True, but you'll always be my girl. You'll understand, when you have children of your own."

Siera rolled her eyes.

Fede leaned around Siera to look at her husband. "Dear, is Rami still here?"

Abarron raised his brows. "I think he still is… last I saw, he was with young du Aquino."

Fede sighed. "Du Aquino's boy is just such a troublemaker. Still, it's good that Rami makes well-connected friends."

"Hmph, if only well-connected meant well-bred. Poor manners seem to be going around more and more," said Abarron, flicking his fingers.

"Oh, Primo's not that bad, Father," said Siera.

"Hm? Oh, I was thinking about the Duchess du Arista," said Abarron.

Fede raised her brows. "Oh? Has she been making a scene?"

Abarron nodded. "She was having at Alejandro du Salamanca, refusing to call him 'du'. I know their families have quite some enmity, but she does this every time."

Siera rolled her eyes. "Just don't invite him, father."

Abarron shook his head. "His family stood against Reimar, but that was then, and this is now. He's worked his way through the Navy to Rear Admiral, Reimar can't afford to turn down talent. Not when so few join the Guard or the Navy."

"At least he worked for his title, I suppose. Still, as viperish as Zaballa is, the du Aristas have always supported Reimar," said Fede, brushing back a stray hair from her face.

"Was Alejandro much perturbed?" asked Siera, looking around her to see if she could spot the Rear Admiral.

"Usually he gets quite annoyed and demands the proper appellation to his surname, but this time he didn't seem to care. He was even smiling. Probably just in a good mood."

Siera grinned. "There're few sour faces at your parties, Father. Not when you put on the spread that you usually do."

Abarron's eyes lit up. "Ah, that's what I had forgotten to

say. Sia, have you tried the peppered hen yet?"

Siera's face went blank. "I... hadn't. Just hen? Chicken doesn't really seem–"

"Oh, you must try some, Sia," said Fede. "It's not actually peppered, it's been soaked in some spice – I can't recall the name – oh, it's fiery, but delicious."

Siera shrugged. "Alright, I'll get some soon."

Fede nodded. "Before dessert is served, especially."

Siera's eyes lit up. "Pie?"

Abarron's face soured. "You and your pies."

Fede flicked her fingers at her husband. "Complainer. Pies are just fine."

"Even apple?" said Abarron.

"Even apple," replied his wife.

The conversation drifted around, and as the evening wore on, people came and went to bend Abarron's ear. At one point, Siera found herself talking to Henk van Rooijen, the ambassador from Altren.

"You know, I love the way you do things in Reimar," said Henk. "I would take the style back to Altren, but it would never catch on."

Siera smiled. "Which style do you mean, Ambassador?"

Henk gestured at Catarina de Vives. "The way you have the pages bearing symbols of office, or one's court weapons. It's brilliant, I've always thought so. But it would never catch on back home, it's too ostentatious. And we're too proud to change our ways." He paused. "But I mean that as a compliment to Reimar."

Siera nodded. "But of course, Ambassador. I wasn't aware that Altrenese culture disliked ostentation."

Henk shrugged. "Altrenese custom prefers a point and a purpose. Even my own wife says I enjoy coming to Reimar too much, that I over-enjoy the grandiosity of everything here. And I do! I really do. Reimar's way of doing things is so..." Henk stared off at the ceiling as his thoughts wandered. "It's so fanciful. I mean, just last week I was visiting Duke du Greco – wonderful man – and his estate is just so welldone. Everything in its place, never too much or too little. Graceful topiaries, but never too many, and always to accent the architecture of a garden or building. He has an eye for detail that I find in many Reimarans. Reimar appreciates, Reimar loves beautiful things."

Siera nodded slowly. She'd not thought of it that way before.

"I've heard that Shardustur also enjoys a fair amount of ostentation," said Siera.

Henk scowled. "They might, but I've never been to Shar. Never will, either. We won't forgive them for Jurien. It was King Braam the Old who decreed that Altren would forever mourn its lost sibling, and so shall it be."

Siera raised a brow. "That was the Old Arn Empire, though, not Shar that invaded Jurien."

Henk sneered. "Old Arn, Arndustur, Shardustur, they're all the same. I hope they all come back as beggars in their next lives, or cripples."

Siera laughed.

"What's this I hear about Shar, Marquess van Rooijen?" asked Abarron, turning to join the conversation.

Henk turned to Abarron, his teeth bared. "That the sea should take them, each and every one."

Abarron's brows rose as he grinned. "Why Marquess van Rooijen, how cruel of you to wish that on the sea!" Henk guffawed as Abarron continued. "And speaking of the sea, the Duke du Tilmost has expressed an earnest desire to have you visit his new villa, and apparently it's right by the ocean."

Henk nodded. "An excellent proposal, Your Noble Highness. I would love to. I mean, I won't touch boating, not for all the Teals in Reimar, but the sea has a soothing sound. If you're not actually on it."

"Splendid, I'll have the arrangements made," said Abarron with a gracious smile.

As the night deepened, more and more guests retired: some to smaller gatherings, others to bed. Ramiros had disappeared off somewhere after Primo du Aquino had arrived, and Siera was worried that he'd be out all night, which angered Abarron deeply. Her mother had left half an hour ago, claiming tiredness. Siera and her father thus found themselves able to talk at least somewhat privately.

Abarron tilted his glass at his daughter. "Never forget, Sia, even if we've disagreed... even if you have your career in the military of all places..."

Siera looked away from her father. "Where else will I go, Father? Sit around and be useless? Sit around bothering Sura all day in the church? The military is the only place I can make a difference."

Abarron shook his head. "It isn't, but I'm not trying to talk about any of that. I just want to be sure that you know, even if this is the path you've chosen, that I'm proud of you."

Siera looked up at her father, eyes widening. Abarron continued.

"After du Tilmost is gone... don't get me wrong, he does a good job... but I know you'll make the right choices in the future, when you bear those gold stars on your shoulders. I'm proud of you. When Rami rules, I know I can rely on you to do what is right, even after I am gone."

Siera blushed. "Thank you, Papà."

"Myself and Marquess van Rooijen – well, and a few others – are having after-dinner cigars. Will you join us, Sia?" said Abarron.

Siera hesitated. She hated the smoke. "Outside or inside?" Abarron shrugged. "It's a bit cold, and there are no moonlights tonight."

"Well, yes, but just for a little while," she said.

Abarron smiled. "Excellent. I have a bottle of Valencia's Finest open, unless you want port."

Siera scrunched her nose. "I'll take the whiskey."

A few years before, Abarron had arranged for an unused storage room alongside the great hall to be converted into a smoking room. A large window had been fitted, allowing guests to look out into the most recent garden that Abarron's groundskeepers had come up with – a complex arrangement of tiny rivers and flower beds currently planted with Queen Fede's favourite: tulips. The rivers were actually feeding themselves, their overall flow cleverly manipulated by enchanted water-stones, allowing the seeming end of the river to flow back to the source. Amongst both the flower beds and small rivers, a variety of lifelike animal statues abounded.

Inside the smoking room, only a few party guests had been invited, among whom Siera recognised Henk van Rooijen, Nicodemo du Singara, and her brother Ramiros, who apparently had not absconded after all. Siera wondered just how keen her father was to impress the Altrenese ambassador.

After half an hour, the smoke was getting to Siera's nose. She made her excuses, said her goodbyes, and retired to bed.

Chapter 4: The First Night of Ruin

12th Teurnot

This deep in the night, the royal apartments were silent. This section of the palace could only be accessed through a corridor on the uppermost floor that led into a small foyer sometimes used for welcoming especially important guests, but usually just for the royal family to relax. Larger rooms lead off from the foyer, the central one – also the largest – was for the king and queen. On either side were the prince and princess' rooms. Although the foyer lacked windows to ensure privacy, the bedrooms did have large windows with a grand view of Ilmarch. At this hour, there was little to see bar an ocean of small lights throughout the city. Even when Ilmarch slept, it rarely slept too deeply.

Only a few sconces were lit inside the foyer, but they did not bother those who were asleep. For those who were awake, their eyes were long used to the gloom. Those who guarded the Reimaran royal family were well-accustomed to their vigil. Their white berets marked them as the elite of the elite: those handpicked from the Royal Guards' First Regiment, itself made up from veterans of every regiment.

Agurtzane du Firenze resisted the urge to scratch at his well-shaped beard. His wife's endless complaints whenever he did it were starting to get to him.

Bernat Rodriguez, his companion this night, smirked from where she stood, a few metres away. "Thinking about your wife again."

Agurtzane turned to regard her. "And how would you know?"

"You always have the same sour face on if she comes up in conversation."

Agurtazne glared at her.

Bernat gave him a wide smile. "Same as you have now, actually."

Agurtazne didn't return her smile. "Good to know you're keeping a sharp watch on my face."

Halfway across the foyer, Quintus Castell was idly thinking about a certain blonde lieutenant. His wandering thoughts were snapped by a hiss from Hirune Faenius.

"Quintus. Quintus! What was that?"

Quintus' eyes focused on her. "What?"

"Going deaf, Quintus? I'd have thought Hirune's ancient ears would be the first to go," piped up Bernat.

The whitecaps all went suddenly quiet as they heard something from the other side of the door. Only Quintus recognised it instantly.

"Someone's picking the lock," he said softly as he stood up.

The other whitecaps did not nod or speak, but instead moved into position a few metres away from the door to the royal apartments. They each drew out a short wooden stave with a pike-head attached. Each gripped the metal pommel and twisted, causing the stave to extend until it was as long as a pike.

"Shields up too. The guards know better than to play around," said Agurtzane softly.

The whitecaps each touched at a gemstone on the bracer on their left arms, which for all the world looked more decorative than defensive. With a hiss and a fierce white glow, magical energy flowed into the shape of a large rectangular shield.

A dull thud came from the door, along with an odd striking noise. Muffled voices could be heard.

"What're they doing?" muttered Quintus.

"I don't like it. We should move back," said Hirune.

"We need to block them at the narrow of the door," whispered Agurtzane.

An odd clicking noise sounded from beyond the door.

"Shields up!" cried out Hirune.

Even as the whitecaps raised their shields, Agurtzane was about to demand quiet. His words were cut short when the door exploded inwards, the smell of charred wood gushing into the room and the shock momentarily shaking the soldiers.

"Door's down, go!" came a cry from outside, and the room was flooded with masked figures brandishing short swords; easily dozens of assailants from Quintus' disoriented perspective.

Although shocked, the whitecaps fell back a few steps into their well-trained rank, and closed together with their shields up and pikes out. The first few assassins who rushed forward did so into a veritable wall, and got Reimaran steel for a welcome. But yet more assassins spilled into the room, a tide of dark clothing and miscellaneous blades, wordless cries on all lips. The whitecaps rapidly fell back, pikes pushing away any who came near, but as Agurtzane had warned the room was nigh indefensible. Doors led off to different corridors, and the whitecaps could not hold both their line and defend their charges from their attackers.

"Break ranks! Keep them away from the royals!" Agurtzane yelled above the din of the melee.

Quintus made a fierce grin as he moved away from his fellow whitecaps and disabled his bracer-shield. Two assassins quickly made for him, swords at the ready, eager to pick him off.

Quintus grabbed one by the face and tipped him into his companion, spilling both of them to the floor. Moving quickly, he stabbed at both of them while they struggled to rise.

Agurtzane moved straight back to the door to the king's room, his foremost thought to protect his sworn liege. Hirune was at his side and both drew out their shortbows and began to rapidly loose into the mass of assassins tearing towards them. Agurtzane grabbed a handful of arrows each time he reached for his quiver, long practice allowing him to hold spare arrows in the same hand with which he pulled the string.

Bernat had fallen back to guard the door to Prince Ramiros' room, but quickly got caught up by a push of masked attackers moving in the same direction. As quickly as she dodged and parried, too many came at her for her to go on the offence. She fought desperately to avoid just being outright mobbed, but she only had a limited space in which to backpedal.

Caught up against the door to Siera's room, Quintus fought like a lion. Knowing he had nowhere to retreat to, he stood his ground and killed all who challenged him. Even as he began to slowly tire and take injuries, he saw almost no end to his attackers.

Agurtzane and Hirune had dropped their bows and taken up their swords, activating their bracer shields once more. But it seemed that some among the assassins had realised that the door to the king's room would be guarded the best, and had made for the two whitecaps. Their opponents might fight no better than lowly thugs, but they need only have one success. And Agurtzane's shield simply ran out of whatever power kept it in shape.

To his credit, Agurtzane never flinched. He didn't try to dodge, move aside, or parry any of the various blades coming at him. He ignored the cries and howls of his assailants and simply lashed out with broad sweeps, using his longsword with both hands. He felt the blade slip into his side, and it was as though the world had gone dim. Agurtzane dearly wanted to try and attack again, just once more, to stand and defend his king. But he fell towards the floor and darkness took him.

Alone, Hirune gave all she could. She saw Agurtzane fall and knew that it was on her: none other could stop assassins from reaching Abarron and Fede. Like a tigress she fought, bared teeth and steel. But there were simply too many, and she was pushed under her own shield, its humming power pinning her between itself and the door. Unable to much move, she was cruelly cut down and trampled.

"Move!" roared Siera as she pulled her apartment's door open in her night clothes, with sword drawn. Quintus was torn between trying to protect her and hoping that with the princess, he could try and get to the king, even as he saw the first assassin dash into the king's apartment.

Bernat cried out in pain and despair as she tried to keep the remaining assassins from reaching and killing Ramiros, even as she knew that in moments they would kill her liege.

A scream from inside the king's bedroom, and it seemed as though a chill passed through Siera. Even as she saw the first

Royal Guard soldiers enter the foyer and rush at the few assassins remaining at the entrance, she knew she couldn't reach her father in time. Taking advantage of the distraction that the reinforcements brought, she cut down a thug in her path and suffered a deep slash against her back as a blade struck her. As she surged forward and reached the door to her father's room, she saw what would be seared into her heart forever.

Her parents framed against the dark night sky, her father with his head just falling back, a sword through his chest, her mother with her hands clutched to her chest and horror frozen on her face.

And a light broke – not from the windows, but inside the room, with a peal of force echoed through the chamber, knocking back bodies, Siera included. Suddenly Lycea was there, and her face was hatred incarnate. Lashing out with a bright, hissing energy, she simply blew apart assassins even as they rushed at her and the queen, splitting them into pieces with some cruel magical art.

Siera never saw the assassin behind her, wielding the blade that had just struck her, leaning in for the kill – nor did she see Quintus breaking their skull with a blow from the enchanted bracer on his right arm.

Siera saw none of that; only her father on the floor, his eyes glazed, and his body still. As guards rushed into the room and threw themselves at the few assassins remaining, as her brother stared horrified over Hirune's bloodied shoulder, as Lycea began yelling for a healer – for all assistance – for the love of the gods that the king was injured, Siera only saw that her father was dead.

Chapter 5: The Autumn of the Kingdom

13th Teurnot

The day dawned, and the wailing began.

All across the city, across Reimar, and then across the continent of Iber, the news spread: Abarron du Tealdan, King of Reimar, was dead – assassinated, murdered, slain.

Most Reimarans were simply stunned. This was a violence unknown to living memory, a brutal shock to their peaceful, orderly lives. Abarron had been a kind ruler, a just king, and to wake and hear of his death sent Reimar spiralling into misery. Businesses closed, and most taverns opened their doors and their taps for free to patrons seeking to drown this misery and their incomprehension. A full three days of mourning were declared.

The dukes of Reimar were no different, but their sorrow was tinged with fear. Abarron had been well protected; if he could be killed, then any of them could be killed. Those dukes who were outside of Ilmarch made all haste to get to the capital, travelling with a heavier than usual guard and considerable paranoia. Appointments were cancelled, windows shuttered, and urgent messages flooded across the country as the nation struggled to understand what had happened. Later in the day, a shocked and stammering Modesto du Greco, Duke of Reimar and Royal Steward, officially announced to the court's sorcerers a message to be relayed magically to every corner of the kingdom: that King Abarron du Tealdan had been mercilessly slain by unknown assassins.

Siera and Ramiros were in shock, Siera in some pain as well while her injury was attended to. They had both relocated to other apartments in the palace, now mobbed by whitecaps and guards both – General Andrayzn had ordered a triple guard to be posted, all food to be taste-tested, and he personally led a sweep of the palace and later the city. A curfew was declared, and even the most slightly suspicious characters were called in for questioning by Ilmarch's constabulary.

And even though that morning none could imagine things turning even worse, the evening did just that. Rebellion had erupted in Reimar's southern cities and provinces. Some unknown conspiracy had hired and organised a large variety of mercenaries and laid hold to Southmere, San Seras, Ponsurno, and Surmarch. No less than four of Reimar's seven major cities had been claimed by traitors.

The day after, an emergency council was called for all the councillors in the realm, and as the dukes gathered and heated conversations were held, Siera tried to recover herself. She forced herself to go to her parents' room; to see the smashed door, the stained bed, and the bloodied carpet where her father had died. Ramiros had shut himself in his room to be alone with his grief, so it was Quintus keeping a silent vigil as Siera sobbed, on her knees, where her father had been murdered scarce hours before.

And in the afternoon of the day after the king's murder, General Andrayzn broke the news to the royal council: Iln had declared war.

The councillors sat around a table that they had long associated with Abarron's voice winding between their own, the afternoon sun streaming through the windows, and the only disturbances to the stale air being the occasional page or servant slipping in to deliver or take away messages.

"Everything is breaking all around us." Modesto muttered, his head in his hands.

The councillors had been in session all day, hastily making arrangements to search for Abarron's murderers, find out whatever they could about the supposed rebellion, argue about Iln, prepare for Abarron's funeral, and bicker over how to carry it all out.

Modesto's clothing was rumpled and his eyes were dark from lack of sleep. He pinched his nose, feeling another headache coming on. "Du Tilmost, what else can you tell us?"

Andrayzn turned away from the window he'd been looking out of, back towards the rest of the councillors. "There is little else to say. Iln is clearly taking advantage of Abarron's death. They'll do what they always do, just with even more vigour – raid through our northern border, hit our outposts, raze villages, burn crops, and drive off anyone they can."

Zaballa du Arista clicked her nails on the huge rectangular table. "We can sit here and wish them all crotch-rot, or we can take to the field… which we'll have to do on two fronts, Iln in the north and these rebels in the south. Andrayzn, be honest: can the army cope with this?" she asked.

Andrayzn looked around at his fellow councillors, and then to his wife, who had spoken little during the day so far. She nodded slightly.

"We cannot."

There was muttering from everyone after he said that. "E – Excuse me, General?! Are you –" started Gaspar du Covas.

"We simply don't have the numbers," continued Andrayzn, ignoring Gaspar's outburst. "We'll have to take militia volunteers – which won't entirely cure our problem, as they'll have little to no training. At least they'll be in good supply, the people are furious about this. They will want revenge. Still, I cannot lead two campaigns at once, so we will require two commanders, one for each campaign."

"Well, who then? One of us?" pressed Zaballa.

"No. The military's own will lead," said Andrayzn as he glanced at Zaballa, his expression deliberately blank. "The decision is the king's, but most likely Siera will lead the campaign."

"She's untested," said Silvio du Donati, levelling his gaze at Andrayzn.

"She's fared well in all her endeavours thus far, and has brought some good innovation to her command." Andrayzn met Silvio's gaze. "She will meet my expectations. On this, you can take my word. Even in this hour, Reimar may be weakened, but it is far from defenceless."

"The people–" said Silvio.

"The king, Silvio, gives me my orders, and the monarch alone will decide the order of this war."

"You think he wants to throw his sister against some jacked-up rebel trash?" scoffed Silvio.

"He doesn't have much of a choice. Reimar is too used to peace to have enough skilled military leaders, we must use what we have. And the princess, Silvio, is more than aware of her duty." Andrayzn tapped at his sword hilt.

Silvio's jowls spasmed. "Oh, and what's that supposed to mean, Andrayzn? You think I have not tried to raise my levies? You think I've been sitting around eating pies? Good God man, some thugs and apparently an idiot nephew of mine have taken over my whole manor and almost all of my estates!" Silvio shouted as he swung his fist at empty air.

Andrayzn scowled. "Unfortunate, truly, but that doesn't change the fact that those levies might be used against us. This war will divide loyalties badly, what we need is a quick resolution above all else. Siera may not have vast experience, but moving quickly is a skill she possesses in spans."

"My own levies, the same," said Federica du Lucan, her expression carefully neutral.

"As mine, as Zaballa's too, I assume," said Nicodemo, rubbing at his temples.

Zaballa gave a small sigh. "I received word from my major-domo that she managed to save a fair portion of the family jewellery when thugs in mercenary livery burst into my estate. Absolutely disgusting."

Gaspar du Covas flicked his fingers at her. "Robbery is usually disgusting, yes."

"Not that, du Covas. What did I pay those lackwits to guard my estate for? They were useless at everything, including defending my family's ancestral home. And as for the north? All we've ever done is fend off the Ilnians, for all that I ever hear about how perpetually penniless they are. Can we hope to do better now? Godammit," said Zaballa.

Andrayzn gave Zaballa a level stare. "Honestly? I doubt

it. Now, as before, we are hampered by Iln's natural defences, being both its mountains and the outposts that are scattered throughout those mountains. An invasion will need to be the focus of our efforts, and our efforts will be divided for the present time."

Zaballa pursed her lips. "Why not send the Fourth Regiment and their skyship over the mountains?"

Andrayzn stared. "Do you honestly expect the under-strength fourth to go marching into the Ilnians' mountain warrens? Do you think Iln will be felled by their own trick?"

Silence took root for a moment, Zaballa glaring at Andrayzn, who continued.

"My advice to His Highness is that I and the First Regiment take to the north. I have fought Iln before, I know how they work."

Zaballa had not broken her glare. "And yet you've never won, General du Tilmost."

Andrayzn stared up at the frescoes above the chamber's double doors. "The day has not yet come where I have to prove myself to you, you traitor's get. A good dog keeps its mouth shut, you should do the same."

Zaballa's eyes widened. "You – if it weren't against the law for dukes to duel for honour, I would have you repeat those words to me without your tongue in your head."

"Councillors, please!" exclaimed Lycea. Surprised, all eyes focused on her. "I do apologise for the outburst, but we have more than enough enemies at our gates that we scarcely need to fight amongst ourselves."

Even as murmured approval and grumbling met her outburst, Lycea never took her eyes off Zaballa. Even as the other councillors sighed and nodded and other topics rose to the fore, Zaballa could feel the heat of Lycea's gaze.

Zaballa forced herself to look away. One continued annoyance for her in council meetings was the real status of Andrayzn's wife. That she was a foreigner was certain, but her mop of blonde hair belied no Archipelagan ancestry; that, Zaballa was sure of. In conversation Lycea always politely deflected questions about her past with that stupid little smile on her face, and Zaballa's own investigations had turned up nothing. Considering that Zaballa herself had scores of books detailing not only the ancestry of Reimaran nobles but those of most notable foreign nobility, the matter continued to perturb her.

Nicodemo du Singara leaned forward on his elbows onto the grand council table, tapping the tips of his fingers together. "Come now, we need decisions, and without a ruling monarch, the council is hampered. I propose that we do not wait for any mere ceremony for Ramiros to head council sessions. By every right and law, he is already king."

"Ramiros is hardy fit to be awake, let alone –" muttered Andrayzn.

"Yes, well – Your Grace, you've seen the most of Ramiros since the attack, how is he holding up?" said Nicodemo.

"Poorly. Would that we had his sister being fitted for a crown instead…" said Andrayzn.

"Well, now, we can hardly expect anyone to be cheerful after their father being murdered. We still need decisions to be made, we still need Ramiros," said Nicodemo, clasping his hands together.

"An excellent suggestion. And why worry that Ramiros will be less than capable? He has an entire council to support him," said Zaballa.

Berezi De Alencar spoke up. "The decision rests not with me, but the guilds are eager to see Ramiros take leadership. I… I myself am dismayed at the levels of pessimism, even within my own guild."

"Pessimism, Berezi?" said Andrea du Tealdan.

Berezi did not meet Andrea's gaze, and stroked her chin with her thumb. "They worry that Ramiros is inexperienced. Of course, that said, they are in full support of His Highness. There is no doubt of that."

"His Noble Majesty," said Gaspar with a sigh. "Nicodemo is correct, to all intents and purposes, Ramiros is king. Ceremonies are important, but not for us. The ceremony is to cement things in the minds of the people."

"Ceremonies, not relevant for us?" said Silvio du Firenze the Second. "Horse peppers! Regardless, Nicodemo is correct. Even if the timing is terrible."

"I'm amazed to see you express any sensible opinion,

Silvio," said Modesto with a wan smile. "Any other day I would correct you for evidently being wrong, but the situation demands expediency. General Andrayzn, can you bring Ramiros to the council chambers?"

Andrayzn glared at Modesto, who gave a slow shrug. "Well, escort him, or such. We cannot have his head falling off, now can we?"

"Shut up, Modesto. Just shut up," muttered Zaballa.

"Private Aintza." Andrayzn pointed at a First Regiment soldier standing at the chamber doorway.

Aintza saluted. "Yes Sir."

"Inform Hirune Faenius or Maria Ibarra, preferably both, that His Noble Majesty's presence is requested in the council chambers." Aintza clenched her right hand over her heart, and left.

For a long moment thereafter, there was quiet. Every councillor wanted to see if Ramiros would even arrive.

After twenty minutes had gone by, punctuated only by terse, shallow conversation; footsteps were heard outside the council chambers. Private Aintza stood outside, holding the door open for whitecaps Ibarra and Faenius.

"His Noble Majesty the King, Ramiros du Tealdan, is in attendance," said Maria Ibarra as she strode into the room, her eyes sweeping quickly around the chamber.

Ramiros more shambled than walked in from behind them, looking as though he hadn't slept at all since the night of his father's murder. He slowly made his way up to his father's seat at the head of the council table, and stopped. Moving quickly, Hirune stepped around Ramiros to pull the chair out for him.

"Ah… thank you," said Ramiros as he gingerly sat down.

"Your Highness –" said Nicodemo.

"Noble Majesty," said Gaspar with a sigh.

"Irrelevant, just make your point," said Andrayzn.

"Well, if we can –" began Lycea

"Yes, either way, you see, Your Noble Majesty, we have requested your presence as we must resolve the matter of the Ilnians declaring war on Reimar," said Nicodemo.

"Better the rebels first, and Ilnian filth second," said Federica du Lucan, flicking her fingers.

"She's quite right. My holdings –" said Silvio du Donati.

"The fattest of holdings, truly," muttered Silvio du Firenze.

"Council chambers, if you recall your decorum, fellow Graces –" said Andrea.

And as the councillors began loudly bickering anew, only Ramiros and the royal guards were silent.

Chapter 6: In Mourning

15th Teurnot

Black ruled the day as dawn broke, mourners flocking to the Cathedral of Illumination, which had unfurled large black drapes to frame the entrance as people came in their droves to pay their respects to their dead king.

The tradition in Reimar had been for a monarch to lie in state at the palace, but Queen Hirune du Messina had changed that when she arranged for the royal palace to be moved to Ilmarch. From then on, a monarch lay in state at the Cathedral of Illumination, where any mourner, regardless of social rank, could pass by.

The cathedral was flooded with people. Mourners turned up in huge numbers, most weeping openly. People clutched the small bronze disks that most of Sura's faithful wore on necklaces for any churchgoing occasion, some mumbling their prayers, others silent as they passed by Abarron's coffin. The Suranic Church's cantors led prayers throughout the day, but most of the citizenry arrived shortly after noon, when the members of the royal family were due to appear. Now, more than ever, people wanted to be reminded that someone was in charge, to know that someone knew what to do at a time like this.

They did not appear.

Amidst the throngs of people, rumours began to surface. That Prince Ramiros had also been slain, but that the announcement had not yet been made because the dukes were arguing over who would take the throne next. That the prince was alive, but being held against his will. That the royal family had fled, and Andrayzn du Tilmost had enacted a military coup. But the rumour that found the most favour was that no formal appearance by the royal family had been made because it was Siera who would now take the throne, her brother having suddenly abdicated – despite this going against Reimaran law; as usual people simply believed what they wanted to believe.

Siera knocked at Ramiros' door. After a few moments of silence, she opened the door to find Ramiros sitting on his bed, his face blank.

"Didn't you hear me knock?" said Siera.

"Oh… sorry, no. I was… well, thinking."

"I don't know whether I should be thinking about it, or not thinking about it, or… or what, or anything." Siera made to walk over to Ramiros, but stopped.

"Oh, of course – come and sit." Ramiros patted the bed next to him. Siera obliged him.

"I keep thinking that I just need to ask father how to deal with all this," said Ramiros softly as Siera sat next to him. "And if not him, mother would have some good advice. But she refuses to see anyone… I don't think she can deal with this at all, Siera. I think she's breaking harder than I am."

Siera bit her lip. "You're probably right… I don't think she can. I don't even know if she'll be at the coronation."

Ramiros shuddered. "I never wanted to think about being crowned. I always hated it when someone brought that up."

Siera sighed. "Well, of course. You're just a playboy to most of them, Rami."

Ramiros looked up and straight ahead. "Any coronation, any assumption of kingship… would only come after my father's death. And I… Siera, he loved us so much, how can he be gone…?"

Siera leaned over to embrace her brother as both his and her tears flowed anew.

Ramiros wept in deep, heaving sobs, and Siera followed.

"I f – feel like I can't even cry in front of anyone else, that they'll look at me and know that I'm weak… Siera, I'm so sorry…" Ramiros choked out his words, his throat thick with sorrow and pain.

Siera tried to look her brother in the eyes as he sobbed.

"Don't be sorry. Never be sorry. You're king now Rami,

you don't owe them anything."

Ramiros shook his head. "No, no! It doesn't work like that. There's a whole room full of them, those people that Father controlled like – like some kind of wizard. And they all danced to his tune, Siera, but I don't know how to sing that song."

Siera grabbed Ramiros by his shoulders, and he turned to face her, his face red and specked with tears.

"Even if they don't trust you, even if they don't know you, they have to work with you. Never give them a choice. Most of them don't even deserve it! You can do it, Rami."

Ramiros continued as if he hadn't heard her. "There's that stupid fatass du Donati, he's always shitting on the kingdom anyway, and that hatchet-faced bitch du Arista is like a goddamn harpy in council, always trying to score points off people, and du Tilmost always looks at me like a mortician, I swear he's a lunatic anyhow."

"Andrayzn is fine, I know him. He's more your ally than you realise."

Ramiros wiped at his eyes. "How? You mean against the others?"

"Andrayzn hates it when any of the other dukes try to tell him how the Guard should be organised, and they're always trying to make each other look bad. Du Greco and du Covas are often at him for various reasons, and he hates them. Oh, and he hates du Arista as well, she tries to talk bigger than she is. I think if you go into council and openly say that you can't match Father for skill and knowledge, they'll acknowledge that honesty. I... I don't know most of the dukes well enough, even you know them better than I do, but you can easily get Andrayzn on your side. He's a military man through and through, he might have liked Father sometimes but they were... they were never warm. I think that if you promise the military your support, Andrayzn will side with you at every turn. And if you get du Tilmost, you get his wife as well, she rarely speaks but she never goes against her husband. Even if she has no council vote, her support is better than nothing. And I think you can win du Lucan over easily, this thing with the rebels will have her frothing. She hates the established order of things being upset, she always talks like that."

Ramiros pressed his palms against his eyes, and then looked up to Siera.

"You're right, she hates any kind of disturbance. I remember that thing with Serrano talking about possible dockworker strikes had her sharpening her knives for weeks."

"That's two already. And Nicodemo is... was always hanging around the palace, around Father, they were such good friends."

Ramiros laughed, his mouth twisting in a sour smile. "Hah, friends, friends! Nicodemo came to see me this morning. I never realised, all along! Sia, he was father's spymaster."

Siera blanched. "Nicodemo... du Singara? Duke du Singara? Really? He couldn't organise a pitcher in a pub..."

Ramiros snorted. "Apparently he just likes to act that way. He thinks it's funny, however that works, I don't know. But apparently he and Father have been suspecting that this rebellion was brewing for months now... they just didn't realise how far along it was. And now Father is dead... a – and Nicodemo blames himself."

"I had no idea..." said Siera.

"He was so serious with me... but the more he told me about the rebellion, the more he began to get upset. Sia... he broke down and begged me to forgive him... as if I was a cantor, he begged me to absolve him of his sins. He really believes that if he had acted sooner, Father would still be alive. He showed me a list he had, of the suspects that he and Father were discussing. He kept clutching at it."

Siera blanched. "Does it list the conspirators?"

Ramiros sighed, rubbing at his temples with his palms. "He doesn't know, he's not sure. There are some names he's confident of – I'll get you a copy of the list, Sia – but he's not sure. And there could be more. You think he'd be more certain... It is his job..."

Siera bit her lip. "Well, spymaster or not, he's not psychic. I mean, wait, he's not psychic too, is he?"

"No, I don't think so. But he's wracked with guilt. I don't think he's holding together too well... after I was summoned to council today–"

"The councillors wanted you to sit in on a session?"

"Yes, they needed me to resolve their idiot bickering. Sura's grace, they bicker. I never realised how under control father kept everything... never even realised at all..."

"Singara supported you, though?"

"He suggested that I be called to head the council before the official coronation. But... he was barely with it himself. Are any of us with it, anymore? I swear half of them are terrified. I've sat in on council sessions before, but today... it's like a pack of dogs all nipping at each other."

Siera sighed. "I can understand their fear... if father could be killed, then anyone could be. There were so many assassins, even the whitecaps couldn't stop them in time. We still don't even know how they got in..."

Ramiros looked at Siera. "Have you been back to the room? Since..."

Siera nodded. "I... couldn't resist. I... Rami I swear, I went to their room and I expected to see father there, and when I saw him it would be like a nightmare breaking and the dawn rising... but it hadn't even been cleaned up."

"A lot of the palace staff had time off. Everyone has. Everyone... everything is all over the place."

Siera pinched the bridge of her nose, and tried not to cry. "I just... I wanted to see him one more time."

Ramiros nodded. "Half a dozen times I've broken down and given thanks to Sura that I hadn't argued with father before he died."

Siera gripped her brother's arm. "What was the last thing he said to you?"

Ramiros' eyes were blurring with tears again. "He said good night, and he smiled. I don't think I'll ever forget that smile. At least I can live knowing that the last time I saw him alive, he was smiling. What did he say to you?"

Siera blanched. "He, he... he also said goodnight. I know what you mean."

At any other time Ramiros would have seen right through Siera's lie. The last thing she remembered, and the thing she would take to her grave, is that her father had told her he was proud of her. Her brother didn't have that. That, and the last time she'd seen her father was him transfixed by an assassin's blade, his head falling back, against the deep starry night sky.

Chapter 7: Enthroned

16th Teurnot

The coronation was a hastily organised event, but thanks to circumstance was more easily done than normal. Every Reimaran coronation required all nine Reimaran dukes to be in attendance in order for the heir apparent to be declared the new monarch, both for the procession and for the actual ceremony of the enthronement. As all the dukes were already in Ilmarch, the coronation could proceed.

The procession both started and ended outside the palace's main gates, moving down the length of Marchioness Federico du Alecio Avenue and then back up again to the palace, where the dukes of the realm and the heir apparent would move into the palace's central hall, the traditional site of the Reimaran monarch's physical throne. Unfortunately, arrangements had not yet been made for Ramiros' own throne to be built and installed, so he would be declared king on his father's throne.

As such, on the sixteenth of Teurnot, Ramiros' coronation began. Despite minimal announcement beforehand, the crowds still turned out and most of the important guild leaders were on hand too.

It was traditional for Reimaran monarchs to ride down the Avenue in a horse-drawn carriage, the dukes of the realm following in carriages of their own after the monarch. No ranking noble would be seen riding atop such a dirty beast of burden as a horse, after all, but nor could a king or queen be seen to have to walk. As such, carriages were the way to go. Most monarchs took the opportunity to make their faces seen, as the carriages were open-topped, so that those people determined enough to wait at the avenue in advance or get there early enough could see their new king or queen in person.

None in the assembled crowd got to see Ramiros' face. The palace's front gates never opened, and no carriages were forthcoming. People muttered that Ramiros must have fallen ill, or that perhaps there had been some delay. After an hour, people began drifting away, until only a few die-hards were left as the day waned. A particularly ugly rumour even began to circulate that this was all some scheme among the dukes to keep Ramiros from assuming the throne at all; that they had him locked up in the palace somewhere.

Amidst the recent chaos, no one had thought to pass the word that the procession was cancelled. Those throngs who turned out did so for nothing.

The Crown Hall, one of the first buildings completed when the royal palace was originally built, was packed. Everyone who was anyone had rushed to get to Ilmarch in time, or was already there and waiting for the coronation. The news that there would be no procession due to concerns of assassins was already known to all bar the lowest ranking courtiers, and those in attendance waited with bated breath as Ramiros' entrance was heralded.

The hall's great mahogany doors had been ceremoniously closed to await the king-to-be's arrival in front of the rows of standing courtiers, officials, and guild representatives. Slowly the doors swung open, to admit the kingdom's great dukes. Andrayzn du Tilmost and Modesto du Greco walked in first, Andrayzn forsaking his officer's uniform for more stately ducal attire. At his left hip he wore an ornamental longsword with gold filigree. Modesto was dressed no less finely, and bearing his own ceremonial blade with jewelled pommel and all. The dukes entered two at a time, making their way up the long blue carpet in the middle of the hall that led to a single tall mahogany throne, Grand Warden Livio du Nascimbeni of the Reimaran Suranic Church waiting to the left, resplendent in white alb and golden sash. Andrea du Tealdan was the last duke to enter, and was the only one not exercising the right of her station in bearing a ceremonial weapon to court in the monarch's presence. After all the dukes had walked solemnly to stand at the sides of the throne, five on the right and four on the left, Ramiros du Tealdan entered the hall, his sister at his side. Siera had on her dress uniform, while Ramiros was clad in a black silk shirt, black trousers, and black sable cloak. He made his way up the blue carpet to his father's throne at a slow pace. He retained his composure in all but his eyes, which flitted from side to side as he walked, trying to remember the name of any familiar faces he could see on either side.

Behind them, ever watchful, walked the whitecaps Quintus Castell and Maria Ibarra.

As Ramiros reached within two metres of the throne, he stopped, and his eyes flitted from duke to duke.

Modesto du Greco stepped forward.

"As royal steward, I hereby declare that His Noble Majesty Abarron du Tealdan the King of Reimar, has been taken from life and duty and now stands in Sura's light. His throne stands empty, and his heir Ramiros du Tealdan stands before us. Ramiros du Tealdan, do you intend to ascend the Royal throne of Reimar?"

Ramiros breathed deeply, and replied. "I intend to ascend the Royal throne of Reimar."

Gaspar nodded. "Who here among the assembled Dukes of the Kingdom of Reimar recognise Ramiros du Tealdan as the rightful heir to the throne of Reimar?" said Gaspar.

"I, Duke Andrayzn du Tilmost, Lord of Gerva, recognise Ramiros du Tealdan as the rightful heir to the throne of Reimar," said Andrayzn du Tilmost.

"I, Duke Silvio du Firenze, Lord of Sapara, recognise Ramiros du Tealdan as the rightful heir to the throne." Silvio winked at Ramiros, who blinked in surprise.

"I am Duke Gaspar du Covas, Lord of Calinia. Ramiros du Tealdan is the rightful heir to the throne of Reimar," said Gaspar.

Andrea smiled as she spoke, her eyes closed. "I, Duke Andrea du Tealdan, Lord of Fidé, declare that my kinsman, Ramiros du Tealdan, is the rightful heir to the throne of Reimar."

"I, Duke Zaballa du Arista, Lord of Gavar, recognise Ramiros du Tealdan as the rightful heir to the throne of

Reimar," said Zaballa, her expression solemn.

I, Duke Silvio du Donati, Lord of San Seras, declare that Ramiros du Tealdan is my rightful liege and the heir to the throne of Reimar," said Silvio.

Nicodemo spoke hastily and loudly. "I – Duke Nicodemo du Singara – Lord of Guerda – declare that Ramiros du Tealdan is the rightful king of Reimar."

"I, Duke Federica du Lucan, Lord of Espinoza, state that Ramiros du Tealdan is the rightful heir to the throne of Reimar," said Federica.

"And I, Duke Modesto du Greco, Lord of Felde, recognise Ramiros du Tealdan as the rightful heir to the throne of Reimar," said Modesto with a curt nod. "The Dukes of Reimar stand in agreement. Ramiros du Tealdan, step forward to assume the Royal throne of Reimar."

Ramiros slowly stepped forward, turned, and sat down.

"Ramiros du Tealdan is hereby declared the king of Reimar. Long live the king!" called out Livio du Nascimbeni, raising a single golden bell in his right hand, and beginning to ring it.

The assembled courtiers cried out in a great din their own declarations of fealty and calls of "Long live the king!"

After the din had calmed, Modesto du Greco held up his hands for silence, then turned to Ramiros.

"Your Noble Highness, if you would speak to your assembled court," he said softly to Ramiros.

Ramiros nodded, then stood slowly.

"Gathered gentlefolk... I stand here today as your newly crowned king. I..." Ramiros looked for a moment as though he'd forgotten himself, but caught his sister's gaze. Siera smiled and nodded. "I... I swear to you all, Your Graces, Your Worthinesses, you lords and ladies, that I will serve Reimar as king... no matter the straits we find ourselves in, Reimar will... will never falter."

A few scattered coughs came from the assembled courtiers.

Ramiros looked around for a brief moment, then slowly sat down again.

Modesto leaned slightly towards Ramiros, his voice low. "Will that be all, Your Noble Highness?"

"I… yes," said Ramiros.

Modesto straightened and turned to address the court. "His Noble Highness has declared court over for today. All those so assembled may depart this coronation's end."

Slowly the courtiers filed out of the hall, Ramiros spotted more than a few try to turn and look back at him, for reasons Ramiros couldn't bring himself to conjecture.

Ramiros suddenly realised someone was talking to him.

"–ness, are you alright?" said Silvio du Firenze.

"Oh… yes, of course."

"A council session has been called to discuss war plans. Your seal is required to authorise the council's plans," said Andrayzn du Tilmost.

Modesto cleared his throat. "General Andrayzn has formed a plan of action that requires your seal, Noble Highness."

"That plan is far from finalised," muttered Zaballa. As they all filed out, the dukes were already murmuring and discussing back and forth, with Ramiros following silently behind them.

Chapter 8: By the Rope

17th Teurnot, morning

Ramiros stood upon a raised platform in the large square outside the royal palace, and looked over to Gustavo Espinoza, the Luminary Academy's Chancellor, who nodded.

"The enchantments are all in place, Your Noble Highness. You need only touch the gem on your collar to have your voice projected across the square, and when you are standing on the dais, even people in Fortenara will be able to see you."

"And your sorcerers will thus relay my words to every city?" asked Ramiros.

"Yes, Your Noble Highness."

Ramiros nodded, then looked back once more. His gaze crossed the assembled dukes, Andrayzn's stony face, Zaballa's scowl, Silvio glancing over Nicodemo's shoulder.

He took a deep breath, and stepped onto the dais.

"People of Reimar..."

Ramiros quickly looked down at his speech, and it finally struck him. It wasn't just a speech, it was a script. They'd just written him a script, for him to read politely, and do so like a good boy.

And here he stood, in the same place where his father would speak, whenever the occasion arose, before the entire country – and here Ramiros stood looking at a script written by the people who just a week ago had been kept in tight check by his father. The clear paragraphs, the lack of contractions... this was a speech written by nobles to reassure other nobles. And who had his father spoken more highly of? The nobles he saw bicker day in and out, or the common people who made Reimar work?

This was not something his father would read. And if he couldn't speak with Abarron's guile and cunning, he could at least speak with his own passion.

'If I am not King here and now, then I never am. And no king weeps like a child in front of his people.'

He threw the papers on the floor, and leaned forward with his right hand on the lectern in front of him.

"People of Reimar, I come to you today as your new king. Hear me and know that I speak the truth when I say that by all rights, my father should be here." Ramiros licked his lips. "I won't lie. Well that it should be Abarron du Tealdan here, not me. But my father, our rightful king, the man who loved this country like no other, was struck down in his own bed by – by filthy criminals and sell-swords, hired by traitors and rebels!" Ramiros' voice rose from impassioned to roaring, his eyes wild.

"I stand before you as few kings have in our long history, as a king enthroned both in war and because of cruel assassination. I do not come to you in this hour, citizens of Reimar, with kind words and a smile. I tell you this: I am furious!"

Ramiros banged his right fist onto the lectern. "You've likely heard the news that rebels have risen up and declared that the provinces of Espinoza, Gavar, Guerda, and San Seras are now separated from Reimar and are suddenly their own sovereign nations. Traitors and rebels roam the streets of these cities, rightful lords and ladies have their properties stripped from them and awarded to riff-raff with ambitions of tearing our kingdom apart! Honest citizens dragged off the streets to be thrown in jail for daring to refuse to bend their knees to traitors! I tell you this, citizens of Reimar, I may be young, but I have no hesitation. These traitors will not escape their punishment. Traitors one and all! No matter their rank – their now former rank – I will have them hanged for treason. Hanged, hanged! Each and every traitor, that struck at my father, our king, and that wants to break apart the nation that we all work daily to leave to our children, that we all work and live in with pride, will be brought out into the harsh light of day and hanged!"

The silence that had permeated the square as Ramiros spoke suddenly gave way to a vast roar, the assembled people shouting their approval. Ramiros was for a moment taken aback, but as he heard them begin to chant his name, he knew he'd made the right choice. He held out his hands for quiet.

It was slow to come.

"People of Reimar! Citizens! Citizens, quiet for a moment for your king! I also swear that Iln – oh yes, Iln, that viper's nest of thieves and beggars – Iln will also feel the wrath of Reimar! They think they can declare war on us in our hour of weakness? NO! Reimar is not weak, Reimar has never been weak, and while I draw breath Reimar will never be weak. Even now the Royal Guard prepares, even now the Guard will accept militia volunteers, accept all able citizens, and even now plans are laid to bring justice to Iln and to traitors both. Those who live by treason will die by the rope! Those who raise a hand to Reimar will have that hand CUT OFF!"

If the crowd roared before, they exploded now. Ramiros was fifty metres away from the people outside the palace gates and he could feel their voices as a physical force, pushing at and around him. They screamed his name and they screamed their hate and they screamed their demand for him to crush the foes of Reimar, and Ramiros felt it all steep within him.

He smiled. He grinned. This is where he was meant to be. This was who he was meant to be. He was not his father and he would never be his father, but by Sura and Riest both he'd see that his father's legacy wasn't lost to traitorous garbage or sheep-fucking Ilnians.

The dukes were all settled in the council chambers when Ramiros arrived and seated himself. He ignored their stares.

"Your Noble Highness, I... could not help but notice that you discarded your speech," said Silvio du Firenze.

Ramiros' gaze was frosty as it settled on Silvio.

"Those papers had nothing written on them that my father would have read. It contained nothing that needed saying, as well written as it was. I am not my father, and I cannot give my father's speeches. Nor, however, can I give a speech made by a committee."

Gaspar du Covas coughed, then spoke up. "This 'committee' knows a fair deal more than you about speeches, crowds, and what people want to hear. You–"

Ramiros' eyes flashed. "Last I knew, Reimar was ruled by a monarch and the Royal Council, I say again, not some 'committee'! Do you take this for a stevedores' meeting?!"

Gaspar's eye narrowed. "To whom do you imagine you are spea–"

"A man who has forgotten his place. You do not speak through my mouth, Gaspar. None of you do." Ramiros said with clenched fists.

The ducal councillors were silent. Ramiros took a quick moment to survey them; Gaspar's sneer, Andrayzn's stony visage, Zaballa's nigh-perpetually furrowed brows, and Silvio du Firenze's half smile. "I am not my father, nor can the Council run the same way as when he was king."

"Better that you were your father," said Zaballa. "And there's not a one of us here who thinks otherwise."

Ramiros smiled thinly. "Then why do you not snap your fingers and bring him back to life, Your Worthiness? I will wait and abide humbly while you carry out your desires."

Zaballa scowled. "If I could, I damn well would. But–"

"You would what, Zaballa? Will you not repeat that for me?" said Andrea du Tealdan, in a tone that froze the room.

"Well, I did not mean literally," said Zaballa after a long moment.

"See that you never do," said Andrea with a smile that meant anything but joy.

A short silence took root. Ramiros broke it

"It is sudden and it is harsh, but my father is dead. You think I somehow fail to realise this? I watched him die," said Ramiros, his voice steady. "He is not coming back. Now, this Council finds itself a new balance. And speaking of matters of importance, Gener– Duke du Tilmost, might you outline your plan to me?"

Andrayzn's mouth twitched into the barest smile. "Gladly, Your Noble Majesty. I propose that the Royal Guard be split, one force led by myself, the other led by your sister. Some in this room have questioned Siera's leadership, but I have full confidence in her. I will lead the First Regiment, supported by elements of the Second, and take the field against Iln. Siera will lead the Fourth, the Fifth, and the Seventh against the rebels."

"I share your confidence, Your Worthiness. Who better to lead against a rebellion than one of the royal house?" said Ramiros.

Silvio du Firenze coughed as he cleared his throat. "Ridiculous. General Andrayzn has never won against Iln, and Siera is untested. Why not one of the other, more proven captains?"

Andrayzn scowled. "Because there are few in the guard who have fought in a war at all. Reimar has been at peace so long that many officers have not even seen large-scale conflict."

Zaballa waved her hand at Andrayzn. "All the more reason to have an officer with more years and more expe–"

"Duke du Arista, do you doubt Siera du Tealdan, my own sister? Are you suggesting... that my sister is incompetent?" said Ramiros

Zaballa rolled her eyes. "Theatrics do not serve you well, Your Noble Highness, and neither I nor Silvio suggest any such thing. Your sister is young, and there are better choices."

Silvio du Firenze coughed again. "Captain Guistina du Ochoa, for example..."

Ramiros sneered. "Those choices are not yours to make. Duke du Tilmost knows far more than you or I about these matters. He can only be in one place, and that place is on the front line against an enemy he has fought before and knows well: those beggars to the north who call themselves sovereign lords in their mountain holds. My sister will campaign against these motley rebels – she knows full well how to quickly take apart an enemy force and show them that our justice is absolute and unforgiving."

Silvio du Donati nodded. "Yes, yes. Indeed. The few retainers who have remained loyal to me have begun to make their way to Ilmarch, Your Noble Highness. They stand at your disposal, well, at General Andrayzn's or your sister's disposal. As you see fit."

"What good will they do us, Silvio? The retainers of a duke either so foolish as to turn traitor or so foolish as to allow treason?" said Modesto du Greco with a sneer.

Silvio reddened. "I have protested in council about my

family's authority being eroded by the crown and my supposed fellow dukes, but I am far from a traitor. And I do not see your levies encamped anywhere, Modesto."

Modesto flicked his fingers at Silvio du Donati. "I have drawn up what I need to, and they stand ready to be utilised where needed. Until then, why should they march?"

"Regardless, the plan must be decided. I hereby call for Duke du Tilmost to take arms against Iln, and for my sister to take arms against the rebels," said Ramiros. "And let Duke du Tilmost and Siera draw up any plans, then set their requirements. Let us leave matters to the experts."

"The major points are made," said Federica du Lucan. "Let us decide and be done with it. Worthinesses?"

Zaballa du Arista snorted. "I discur."

"I concur," said Andrayzn du Tilmost, not looking at Zaballa.

"I discur," said Silvio du Firenze, looking sidelong at Andrayzn.

"I concur," said Silvio du Donati.

"I concur," said Nicodemo du Singara.

"I abstain," said Federica du Lucan.

"I concur," said Modesto du Greco, extending his little finger to Silvio du Firenze, but not wiggling it.

"I concur," said Andrea du Tealdan.

"I… concur," said Gaspar du Covas.

"Then it is decided," said Ramiros, smiling.

"That said, the budget currently does not allow for such expenditure. We must discuss whether it is plausible to alter the budget to accommodate this," said Gaspar du Covas.

"The military needs what it needs, Duke du Covas. In this hour of all hours, we cannot afford to hold back funding. If we do, we might lose the Helion," said Ramiros.

Gaspar's eyes settled on Ramiros, and for a moment Ramiros was sure the old goat was going to lecture him.

"This is true, Your Noble Majesty. To lose the wealth of the Helion… unthinkable." Gaspar licked his lips. "Yes… let us discuss military expenses… maybe even martial law."

"Martial law? Yes, yes of course… we must call for curfews and militia," said Modesto du Greco. "Harsh times call for harsh measures. We… Reimar needs security."

Andrayzn raised a finger at one of the soldiers standing next to the guards, a staff sergeant. "Felipe, bring me those papers I had set aside." Andrayzn turned to Gaspar. "I have outlined most of the expenses, but if the council wishes assurance that the extra expenditure is necessary, then this will demonstrate the need and purpose. And martial law allows the guard to take volunteers, as although we call them militias, it is a holdover term. These individuals have little to no training in arms but will be trained as much as circumstance and time will allow, nor will anyone be forced into long-term service."

"Yes, of course," said Ramiros, before sighing to himself.

Nicodemo du Singara turned, as one of his retainers tapped him on the shoulder, and whispered into his ear. Nicodemo froze.

"Is something the matter, Duke du Singara?" asked Lycea du Tilmost.

Nicodemo seemed to deflate as he folded his hands on the council table. "It pains me to announce this, but Mordeno has forsaken us."

A sudden, deep silence reigned.

"Whaaaat?!" said Gaspar du Covas. Ramiros was startled, he'd never heard the old man say anything so loud. "How *dare* they refuse a call to arms?! How *dare* they go against our alliance! We own them, Sura scorch their *souls*, we OWN them! They think they can reap the benefits of friendship with Reimar and turn on us like this?! Those… those…" Gaspar trailed off as he bit into his thumb, his face reddening.

Silvio du Firenze nodded. "As loud as Duke du Covas is being, I concur. Mordeno expects–"

A page burst into the room. The whitecaps had their swords drawn and were standing in front of Ramiros before anyone else had even turned to look.

"Your–" the page froze, staring at the whitecaps' drawn blades.

"Young du Cipriani, is it? Speak quickly now," said Federica du Lucan, as the whitecaps sheathed their blades.

"A message from sorcerer Aurelio. They say to tell His Noble Highness immediately that Mordeno has refused

Reimar's call to arms."

"Confirmed, then!" screeched Gaspar du Covas. "Mordeno is faithless! Faithless trash!"

"Page… du Cipriani, is it? Do not repeat what you have heard here to anyone outside this room," said Ramiros, rubbing his forefinger and thumb together.

"Y–yes, Your Noble Highness," he squeaked.

Ramiros nodded, his eyes still on the page. "Good."

Gaspar du Covas pounded on the council table. "We must decide on action. Mordeno must be punished for their faithlessness!"

"Agreed," said Silvio du Firenze.

"Such a break with a long-standing ally is never acceptable. Wars have been started for less," said Federica du Lucan.

"True, but we barely have the ability to fight Iln and the rebels," said Andrayzn du Tilmost.

"No need for soldiers, Duke du Tilmost," said Gaspar du Covas, breathing heavily. "We should deny them the use of the Helion. Completely and utterly."

"What, all use?" said Berezi De Alencar. "But then we cannot tax them."

Modesto gave a short, sharp laugh. "They can keep their petty coins, we gave them a generous discount on Helion trade tax, and this is how they repay us? We should deny them any traffic through our land. Let their trade wither. Let them wither."

Ramiros nodded. "A faithless ally must be dealt with harshly, lest Reimar be seen as weak. We cannot afford such. Arn and Shar are watching."

"What news from Altren?" asked Andrea du Tealdan.

"Nothing yet," said Nicodemo du Singara.

"Altren, too, might prove unreliable. We should demand an answer," said Zaballa du Arista.

"We have not asked them a question," said Gaspar du Covas, staring at the ceiling.

"Don't be pithy, du Covas, you know what I mean," snapped Zaballa.

"Well, we have to know if Altren stands firm or not," said Federica du Lucan.

"And there are diplomatic ways to go about it," said

Gaspar. "Duke du Singara–"

"Enough, enough!" shouted Ramiros suddenly. All eyes turned to him. "I will go to Altren myself. We can't afford to lose them as an ally, we have to make sure."

"Should a Reimaran king stoop to visiting other nations, smiling with cap in hand?" said Modesto du Greco. "They owe us. We should not even have to ask."

"I will worry over manners when Reimar is safe. Now is not the time for manoeuvring on position and privilege, we need action."

"Agreed," said Andrayzn du Tilmost. "If Altren marches alongside us against Iln, we have a much better chance."

"And why ever not bring them to heel personally?" said Zaballa. "It is a sound proposal."

"Any other objections?" said Ramiros. Duke du Greco muttered under his breath about who owed whom, but Ramiros pretended not to hear him.

"Your Noble Highness, you will be needed here. If you leave for Altren – what about decisions that must be made? This is why we have diplomats to send in your stead."

Ramiros shook his head. "No diplomat will impress enough, it should be me who goes personally."

"If Your Noble Highness is interested, I can arrange far faster transport than even a skyship," said Lycea. All eyes swung to her.

"Oh?" said Ramiros. "Is this some magical art?"

"If I might interject, Your Noble Majesty," said Gustavo Espinoza, head of the Luminary Academy. "I assume that Councillor du Tilmost refers to the warlock's art of transplacing things."

"Of course, Gustavo," said Lycea, smiling.

Gustavo licked his lips. "A dangerous proposal. Such an art is highly inaccurate."

Lycea's smile did not waver. "Inaccurate for most, but I have a great and refined skill in this matter. If His Noble Majesty is willing, I can have him and any companions in Altren within moments."

"Done," said Ramiros.

"Your Noble Majesty, I–" said Gustavo.

Ramiros glared at him. "My mind is set. I will not be

dissuaded by objections about 'inaccuracy' and so on."

Zaballa shrugged. "If the councillor says she can do it, then she most likely can. How can magic be inaccurate, anyhow?"

"Yes, a most practical plan, councillor," said Nicodemo du Singara. "This way we can impress upon Altren the need to maintain our alliance, as well as have our Noble Highness be away from court for as short a time as possible."

"If this art – this transporting trick – if it works so well, why not do it all the time? Why, we could make a fortune," said Gaspar du Covas.

Lycea smiled. "Well, Your Grace, I am not a carriage conductor, after all."

"Well... yes, but more's the pity. Gustavo, why aren't we training mages to simply transplace things?"

Gustavo scowled. "Because the skill is difficult to use, and quite dangerous. It's too dangerous to be employed casually, very few have mastered it."

"Myself being one of those few," said Lycea.

"Well, if Headmaster Espinoza says that is dangerous, maybe we should not risk His Noble Highness being transported in such a manner," said Silvio du Firenze.

"If the councillor says she can do it, then I will assume she can. We must have Altren on our side," said Ramiros.

"We could have councillor du Tilmost take someone else, though," said Modesto du Greco.

"I volunteer myself, of course," said Nicodemo du Singara. "I – I wouldn't want anything to happen to His Noble Highness."

Ramiros scowled. "Do you think Altren will be as pleased? Er, no offence, Duke du Singara."

Nicodemo stared at Ramiros, face flat.

"If Councillor du Tilmost can do it, then send them both," said Silvio du Donati, thumping the table with his fist.

"Both?" said Nicodemo.

"Wait, I want to know just how risky this–" said Federica du Lucan.

"Of course send them both," said Andrayzn. "We cannot afford to lose Altren as an ally."

"We still don't know if we do risk losing them, or not,"

muttered Gaspar du Covas.

"We cannot risk it. Duke du Tilmost is right, both Duke du Singara and myself should go."

Nicodemo nodded. "It's best to be safe in this matter. Besides, I speak fluent Altrenese."

"Might as well all go at this rate," muttered Zaballa du Arista.

"I still want to know if any of this is safe," said Federica du Lucan.

"It seems they are decided, regardless," said Silvio du Firenze.

"Exactly so," said Ramiros. "We should not delay. When can you be ready, Councillor du Tilmost?"

Lycea smiled. "Whenever you are, Your Noble Highness."

"Duke du Singara?"

"Well... is now too soon?"

"Seize the moment... Father always said that. And the moment is upon us. Let us leave this very day."

Chapter 9: To Arms

It was a beautiful morning in Ilmarch, the well-risen sun flickering gentle gold between the spires and roofs through the city.

Few stopped to appreciate it.

On the Eighth Spoke Street of the Marble District, Siera du Tealdan gave a brief nod to the two saluting gate-guards as she stepped into the Fourth Regiment's central courtyard, and turned, towards what had been the officer's cloakroom. Despite its original purpose, Siera had begun using it as a meeting room for herself and her officers. Siera's actual office, although it commanded a well-framed vista of the city, was up two flights of stairs and didn't afford her a level view of the parade grounds.

As she stepped into the room, Siera happened to meet Ermanno's eyes. She saw only pity in that flint-grey stare, and for a moment she hated him. But she nodded and continued on.

"Captain, I can only offer my cheap condolences. He was a father to us all," said Adalberto as he stood. Siera noted that he didn't look as though he'd shaven or bathed.

"Captain." Gretchen saluted. "My condolences on your father." She looked like she wanted to say more, but a moment of silence stretched, and Siera filled it.

"My thanks, but I've no more time for tears or wailing. It wasn't the spirits who killed my father, it was people with flesh and blood. And that I can deal with. We will be at ashes all too soon, as I am sure you know."

Ermanno rubbed his chin with his thumb. "No disrespect, Siera, but are... is your brother up to it? What are his thoughts, now that he has taken the throne?"

Adalberto glared at Ermanno. "God, Ermanno, even at this

time?" he muttered.

Siera levelled her gaze at Ermanno, her expression flat and her eyes stony. "My brother is furious. Do not take his speech for an odd outburst, he means all the steel he speaks with."

"And if some nobles do not agree?" said Gretchen, looking away from Ermanno to Siera.

Siera made the tiniest shudder, which only Ermanno realised was actually her suppressing a laugh. Siera turned to Gretchen and flashed a thin smile.

"Then they will be publicly hanged as traitors. My brother's words to me, not mine. Not that I in any way disagree," replied Siera.

Ermanno nodded. "I don't see anyone disagreeing. The mood on the street is raw grief, and hatred."

Siera nodded. "The rebels haven't claimed responsibility, but that's beside the point: they imagine they can do as they will. The Council has just agreed to institute martial law, which will be announced within the week." Siera held up a letter from her desk. "With martial law, we can accept militia volunteers – meaning that even the lowliest private will be put to training the militia during their off-hours as soon as the announcement is made."

"Fresh, white troops... I don't doubt they'll be red before long," said Ermanno.

"Don't doubt it. We have siege work ahead of us, which means your greatbows, Adalberto, will be knocking down walls in a matter of weeks. Ensure that we have ample supply of enchanted bolts, and don't halt for costs – we'll have all the funds we require."

"What of the ringleaders? On your word, captain, not a soldier will take a prisoner," said Gretchen, her right hand beginning to drift towards her chest.

Siera shook her head. "No. There are to be no accidents, but nor will there be any honourable beheadings. My brother has given me a list of the suspected traitors, and one by one we will get our answers as to who is or isn't behind this. And with martial law, I can have them strung up whenever I want." Siera's fists clenched. "Every traitor taken alive will hang, they will kick, and will gasp until their eyes pop out of their heads and they starve for air. I want every soldier and citizen to see a traitor's reward, to know that their battlefield sacrifices will not be rewarded with some limp, tame justice upon these traitors. Justice with honour is for a time of peace, and my brother has made it clear that we will not have some half-baked war. We will have ash. We will hang every single one of them."

Gretchen smiled, and Adalberto paled. "Captain, your father…"

Siera gave him a hard look.

Adalberto swallowed. "Never mind, Sir. My apologies. If your brother commands it, if you command it, then I will hasten to obey."

Siera nodded curtly. "Good. And as callous as it sounds, Ramiros wants to reassure the citizenry, especially the common folk, that Reimar remembers how to use its steel outside the kitchen. This will not be a campaign of months, it must be a campaign of weeks. I don't see many reasons not to come at them from the air, we might not even need any sieges at all unless they have greatbows or arched ballistae to oppose us. My brother plans to have General Andrayzn take the northern front, and myself the south. The people will see the royal family directly punishing this treason, and be emboldened by it."

"Sounds as though this should come with a promotion, Siera. Captains don't usually command wars," said Ermanno.

"It does, Ermanno. Major, second only to General Andrayzn himself."

Adalberto, Ermanno, and Gretchen all saluted.

"Congratulations, Sir," said Gretchen and Adalberto. Ermanno nodded.

Siera smiled. "The exact division of the regiments is yet to be decided, but both ways we'll have all the funds we need. We'll also have support from the Luminary Academy and any other mages who sign up. A limited contract will be available to all militia volunteers requiring service for the duration of the war, to make sure no militia fighter is afforded more service time than we need. We need more soldiers, but after the war we can't afford to have unsuitable recruits remaining in the regiments. We'll also be working with the Seventh Regiment, using whatever mercenaries Captain Parrino deems fit."

"I realise it sounds odd, but hopefully few Archipelagan mercenaries will sign up," said Gretchen, scratching her chin.

Adalberto coughed. "I doubt you have an issue with seeing fellow Archipelagans die…"

Siera and Gretchen's eyes met for a moment. Gretchen looked away, and clicked her tongue at Adalberto. "It's not that, it's that I don't want to have to separate my own soldiers and Archipelagan mercenaries in the inevitable fights. Tensions will be too high. We might as well hire Ilnians, for all the terrible idea that is at this time… not that they're much noted for selling their swords to Reimar."

Siera nodded. "A fair point. If Captain Parrino takes on any Archipelagan bands… no, I will send word to him to avoid taking on any at all. The gain in troops will not be worth the loss in morale and discipline."

A long moment stretched out, and no one spoke to fill it. Eventually, Siera shrugged.

"Ensure that the initial logistical necessities are made, and meet me in one hour in my office to plan at least our major moves. I already have an overview drawn up, but I want your opinions in case there is anything that I have overlooked."

Ermanno, Gretchen and Adalberto saluted as Siera walked out.

"Well, I'm off, then. See you in a hour," said Adalberto as he too took his leave.

Gretchen watched out of the corner of her eye as Adalberto left. "Soft hands," she muttered when he was gone. "Thinking of how her father would have handled it instead of just taking his damn orders."

Ermanno let out a low laugh. "He never changes. Sometimes I don't really know what Siera sees in him. Or me, for that matter."

"Oh, but not me?" said Gretchen. "Don't hold back."

Ermanno grinned. "I believe I know full well what she sees in you, it's the same as what I see when I look at you. A nice young Archie lass with big, fulsome… blue eyes, and the largest… nice blonde hair."

Gretchen smirked. "Don't play the rogue with me, Erman. Come, tell me what you were thinking."

Ermanno's grin fell immediately. "I think she sees someone who no longer has a past to go back to. Someone who will only ever go forward. She sees that, and you should never think that she doubts you. She knows what makes you tick, when it matters. I think she knows us all better than she lets on."

Gretchen shifted in her seat. "I won't deny it, but that's cutting close to the bone, there. But no, I don't suspect that she really doubts any of us," said Gretchen.

Ermanno nodded slowly. "We've all proven ourselves for longer than she has, no insult to Siera there. She looked up to Dante du Vives a lot when he was captain, and if he was fine with an old man, a limp wrist, and an Archie – well, no wonder Siera has never complained."

Gretchen shrugged. "You know, I always assumed that the big countries were really serious about their militaries. Then you see them up close… they're all just people. I mean, damn, when I was being trained in the First, we had drinks sometimes with the sergeants. Hard as anything during the day, but come a night at the pub and they were full of old war stories, old good luck habits, advice, everything." Gretchen smiled as she leaned back. "The First is a great regiment."

Ermanno tapped his index finger against his forehead. "I'll second that, even if they are a bit up their own asses sometimes. But what do you mean, big countries?"

Gretchen sucked her teeth. "You know, Reimar, Shardustur, Arndustur. Zarann too, I guess, for all that they're so far away. The real countries, not like the Archipelago, or places like Jurien."

"Hmm, I see. Well, that said, I don't get paid to jaw. Time to get the sergeants earning their keep," Ermanno said as he stood to leave.

Gretchen sighed. "Too right. See you in an hour."

Chapter 10: See It Done

Just over an hour after Siera had left, her lieutenants convened in her office on the first floor.

Siera had unrolled a large map of Reimar on her table, and motioned for her lieutenants to sit closely. "We have days yet to prepare, but let's go as quickly as we can. The rebel mustering has been quick. They must have been working towards this for some time, they have a lead on us. And in addition to the Seventh, we have the Fifth coming in to assist us with any siege work," said Siera

"Any idea of who's behind all this?" said Ermanno. "Rumours are flying around, but nothing's official. And earlier, you mentioned a list..."

Siera nodded. "It seems the Council is debating on whether to tell the citizenry what they know, and if so, how much of what they know. That said, I do not give a wooden teal what the Council thinks, so I will tell you that some of the conspirators have been confirmed. Federico du Arista, and Enio du Donati, are apparently both thickly involved with all of this. My fa– my brother has reports that Enio, especially, has been seen with several Shardustan individuals, mostly minor nobles with known connections to some more... aggressive factions within their court."

"Never heard of Federico or Enio," said Ermanno.

Siera flicked her fingers. "Federico du Arista is some distant cousin, or somesuch, of Duke du Arista, and Enio du Donati is Duke du Donati's nephew."

"And Shar, eh? Makes sense. Do you think they'll move as well?" asked Gretchen.

"I would assume so, but apparently Shar has been having their own problems over the last few years, some dispute or other with Arn. Probably about who the rightful heir of the Empire is, as usual. It seems that their army is mostly encamped on the Shar-Arn border, but I would not put it past them to try something underhanded."

"So, where to first, Major?" asked Adalberto.

Siera tapped her right index finger against the map on her desk. "Taking Surmarch would be easier than the others, I know of a weak point in the keep from a personal visit there. But it is not an ideal first target, so it will have to wait until later," said Siera. "Rather, our first target will be Southmere. With the Navy backing us, we'll be able to land the Third Regiment at the harbour and make sure the rebels and their sell-sword dogs have nowhere to run to. Once we have Southmere, our supply train becomes more reliable."

"No marching on an empty stomach," muttered Ermanno.

"Indeed. That said, the Guild of Merchants and Lenders has offered the use of two skyships, one from the Far West Trading Company and the other from Antonio Beluschi. The *Airsprite* and the *Broadgull*, as I recall.

Gretchen laughed. "I've heard of him, doesn't he have that free circus once a year in Ilmarch and Valencia? At least he's throwing his money around in a more practical way with this."

Siera nodded. "Rich enough that his trading concern has an entire skyship, now for us to use. With two transport skyships and Southmere in our hands, we can all but guarantee that our supply lines will be robust. And after Southmere, I'll see what new reports have come in. Either Surmarch or Ponsurno, and then San Seras."

"Oh?" said Ermanno. "Not San Seras second after Southmere?"

"I thought so initially, but I just received a report by sorcerer that San Seras has a profusion of Archipelagan ships in the harbour, likely mercenaries. The longer they sit around, the more it will drain the rebels' war funds, which I suspect are from Shar anyhow. We will see how long the Sharans like spending money on traitorous garbage."

"I thought they're called Shardustans?" said Gretchen.

Siera shrugged. "The '-dustur' appellation is apparently some old Vig word for 'heritor'. Personally, they can call themselves limp pigs in blankets for all I care."

Ermanno coughed. "Seems like a sound plan, but are you

convinced of Southmere? Not leaving any chance for the mercenaries to escape means they'll put up a brutal fight."

Siera nodded slowly. "That is true, but every one of them that escapes will thus live to fight us another day. Also, even with mercenaries, I doubt the rebels have all that many troops, our own lack of numbers will not be as much of a hindrance as it appears. This does mean that we will certainly have to storm the city, they will not cleave to honour and meet us outside the walls."

Ermanno nodded. "What's our battle order?" he said.

"For Southmere, I want to gauge how many they have on the walls once the Navy is in position." Siera looked up at Adalberto. "If they split their forces, then we knock a few holes in the walls and if they insist on sticking around after that, it's the first and Third Battalions into the breach."

"Not the militia volunteers?" said Adalberto, who spread his hands in the air as he spoke. "I'm merely noting that, well, we might just want to save our trained soldiers for later battles. Even if we try to make the war as quick as possible, we can't afford to lose too many soldiers of the Guard."

Gretchen scowled. "It's ours to do or die, Adalberto. Not those who signed up to defend their country and have no real training."

"As you say, they signed up, Gretchen," said Adalberto, rubbing his thumb and index finger together. "They want to defend their nation, they should get their chance."

"Enough," said Siera. "The conscripts are kept largely aside for my plan for Southmere as we don't want too many holes in the walls, or we'll just have to repair them afterwards. Furthermore, do not forget that it's Teurnot. And this early in Autumn, our best source of people is out harvesting grain, so in all likelihood we will not get many militia volunteers in any case. And this will not be an open battle of clashing armies, so greater numbers will only slow us down. And besides, I intend to have the *Wrath* moving over the city, striking at any ballistae or troop formations below."

"You're not worried about siege weapons turning on the *Wrath*?" said Ermanno.

"What about risks to civilians?" said Adalberto.

Siera nodded. "Ermanno first. I am, but the heaviest devices will be facing the docks. Southmere, like Ponsurno, is dominated by an artificial hill in the centre with a keep atop it. If we move with the keep between the ship and the harbour, they will not be able to loose anything at us. And besides, the Navy will be coming in with a nice hot apple pie at the harbour."

"That's an odd way to say 'horrible beating'. Still more than they deserve," muttered Gretchen.

Siera continued. "And as for Adalberto's question, greatbows are for walls only, as usual. That tradition stands for good reason. The citizenry are unlikely to stand around gawking at a battle in their midst, and they should be safe inside their houses. And holed walls need repairs, so I'll have the Fifth Regiment stay behind after we move off to repair what they can. And speaking of deserve–" said Siera as she sat back down, and motioned for her lieutenants to sit as well, "–after Southmere is taken, we need to prevent any rebel leaders from escaping. When we reach the keep, if there's no surrender, I will likely call for the Third Battalion over the walls and to spread out, looking for any ringleaders. Gretchen, do you think your troops can handle this?"

Gretchen nodded, her face solemn. "There won't be any escapees. How do you want them treated?"

Siera shrugged. "As long as they live to see the noose, I don't care. If any soldiers feel the need for some quick justice through their boots, well... I can hardly punish their enthusiasm. Not after what the rebels have done." Siera's fists clenched. "We will have a special group of judges with us, put together by Duke Federica de Lucan, coming in after we retake Southmere and any other city later on as well. Most of them are travelling judges, used to moving through the countryside to hear cases. They know how to get things done with a crowd. We need only secure the trials, which I have been assured by Duke de Lucan herself will not take more than an hour at absolute most."

"Even if there end up being dozens of ringleaders?" asked Ermanno.

Siera smiled thinly. "The judges need only find enough evidence that the suspects are ringleaders, or traitors in any way. The wages of treason are death."

"You mentioned mercenaries, Major. Any idea of how many?" said Gretchen.

Siera grimaced. "Unfortunately, I have only an estimate. The rebels have taken on at least four hundred Archipelagan mercenaries, although half of that number appears to still be sailing to San Seras. As for more typical mercenary numbers, I have estimates ranging from three to five hundred soldiers, but with no indication of where they are focused, though."

"Where are these reports from, Siera?" said Ermanno.

Siera raised a brow at him. "Most are from sorcerers with either the Guard or the Navy. There are a few others from… alternate sources."

"What about word from the garrisons?" said Adalberto.

Siera bit her lip.

"There aren't any, are there?" said Ermanno quietly.

"No, there were some," said Siera. "Hastily sent and half-garbled. The majority of the Second Regiment's garrison forces were overrun before they realised anything had gone wrong. Not many sorcerers are stationed with the Second, they tend to be more often placed with the Third. We have no word if those soldiers are captives, or…"

A quiet coldness crept into the room.

Ermanno's face was stony. "That's most of the Guard. If the remainder of the Second is used to defend the Reimaran heartland, we won't have many soldiers to take to the field with."

Gretchen scratched at her chin. "Just kind of assumed every regiment would have some sorcerers, the same amount. Probably wouldn't have helped…"

Siera nodded. "Well, that is the overarching plan. For now, until I can confer with Captain Parrino and Captain Cipriani, specific deployments will have to wait. Make the logistical arrangements necessary and have whatever you need me to sign on my desk as quickly as you can. Let us not have logistics delaying us," said Siera as she stood, and her three lieutenants saluted her.

Siera had been at paperwork for the last two hours, arranging to have the various nobles' levies assigned, quartered, and fed. *No paperwork: no army*, she mused.

A knock came at her door.

"Come in," said Siera as she looked up, before she went right back to writing.

Tomasso entered and saluted. "Major, I have word from Captain Parrino. He…"

Siera stopped writing, and looked up. "What, are there delays? Bad enough we have to hire mercenaries in the first place," Siera muttered as she flipped between half a dozen reports of expected expenses and claims.

"Er, no, major. He… says that there are no mercenaries to hire."

Siera frowned. "How? That… should be impossible. What conflict has got them all so interested?"

Tomasso sighed. "He didn't say, Major. He just said that he'd tried every reputable band he knew, and none of them were available."

Siera stared at her desk. "Not even the Orange Band? I doubt they are all off on some tavern crawl. This is not right… something is wrong here," muttered Siera.

"Major?"

Siera looked up at Rossi. "Find Lieutenants Gartzia, Gallo, and Ailbhe. Have them meet me here. And kindly relay a message to Captain Parrino… hmm… If he can at all, have him try to investigate this. I would do it myself, but I flat-out do not have the time. Please give him my apologies on that score."

"Yes Sir." Rossi saluted, and left.

Siera slumped back in her chair, and stared off into the distance. Slowly her gaze drifted back to her desk, and to the paperwork awaiting her.

She leaned forward and slammed her fist onto her desk, jostling her inkpot. Siera immediately cursed and massaged her hand.

Her office door suddenly opened, startling Siera. Ermanno strode into the room.

"News, Major?" asked Ermanno as he pulled himself a chair.

"Do take a seat, Ermanno. Do relax."

Ermanno halted as he was about to sit down, blinking as he looked up at Siera. She scowled at him.

"Just sit man, you look like a frog. Yes it's news; somehow, every god-damned mercenary has already been bought up. They are all unavailable, all, and they are being unusually tight-lipped about it... which means they are likely already on the march. I told Rossi to get back to Captain Parrino and try find out anything he can about who has bought up all these contracts, but... I have a bad feeling about this. If Parrino does not yet know anything else, I doubt he will discover anything new." Siera slowly seemed to deflate as she talked, leaning back into her chair, and using her arm to prop her head up.

After knocking, Gretchen popped her head around the doorframe.

"Come in, take a seat," said Siera, waving a hand at her.

"Apparently, all the mercenary contracts have been bought up," said Ermanno as Gretchen pulled up a chair.

"Alas, everyone is here before me," said Adalberto as he arrived.

"Come in, Adalberto, and close the door behind you," said Siera. "And to reiterate and confirm, yes, apparently all available mercenary contracts have been bought out. People are not talking, not even the more unsavoury sell-swords."

Gretchen rubbed her knuckles under her chin. "Maybe it's for the best that there are no mercenaries. But it couldn't have been the rebels, Sir. There's no way they have access to those sorts of funds."

Siera massaged her temples. "Who else could it have been? There's been no word of clashes between Arndustur and Shardustur, no overt moves on Jurien... just us. Us, Iln, and some – some jacked-up halfwits who actually think they can carve out their own little fief out of Reimar's hide!"

No one spoke.

Siera clenched her fists, and slowed her breathing. "We must assume the worst. I will meet with my brother and try to think of another way to find more experienced troops. I refuse to throw the militia into battles like pigs into a sausage grinder."

"But who else is there?" muttered Adalberto.

"There is one other, but I don't think they'll agree. Either way, I have to try. I'll call for you again when I know more. If you have any brilliant ideas do not hesitate to tell me. Dismissed."

After her lieutenants had filed out, Siera leaned back in her chair. All of a sudden, the room seemed too large for her, her chair and her desk oversized. It reminded her of when she was a child, sitting on her father's knee while he worked away, his desk awash with papers, words and numbers filling up the pages. Siera pushed her knuckles against the sides of her head, feeling the beginnings of a headache coming on.

No matter how small she felt, she reminded herself, there was no one else who could pull this campaign off. Andrayzn went north, and it had to be another high-ranking officer who went south. Siera knew it wasn't entirely her skilful command that had her leading this part of the war, but her position and family name that would inspire the soldiers and militia.

This was what she had chosen. She had to see it done.

Siera steepled her fingers. If there were no mercenaries, then there was only one reliable organisation she knew of with trained troops: the Noble Order of Eneco. But they were church soldiers, sworn to hunt down and execute necromancers. The church would surely never authorise their use for human opponents...

Siera scratched at her nose. If only her mother was here, she'd be able to help immensely. Livio du Nascimbeni was a close personal friend of her mother's. But apparently Fede du Tealdan had completely lost herself since watching her husband brutally murdered in front of her. She had left for some conservative Suranic retreat – simply upped and left in the night. Siera repressed a sudden and intense desire to cry, shuddering and feeling the tears ready to spill. She'd never really realised how well her parents had worked together, her mother's socialite skills shoring up her husband's support and ensuring for him the right allies at the right time.

Siera pressed the palms of her hands against her face, forcing herself to calm down. Livio wouldn't turn her down for an audience, and everyone has their price. If her father taught her anything, it was that.

What mattered was whether or not you were willing to pay it.

Chapter 11: The Price of Honour

Ramiros slumped into his chair in a small study near the Royal Hall. Various people kept trying to meet him in the Pearl Study, his father's old favourite, but he had refused. He'd had his page move everything down here instead.

Ramiros massaged his temples. He hadn't been back to his father's old study since that night. Nor would he be badgered into using it.

Ramiros started and straightened up in his seat as a knock came at the door.

"Who is it?"

Maria Ibarra called out from the other side of the door. "It's Councillor du Tilmost to see you, Your Noble Majesty."

"Oh… yes, send him in," said Ramiros, who then blinked in surprise when the door opened and Lycea du Tilmost walked in.

Lycea made a small bow. "It's me, Your Noble Highness, not my husband."

Ramiros blinked. "Oh, of course, my apologies. I… well…"

Lycea smiled. "I understand. The Council has somewhat thrown you into matters, and far too soon," said Lycea.

Ramiros shifted in his seat. "It is unavoidable… we do as we must."

Lycea took a step closer to Ramiros. "True, which is why I felt that it was best if I approached you in person, Your Noble Highness."

Ramiros looked up at Lycea. "Oh, where are my manners, Councillor? Do have a seat. So, what matter brings you to me?"

"Thank you," said Lycea as she sat down, then leaned in towards Ramiros. "I realise that you were likely unaware, Your Noble Highness, but your father and I had a particular arrangement that I can now offer to you."

Ramiros blinked. "What? An arrangement...?"

Lycea nodded. "I speak in an official capacity, but not for the Royal Council. Your father found it most advantageous, which is why I am here to offer it to you as well."

Ramiros blinked. "Councillor... if you are here to say that you and my father were... in any way..."

Lycea blinked, then frowned. "Oh, no, not at all. No, never." Lycea forced a smile. "I am... not sure whether to be flattered or offended, so let me speak more clearly."

Ramiros coughed. "Yes, Councillor. It would be better if you did."

Lycea smoothed her skirt before continuing. "I represent an organisation that seeks to expand magical knowledge to any who seek it. In the past, it has allowed Reimaran mages to make some wonderful... innovations. If you believe that Reimar would benefit from such an association in the future, then we can continue further."

Ramiros frowned. "Do you mean to say that recent inventions have been because of this... organisation that you represent?"

Lycea shook her head. "Not entirely. Most Reimaran innovations are entirely their own. However, my organisation is able to provide some of the... finer details when it comes to putting everything together."

Ramiros sucked his teeth. "Siera said she couldn't get the Luminary Academy to make those ropes stable enough, the ones they use to drop down from the skyship... that was your group, then?"

Lycea nodded. "Usually, the academy is able to perform to an excellent standard. Still, my organisation has an immense store of knowledge, some of it lost to the world at large. I supervised the Princess' drop-line project personally, at your father's request."

Ramiros absently brushed at his chin with his knuckles. "I always thought he was against it... but only now do I realise that he wanted it to work all along. I should have realised..."

Lycea smiled softly. "Your father hated that magic can be used for war as well as building and improving a nation, but knew that other leaders rarely shared his views. Especially in light of Iln's use of flying armour, Reimar cannot afford to lack in innovative weaponry."

Ramiros absently gestured at Lycea. "Hm, true... and now, with the rebellion... do you think this... ties together in any way? Events seem... well, it might just be me, but events seem to be running together of late."

Lycea paused.

"Well, Your Noble Highness, I must admit that there are people who are not as interested in magical advancement as my organisation is. Some who would prefer that magical knowledge be kept to those whom they believe deserve it."

Ramiros scowled. "Oh? And this other shadowy group – could they have been behind my father's murder?"

Lycea's face went blank for a moment. "In all likelihood, no, Your Noble Majesty. They prefer to use poisoned words over steel. Direct action is not their preference."

Ramiros sucked at his teeth. "And what is this organisation called?"

"Which one, Your Noble Highness?"

Ramiros shrugged. "Either. Both."

"I represent the Circular Order of the Tower. Our–"

"What a bizarre title. Why 'circular'?" said Ramiros.

Lycea's smile did not waver. "Well, the... master of our organisation claims that circles are an underutilised format in ritual magic, and likens our organisation to a circle in balance."

Ramiros was nodding before Lycea had finished. "Yes, of course. Do go on."

Lycea smiled thinly. "Our... ideological opponents are known as the Hermetic Pact of Transcendence. Our differences cannot be reconciled, but that is hardly Reimar's problem, or yours. Regardless, we offer the same assistance we have before."

Ramiros thought for a moment, then sighed.

"My father always hated conflict, but as I sit here, I can't see anything but that. I have people spouting off bizarre theories about Shar murdering my father, about Arn possibly funding the rebellion, about some Archipelagan group being behind it all. And now, with Mordeno forsaking us... we can hardly turn away allies. No matter how strange or sudden this all is."

Lycea smiled softly. "The Circular Order offers knowledge, not military force. It is… not strictly an alliance."

Ramiros looked up sharply. "Oh? Just words, then?"

Lycea's mouth twitched. "We offer more than mere words, or rather, our words can shape the course of a great many things. Even if we will not stand at your side in battle, we can offer you knowledge of how to prevail over your rival's machinations."

Ramiros looked at Lycea from under hooded eyes. "If you do not offer formal alliances, Councillor, then how am I supposed to be sure that your group does not have another representative offering the Circular Order's knowledge to Arn, or Shar?"

Lycea made a slow shrug. "We offer to all who care to accept. Thus far, both Arn and Shar have seen fit to rebuff us, considering counter-offers from our rival to be more to their taste."

Ramiros smirked. "And so Reimar is the only great power on Iber that you can work with…"

Lycea smiled anew. "Largely so, Your Noble Highness. And your father… was wary of some of our offerings. He considered them too dangerous."

Ramiros's eyes widened slowly. "What… what kind of offerings?"

Lycea smiled broadened. "Skyships are only the beginning, Your Noble Highness. Are you aware that the captain of the Fifth Regiment has devised a way to enchant a great-ballista with the same explosive qualities as a greatbow?"

Ramiros stared. "I… was unaware of this…"

"We can offer the precise techniques to turn prototype into standard. That, and more. Imagine a skyship equipped with dozens of such ballistae… it would be able to demand surrender from any foe. No army has the ability to resist that kind of power."

Ramiros' mouth twitched. "Yes, but… well, to use greatbows and such on soldiers is… is despicable."

Lycea met Ramiros' gaze. "Fearsome."

Ramiros rubbed at his face. "We would be held up as barbarians, to do such. Why–"

"Barbarians, no. Barbarism is for those holdouts north of Iln. What was yesterday called barbarism, by sages and bards, Reimar may turn into a strength that cannot be denied. A power that shakes the knees of your enemies."

Ramiros licked his lips. "Well... a weapon like that would certainly be fearful. How much... would such a device cost?"

Lycea's smile showed just a hint of teeth. "I will send for the designs immediately, so that the Luminary Academy can assess the necessary material requirements."

Ramiros nodded slowly. "The Council..."

Lycea gave a slow shrug, her eyes never leaving Ramiros'. "The Academy falls under royal jurisdiction, not Council oversight. Your jurisdiction. And Duke du Singara does not answer to them either, so they will not know until it is too late, if you order Headmaster Gustavo to mind his tongue."

Ramiros scowled. "Wait, how did you know he worked as my fa–that he is the royal spymaster? Did my father tell you?"

Lycea shook her head. "He did not, I simply deduced that your father would as a matter of course have someone close to him whom he trusted to handle informants and spies, and that person must be Duke du Singara. Your father and I had a practical agreement, but I was not his confidante." Lycea smoothed over her skirt again, then sighed. "If only he had confided in me, I could have been of more use to him. Your Noble Majesty, I hope you will take me into your confidences, so that I can further earn your trust. And Duke du Singara does not know that I know of his covert role, however, so whether or not you tell him is up to you. You may wish to delay telling him, even if you desire to do so, but the choice is yours, Your Noble Highness."

Ramiros tilted his head. "Oh? Why might I wish to delay telling him?"

"The Irregular Intelligence Office that your father created is underfunded, but well run. If Duke du Singara believes that you prefer the Tower to his own efforts, he will feel rebuffed. Instead, you might cultivate him as an ally even further by pushing him to work even harder to keep his network of informants busy."

Ramiros slowly leaned forward, and clasped his hands under his chin.

"You have done far more than just deduce. Were you more than just a councillor to my father? How much did you really advise him?"

Lycea leaned forward. "Your father was a brilliant and astute ruler, he had no more use for me than my Tower connections, and my knowledge of some of the more… covert dealings of certain societies and groups. However, you have been thrust into power during a time of uncertainty. If I can make myself more useful to you, Your Noble Highness, then I must attempt to do so. After all, my husband would be most wroth if I failed to aid his rightful lord."

Ramiros leaned back in his chair, his eyes never leaving Lycea's. "So… Duke du Tilmost knows you work for the Tower?"

Lycea nodded. "He does, Your Noble Highness."

Ramiros shook his head. "I can scarce believe that my father kept all this under control… I had no idea."

Lycea smiled. "Rulers have immense burdens, Your Noble Highness. It is through no fault of your own that you were unprepared for this position."

Ramiros stared at the ceiling for a moment. "You know, Councillor, you make a great deal of sense. And unlike the rest of those domineering bunch – no offence to your husband, of course – but I think that you and I might well speak in the future."

Lycea smiled, and reached into a pocket to produce a small silver ring.

"Your father had one of these, although unfortunately I arrived too late to do enough. If you ever have need of me, press into this groove in the ring, and I will come to your side as soon as I can."

Ramiros reached out to take the ring. "Too late… that is right, you were there when…"

Lycea bowed her head to Ramiros. "Yes, and I curse daily that I was not fast enough to save your father."

Ramiros thought for a moment, silent, then slowly shook his head. "Hardly your fault, Councillor. I suppose you are unaware of the identities of the assassins? They were all killed during the attack, if just some had survived, we could have questioned them..."

"I do not know, Your Noble Majesty, but I can attempt to find out."

Ramiros smiled slowly, and although Lycea smiled back, inwardly she was alarmed at Ramiros' toothy grin as he leaned towards her.

"Yes... if you can. You must find out. I do not care how you do it, Councillor, I do not care how you find out, if you need to break them in half to do it. I want to know who killed my father and then by god, I will use everything I have to crush them into dust. I will have it known throughout Iber, throughout Brisia, that those who struck my father down were annihilated without mercy or restraint." Ramiros unclenched his fists and leaned back again, his gaze level with Lycea's.

"I will do all I can, Your Noble Highness," she said.

"Very well. That will be all," said Ramiros.

Ramiros nodded curtly, and Lycea rose to take her leave.

17th Teurnot, afternoon

Tomasso leaned forward and opened the carriage door, then stepped out and held the door for Siera. She stepped out, and immediately squinted.

Even up close, the Cathedral of Illumination was a grand sight. The off-white limestone and the golden bas-reliefs had amazed her as a child, and even though she was no longer comforted by the church as she had once been, the cathedral impressed her still.

Siera walked up to the large oak double doors, and stepped through. As she did so, an acolyte hurried up to her and Tomasso.

"Excuse me, ah… Sir, but there's currently no sermon planned for the rest of the day. However, there's a small scripture reading by Cantor Silvio in one of the studies, if you like."

Siera glared at him. "I'm here to see Grand Warden du Nascimbeni. I have an appointment."

The acolyte stared at Siera. "Uh, I see. And you are…?"

Siera gave him a level gaze. "Her Highness, Major Siera du Tealdan."

The acolyte did a very quick double take. "O–oh! Your Highness, please forgive me, I– I didn't realise… P– please, come right this way."

The acolyte led Siera into the nave, the high vaulted ceilings resplendent with golden discs representing Sura, the creator of humanity. More recent artistic additions in the form of paintings adorned the sides of the nave, being various depictions of Sura or the avatar Riest, all of them with shining golden disks or stylised suns in place of their heads. Siera approved of the Suranic Church's change of stance in regards to depictions of god into allowing paintings of Sura following certain guidelines, even if they still forbade faces. Although the du Tealdans were all devout Suranists, Siera had been sorely tempted by Riestism as a teenager, as it allowed artistic depictions of Sura and Riest. The sect certainly knew what more easily moved people to even greater reverence for god.

The newer artwork on the Cathedral of Illumination was gorgeous, and served to remind her of the nobility and grace of the human form.

"One moment, Your Highness," said the acolyte, before hurrying off to another nearby priest. After conferring with the priest, the acolyte turned back to Siera, who had quietly walked up behind them.

"Oh– ah, there you are, Your Highness. The Grand Warden is currently conducting some business in the vestry anteroom, but will meet you in the Ciro du Vescovi library. Would you care to wait there?"

Siera nodded curtly. "Very well."

"It's past the pipe organ, and just up the stairs. I'll come up with some refreshments for you and your, um, lieutenant," said the acolyte, who then hurried away.

Siera turned to Tomasso and smirked. Tomasso tried to fight a grin, but failed.

"You wish, Tomasso," said Siera.

"Maybe one day, Major... a man can dream," Tomasso said as he shrugged.

Siera left Tomasso outside as she waited for Livio du Nascimbeni in the library. She assumed that it had been sponsored by Ciro du Vescovi, whoever that was, or had been. A small room with no internal dividers, three of the walls were covered by bookcases, the centre of the room having half a dozen chairs and a few small side tables. It was probably used as an informal meeting room for the local clergy. She walked over to one of the chairs. The room smelled of cigar smoke, and an empty bottle of port had been left on a side table next to Siera.

Siera was about to sit when she heard the door open behind her. She turned to see the slight figure of Livio du Nascimbeni, who retained a firm posture despite his seventy-something years of age.

Siera bowed formally. "Your Excellency, I hope I have not come at a bad time?" she said.

Livio gave a slow, wide smile as he strode over to Siera. "Of course not, Your Highness. It is wonderful to see you again. Please, accept my condolences."

Siera nodded curtly. She had no need to remember her father's death right now.

"Let us sit, Your Highness." Livio smiled as he gestured for Siera to take a chair.

"I must apologise for the state of the room. I had asked for an acolyte to clear it before you arrived, but I think they are still studying." Livio's apologetic smile was perfect.

"No trouble at all, Your Excellency," Siera said as she sat down, and tried to breathe through her mouth. The deep-set stench of cigars made the room feel stuffier than it was.

"So, how fares your family, Your Excellency?" said Siera, as Livio took a seat for himself.

"Well, very well. My brother has made several inroads in the Zarranese lumber industry in the last few years," said Livio with a well-practiced blank expression.

Siera nodded. "Good, good. My brother is firmly in favour of trade with Zarann." Siera looked down at her lap before looking back up and continuing. "It seems that my mother has... decided to join a retreat. High Light Peak, I believe. Unfortunately, I do not know much about the location..."

Livio's mouth twitched slightly. "It was very sudden, to hear that your mother wished to seclude herself from the world. Please rest assured, Your Highness, that High Light is well-furnished, despite being in the Catra mountains. She will be left to heal her soul as best she sees fit."

Siera nodded, momentarily lost as to what to say next. She felt that if she were to return to the palace, just right now, she would see her mother once again. But Fede du Tealdan was half the country away, near Evenith. It didn't seem real that she was so far away.

"Yes... my father's death has left her... well," said Siera.

Livio extended his hands outward, palms up. "The world can weigh heavily on us sometimes, Your Highness. The soul is a thing of pure, blessed light, and even though the body is a divine work after Sura's own form, the world weighs us down at every turn. The church does whatever it can to uplift those who feel their spirits fall, especially at a time like this. If you have doubt, remember that it is human nature to feel this way. As always, the church is here to help."

Siera wanted to feel lulled and comforted. As a child she had loved the church, and even imagined one day joining the priesthood. But her comfort in the church had lessened the more she saw of the world, and realised that the church's kind words and high ideals sometimes meant little in practice.

Siera swallowed. "Would that all the world was as nurturing, Your Excellency. But unfortunately... the world is often a cold place."

Livio nodded slowly. "Your Highness, do you feel yourself weighed down by your duties as well?"

Siera looked up, blinking. "Do I...? Well... sometimes."

Livio nodded again. "Sura did not make us to walk alone, Your Highness. It is written multitudinously in the Etmarl that we must find solace in one another. Alone we are like a candle, together we are like a sunrise."

Siera found herself nodding in reply. "Sura's own holy scriptures do say this... Your Excellency–"

Livio waved away her pleasantries. "Please, Your Highness, Livio."

"Very well... Livio... how can God forbid slaughter yet condone warfare? Even if god condones self-defence..."

Livio smiled softly. "God condones defending not only one's own life, but family as well, and property, and one's nation. You should not feel that God condemns your impending campaign against the rebels, Your Highness, nor condemns any of your actions. Remember, Sura sees not only deeds, but intentions as well. You desire to defend Reimar, and the rebels desire to bow to mere greed and violence. They have risen against their lords, and defied the proper feudal order. Riest proposed that order, when the first humans basked in her light and bowed to her deep wisdom and learning. These rebels defy their place, their lords, and so in turn they defy God. Your actions are just, Your Highness."

Siera nodded, feeling better despite her misgivings. But she had not come here for comfort.

"I believe this, but, it is hypocritical of me to want such

sanction and yet come here, to you, today."

Livio lifted a brow. "God offers what God offers, Your Highness. There are no conditions to Sura's love. But, what other purpose brings you here today?"

"Grand Warden – Your Excellency – Livio, as much as it pains me to ask this, I am here to request assistance in bringing an end to the rebellion."

Livio's expression did not change.

"Well, I can understand your position, Your Highness. However, the church is not a military organisation. We pray for your success, of course... but would not mercenaries serve your purposes better?"

Siera shifted in her seat. "They would, however, such an option is denied to the Guard. There are mercenary contracts available, but they are for smaller and much less reputable bands. Not, of course, that any mercenaries are ever reputable, on the whole, but we would be taking on very dubious allies of minor strength. We need allies we can count on, and aside from the Royal Guard... it is widely known that the church's own guard are both reliable and well trained."

Livio smiled softly. "The Faithful Order of Eneco keeps their training to the highest standard, but they are no military force."

"I know, Your Excellency. I do not come to you out of any misunderstanding, I know they are intended to only hunt those who practice the unhallowed art of necromancy. Still... these rebels might well have allied themselves with such wayward types."

Livio slowly shook his head. "Yet, there is no proof of that, Your Highness. And it defies church policy and doctrine to send the Noble Order into battle against those who are innocent of unhallowing. It would be... very difficult for the church to intercede in this matter."

Siera swallowed. "This is true, Your Excellency, but even scripture recognises the need to defend one's self, and one's loved ones, as you have said. As a member of the royal family, I would be remiss in my duties if I did not quickly put an end to the chaos that the rebels have brought to our nation. And defend ourselves we must, who but the rebels had reason to murder my – our rightful king?"

Livio began a slow, soft smile. "This is true, and rebellion certainly brings chaos. The rebels certainly have gone against the rightful peace and prosperity of both Reimar and humanity. Perhaps…"

Siera met Livio's gaze. "Yes?"

Livio stroked his chin with his thumb, his eyes downcast. "Perhaps the Order could be positioned to investigate these rebels. They have, as you say, possibly allied themselves with unsavoury groups. And such an investigation could only be conducted under peacetime conditions… so if the rebels refuse to lay down their arms, then that would all but confirm their guilt. At that point, the Faithful Order could render battlefield assistance, even if only in a limited capacity."

Siera leaned forward. "I believe that this would certainly be in the interests of both the church and the kingdom, Your Excellency."

Livio nodded. "However… this would take no small effort on the part of myself. The Order is beholden to me, but I can't demand that my subordinates carry out such actions if my reasons look to go against church teachings. And they would be right to question my edicts on this… this difficult matter."

Siera leaned back in her chair, and met Livio's gaze. "Perhaps there is something I can do, to help assure everyone in the church that such an action is merited."

Livio's smile deepened. "Your Highness, this is a wonderful idea. There is such an action…" Livio flicked his fingers against each other.

"Do continue, Your Excellency. My brother is also anxious to ensure the success of my campaign, and he is a firm believer in the mission of the church."

Livio didn't even bat an eyelid at Siera's outright fabrication. "Of course, Your Highness. And indeed, both the Cardinals of the Grand Assembly and I would be put at ease if you could convince His Noble Majesty to bring his attentions to the matter of the Cult of the Second Dawn…"

Siera's eyebrows rose. "The Chu– the Cult of the Second Dawn? Is there an issue in need of resolution?"

Livio flicked his hand dismissively. "The so-called 'Church' of the Second Dawn is nothing more than an upstart cult, preaching heresies and lies, claiming that the other lesser gods are equal to Sura. However, of late they have been attracting more and more support, and have even been petitioning the most virtuous Duke du Tealdan herself to speak on their behalf. Of course, as a devout believer she has little time for their blasphemies... but she is a benevolent woman, and does not condemn them outright. Now of course the church does not seek to tell Duke du Tealdan her business, but we would be put much at ease if a strong message were to be sent to the Second Dawn."

Siera looked down. Reimar was, as many other nations, tolerant of most of the offshoots and sects of Suranism. Rarely did a monarch become involved in matters of faith – in fact, it had been on one such rare occasion that a monarch had intervened to give the Suranic Church of Reimar more leeway in organising their chapel guards, and the Faithful Order of Eneco had been created as a result. The throne did not meddle in the authority of the churches, by wise tradition. In return, the churches, especially mainstream Suranism, lent the throne legitimacy in the eyes of the public, and in many ceremonies.

Siera did not meet Livio's gaze. "My brother is willing to consider this. What form of message did you have in mind?"

"That they be banned."

Siera looked up sharply. "Banned? To my knowledge, no monarch outright banned a faith, no matter how heretical their ideals become. The common policy for generations, and as was for my father, is to let the churches decide amongst themselves."

Livio nodded. "Indeed, and it is a wise policy, Your Highness. The church never questioned your father's leadership, nor do we question your brother's leadership. However, as you have said, these are trying times... and such times call for swift action. Decisive action. And if the church were to see such action on the part of your brother, well, we would certainly be moved to take our own swift action in pledging you the assistance of the Noble Order."

Siera bit her lip. Reimar had, under her father, experienced even more wealth and prosperity than ever before. If Reimar's prosperity was to continue... perhaps this small sacrifice would be acceptable.

"I suspect that a ban would be difficult for my brother to make. However, he could easily deny the Second Dawn any royal funds should they seek such, and as such their petition to my... I always forget if Andrea is my third or fourth cousin – their petition would be useless. My brother could also publicly rebuke the Second Dawn's actions as disrespectful to the Suranic Church, and Reimar as a whole. He might even go so far as to say that the Second Dawn is a disgrace to Reimar in such a dire time... or something similar."

Livio stroked his chin with his thumb. "This... would send a clear message to both the Second Dawn and the faithful of the Suranic Church that the former is not welcome, while the latter is privileged above all others. Yes... this will work. Especially if your brother were to inform the people that Mordeno has abandoned our alliance due to the heresies of the Second Dawn."

Siera's eyes widened. "Mordeno has forsaken the alliance? What?! I– I have heard nothing of this!"

Livio raised a brow at Siera. "I see... my apologies, Your Highness, I did not mean to speak out of turn. I myself heard only a short while ago, and perhaps General Andrayzn has not yet heard the news. Apparently Mordeno has proven faithless, claiming that they cannot aid us against Iln. Some nonsense about not being able to prevail against Ilnian dragoons."

Livio flicked his fingers, his voice cold. "Cowardly. To betray a trust is a sin. When you break faith with one, you break faith with humanity."

Siera swallowed. Of all the times... she could only hope that Reimar's alliance with Altren held firm.

Now or never.

Siera looked up at Livio. "If my brother could be convinced of... something like this – and I am certain that he can, no – I *guarantee* that he can – there must be no pogroms in the streets, nor any underhanded violence. He will not condone violence and disorder."

Livio smiled softly, his eyes bright. "The church is in complete agreement, Your Highness. The followers of the Second Dawn are lost souls, they need the comfort that only the Suranic Church can deliver. No church official, myself or any other, would ever condone violence done against any such individual so desperately in need of the light and the way. The cult leaders, though… it is clear that, at least, they should receive no royal funds or support for their deceitful charlatans' displays, only condemnation."

Siera closed her eyes. "I will speak with my brother. He… will ban any funds going to the Cult of the Second Dawn, and condemn their actions at all levels of their organisation. The Second Dawn will find itself paying in any popularity they have after they are accused of heresy so great that Mordeno has failed to honour our alliance. And at this time of uncertainty, the dukes will agree that actions like this are… necessary."

Livio rubbed his index finger and thumb together. "I am confident in both you and your brother's ability to ensure this, Your Highness. Are you… certain that the dukes will bow to your brother's will on this matter?"

Siera leaned back in her chair. "Duke du Tealdan, as you say, is a pious woman with no love for the Second Dawn. The other Dukes… understand practical measures. I am certain of it. And the guild leaders will be eager to ensure stability, this time above all times."

Grand Warden Livio Nascimbeni smiled, and bowed in his seat. "The church is grateful for your wisdom on this matter, Your Highness. With this, our confidence in His Noble Majesty's rule will be unshakeable, and we will commit the faithful to fight under your command."

Siera realised that she had slumped in her chair, and straightened up. "I confess I am somewhat surprised that you did not request that Whitechapel be treated in the same way, considering their extraordinary blasphemies."

Livio's face did not change, but his eyes went dead flat.

"The heresy of the Second Dawn is reprehensible, but to claim that Riest and Sura were once human? To deny the fundamentally divine origin of the creator and her avatar?"

Siera stared as Livio's hands began to shake. She had

never seen him actually riled up before.

"They speak words beyond mere heresy. I will not dignify them with any attention. Their time will come, both I and the church will make sure of that. Their words, their deeds... all filth, all unclean. They are lower than – lower than elves or snakes or beasts. It would offend me less to drink sewer water than to speak their name ever again."

Livio went silent, his mouth twitching. Siera stared at him silently grateful that she hadn't gone into the priesthood.

Siera bowed slightly. "With that, I must take my leave, Your Excellency. I have much to attend to."

Livio closed his eyes for a brief moment, composing himself.

"Of course, Your Highness. After His Noble Majesty has made the announcement, I will have a cantor come by to deliver a letter offering the services of the Noble Order of Eneco. One copy to your brother, one copy to you."

"Perhaps you should send my copy to General Andrayzn, instead," said Siera.

Livio shook his head. "You have approached me, and the Noble Order will be seconded under you. The authority falls to you, Your Highness."

Siera nodded as she stood. It felt odd, almost too early, to have this kind of power and authority.

"I will notify my brother immediately,"

Livio stood, and bowed. "Excellent. As always, Your Highness, the church offers succour to those who are assailed by the travails of the world."

Siera bowed slightly, then turned to leave.

As she stepped out of the small library, Tomasso saluted and proffered a rolled up parchment.

"A messenger came for you, Sir, from His Noble Highness," he said.

"Did they say what this was about?" said Siera.

"No, Sir."

Siera frowned and tried to break the wax seal binding the parchment, but it refused to budge. Siera had a brief moment of incomprehension, then realised that it was warded. She pressed her own signet ring to the wax seal, and it fell off the parchment, melting into a small puddle as it did so.

Sia,

Alas, Mordeno has proven faithless. They will not come to our aid. I leave later today for Altren to ensure their steadfastness.

I've spoken to N again. He says that he has word from an associate of his, a sorcerer, who is in P. city. The rebels need mercenaries to keep the people quiet, the revolution is not popular. This should help, the citizenry know where their loyalties lie.

Love,

R.

"Something important, Sir?" said Tomasso.

Siera smiled. "Something important, and useful, even if poor news overall. Let us head back. Actually, Tomasso, let us finish early this day. I think we could all use dinner and our bunks."

Tomasso saluted enthusiastically. "Shall I inform the lieutenants, Sir?"

"No, I'll head back and tell them myself. I cannot slack while they work, although I will stay at the palace again tonight."

Chapter 12: Gamble

The next day, Siera arrived at the barracks early, had breakfast in the officer's mess with her lieutenants. They all then moved to her office to get down to business.

"New plans, Siera?" said Ermanno.

Siera rested her fists on the table.

"I have been racking my mind for an idea, something, anything... We cannot buy mercenaries, the Second Regiment has suffered immense losses, and the First Regiment is marching against Iln. We have the support of the Third and the Navy when we fight at Southmere and San Seras, the Fifth and the militias for the whole campaign... and the Seventh, for whatever the Seventh is worth with a handful of troops. Unfortunately, only a few hundred militia volunteers have signed up. Some of them are being put under General Andrayzn's command, the rest will be assigned to us once the First Regiment has given them some rudimentary training."

Ermanno's face was neutral. "I've seen some outside Ilmarch, where the First has its temporary training camp. They look like drowned rats."

Siera clenched her teeth and ignored Ermanno. "I've also been able to convince the church to lend us the support of the Noble Order of Eneco."

"How did you manage that?" said Adalberto, blinking.

Siera did not look at her lieutenants. "Everyone has their price. I am not especially proud, but I will be even less proud if we fail to stop the rebels. I do not wish to say more."

Adalberto chewed his lip. Ermanno said nothing. Gretchen nodded. "Everyone does what they have to, Major."

Siera nodded. "Still, that's not enough. Here's my trick: I'm going to bet it all on somewhat of a gamble. That's why I want your input, because if I'm wrong, we will not live to rue our mistake."

Silence took root in her office. Siera pushed on.

"There's no way that the rebels have the money to pull this off. They must have bought up all the mercenaries with someone's money, and my bet is that it is Shar."

"The Shardustans have long wanted the Helion, but they're not the only ones," said Gretchen.

"True," said Siera. "But they are the best positioned to take advantage of the border, so they are my main concern. As such, I must acknowledge that they might well be marching forces against us even now."

"Have there been any reports of this?" said Ermanno.

"No," said Siera, shaking her head. "But it is what I would do, if I were them. The position that we are in is precarious. They would be fools not to take advantage of that. This business with mercenaries, all of them... I fear that we might be fighting Shar as well, before long."

"We can't hold the border, retake the cities, and eliminate the rebels," said Adalberto.

"And retake the Helion. We cannot ignore the lost revenue, especially during wartime. It could make or break the war," said Siera, who grimaced. "Which is why I am willing to take a great risk. We cannot march past Southmere and Ponsurno, so we will fly past."

"What, on the *Wrath*?" said Gretchen.

"Yes. We fly low over Surmarch, drop in on the keep's courtyard, and take the keep directly. Once we have the keep, the rebels will be boxed in and out."

Ermanno sucked his teeth, and shook his head. "They'll close the portcullis on us, Siera. Even if they have only a few archers, we'll mill around and they'll roast us like a duck in a pot."

Siera smirked. "The keep's portcullis is broken, it has not worked for years. The last time I was visiting with my father, Duke Federica de Lucan had been too busy building gardens and statues to repair it. I doubt the rebels know this, there's no indication anyone in her family has joined the rebellion. Duke du Lucan joked that she hadn't told the mayor about the broken portcullis because she despised him as a toady, so he cannot tell the rebels either, even if they have not disposed of him. Thus, I doubt the rebels are aware of this. We can sweep into their forces and take them largely by surprise. Once we have the keep–"

"They'll retake it. The portcullis is broken, as you said," said Ermanno.

Gretchen pointed at Ermanno, then Siera. "Wait, is it only the inner portcullis? Is that why you said we should drop down in the courtyard?" said Gretchen.

Siera smiled thinly. "Exactly so. The outer portcullis will be dropped when they see us coming. Gretchen, securing that portcullis will be your Battalion's duty."

Gretchen saluted, right fist over her heart, head lowered.

"And what if they've discovered that it's broken and they've fixed it?" said Ermanno.

"Then we'll have to use greatbows, which will disadvantage us later on if we have to go on the defensive," said Siera with a shrug. "But there's nothing for it, we must take Surmarch, we must have the keep."

"Adalberto, I want your Battalion picking off anyone you can see while we're in the air. Ermanno, I want the First Battalion moving as soon as they hit the ground, and securing the keep."

Ermanno nodded. "Are there any other interior defences?"

"In terms of gates, no. Doors, yes. There is also a central armoury, but I happen to know that it only has munitions armour and polearms. They will not have any ugly surprises lurking in there, unless the rebels have upgraded the stores themselves."

"Which is unlikely… We should be able to take the keep quickly, then. What word on enemy numbers?" asked Adalberto.

"I have a short report from my brother on that matter. The rebels apparently still need mercenaries patrolling everywhere to keep the citizenry at bay, except for San Seras, where apparently some citizens have even hailed the rebels as liberators. Disgusting. They will be humming a different tune in short order," Siera growled. "However, that should mean fewer enemy troops in the keep than our own, even. The keep was designed to be the locus of the city's defence if an attack came or as a retreat if the city was taken. It has no advantage against us storming it from the inside. And I will wager Reimaran training and courage over a sell-sword's greed any day."

Siera tapped on the map on her desk again.

"Once we have Surmarch, the rebels will be much more dismayed. I suspect that they will send more of their forces to secure the Helion, so the same night as our attack on Surmarch I want to be away, to Ponsurno. While we fly, the Seventh and the Fifth will bring up the militia along with the Noble Order and settle into Surmarch, keeping it from being recaptured. The Fifth can also repair the inner portcullis so we do not fall victim to our own trick."

Siera stopped for a moment to collect her thoughts.

"Originally, I was thinking Ponsurno would require a more traditional siege, as the keep is recessed into the actual mountainside. However, time is of the essence. If Shar is motivated to send their own troops to oppose us, it will be sooner rather than later. If we hold Ponsurno, however, things turn in our favour in the event that Shar attempts any invasion. They won't be able to cross over into Reimar unannounced if we have both Monai and Ponsurno, and the Second Regiment's soldiers in Monai are certainly vigilant for any such attempt. Once we have Ponsurno, we move on either Southmere or San Seras, whichever seems more promising. I'm thinking Southmere first, but we will have to see."

"What strategy for taking Ponsurno, then?" said Ermanno.

Siera sucked her teeth. "The keep is recessed into the mountain, there's no way to come at it from the air at all. We could drop into the assembly grounds and get past the outer wall that way, but we'll be too vulnerable. So, this is something that I want you all to think about. My ideas thus far are lacking in innovation, Ponsurno is too easily defensible. If anything cunning strikes you, let me know. Otherwise, we have enough time between then and now to plan. We have our first move, and our last will likely still be San Seras. Southmere we can arrange to move on with the Navy, as before. We just need a way to crack Ponsurno in short order. Until then, you have your duties."

Her lieutenants saluted, and Ermanno and Adalberto left.

"Something on your mind, Lieutenant?"

Gretchen turned to check that Ermanno and Adalberto had left the room.

"Well, an idea strikes me, Major, of a way that we could get into Ponsurno with a lot less risk, and a lot fewer lives lost."

Siera raised her brows at that. "Oh? Do tell."

"The gate guards are probably going to be mercenaries. They'll hear that we've just jumped on Surmarch and they might be feeling a little nervous. So, with your permission, that's when I and the Third Battalion could head up to the gate under cover of night and bluff our way in, claiming to be a new band of mercenaries looking for work."

Siera stared. "That seems... highly unlikely. Why would they take you on?"

Gretchen smiled. "All mercenaries are greedy, but some are smart too. If they're greedy they'll let us in so they can hold us up for our gear. If they're smart they'll claim to be taking us on, then have us take the front line in an attack while they sit back and get paid."

Siera frowned. "Perhaps... well... but no, of course it will not work, even in the dark, they will realise that you are the Guard. Your uniforms will give you away."

Gretchen shifted as she stood. "Well, I was thinking that we might try for a subtler approach, go in with our civvies."

Siera stared. "What?"

Gretchen shrugged. "Just an idea."

Siera glared at her. "It is an idea, but it is an unacceptable one. Lieutenant, I confess I am disappointed in you. The Royal Guard's reputation is borne by the colour, on uniform and standards both. I will not discard that unless there is no other choice."

Gretchen shrugged again. "You did say you wanted an idea of how to get in... mercenaries are even worse than soldiers at guard duty. It just might work."

Siera shook her head. "It might, it might not. It is still risky and – risk aside, to hell with risk, I cannot approve of discarding the Guard's colour just so we can have a quick advantage."

Gretchen nodded. "Fair enough, Sir. Figured I'd mention it."

Siera sighed. "I am not offended, if that is what you are thinking. I just dislike that things have become so bad that… that to be honest, this is not an unattractive idea to me. Still, no, I cannot endorse such an idea. I appreciate your initiative, but… no. Carry on your way, Lieutenant."

Gretchen saluted, her expression flat. "Well, at least we aren't taking on any Archipelagan mercenaries." With that, she left.

An hour later, and Siera sat grinding through paperwork. A signature here, a report there. Notes from meetings earlier in the day – thus more expense than anticipated, a quartermaster needing more money to buy up enough stores in a short time, a delay in enchanting the deflection rings for new recruits… the problems and delays went on, and Siera ground on with them.

She looked towards a small metal hourglass on her desk as it began to light up. Of the twenty four crystal orbs evenly spaced along its face, divided into three segments – morning, afternoon, and evening – afternoon slowly lit up to the fourth orb.

Siera leaned back in her chair, massaging her temples with her palms.

A sudden knock at the door had Siera halfway to her shortsword before she thought to even say anything.

"Who calls?"

A brief silence had Siera suddenly thinking of assassins, coming for her now to finish what they had started with her father. Her hand was already drawing her blade before Tomasso spoke from the other side of the door.

"Ah, Sir, it's General Andrayzn here to see you."

Siera slumped. "Yes, of course. Thank you, Tomasso, admit him."

Andrayzn entered a moment later, having simply opened the door himself.

"Afternoon. I won't make this long, Siera."

"I won't object if you do, I've only paperwork to return to." Siera stood and walked around her desk to pull out a chair for Andrayzn, and as he sat, she noticed him very deliberately eyeing the decanter of whiskey on Siera's desk.

"Aah, let us have a glass then. A present from distant relative for my birthday a few years ago," said Siera.

"Years?" Andrayzn raised an eyebrow as Siera poured a glass for each of them.

"I might have inherited my taste for it from my father, but I very rarely feel the occasion calls for it. Ice?"

"If you have any, do not exercise any especial effort for something so trifling… aah, you have a little… hmm, very convenient," said Andrayzn as Siera opened a small case the length of a forearm, with five circular indentations inside, a small sphere of ice nestled in each. Siera dropped two spheres into each glass. "The ingenuity of mages never ceases to amaze me," Andrayzn said as he shook his head.

Siera smiled. "This I had made for me, I only really enjoy whiskey with ice. Cost a fair teal, but you get what you pay for." Siera passed Andrayzn's glass to him, and seated herself.

Andrayzn took a sip, and grinned as he leaned back. "Paperwork, the bane of every officer, and the underpinning of every good military. Any particular difficulties?"

"Well, there aren't enough rings for all the recruits. The academy tells me they're working as fast as they can, even with some old alumni signing up to help with the war effort they simply can't make them fast enough. And it's focus on that or focus on those charger's boots that Gretchen's had some success with."

Andrayzn frowned. "Those boots that you can use to ah… leap forward with? They're practical, but I don't relish choosing between them and deflection rings…"

Andrayzn shook his head. "And the war will be an ugly business. The rebels are likely to hole up and use archers as often as they can, I doubt they have the numbers to win a straight fight. Those rings will aid considerably, although against volley shots they aren't as effective as we were led to believe."

Siera nodded slowly. "Oh, I know. And I have a…

report… that there just are not enough of them to take to the field, not that I put my faith in reports alone."

"Which is its own worry…" said Andrayzn.

"Exactly. Why stage a rebellion if you don't have the manpower to pull it off?"

Andrayzn and Siera didn't speak for a moment.

"General, if I may… perhaps it's my father's murder, perhaps I'm still blinded by grief. But I have a theory I'd like you to hear."

Andrayzn shook his head. "On the contrary, you've held up well for someone who has quite brutally lost a parent. Still, continue."

"I am convinced that someone has told this filth that they will get reinforcements. Someone has told them that they can pull this off, someone has made this situation. It does not make sense, this rebellion… it honestly seems to have sprung from nowhere."

Andrayzn thought for a moment, then sipped at his whiskey. "Not quite nowhere, there are those who hate Reimar, and claim they lost their independence over the kingdom's greed."

Siera looked down at her glass. "You almost sound as though you have a shred of sympathy for them."

Andrayzn wrinkled his nose. "Not in the least. Everyone politicked, everyone fought, Reimar won. The matter is quit – and few can say that life in the old baronies and city-states was better. Constant strife, bickering, embargoes, shortages… people live far better off under Reimaran rule."

Siera tried to catch Andrayzn's eyes. "What do you think of there being some agitators of some form?"

Andrayzn gave Siera a level gaze. "The only reason there isn't wider talk about outside involvement in this matter is because there are too many to blame. People will point a finger at Iln, but although Iln is an old thorn in our side they can hardly finance an entire rebellion, and anyone with sense knows it. Shar or Arn could be behind it, as could any of the nations that border the south-east, although I doubt it. Neither Iltraya nor Arnagol has the funds alone, although together they might. Or the Archipelago, or the even less likely parties – Zarann, or Ronae, as much as both of them are half a world away there's only one Helion, and whoever holds it has considerable power. Or some other group we've not thought of, or don't know of."

Siera sucked at her teeth. "Do you recall just a few days ago, I mentioned that it was likely that the Archipelagans knew our patrol routes?"

"I do. And I suspect you're right, as much as I try to keep myself from paranoia… the timing is too suspicious. And the Archipelagans are a good tool, for the purpose of weakening Reimar."

"I'm keeping my knife to Old Arn, Arndustur and Shardustur. They have the money, the troops, and the gall to pull it off. Iln doesn't have the first two, or if they do it will nigh bankrupt them. And both Iltraya and Arnagol have their own bickering to attend to, I doubt they could pull off an alliance."

Andrayzn shook his head. "I will not commit even a guess. There are too many factors, and they are beside the point for now: we know where the rebels are, we know we can crush them, and thus must do so."

Siera nodded as she sipped her whiskey.

"Aside from the possibility of another nation involving itself, and the ring shortage, what else?" he continued.

Siera thought for a moment. "I assume you already know, although – oh, I completely forgot to send word to you. My apologies, Sir. There are apparently no mercenaries for hire, none at all."

Andrayzn laughed, and flicked his fingers at Siera. "Parrino had that bit of news on my desk before yours, I will wager. You know… just a few days ago, if anyone had told me that I would very shortly be rueing a lack of violent beggars with inflated self-worth, I would have laughed in their faces and told them to hike into the sea."

Siera did not echo Andrayzn's laugh. "I had honestly expected that we would pick up a few hundred mercenaries, or even a thousand, and be free of any concerns about using them unjustly or openly sending them in first… and then, nothing. Still, I did get some assistance."

"Oh?" said Andrayzn.

Siera nodded. "The Noble Order of Eneco."

Andrayzn's brows rose. "The church authorised their deployment? There is not a hint of any necromancy, or such, that I know of... how did you do it?"

Siera blinked. "Well... as long as they render assistance, it is good."

Andrayzn looked at Siera, then shifted to look out of the window to her left. An uncomfortable moment passed as Andrayzn sipped at his whiskey again before speaking.

"I understand if it is something you prefer not to mention, but I trust that the Guard's honour has not been tarnished."

Siera stiffened. "Never. The honour of the Guard remains unquestioned."

Andrayzn shrugged slowly and deliberately. "Then it is on you, Siera, and I trust that you have dealt well and for a good end, however you accomplished this... feat of diplomacy. I can only hope you do not come to regret whatever deal has been struck."

Siera took a long sip from her glass. Andrayzn followed suit.

After a long moment, Andrayzn spoke again.

"Then, another issue: prisoners."

Siera nodded. "I've told my officers directly, no accidental deaths if there are surrenders by the rebel ringleaders."

"Of course. However, with martial law declared, you have the authority to dispense summary justice."

Siera nodded. "And I intend to use it."

Andrayzn took another sip.

"Sir, if I might ask... a question that only a commanding officer can answer. I have my promotion to major, but how best to wear it? What... precise authority does the rank have, considering it hasn't been assigned in decades?" said Siera.

Andrayzn looked down, mulling over the question.

"To be honest, in the Royal Guard the difference between a major and a general is not a vast distinction. Even though your promotion occurs out of need, it is nonetheless permanent. A major you will remain, even though you command only the Fourth after the war is over. The responsibility weighs on you, but so do the privileges. Only you can decide how best to use your authority, now that you are no longer of equal rank to the other regiments' captains."

Siera nodded, her gaze distant.

Andrayzn continued. "I will note that attaining the rank of major at twenty five years of age is no small feat, no matter that circumstance has required thus and thrust this upon you. Still, you cannot claim youth for any indiscretions. That said, at this point there are only two people to gainsay your commands: myself, and your brother."

Siera nodded, then looked up to catch Andrayzn's gaze.

"At the least I can use it to bring a swift end to this rebellion. As you have said, the authority is mine, and I will use it to put Federica du Lucan's judges to hanging work," she said.

Andrayzn bit at his lip.

"I cannot say I am surprised, although I suspect you will get a few visits from people asking you to do otherwise."

Siera frowned at Andrayzn, then blinked as her eyes widened.

"Of course... why did I not think of that? Some fool's relatives are going to try to get this embarrassment to the family removed in a more polite fashion. Well, I will not have any of it. Every traitor will hang."

Andrayzn shook his head. "You might find that attitude more difficult to hold if things become more political." Andrayzn paused as he leaned forward, his elbows on Siera's desk. "Ultimately, your brother has placed you in charge of this campaign, and although I am still your commanding officer, I speak only as a comrade when I implore you to end this as quickly as possible. If this stretches on, the political ramifications will only become more and more ugly, not just for Ramiros, but for all Reimar."

Siera met Andrayzn's gaze.

"I do not intend to give them a moment's rest. Not a traitor will cool their feet before they are kicking in the breeze. My plan is to first take the *Wrath* directly to Surmarch."

Andrayzn took a long look at Siera. "Directly into their midst, scattering them. A bold move, with a great risk. I can hardly caution you, at this time... we need to be as bold as we dare. We cannot afford anything less. What after Surmarch?"

"Ponsurno, although I am not certain how to get in."

Andrayzn leaned back in his chair, stroking his chin with his thumb. "Your advantage will likely be the same, now that you have proven that your idea of drop-lines works. Not a castle in all the world has been built to withstand that kind of assault, although defensive ballistae might make you more cautious. You have an ace in that skyship. Although for Ponsurno you will likely only be able to drop into the city itself…"

Siera nodded. "The keep is recessed into the mountain, yes."

Andrayzn looked at Siera a moment longer, and she was certain he had something else to say. However, he nodded, and stood, Siera standing right after him. "I have other business to attend to, but if anything else comes up I will pass that along. Keep me informed."

Siera saluted, and Andrayzn nodded in reply before turning to leave.

Not half an hour had gone by before Siera looked up again as another knock came at her door.

"Who calls?" she said.

The door opened slightly and Tomasso poked his head around it.

"Someone to see you, Major. Elodia du Covas."

Siera frowned. Elodia was not known to her, but the du Covas name most certainly was.

The du Covas family had been counted as the weakest at the time of Reimar's founding in C.E. 571. But having kept their family line intact, exploited their holdings' mineral wealth, and funded expansion of their familial seat at Evenith, the du Covas family was now amongst the most prominent in the realm.

Siera bit her lip. "Send her in, Tomasso."

Elodia du Covas entered, flanked by two foppishly dressed courtiers, neither of whom Siera recognised.

Elodia made a quick bow. "Good afternoon, Your Highness! I am so terribly sorry to drop by and interrupt you but there is a most important matter that I must raise to your attention."

Siera blinked. She could almost place Elodia's face, surely

she was one of the more relevant du Covases… but Siera couldn't quite remember her.

"Yes, well, do take a seat…" said Siera.

Elodia smiled as one of the courtiers flanking her pulled out a chair, and both stood behind her.

"Your Highness, it is just – just dreadful to hear about all of this rebellion, and your poor father as well – please accept my heartfelt condolences!"

Siera nodded slowly. She still couldn't place Elodia. She obviously wasn't a 'Your Grace', but wasn't there a branch of the du Covas family that were actually marchionesses under the main du Covas line? Siera couldn't recall. "Trying times, yes… of course, of course…"

Elodia gave a wide smile. "Yes. But it gets even worse, Your Highness! My brother has flat-out lost his mind and decided to join the rebellion!"

Siera's expression went flat. "W–what?"

Elodia went on as though Siera had said nothing. "He wrote a letter to me, saying that his best friend Enio had implored him to join them, saying that their cause was just and faithful, and that he could not deny his dear friend in his cause!"

Siera stared at Elodia.

"Are you saying…" said Siera.

"It is truly terrible, Your Highness, but might I implore you to bring my brother to his senses?"

Siera stared at Elodia.

"What?"

Elodia's expression changed to being perplexed. "What do you mean 'what', Your Highness? My brother must be brought to his senses! His Noble Majesty has declared that you will be leading the Royal Guard to put an end to the rebellion, surely you will find my brother at some time during your efforts? Oh, I worry about him. He is impetuous, but he has a kind soul. He would never hurt anyone, Your Highness. Please, bring Francisco home to me." Elodia's smile and hopeful expression would have brought a tear to any eye.

However, after waking in the dead of night to witness her father's murder, after all the long nights since with barely any sleep, after wondering if she was planning and preparing for a doomed effort that might see her command wiped out and Reimar still burdened by this surge of rebellion, something in Siera snapped at Elodia's words.

Siera slowly stood up. "You mean to tell me... this story about your brother... who has joined a rebellion that in all likelihood was behind my father's murder?" Siera's mouth twitched. "That your brother has joined a force that has expressly committed treason against the kingdom of Reimar? You come here today, and you come here to tell me to my face that you want me to find your godsdamned brother and bring him back to you in anything other than a fucking NOOSE?!"

Elodia baulked. "Y–your Highness please, I–"

Siera's knuckles were white as she gripped her desk. "You can see your brother at the end of a rope when I HANG HIM. Now get out. Get out!"

"Your Highness–" said the courtier to Elodia's right.

"You can go hang as well, you impertinent little shit! Every traitor will be hanged, every one!" Siera swept her hand at Elodia in dismissal. "Your brother is a traitor and a coward and a fool! His death is deserved a thousand times over, and I will damn well see to it personally!"

Elodia raised her hands to her face to hide her tears as she stood and fled the room, followed by her courtiers, their faces pale.

"I hope Sura reincarnates your brother as a lice-ridden beggar, or a whore!" Siera shouted after Elodia.

Tomasso slowly leaned around the doorframe to look into Siera's office, eyes wide. "Er... is everything alright, Major?"

Siera's face could have cracked stone. "That goddamn little cur's brother apparently joined the rebels, and now she wants me to bring him back to her like a wayward puppy that pissed on the carpet!"

Tomasso baulked. "W–what? I... She must have lost her mind, there's no way that treason can be dealt with any other way... what did she even think..."

Siera pinched the bridge of her nose. "I highly doubt that there are many among the nobility who have joined the rebels, but if I get anyone else in here trying to get their idiot relatives out of trouble I will be sorely tempted to throw them out of my window. Face first."

Tomasso stood in the doorway a moment longer, before slowly closing the door to Siera's office, unsure of what to say, or whether to say anything at all.

And here he had thought that a short stint in the army would be all that he needed to get his parents settled for citizenship. He bit his lip.

Tomasso turned as a cough came from behind him. A portly man, flanked by two well-dressed men in feathered caps, had walked in.

"Is Her Highness here?" he said.

Tomasso baulked. "I... she is, Sir, who might I say–"

"Duke Silvio du Donati."

"Uh, of course, Your... Worthiness."

"Your Grace," said one of the courtiers behind Silvio, his tone frigid.

"Oh, Your Grace. Right, of course," said Tomasso with a lopsided smile.

Tomasso opened Siera's office door again, poking his head into the room.

"Sir, Duke du Donati has arrived to see you."

Siera looked up sharply. "What? Well... well, send him in."

Tomasso opened the door for Silvio and his two attendants, and bowed as they passed by him to enter.

Silvio entered and waited to be offered a seat. Siera neither stood nor looked up at him.

Silvio scowled. "Your Highness, it–"

Siera looked up and pointed at the two courtiers flanking Silvio. "Send those two out. I will not have every dandy courtier blundering into my headquarters, today or any other."

Silvio's face went blank. He turned and muttered, "Very well, gentlemen, let us meet outside afterwards."

They left, and Silvio strode forward to take a chair for himself. "Have I found you at a poor time, Your Highness?"

"You have," said Siera as she stopped writing, and put aside her quill. "Why are you here, Your Grace?"

Silvio glared at Siera. "I will assume your poor manners are due to your father's recent passing, Your Highness. And I come to ask a favour."

Siera's mouth twitched.

"If this, by any chance, is about your nephew…" said Siera in a low tone.

Silvio nodded curtly as he pulled out a caramel candy from a pocket and unwrapped it. "It is. Hang him for me, will you?"

Siera blinked. "W–what?"

Silvio popped the candy into his mouth as he gesticulated at Siera. "You must know that he has sided with the rebels. Blinding God, every stable hand and beggar in the kingdom has likely heard by now! Disgraceful. And worse, he has made off with using my estates as a headquarters and has run anyone in the family who is not sympathetic to him off the land. The gall, by Sura! And I think that he is deeply involved, too, and not just some flunky of the ringleaders. He is a ringleader himself, mark my words."

Siera leaned back in her chair. "Well, this is a pleasant change of tone for a visitor. I am pleased to hear that you understand that the wages of treason are death."

Silvio nodded, rubbing his fingernails on his shirt. "I have frequently asked of the Council to consider the particular status of my lineage and the greater sovereignty that it deserves, but I am no traitor. My nephew is a fool and scum of the lowest order, I want no doubt of my position on this matter."

Silvio looked out of Siera's office window. "I can only imagine what they hope to gain from this. Too many spare second and third children, or fourths and fifths, too mean and too churlish to go into business and establish their good name. And none want to enter the military, 'There's no grand riches there', they complain. No insult to you, Your Highness. They want power, do they? Fools. The old palatine dukedoms are not coming back, the old order will not return. And they would not last five minutes against everyone else even if they somehow resisted Reimar." Silvio's mouth wrinkled in displeasure.

Siera nodded. "Duly noted, Your Grace. Your sentiments

echo my own position, I have no intention of letting a single traitor go unpunished, not–"

"By hanging? You aren't going to just politely chop their heads off, are you?" said Silvio.

Siera raised her brows. "Well, yes. The only just punishment for treason is the rope."

Silvio made a thin smile. "Good, good. Let them all see him twist in the breeze, the bastard!"

Siera found herself smiling. She'd written Silvio du Donati off as an old blowhard, raised on his father's stories about how things were better before Reimar ruled over San Seras. Yet here he was, demanding the sort of justice she could well get behind.

Silvio licked his lips. "And before I forget, Your Highness, I have managed to raise a small contingent of household guards. They fled when my nephew took over my estates, and the others I had here with me in Ilmarch. They total a mere seventy four, but they are at your disposal."

Siera blinked. "Are you denuding yourself of your guards, Your Grace?"

Silvio shrugged. "I keep a mere dozen around me at the moment, but I can hardly keep myself better kept with eighty or more guards milling about. Far better than you have them. They have been trained with the pike, sword, and the bow; and their sergeant will be here tomorrow at eight to report in and follow your orders to the letter, to the last. It pains me, but they were right to run. They couldn't win then, but under you they will fight well. Yes, and they will arrive with a variety of coin purses, totalling four hundred and seventy-two teals in writs and deeds. I would offer more, but as my nephew has outright stolen my familial seat and familial treasury, I cannot."

Siera bit her lip, then smiled. "They will be well received, Your Grace, troops and coins both. Well received. And tonight... well, I will be staying at the palace, and I will be certain to let my brother know of your considerable contributions, and your faithfulness to Reimar. You have my thanks."

Silvio smiled thinly once more. "Best of luck in your campaign, Your Highness. I anticipate word of my nephew –

and his wretched cohorts – swinging by their rotten necks."

Silvio nodded, and stood to leave, pulling out another caramel candy for himself as he did so. Siera stood as he left, but her mind was more on the extra few troops and funds she would receive tomorrow.

Chapter 13: The Teahouse, the Mess, or the Tavern

As plans progressed, the lieutenants met with their sergeants, who in turn informed their corporals. However, each lieutenant had their own preference for raising morale and hearing from their subordinates before a campaign, and now was not a time to go changing one's habits.

Adalberto du Gallo, along with his staff sergeant, Cecilia Perez, met his seven field sergeants at the teahouse.

Normally, Adalberto met his sergeants to strategize or carouse at Esmeralda's, a small bar in the Almoner's borough. However, he had promised them that if ever a real war came, that he would treat them to a meal at the teahouse.

There were many teahouses in Ilmarch, and going to one was no distinction. But there was only one teahouse prominent enough to be called 'the' teahouse, that being the teahouse of the Reimaran Guild of Merchants and Lenders.

The Guild had similar teahouses all over Reimar, the use of which was a privilege for members and associates, and offered far more than tea alone. The capital's was no exception.

Situated in the south of Ilmarch, it enjoyed far more greenery than the older north-western parts of the city, which were overgrown with more limestone and cobble than with trees. The teahouse itself was a multi-storey building, the ground floor a variety of seating areas, a streetside view of the coming and going of Ilmarch, a full bar that never closed – not day or night or Highsun – restaurant tables, and outdoor seating by the lake and in the gardens. Even if the 'lake' barely qualified as a large pool, the teahouse staff insisted that it was a lake, and would ignore commentary to the contrary.

The second floor featured a full kitchen that only closed after midnight, as well as private meeting rooms for formal or informal gatherings. The third floor had short-term residences for guild members and associates who were staying overnight or less than a month. The guild even had a few sorcerers on hand to relay and receive any urgent messages.

Although any guild member could invite whatever guests they wished, you would be rebuffed at the door if you weren't in favour with the guild, a notable associate of another major guild, or at least known as an investor of importance.

The guild teahouse did not take casual visitors or members of the public, not even those brave souls who served in the Royal Guard.

The du Gallo family, though, had a long association with the guild, going back some one hundred and fifty years of investment in various industries, and counting for thousands of teals of business every year. A du Gallo had even been a former guild master.

So although Adalberto himself had as much mercantile skill as a dead rabbit, and was a relatively unimportant third son of the main family to boot, he had no problem in walking through the front foot gate with his eight sergeants. Those same sergeants gave low whistles as they walked up the paved drive and past the various fanciful topiaries, and approached the main entrance to the teahouse proper.

"No fuss to you, Sir, but I always thought you might just be joking when you said you could get us in," said Cecilia Perez.

Ramiro Santos was about to spit before he remembered where he was. "Hey, Esmerelda's was fine by me. Fiery fucking Sura, the waiters here have fancier uniforms than we do."

"And they're better looking than you too, Ramiro!" said Primo Vivas.

Adalberto turned and smirked. "Watch your tongues in here, they'll happily throw us out if we disturb anyone."

"Right, Lieutenant," said Cecilia.

"Yes, Sir," said Ramiro.

As they walked into the foyer, Adalberto saw the major-domo standing off to his right, chatting to a few waiters. The major-domo, a tall man with a bright red blazer and a white sash, saw Adalberto enter. He held his palm up to the staff, and walked over to Adalberto, noticing as he walked the silver bars on Adalberto's shoulders, and the silver ring with a red garnet in the centre that he wore on his right index finger.

"A good day to you Lieutenant... du Gallo. What can we offer you today, Sir?"

Adalberto imagined he could hear the surprise on his subordinates faces. "Table for eight, please."

The major-domo bowed slightly. "Certainly. Do you have a seating preference, Sir?"

Adalberto grinned. "Anything available in the gardens?"

"Yes, we have some free tables close to the lake." The major-domo signalled to a passing waiter. "Take Lieutenant du Gallo here and his... sergeants to one of the lakeside tables."

The waiter escorted Adalberto and his sergeants through and around the cluster of tables and smoking booths, clattering dishes and muttering lawyers, merchants, and traders; exiting through thin stained-glass doors to the teahouse gardens. Closed off from the hustle and bustle of the streets outside by high walls and hanging vines, the gardens were the very image of peace and quiet, even in the midst of Ilmarch. The various tables outside were also well spaced apart from each other, to ensure that the quiet was not unduly broken by too many conversations in close proximity.

"So, wait," said Kemen Elizondo as they all sat down. "Can we smoke outside? Or do they just smoke inside to be fancy?"

Primo glared at Kemen. "Next you'll ask for an apple pie, Saparan. Of course you can smoke, all the rich are mad for it. Everyone knows that."

Adalberto rolled his eyes. "Yes, you can puff away like a chimney, no one will bother you." Kemen winked and quickly started rolling a cigarette.

"So, Lieutenant, is planning finished? Where in the Gods'

names are we heading off to, anyhow?" asked Silvia Abana.

Adalberto nodded solemnly. "Major Siera has been assigned the southern campaign against the rebels, as you know. We'll be marching in six days, and you'll only be briefed as to our destination once we've assembled."

"Where do we assemble, Lieutenant?"

"Same place as last time: skyship docks."

"Oh, we're off on the *Wrath*? Aren't we marching with the other regiments and all the levies and that in two weeks?"

Adalberto leaned in close to the table, indicating to his sergeants to do the same.

"That's just a rumour. The major suspects someone is giving away information, and you didn't hear it from me, but she thinks it might be in the Admiralty. Now, don't breathe a word of it to anyone else. We'll be flying out to take the rebels by surprise, final destination to be announced after we board the *Wrath*."

Silvia nodded. "You know, that's the major for you. She's never straightforward, always has a trick up her sleeve."

Jessenia Cabrera clicked her tongue. "Rebels won't see us coming. Major's gonna rip 'em a new one."

Adalberto grinned. "The rebels might have the advantage of surprise, but they're not the only ones with surprises. The major has some wide plans for them, don't you worry. I realise that everything sounds a bit hushed, but it's all for good reason."

"Too hushed to decide formations?" said Silvia.

"No, not too hushed for that. Cristóbal, you'll be getting in a new consignment of greatbow arrows, although not as many as we'd like. Cecilia will sign for them once they come over from the Luminary Academy, but don't get carried away. We'll need them for siege work. Otherwise, the only other change is that we might be shooting from the deck of the *Wrath*, so that will be a challenge."

"Any idea of ranges, Sir?"

"We'll be seeing all sorts before this is over, there's no way we can dodge some ugly urban fighting either. Regardless, the basics are the same: make sure everyone has their gear and looses a volley in time. If there are no vocal orders, then loose after my shot is launched. If there are no target orders, then repeat at last target or pick your own." Adalberto grimaced. "We'll likely be doing a lot of that before this is over. No nice easy shots on fields, things are going to get close and ugly, and those greatbows will bring down a few walls before everything's quit."

"Better than using them on ships. It's not right, I still say. Those things should be for actual structures only," said Primo.

Adalberto spread his hands and shrugged in reply.

"Well, I'll have everyone doing at least some shortsword training again. Honestly, I forget we have the things sometimes," said Pepito Casales.

"That is a good plan, we might well find ourselves in such a situation. Let's not get caught out in an enemy flanking or charge with just our bows out," said Adalberto.

Ramiro snorted. "Huh, good reasons are one thing. The talk around the barracks is that we're taking on Archipelagan mercenaries, having them hold the front for us."

Adalberto shifted sideways in his chair, scowling. "Rumours are just that: rumours. If you hear them, stamp them out, we can't have that sort of talk proliferating. The major has specifically mentioned that there are to be no Archipelagan mercenaries. She doesn't want morale to suffer."

The sergeants all visibly relaxed, except for Ramiro.

"But, we'll still be fighting with sell-swords?"

Adalberto sighed. "No, none will be hired. Or can be, either. Someone has bought up all the mercenaries."

Kemen started almost out of his seat. "Eh–what, all of them? Sura's fiery backside, how? That would cost a fortune!"

Adalberto scowled. "I don't know how, and neither does the major. But the mercenaries have all been busied by something else, heh, we'll likely be fighting some of them."

Silvia sighed. "That's a bad business, Lieutenant. I don't care for them, but I'd rather have them on our side."

Adalberto looked around for any passing waiters, but saw none. "Yes, well, I know, but we can't get them, so no use wanting them either. And besides, we all know the true mettle of a mercenary."

Laughter greeted Adalberto's comment.

"Worthless, each and every one." Ramiro smirked. "My idiot second cousin's kid wanted to join the Guard, but he can't count higher than five. Some recruiter convinced him to sign up with the Orange Band. Probably dead now, the fool."

Silvia rolled her eyes. "You're not even drunk and you're telling that story already."

Ramiro glared at her. "Why not? It's an embarrassment to the family! How am I supposed to be out fighting for Reimar when any little shit can sign their life away to some mercenary scum?"

Pepito made a lopsided smile at that. "I suppose it can be a bit strange to have mercenaries in the family, if you're in the military."

Adalberto clapped his hands once as a waiter approached their table. "True, but let us talk as we eat."

"Eat what, Lieutenant?" said Jessenia.

Adalberto grinned. "Us brave defenders of the realm will be putting everything on the family tab, so dig in to whatever daily offering you like."

"Maybe ten plates of pickled eggs?" said Cecilia with a smile.

Adalberto laughed along with his sergeants. Soon enough there'd be precious little laughter.

What Ermanno Gartzia lacked in wealthy relatives, he made up for in pragmatism.

He met his sergeants in the regimental mess.

"Tell me you got something special for us, Sir!" said Silvio du Cipriani, Ermanno's staff sergeant.

Ermanno looked straight at Silvio. "Of course, so you can eat heartily for sure. I had the cook whip up a nice apple pie with a side of dog peppers."

"Fuck off, Lieutenant," said Eugenio Passerini.

Ermanno flicked Eugenio's ear. "You've got too much of your corporal's manners. I'm not your sergeant, Eugenio, I'm your lieutenant. Casual's one thing, but I cuss you out, not the other way around."

Eugenio rubbed at his ear. "Fine, fine, Lieutenant."

Ermanno ignored him. "To answer your question, yes, I had the cook whip up a nice thick stew for us."

"What, like the one last night?" said Carmine Brunetti.

Ermanno's face remained blank. "Thankfully not leftovers, this one's fresh. And it has actual meat and beer in it, I made sure."

"I swear the one last night was dog," muttered Nico Labriola.

"Nah Nico, just your mother's flank!"

"Quiet down, let's talk business before we eat. Can't flap your gums with a mouthful of stew. Pacifica, volunteer to grab the grog out the kitchen," said Ermanno as the cooks brought out everyone's food. Pacifica gave Ermanno a half-hearted salute.

"I heard that we're marching in two weeks down King Eneco's highway, Lieutenant," said Feliciano Airaldi, a nervous smile on his face.

Ermanno barked out a laugh. "Major's played everyone for a fool. We leave in under a week, and we're not taking the Gold Road."

A moment of silence took hold, then sighs and scattered laughter broke out.

"Damn, goddamn! Captain had me going there, I really believed it! Uh, Major, I mean."

"Hah! Canny as her old man."

"I should have known, the major wouldn't lead us down the Gold Road like a pack of mummers!"

Ermanno nodded. "The Major thinks there might be rebel sympathisers on the lookout, so she had the announcement made that she would be leaving in two weeks by the Gold Road, straight to the Helion. Truth is, we move sooner, in just six days – and on the *Wrath*."

"The *Wrath*? To go where?" said Vincenzo di Vitis.

"Surmarch," said Ermanno with a grin. "We'll drop down from the air and take it in the early hours of the morning. Rebels won't see us coming, and we won't have to blow down the gates that way. When the militia and the Fifth Regiment arrive after us, they can hold the city while we away to our next target."

"What's that, Sir?"

"You'll see when we get there and kill every rebel in sight."

Pacifica Sastre walked back to the table with an entire tray of wine bottles and mugs. Alcohol was forbidden while on duty, but when off duty the lieutenants could authorise consumption on the grounds of morale or special occasion. "All well in the end for the where, but what about the who?" she said.

Ermanno sighed. "Most likely mercenaries."

"The rebels likely don't have the money to hire too many. We'll have them for supper," said Nico, reaching out for a mug.

"You wish. Major said that Captain Parrino found out that there's none to be hired, someone's bought them all. And I won't give you a wooden teal to bet against who did it."

Vincenzo scowled as he poured himself some wine. "Parrino? He's an old man, he probably made a mistake." Ermanno gave him a flat stare, but Vincenzo was too busy stuffing his face again to notice.

"Yeah, no way that the rebels could hire every actual mercenary. That's ridiculous. Where'd they get the money?" said Pacifica.

Ermanno did not look up at Vincenzo. "Old men may yet surprise you, young mister haven't-seen-my-twentieth year."

"Well... no disrespect, Sir. But—"

Ermanno flicked his fingers at Vincenzo. "No buts. Parrino made sure, and the Major made sure. General Andrayzn likely made sure as well, for all I know. We're likely fighting a horde of goddamn sell-swords."

Pacifica sighed as she raised her mug. "Well, here's to coming back safe and in one piece."

"Here's to that," said Giovanni Marino, the other sergeants chiming in.

"Lieutenant?" said Pacifica, as Ermanno stared into his mug.

Ermanno looked slowly around the table at his sergeants. "I'll give you your toast, but for me, here's to dying a hero."

"Can't imagine you'd ever die, Sir," said Vincenzo.

Ermanno stared at him, his face blank. "We all go, sooner or later. Only concern is how you do it."

"Morbid talk here," said Giovanni, after a long sip.

"True that, Sergeant Marino. And here's the cook with our stew, so dig in. Soon enough it's whatever the cooks on the *Wrath* brew up, and you won't be eating the Major's biscuits either."

Ermanno smiled faintly as his sergeants grumbled.

Gretchen left the barracks with her sergeants in the afternoon, making their way to the Wreck. Built out of the hull of an old fishing vessel, the Wreck was a popular tavern for dock workers and off-duty sailors. Gretchen preferred it both for its low prices and for the rumours that wafted in with the tide.

That, and the stink of the harbour had a comfortable familiarity.

Gretchen and her subordinates had arrived during a lull in ship loading, so the bored dockworkers had spilled into the Wreck. Their raucous drinking made a bizarre backdrop for the seven soldiers sitting in a booth near the rear of the room.

Mario Corvi looked around the interior with a sullen face. "Loud in here, Lieutenant!"

Gretchen grinned at his poor mood. "Just like every other time, Mario. And this way, no one can overhear us. Besides, the dockers will leave soon when another ship comes in. But let's all have drinks first."

Gretchen motioned to a flustered barwait, who made his way to Gretchen's booth.

"Get your drinks ordered now, can't talk with a dry tongue," said Gretchen.

"To each their own, Lieutenant, or...?" said Domenico Arnoni, Gretchen's staff sergeant.

Gretchen smiled. "For all but the first round, that's on me."

Smiles met her reply.

After they had placed their orders, Paz Santiago, Gretchen's longest serving field sergeant spoke up. "So, what're our marching orders, Lieutenant?"

Gretchen leaned in closer over the table, indicating for the others to do the same. "Six days from now, before dawn, we meet at the skyship docks. Further orders come down after we board."

Celio Espinoza wrinkled his hooked nose. "What? We're off on the *Wrath*? But–"

Gretchen pointed at him. "No buts from you, Celio. The Major wants this kept quiet, she's got something up her sleeve."

"Well, did the Major tell you, Lieutenant?" said Celio.

"Of course," said Gretchen.

"So, tell us then!" he said.

Gretchen smirked. "Not a chance. Major wants things kept quiet, and if that's not good enough for you, then request a transfer."

Mario chuckled, almost too softly to hear over the low din of the tavern's other patrons. "Not on your life, Lieutenant. I wouldn't be serving under you in the First, that's for sure."

Giacinta Caivano smirked. "Ho, he'll have his lecher's grin out in just a moment."

Gretchen's eyes were lingering on the barwait coming back to their table. "No time for grinning, our pitchers have come."

"Like birds home to the roost," said Paz.

"Before you start, let's have a cheer for the Major," said Erasmo Marino.

Erasmo snatched at his pitcher and raised it high. "To the major's promotion!"

Paz gave a solemn nod as she raised her own mug. "To Her Highness, long may she live."

Mario smacked his lips. "Here's to Her Highness whipping those rebels."

Gretchen grinned. "To the best captain I've served under, and the best major I'll ever serve under."

"For a moment there I had thought you'd forgotten the major's new rank," said Domenico.

Gretchen chuckled. "I keep almost slipping, but not yet. Damn good captain, damn good major."

Mario waved his hand at Domenico. "Never mind that. Lieutenant, level with us. There's a rumour going around that we're getting in Archie mercenaries. No offence."

Gretchen nodded. "None taken, and no, there's no mercenaries coming."

Mario let out a breath. "Well, that puts paid to my worries

then. Er, you mean no Archies? I mean, Archipelagans."

Gretchen leaned back in over the table. "Archland or otherwise, none at all. Apparently they're all off busy getting killed somewhere else."

"Useless bunch of thugs anyway," muttered Celio.

"They're good for going in first," said Giacinta, raising her mug again.

"They're better at running the fuck away, never there when you need them. No pride," said sergeant Erasmo.

"And it's pride that will carry us yet. Rebels don't have any brains or sense, let alone pride," said Gretchen.

Mario clicked his tongue. "Why, though? I don't get it."

Gretchen gave a slow shrug. "Apparently it's some leftover southerner nobles who've decided they've had enough."

Paz cleared her throat after a long sip. "What makes them think they can win, though?"

Gretchen shrugged. "Too arrogant to think they'll lose. And there's Iln, convinced we can't get to them behind the mountains."

"Hardly fair, they can fly, with that armour they have," said Erasmo.

"Hardly fair is right, but there's no fair in war. Besides, the general won't let them run around burning everything," said Gretchen before she took another sip.

Paz sighed. "Not sure how he's supposed to stop them. Every other time he just runs them off after a few months. Fucking Iln."

"If the major can come up with a way to squash the rebels, the general will think up a way to swat some Ilnians," said Gretchen.

"A good swatting is what they need. I don't understand how their mages can come up with flying armour, but ours can't," said Domenico.

"I've no idea. And if I'd been born a mage I'd be getting paid a lot more than I am now," said Gretchen. "So there's no use worrying about it. Besides, we're off to fight rebels, not Ilnians, so we should focus on the foe at hand."

Mario glared at his empty mug. "Are we going in with those boots, Lieutenant?"

Gretchen nodded. "Damn right we are. Major has pulled out all the stops for whatever gear we need. The Luminary Academy is enchanting up all sorts of stuff for us as always, those stampeding boots are high on the list. Right after those arrow-deflecting rings."

"Just like Highsun's day," said Paz.

"What, did you get magic shoes for Highsun? At least then you could run away from your husband's awful cooking," said Giacinta, which drew soft laughter from everyone but Gretchen, who failed to conceal her smirk.

Paz shrugged. "I've told you, a man can only have two of three important attributes – good in the kitchen, good with money, or good looks. Or a woman besides, the best is two of three."

Mario grinned. "So which ones does your husband have? Both length and girth, or…?"

Paz made to throw her beer at Mario, but her mug was empty. "Where's your husband, eh Mario?"

Mario's grin didn't fade. "Don't have one, but my parents have a few nice girls lined up. Maybe I'll send some your way."

Paz snorted. "Speaking of that, what's-her-name in the Second Regiment has that new necklace. You reckon Adalberto'll put it on her wrist?"

Mario smacked his lips. "I wouldn't mind moving something lower down on her myself. Bertie's a smart man."

Gretchen rolled her eyes. "Less husbands and wives, more trade talk. Now, last time we only had fifty or so, but this time we'll all have enough. They're supposed to arrive in two days, so I'll assemble everyone in the afternoon and we'll all practice again."

"Not me that needs practicing, Lieutenant," said Erasmo, as he smiled at Mario.

"Piss off, 'Rasmo, it was an accident," said Mario.

Erasmo rolled his eyes. "You tried to do a fucking cartwheel and rammed a wall, what do you call that?"

Mario flicked his fingers at Erasmo. "They're tricky things, that's why. Too hard to use."

Gretchen tapped her mug against the table. "Horse peppers. Take your time, go slowly, and you'll get the hang of it. Before you know it, you're charging across the field, every stride is five metres. And whatever the mages have done to them makes sure you don't break your legs. Enemy won't know what hit them."

Paz sighed after failing to attract the barwait's attention. "Eh, we've got a lot more gear these days, Lieutenant. D'you think… d'you think that fighting is changing?"

Gretchen nodded, frowning. "Of course. Major has us jumping off a skyship to kill pirates. Iln has had that flying armour for almost a decade now. Change with the times, or you'll get rolled. Just what the major says," said Gretchen.

Mario shrugged. "Still comes down to you and your weapon, you got skill or you got courage. No mage'll give you either."

"True enough," said Gretchen. "Now if the mages could make swords run around and attack people by themselves, we'd be out of a job. But they can't, so here we are."

Gretchen tried to wave over a barwait, with no luck.

Chapter 14: To War

Late autumn gave the pre-dawn air a definite chill. Siera resisted the urge to stamp her feet.

Before her, the Fourth Regiment's soldiers filed onto the *Sky's Wrath*, yawning and shambling as they went. Even her lieutenants were too sleepy to chide the troops into a quicker boarding.

Siera looked up, to the *Wrath's* main sail. The Royal Guard's insignia was hard to make out in the gloom, but the sight of it comforted her slightly. The large white shield with a silver spear crossing over a black bow, with three Gold Teals underneath, the motto on an arcing scroll at the very bottom: "*Reimar, Vigilance, and Honour.*"

"What's that, Sir?" asked Adalberto.

Siera blinked. "Oh, thinking out aloud. Wish I was in my bed, to be honest."

Adalberto nodded. "Orders are orders, and need is need, but I'd – I would trade a fair coin to be still in bed, warm and asleep."

"More the pity that regulations forbid a nice spot of spirits when on duty," said Ermanno as he rubbed his hands together.

"Oh? I just realised, I have no idea what your preference is, Ermanno," said Adalberto.

Ermanno smacked his lips. "Have you tried that Arnageli… Arnagoli, people and things from Arnagol, whatever they're called – that rum?"

Adalberto's eyes lit up. "Rum, great stuff! The spice of it, it's wonderful. Delicious and sweet. Love it."

Ermanno grinned. "Good to see a man of taste around here. I tried to get Gretchen to have some last time we had leave, and she came back and said she wished she could have spat it in my face."

Siera shook her head. "I tried it a few years ago, awful stuff. It would be best put to use stripping varnish from wooden furniture. A proper liquor is fiery."

Adalberto shrugged. "You're a whiskey drinker, right Major?"

Siera nodded. "Picked it up from my father, never looked back."

Ermanno looked at Siera. "Hmm... if it's your old man's taste, it can't be Old Arn Highland, or that thick old Jurienese stuff. He'd drink a proper Reimaran liquor."

Siera smiled softly. "Truly said. My father loved Valencia's Finest, myself, I prefer Ilmarch Old Harbour. Still, I remember seeing a small bottle of a Favrian whiskey on his desk once. I cannot recall the name. I hope he got to try some, before..."

Siera didn't continue. No one else spoke again until Gretchen walked up and made a quick salute, fist over heart, to Siera.

"All done, the last soldiers are on board. Commodore Terciero says we can cast off any time."

Siera nodded, rubbing her hands. "I wish we could have had a normal send off. Relatives and others cheering as we depart makes for a good morale booster."

"True, but that's for our regular patrols. Wartime is different," said Ermanno.

"That sounds bizarre. Do the troops somehow not need a morale boost during war?" said Siera.

"It's not that. It's the wailing," said Ermanno.

"Wailing?" said Adalberto.

Ermanno grimaced. "You can keep all that patriotic talk for the good times. No disrespect, of course. There's not a parent in the world who's so blind to think that all their children will be coming back. Parents, spouses, children, lovers, friends, anyone. Mood in the crowd can turn dark quickly. It's depressing."

Siera frowned. "Either way, we leave quietly this time. Hopefully I am wrong, and there is no spy or informant to let loose our advertised departure. But far better safe than sorry."

There was no further talk as they boarded the *Sky's Wrath*. As the last guide ropes were cast off, the ship slowly lifted out of its dock and into the air.

The *Sky's Wrath* rose into the sky, slowly turned south, and sailed to war.

Chapter 15: The First of the Ashes

27th Teurnot, hours before dawn.

The *Sky's Wrath* kept a steady pace, arriving on schedule. Commodore Terciero had kept the ship slower than usual, to arrive well after nightfall.

The *Wrath* was slowly closing in on the city below, all but the most essential lights on deck having been extinguished. The ever-present faint creaking of the hull was the only giveaway of the vast bulk of the ship descending on Surmarch, faintly silhouetted against stars in the deep night sky.

Boots began to tramp over the deck as the troops started to assemble to present arms, drop-lines prepared and ready, and Siera smiled.

She still remembered the first time they'd tested the prototype drop-line. She had wanted to volunteer; after all, it was her idea. But she knew that it would look bad, as the risk of an accident was too great.

Can't have Her Highness breaking every bone in her body and dying in a puddle.

Siera remembered the volunteer, a private. Enrico Messina. Siera was certain that Ermanno had 'volunteered' him, but had said nothing.

She remembered his nervous smile, and his salute before he dropped over the side of the *Wrath*, a hundred metres above the ground. They had all known the reality of it: despite safer tests with bags of flour and the assurances of many learned mages at the Luminary Academy, if Enrico had turned into a pile of sausage meat when he hit the ground, well, that would have been the end of Siera's little idea.

Enrico twisted his ankle.

Siera had laughed upon hearing the news, feeling guilty as she did so, but relishing the weight falling off her shoulders, her stomach un-knotting as she realised that it worked, *it worked.* Twisted ankle be damned, the lines would slow anyone dropping down it if they had the buckle to do so, and would adhere to the ground it touched until pulled away by hand. The buckle was even enchanted to tarnish itself when the enchantment wore out, and did not need to be manually replaced by a mage. Sturdy, reliable, and fast.

Now, almost six months later, she had seen the first practical use of the drop-lines – and over a stormy sea, no less. The lines worked excellently, continuing to perform as expected.

'The ingenuity of mages, indeed', Siera thought to herself. That, and the dozens of drills that the soldiers of the Fourth had undertaken since the first successful prototype test. No more twisted ankles.

Siera stood near the helm, her lieutenants out on the crowded deck making sure all was in order for the landing: harnesses firm, weapons ready. Below her, the dark outlines of Surmarch drew closer. Siera could make out torches all over, but from even this low above the city, it all looked quite dark.

Siera felt that roiling unease in her gut, that same old sickly feeling whenever the moment for action came. No matter how many times she went into battle, it never stopped happening.

She waited for the cry, for the alarm, for the distant clattering of boots and shields as the *Wrath* was sighted coming in.

None came.

Siera was still surprised that Ermanno hadn't objected to this approach, coming in over Surmarch at night. But who could say what was crazy anymore? Ilnians flew and Reimarans leapt off the sides of skyships. Or as her father had tried to remind her, skyships in their entirety still disturbed some people. Not a single one had existed when he was a boy.

The world was changing. "Change, or be rolled".

"Sir?" said Tomasso.

"Hm? Oh, was I thinking out aloud again?" said Siera.

"Yes sir. Something about being rolled, I think. We'll certainly be doing some rolling tonight." Tomasso smiled nervously.

Siera grinned suddenly, her eyes wild and bright.

"Damn right we will. This is our land. Rebels want the legacy of their forebears returned? I will shove it down their goddamn throats until they choke."

Tomasso blinked.

"Well, time to address the troops, before we get too close to Surmarch. Pity we cannot have everyone on the deck together."

Siera walked out onto the deck, packed as it was with soldiers, and touched a gem on her collar similar to the one her brother had.

"Soldiers of the Fourth! You have left in silence and arrive in silence. Our battle today is one of surprise, and our enemy does not expect us. Even so, stay on your guard. The rebels have likely hired a multitude of mercenaries to stand watch, and the fighting ahead may be bloody. I do not say this to warn you, I say this to encourage you. Even as you look around and see how few we are, remember this: you do not stand alone. All of Reimar stands with you, all of your families stand with you. You go on today to reclaim what is ours, you go on today to ensure all of our families' futures."

In the dim light, Siera could see some of her troops nodding, some mouthing prayers, others holding good luck charms. Siera grimaced as she remembered how she'd disdained such things when she was a lieutenant, thinking them small-minded and provincial.

She'd changed her mind. Almost any comfort that her soldiers could have was a good thing.

Tomasso looked to his left as one of Terciero's aides approached.

"Major du Tealdan, commodore Terciero says that we are almost over the keep's courtyard. He will lower the ship to fifty metres, but that will only take a moment. Your soldiers can jump anytime."

Siera nodded. "Good. Carry on." Terciero's aide saluted, and left.

"Your harness all ready, Tomasso?"

Tomasso baulked. "Yes, sir, but we won't be jumping this evening, will we?"

"Not if all goes according to plan, but when does that ever happen?" said Siera with a smile.

Siera turned to see that all of the first group of soldiers under Ermanno's command were waiting at the port and starboard sides of the ship. As large as the *Wrath's* deck was, it could certainly not accommodate every soldier in the Fourth Regiment.

Siera drew her sword, holding it high.

"Stand ready, soldiers of the Fourth! When you hit the ground, do not hesitate! You have been trained by the best, and your king trusts you to drive back these traitors and cowards hiding behind their mercenary dogs! For Reimar, and for honour! Drop now!"

Soldiers on both port and starboard sides turned, muttering quick prayers, running last-second checks of their belt harnesses, and dropped over the side to the courtyard fifty metres below. As each had their feet on the ground they moved away, so the next soldier would not land on top of them.

Ermanno grimaced as he landed, his knees creaking. "Form up! Squads, form up!" he cried. All around him, the First Battalion's soldiers came into formation, shields up, swords out.

"Hey, who goes there? What's all that noise?!" came a call from near the keep.

"Forward advance at pace! At pace!" cried Ermanno.

"A–attack! We're under attack! Sound the alarm, close the gate!" came a cry.

"Good Sura, may Siera have been right about that portcullis, gracious God," muttered Ermanno as he marched forward in the midst of his troops.

Fifty metres above, as the last of the First Battalion's soldiers had dropped over the side of the *Wrath*, Siera felt that same old twist in her gut drop away. No more time to contemplate if her gamble was on the money or not; now came time only to do or die.

Siera nodded as Adalberto hustled his troops onto the bowcastle so they could loose arrows down on any foes they saw. Even if the dark precluded any accurate bow work, it was better to have them in position and not need them than the reverse.

"No slippery fingers until my mark, no wild guesses and hopes for luck in the dark." Adalberto called out. "No nervous fingers, private Gustavo."

"Is that Lieutenant Ermanno leading the attack, at the front there?" asked sergeant Vivas.

"I… think it is. Unusual. I swear that's some fool with a crossbow down there… Cecilia, hand me my longbow.

"Sir."

"As much as I ordered no shots in the dark…" said Adalberto as he nocked an arrow and took aim in the deep gloom, and loosed.

His arrow snapped out and downward, finding its mark in a mercenary who was eagerly bringing a crossbow to bear against Ermanno's attack.

Cecilia craned her neck over the side. "I think you hit them, sir."

Adalberto nodded, smirking.

Yet more boots thumped across the deck, as Lieutenant Gretchen led her Battalion up to the drop-lines.

"Buckle and over, buckle and over! Move aside when you hit the ground, let's have no one eating boots!"

Gretchen's troops dropped over the side, landing and forming up.

"All form up, forward at half pace. No stampeding until my signal."

"Wish I had a pike right now. Nothing like a nice, solid pike," said Giacinta Caivano.

"You won't be wishing so hard when we're leaping onto them, swords first. Break your damn arm, trying to wield a pike like that. It'll be just like we practiced, you'll see," said Gretchen.

Back at the keep's gate, the mercenaries of the Ardent

Company had tried to close the portcullis and found, to their horror, that the mechanism would not budge.

Before the tight formation of the First Battalion, the dozen mercenaries who just moments ago had been playing cards and chatting idly were either dead or running.

At the other end of the road leading to the keep, the outer portcullis was far better staffed with mercenaries. The first challenges came out when Gretchen was scarcely fifty metres away from the gate.

"Who goes? Adolphus, is that you?"

"Boots, jump up to the ramparts and take the gatehouse!" cried Gretchen.

Her troops came to a brief halt as they fumbled at their boots, a short slap to the side activating whatever dormant magic was embedded in them. A soft light came from the variety of bizarre indentations and markings along the metal plates on the sides of the boots, and Gretchen's soldiers took it in turns to leap forward towards the gates, Gretchen at the head of the charge.

"Up, up!" she cried as she came to a halt near the base of the gatehouse, well-wrought brick and mortar doing nothing to stop her as she simply leapt ten metres in the air to land softly on the ramparts above her.

Shocked mercenaries, in the red and orange livery of the Ardent Company, sat in the gatehouse itself to Gretchen's left, mouths' agape and halfway through some game of cards.

A wild dare slipped from Gretchen's thoughts to her lips.

"No one moves, or you all die! Hands away from swords, keep still!" she yelled.

Gretchen's troops by now were all around her, pushing into the gatehouse and shoving mercenaries aside with the flats of their blades.

Gretchen had the gatehouse with not a single casualty.

Ermanno and his Battalion had pushed through light resistance throughout the keep, and things were becoming more of a mop-up than a battle.

Turning from one large hallway to a grand foyer of some form had Ermanno feeling wary.

"Giovanni, have the troops stop their advance."

"All halt! All halt!" Giovanni cried out.

Ermanno snapped his eyeglass out of its case on his hip, and got a closer look of the upper level of the foyer. It wasn't obvious as one first walked in, but there was a wide area up above that appeared to be just a narrow walkway from the ground. The banner placements were too regular...

"Broad shields out, all squads, broad shields out! Then advance," Ermanno called out.

"Broads to front, out to front!" cried the sergeants, as soldiers fumbled at the broader wooden shields that they wore on their backs, exchanging their smaller metal bucklers for them. "Forward!"

As his soldiers pushed on, shields held in front of them, Ermanno turned to put his eyeglass away. He saw movement from up above, out of the corner of his eye.

Ermanno straightened just as dozens of soldiers bearing crossbows rose from kneeling and loosed a volley of bolts at the Reimaran advance. The flutter of the first shafts brought the whip-snap sound of crossbow strings and screams, but few soldiers fell, thanks to their waiting shields taking the brunt.

A clamour erupted around Ermanno, calls for orders and cries of confusion and pain came from all around.

"Sir, should we pull back? They have crossbows!" shouted Pacifica Sastre as she looked over to Ermanno.

Ermanno drew his sword. "Shields up, sprint to the staircase! Take the fight to them! Charge!" he roared.

These orders were all his soldiers needed. The Reimarans let out a battle cry, the few clattering crossbow bolts drowned out by the stamp of their boots.

Dozens of mercenaries lined the broad walkway as the First Battalion charged up the stairs. Ermanno could see now that the banners he'd seen from down below hid crenellations, great cover for archers – or crossbows.

"Charge! Show them your steel! Charge!" shouted Ermanno as he paused to pull up a private who'd tripped on the stairs as they ran up.

"Go, give them what they deserve!" The mercenaries baulked in surprise at the Reimaran advance in the face of their ambush, and begin to break ranks.

Ermanno didn't bother calling out further orders. The mercenaries had nowhere to run.

The pre-dawn half-light slowly gave way to day in the early hours of the morning as Ermanno returned to where he'd dropped down from the *Wrath*, a single squad accompanying him. Siera, Tomasso, Quintus, and one of the sorcerers under Terciero were in the small guardhouse next to the broken portcullis, standing around a table with a few maps spread out over it.

"Tell Commodore Terciero to take the *Wrath* on one more patrol around the city, then report back here," said Siera to the sorcerer next to her, who bowed in return.

"First Battalion reporting back, Siera. Nothing but mopping-up inside the keep. A few well-dressed types tried to leave without permission, I've got a squad bringing them along."

Siera nodded. "Good, if there are any others then Gretchen will find them. She has a sorcerer with her as well, just in case. The keep is under our control?"

"As far as I can tell, yes. I've got a squad at each of the entrances, the interior is clear, armoury remains locked – don't think it was ever opened, strange as that seems."

Siera laughed. "Incompetence is a welcome trait in an enemy. How many mercenaries did you find?"

"That's the strange part, Siera, we found..." Ermanno turned to his aide. "What, maybe... five dozen?"

Siera frowned. "What, so few? That does not sound right... surely they must have hired more?"

Ermanno scratched at his chin. "You'd expect so, but apparently not."

Siera shook her head. "Gretchen managed to get the outer gatehouse without a single loss through surprise, then moved through the streets to find any others."

"And Adalberto?" said Ermanno.

"The *Wrath* moved off to patrol the city outskirts, making sure that no surprises are encamped outside the walls. Apparently, all is well. The gatehouses that were staffed with mercenaries either surrendered or put up a poor fight, apparently no-one thought to train the Ardent Company to use siege weapons. The *Wrath* was never in even the slightest danger."

Ermanno gave a low whistle. "Have we done it, then? Do we have Surmarch?"

Siera smiled. "I think so. I can hardly believe it... well, let us wait on Adalberto and Gretchen."

Siera and Ermanno busied themselves with waiting until the *Wrath* hove into view.

"Aah, and here he comes," said Siera.

Fortuitously, Gretchen arrived with a squad in tow after Adalberto had dropped down off the *Wrath*.

"Well, let us have all reports now, then," said Siera. "Ermanno?"

"Keep's well, half a dozen surly captives supposed to be coming along. They're late, though," said Ermanno.

Gretchen coughed. "Well, all those locations we suspected the rebels might have established themselves are clear. Courthouse was empty and locked up, constables had been pressed into service and had mercenaries with them on all patrols, soon as they saw us they turned on the mercenaries. It got bloody, but we've cleared them out so far. No-one at any of the markets, although there were a few signs claiming that Surmarch was under the rule of its rightful lords now. Tore those down. Rest of the Battalion's broken up and leading the local constables to make the rounds and have the citizenry know that the city has been liberated," she said.

"Well enough, but what is our tally of losses?" said Siera.

"Three," said Ermanno.

"None," said Adalberto.

"Four," said Gretchen.

Siera stared. "Three, none, and four? Have we really lost only seven soldiers in retaking the entirety of Surmarch?"

A slow, broad smile spread across Siera's face. Her lieutenants slowly echoed her grin, looking to each other as the realisation sank in.

"We've did it – done it. We've taken all Surmarch, haven't we..." said Ermanno.

"How, how..." said Gretchen as she started to laugh.

Adalberto chuckled. "I think we've overestimated these rebels. You must be right, Major, someone has put them up to this."

Ermanno pointed away from the group. "And there's our pretty pigeons."

Siera turned to see a squad of First Battalion soldiers flanking a group of five captives, only two of whom were dressed in anything but nightgowns. Behind them came a well-dressed man in the colours of the Ardent Band, without any armour but with a far better cut of cloth.

"Sorry for the delay sir, but we found this one–" the soldiers pointed at the man in the Ardent Company's livery"– skulking around the solar."

"I am Jannick Hummel, and I was only trying to obtain our agreed-upon wages," he said, making a short bow.

"You worthless shit," muttered one of the captives.

"You." Siera pointed at the one who'd spoken up. "What is your name?"

"Imanol du Salamanca, and more curses to you, du Tealdan."

Siera smiled thinly. "Where is Mayor de Affini?"

Imanol laughed. "He was un-cooperative, cleaving to the throne over a much wiser changing of loyalties. We sent him packing to the keep's dungeon. We never sent him any food, so I doubt you will find him alive."

Siera grimaced. "And the commander of the constabulary?"

Imanol grinned. "Likewise. Maybe one of them ate the other. You should go see."

Siera reached out and struck him across the jaw with a clenched fist. "Show respect to your betters, traitor, or you can talk without teeth."

Imanol breathed deep through clenched teeth, scowling as his lip bled. Siera turned to another captive.

"I know you all too well, Itsaso du Lucan. From the Marchioness du Lucan's, are you not? Wretch. You will be pleased to know that Duke du Lucan herself has arranged the special contingent of judges I have with me to preside over your treason trial. You will be tried before the public that you tried to sway from their rightful lords."

"A show trial," muttered the third conspirator.

"And yet still more than you deserve, Sendoa du Bianchi," said Siera, her eyes flashing as she glared at him.

"I assume you have our punishment already laid out?" said Itsaso, her eyes defiant even as her hands shook at her sides.

Siera smiled. It didn't reach her eyes. "You will most assuredly be found guilty and then hanged."

Imanol sighed. Sendoa broke suddenly into quiet tears. Itsaso bared her teeth.

"A barbaric punishment. How dare you call us traitors? My family rightfully owned this land until a Reimaran invasion turned us into mere marchionesses! We even had to marry into the damned du Lucan's to guarantee the noble station we deserve!"

Siera's face was stony. "Your family swore allegiance to the Reimaran throne, and that same family seems to be nowhere near you in your time of faithlessness. You greedily tried to usurp your lord and take power for yourselves. And now you will receive your just reward: the noose."

With that, Siera turned away from them. "Put them in the hold, and assign a guard to them," she said to Ermanno.

"Er, Captain, is it? Major?" called out the Jannick Hummel.

Siera turned to glare at him. "I have no care for the complaints of mercenaries, you can join the rest in the hold."

Jannick gave a nervous smile. "Well, you see, I myself am not Reimaran, so, I cannot be a traitor."

Siera's gaze met his. "You conspired to take money from traitors, and conduct violence against Reimar. You also did not surrender to us," said Siera.

Jannick rubbed his hands together. "Well... yes, but now that we're not being paid, we won't make any trouble. It's not worth our while, see?"

"Your mercenaries can hardly make trouble, as they've been killed or captured, you mean," said Siera.

Jannick blinked. "Well, the ones who remained here in Surmarch, yes."

Siera scowled. "What do you mean, remained?"

Jannick licked his lips. "Six hundred marched out on to the Gold Road to ambush you."

Siera blanched, her rejoinder dying in her throat.

Whether they were Reimaran or not was irrelevant to her, any foe that raised their blade to Reimar would be struck down. What was it that her brother had said...? 'Those that raise a hand to Reimar will have that hand cut off', or such. Still, here was a fight with six hundred troops that she could avoid…

"You weave a fine tale, but for now you can sit in the hold with the others. Take them away," Siera said.

Back on board the *Wrath*, Siera held a hurried meeting with her lieutenants.

Ermanno was the first to respond to the news of Jannick's mercenaries on the Gold Road. "It's not right, Siera. We shouldn't let them escape, just because it's inconvenient to fight them."

Siera's eyes flashed. "I complain about no mere inconvenience here, Ermanno. We have only so many Royal Guards, and every day we fail to completely crush the rebellion is another day that we will live to rue."

Ermanno shook his head.

"A battle that can be avoided probably should be, I'd say," said Gretchen. "What will we really gain by fighting? Is it going to get us Southmere, or Ponsurno, or the Helion?"

"Exactly so," muttered Siera. "I do not like it, but I must take the best course possible. And I will not throw soldiers at problems I can resolve in other ways."

Ermanno scowled. "By that reasoning you could best save us all by never fighting and giving the country to the rebels."

Siera's eyes widened, and Ermanno realised he'd gone too far.

"Never, not once, not ever say such a thing again. Never suggest nor even dream that I would not do everything to save Reimar, from rebels or Ilnians or the very spirits of wrath and fire themselves. Not in my hearing. Or I will throw you off this skyship after I have you whipped for insubordination."

A short, intense pause took root in the room.

"Understood," said Ermanno, his expression flat, as Siera glared at him.

"W–well, there's no easy answer, I think can all agree on this," said Adalberto, putting his palms out. "But if we can just get rid of this lurking Ardent Band, then–"

"The Ardent Company," said Gretchen.

"Yes, right – if we can just get rid of them by unloading this unctuous fellow, then... why ever not? We can win without fighting. Take their surrender and throw them out of the country. All's well that ends well."

Ermanno made as if to speak, but said nothing. Siera's eyes flicked over him as he did so.

"Let me guess, Gartzia: 'General Andrayzn would say that it dishonours the guard', or somesuch. Well, General Andrayzn is not leading this campaign, and the true dishonour to the Guard is pursuing some idiot mercenaries, dragging their balls through the mud as they wait to spring an ambush that will never come!"

"I wasn't going to say that," muttered Ermanno.

Siera glared at Ermanno. "Either way, my decision is made. Let us be rid of this band of mercenaries the quickest way possible. We will send word that they can leave Reimar if they surrender," said Siera, tapping her index finger on the desk.

"I'll have that commander of theirs brought up, or whatever they call him," said Ermanno with a sigh as he made to walk.

"Before you go, we have... just under five hours, I think, until the trials begin," said Siera. "Adalberto, the Second Battalion will remain on the *Wrath* and watch for any rescue attempts, unlikely as that may seem. Gretchen, your Battalion will be on patrol around the city. Ermanno, you will arrange for the First Battalion to secure the square. If the crowd gets ugly, leave things to me, and do not act without my signal. If any rescues are attempted, though, do not wait for my orders before you cut them down."

Adalberto bowed. "Yes, sir."

"Just like we planned, Sir," said Gretchen with a salute.

Ermanno nodded. "We'll keep the peace."

"Good. See you at the hanging," said Siera with a faint smile.

Siera waited until after her lieutenants had left her cabin, and then herself exited into the hallway. She checked left and right, they were gone.

She turned to Quintus, standing guard just next to the door. "We have guests awaiting our hospitality in the hold," she said.

Quintus nodded.

They made their way down into the hold, and easily found an alcove that had bags of flour as well as Siera's four captives seated on the floor, with two guards from the First Battalion standing over them. As Siera approached, she realised that they were actually beating Sendoa.

"You cheap little *fuck*, you *cunt*," hissed one soldier as he held him by the hair and used his other hand to punch him repeatedly in the face.

"P– please, stohp–" he pleaded through bloodied lips.

The soldier's comrade egged him on. "Show him, Ramo, show him. Fucking little traitor highblood, eh? Who's the big man now, eh there, boy?"

"You two!" At Siera's voice, both men jumped and turned to her with surprise and fear across their faces.

"S– Sir! We were just–"

Siera nodded as she walked up to them. "Welcoming our prisoners on board. Good work. Wait at the stern stairway, and we will not need to mention any of this to Lieutenant Gartzia, will we?" said Siera with a thin smile.

"I – yes, yessir. Yes Sir," they said as they quickly walked away.

Siera's captives sullenly regarded her, except for Sendoa, who was weeping quietly.

"Well, we have business to attend to. You, Ardent Company. I find it more practical to have you spared and your filthy company dispersed from Reimar, but I can hardly trust you to keep your word."

Jannick lifted his manacled hands. "I've no reason to lie, Your Highness. And besides, if we don't get paid, we don't fight."

Siera slowly paced around to his side. "You might make your way to another city held by rebels. I cannot afford that. What assurances can you offer me?"

Jannick licked his lips. "Well… how about you hire us, instead?" he said with a toothy grin.

Siera's face was impassive. "As enjoyable as it would be to march you to your deaths, I can hardly trust you. You might well be a mercenary, but–"

Jannick spread his hands as widely as his chains would

allow. "But switching sides is what we do, Your Highness. And besides, everyone knows that the throne's good for it, in Reimar."

Siera frowned. "Good for what?"

"For delivering pay. Reimar's Helion-rich."

Siera shook her head. "Even so, I cannot trust your group."

"Well, err, how about this: you let me send word to my troops to stand down, no money in it, heh, and they all report to uh... anywhere you like, really. Then you'll know we're not taking a hike to San Seras, right? Then you let me go, and I'll march the Ardents out of Reimar."

Siera sucked her teeth. "An unreliable arrangement, but I will take what I can get. I will escort you to a sorcerer shortly. But for now... well, let us have a demonstration of why it is best to not go against Reimar. Quintus..."

Quintus Castell's stony face broke out into a savage grin.

"Which one first?"

Siera pointed to Imanol. "Him."

Imanol looked quickly between Siera and Quintus. "What do you mean? What do– no, let go of m–"

He tried to squirm away as Quintus reached forward and grabbed his nightgown, as the captives were all still dressed in what they'd been found in. It tore, but by then Quintus had him by the back of the neck.

"Now we want to know, see–" Quintus rammed his fist into Imanol's face with a dull smack. "Quit your squirming, behave! Now we want to know: who ordered King Abarron killed?"

"It wasn't me it wasn't me, I swear, we didn't know we didn't, we–"

He squealed as Quintus took him by the throat and shook him.

"That's not a good answer. Try again," Quintus said, dropping him to the floor after one last shake.

"W– we all– we wanted– to secede– but no one– knew that– there was– a plan to– to kill Abarron–" he said, as he gasped for breath.

Quintus leaned down and pulled at the prisoner's ears. He shrieked.

Quintus pulled harder.

"No no no no—" he screamed.

"Names!" Quintus shouted into his face. "I want NAMES!"

"I don't know I don't aaaaiiiiiiiiii—"

"Enough," said Siera calmly. "He truly might not know, perhaps there is a conspiracy, even within the rebels."

Siera's gaze shifted. "Try Itsaso."

Itsaso's eyes widened. "N— no, no, I don't know— please, I don't k—"

She gargled as Quintus grabbed her by the throat and hauled her to her feet.

"Her Highness wants names. Be polite, and give her some names!" he grunted as he began to shake her.

"U— ugh— I— ugh— do— n't— ugh."

Siera examined her fingernails. "She cannot speak if you choke her, Quintus."

Quintus dropped Itsaso to the floor, then crouched over her as he took her by the hair and pulled her face close to his.

"I'm losing my patience, girl, don't make me angry! Tell me who had Abarron killed, or I will make you beg for the clean death of the rope."

Her eyes shone through her tears. "Enio will know, he'll know!"

Quintus nodded slowly. "And where is this Enio?"

"Enio d— du Donati, l— last I knew, uh, he w— was in Southmere. I swear all I heard was that he was in Southmere, he said— he said that he wanted to make sure there were n— no Reimaran spies lurking in t— the city. Please, I…" she trailed off. Siera looked up, avoiding Itsaso's eyes.

Quintus didn't stop glaring at Itsaso. "Sir?"

Siera nodded. "It is more of a lead than we have so far. Very well. Let us leave this wretched lot. I will have some guards escort Jannick to whichever sorcerer is least busy." Siera turned to Jannick, not a trace of pity in her eyes. "I hope for your sake, mister Hummel, that you choose to stand by your word."

Jannick smiled weakly. "But of course, Your Highness. Of course."

Siera strode away sternward to the stairs, Quintus right behind her.

"You two." Siera called out to the First Battalion soldiers who stood fidgeting next to the stairway.

"Return to your post, but remember: we need them in good enough shape to stand trial," said Siera.

"Yes Sir, sorry Sir."

"Yes Sir, won't happen again Sir."

Siera nodded as she took the stairs, Quintus at her side.

"I almost feel dirty, after that," she said softly, then grimaced. "But justice with honour is for peacetime, for those who can afford it. I will not stay my hand from finding my father's murderers, or from those who have betrayed Reimar."

Quintus nodded. "I'll always stand ready to do what needs to be done,Sir."

Siera smiled as she looked over to him. "Your loyalty is as reassuring as ever, Quintus."

Chapter 16: Liberation and Death

27th Teurnot, dawn and morning

Surmarch awoke to find itself liberated.

Citizens from all walks of life flocked to the boulevards and markets to spread the news and see the Surmarch constabulary on patrol with Reimaran soldiers of the Fourth Regiment. More than a few taverns opened their taps to cheers for King Ramiros, and Princess Siera.

And at noon, a massive crowd had assembled on the word that there was to be a trial in the city's main plaza for the traitors who had sought to cleave Surmarch from the kingdom.

The square itself was packed, as well as the buildings overlooking the square. The two taverns that were adjacent to the plaza were doing a roaring trade in wines and roasted jackalope.

Siera shifted uncomfortably as the judges filed onto the large, creaky wooden platform that had been hastily erected in the plaza, wood scraping over the bare cobblestones. It had been assembled in mere hours by a dozen eager carpenters, but didn't feel entirely sturdy. Apart from the gallows itself, there was, on the platform a plain wooden table with five seats, one for each of the judges.

Siera had felt it essential that she personally preside over the proceedings. Tomasso, Quintus, and Igon Tapia, one of Commodore Terciero's assistants, were with her.

Along with, of course, the five judges hand-picked by Duke Federica du Lucan, as well as the executioner that they had brought with them – a squat, bearded man who looked more like a baker than a hangman.

"Sir, Princess! Sir, Princess!" called a young boy who wound his way through the crowd towards Siera.

Quintus loomed over the boy as he tried to make his way

up the wooden platform.

"What do you want?"

The boy craned his neck upwards to see who had spoken. "Message from Cantor Cristoforo for Her Highness," said the boy.

"I'll give it to her," said Quintus.

"Cantor said to hand it in person."

Quintus glared at the boy. "I'll give it to her, so hand it to me or you won't get a tip."

"'K," the boy said as he handed the sealed letter over, then pushed his palm at Quintus.

"Off with you," said Quintus as he flicked a silver teal at the boy, who had pocketed the coin and run off before Quintus could turn to walk up the platform.

"Who is it from, Quintus?" asked Siera.

"The boy said it was from some Cantor."

"Hmm," said Siera as she pulled the seal away from the parchment, and began to read.

Your Highness, Siera du Tealdan, Defender of the Realm,
I heard with joy of your arrival in Surmarch, and your relentless charge to liberate our fair city from the clutches of these rebels and their mercenary lackeys. But I now write to implore you to keep God in your heart and mercy in your thoughts: please, Your Highness, do not commit to such a gross parody of justice as a cruel public hanging. True, a traitor deserves no clemency, and they have transgressed the laws of Sura as surely as they have transgressed against the laws of Reimar. But even debased cravens as these deserve a fair trial, not a cruel hanging before a mob.

Your eternal servant and faithful admirer,
Cantor Cristoforo Cuevas

Siera scowled as she finished, then tore up the letter before stuffing the strips in her pocket.

"Bad news, Sir?" asked Tomasso.

"Some preacher who wants a fairer trial for the traitors. A nice sentiment, but the time for tame justice has ended.

Judge Noguerra?"

Judge Baltasar Noguerra was a slender man in his late forties, the last traces of his formerly black hair struggling against a mass of grey. He stood from his chair and bowed slightly.

"We stand ready, Your Highness. Please deliver the accused at your convenience."

Siera nodded. "Bring up the accused!" she cried out.

Ermanno's troops led the three accused, somewhat the worse for wear, to the platform.

None resisted.

They stood shivering in the late morning air, though not from any cold.

And Siera wondered, for just a moment, why she felt no pity for them.

Baltasar stood, and activated at his neck a charm similar to the one Siera wore.

"Citizens of Reimar, we five justices have come here today to bring judgement against these accused traitors!"

Siera was amazed at his tone. He had been so demure and polite when addressing her, and now grated and brayed across the mass of people in front of him with a cruel edge in his voice.

"Now settle, please, all you assembled – settle and bear witness! You stand here to witness the justice of Reimar, the justice of the throne! Now are there any here today who claim to have observed and noted the actions of these three accused?"

A low mutter rumbled through the crowd.

"I do! I do! I saw them!" screamed one man, who pushed himself to the forefront of the crowd.

"You there, come up, come up and give testimony!" cried out Baltasar.

The man scrabbled at the wooden stairs, and quickly crossed the platform to the judges' table.

"I saw all three of them in this square, right after they had put those sell-swords all over the town, they were laughing when they led out the Guard, and when they had them killed!"

Baltasar, to his credit, did not baulk. "Which soldiers were these?"

"They– our soldiers, Reimar's Guard. These three, they had their mercenaries bring out some officers and said that they were all traitors to the trium– the triumvirum, or the triumviral, or something. And then they ran them through, all five of them! Just ran them through with their swords until they died, over and over!"

"Your testimony has been recorded, now return," said Baltasar with a curt nod.

"Disgusting," muttered Siera.

Tomasso nodded. "They had the Second's garrison in Surmarch under control, but wanted to make an example... Why be so cruel?"

Siera coughed. "People are cruel to show off their power. What they did was needless."

Siera was certain that if she turned to Quintus, she would not be able to look him in the eye.

As the trial continued, the crowd began to get more restless. Testimonies came of the so-called 'Triumvirate of Surmarch' executing the Second Regiment's officers in public, and of arresting merchants who were seen as being too close to the throne. Even in such a short space of time, this triumvirate of pretenders had wreaked havoc.

It was when one witness was claiming that the Ardent Company had flat-out robbed a local florist that things began to get ugly.

"Where're the sell-swords?!" someone screamed.

"Hang them too! Hang the Ardents!"

The crowd began to get restless. For just a moment, Siera was struck at how a large group of people ceased to look human and became a large, unruly thing with its own mind and shape.

"Order, settle down! Settle!" cried out Baltasar, but to no avail.

"Where did the Ardents go?! Get them too!"

"Sell-swords for hanging!"

"Hang them too!"

People began to scream and shove. Siera realised that if

people tried to stampede off to find mercenaries to hang, anyone so much as suspected of guilt would earn the rope.

"Godammit," Siera turned to Igon Tapia. "My speaking charm is no louder than Baltasar's, can you make it louder?"

"Well, I... uh... I don't really know which uh... the enchantments used. But I can try, although you might want to get a new one afterwards. I might break it."

Siera handed over her necklace to Igon, who brought out an odd silver stylus and attempted to pick at the necklace.

All around her, Siera could feel the mob's cries grow louder. Baltasar tried to calm the crowd, but they had all misjudged the citizenry's anger at recent events.

Siera wondered if the mob would storm the platform and try to hang the traitors themselves, then realised she might well be crushed; the platform would certainly collapse.

"Hurry, if you can," said Siera.

"I, well– oh!" said Igon, as the pendant abruptly cracked in his hands.

"Oh for *fuckssakes*!" cried Siera.

"Your Highness, things are getting ugly. We should–" said Quintus.

Siera looked around, eyes wide. "Leave, Quintus? How? We have no way to signal the *Wrath* to send down a line, or to leave the square by any normal means."

The baying of the crowd had grown insane. Siera could feel the platform shift abruptly as dozens of people shifted against it, cries coming from all around for the red caps, the traitors, for every rebel to be hanged, hang them all right now.

From above, an ear-splitting thunder pealed out.

The mob went quiet as people gasped and stared around, the atmosphere in the square abruptly descended into low muttering, peppered with the occasional indignant squawk of surprise.

Siera looked up, grinning wildly.

Fifty metres above her, Lieutenant Adalberto could not conceal a smug grin at his soldiers' reactions as he lowered his greatbow.

"S– Sir! You told us never to do that!"

"Sura's arse, I thought we were all going to die…"

"Sir, I always wondered – no offence – but you've got the biggest ba–"

"Enough, enough," said Adalberto, waving at his subordinates. "And I did mean it, at no point should you ever do that. However, I can't really stand around while the crowd gets unruly around the Major. And I hate to make a 'Do as I say and not as I do', but there you have it." Adalberto shrugged.

"It's what was called for, Sir. Still, I almost had to change my trousers."

"If he'd cocked it up you wouldn't be alive to have trousers," said Cecilia, wiping sweat from her brow.

"Greatbow arrows are dangerous tools, damn sure."

"Greatbow arrows, or greatarrows? I always wondered."

"Well," said Adalberto "they don't work as intended unless you loose them from a greatbow. But–" he added, pointing to the dissipating cloud of obsidian dust, "– a whack to the tip will make them unstable."

"I never knew that you understood how they worked, Sir."

Adalberto made a slow shrug, a smile creeping across his face. "Well, I can't use such a powerful weapon with some merely superstitious understanding of it."

"Man, the way he just… he just whacked it on his boot… good God…"

"Heh, I was ready to be judged by Riest, right then."

"Well, crowd's quietened down. Looks like the Major has called for the sentence to be passed, too," said Adalberto, peering over the side of the *Wrath*.

On the platform, Siera had quickly called for the judges to declare their sentencing.

"The rightly appointed and upstanding judges of this council declare these three accused, Sendoa du Bianchi, Itsaso du Lucan, and Imanol du Salamanca, to be guilty of treason against the Kingdom of Reimar. As a duly appointed representative of the throne, I hereby condemn these wretches to death."

Siera looked over at the accused. Itsaso seemed to be reciting a prayer, Imanol had a dull, blank expression on his face, and Sendoa was again weeping quietly.

"In accordance with law and tradition, no civilised beheadings are offered to those guilty of so vile a crime. The barbarism of the noose is the only righteous punishment for treason."

The crowd, although quieter after Adalberto had detonated a greatbow arrow over their heads, was still nigh deafening as they roared their approval. Siera could see a variety of citizens, one hand holding a mug, the other hand raised in a fist.

It was then that it struck her.

No matter how many witnesses there were, this really was a show trial. Siera felt as though everything around her quietened, and she slowly turned to see judge Baltasar pointing towards the former triumvirate; their cold, pale faces, their wide eyes.

Siera saw the hangman step forward – she couldn't remember his name – his black hood unmistakable, slowly fitting each accused with a noose.

Siera dully felt the crowd roaring again.

This is what the Cantor had meant, this is why Adalberto had blanched at her heavy talk of public hangings. No matter the justifications or reasons she had, this was mob justice. She might as well personally throw each of the former triumvirate to the crowd and call for the citizenry to tear them apart with their bare hands.

Siera realised that they'd do it, too. Those farmers and carpenters and traders, those florists and bakers, those tanners and stable hands – put them in a crowd, whip that crowd into a mob, and they would rip any perceived enemy apart.

Siera felt as though she would vomit.

She forced herself to watch as the hangman grabbed the rope of the noose around Sendoa's neck, threw it over the strut that stood over the platform, and wound the rope around the crank.

The executioner leaned forward, and rapidly turned the

crank to hoist Sendoa into the air, kicking and flailing.

Siera dared a look to her left, where Quintus was watching the proceedings. She saw no pity in his stony gaze.

One by one, the executioner hoisted them up and dragged on the rope until they had at last expired.

Kick and struggle as they might, all three of them were hanged until dead, as the assembled crowd roared and jeered.

The aftermath of the retaking of Surmarch was, all things considered, an orderly affair. The initial rebel takeover had focused on the Second Regiment's garrison and notable noble holdings, with few appointed figures being hauled off and removed from office.

Siera was rapidly becoming convinced that even if she had not arrived to liberate Surmarch, the local guilds would have put a serious dent in the rebels' attempt to hold control. Taking over their relatives' holdings seemed to have been the rebels' long term plans, but they had made little progress, as those citizens who worked the land or a trade had outright refused to obey their new overlords. Once the money for mercenaries ran out, the rebel triumvirate would have been ousted immediately.

The day after Siera had wrested the city from the rebels both the *Airsprite* and the *Broadgull* had arrived, bearing Siera's only troops apart from the Fourth Regiment itself. Some hundred hastily-trained levies, the dozen engineers and magewrights of the Fifth Regiment, Duke du Donati's seventy-four household guards, and the forty-strong warriors of the Noble Order of Eneco. These forces would hold the city until Siera could retake Southmere, and then move troops from Surmarch to Southmere to defend the latter as well.

Siera and her lieutenants had convened in her cabin to make plans for a hasty departure.

"I have sent orders onward to Captain du Cipriani as to the Fifth Regiment's duties, seconding them the Noble Order and what few levies have been raised as well, for now. We go on to Southmere with just the soldiers of the Fourth Regiment for now."

"Can we land properly at Southmere?" said Adalberto.

Siera shook her head. "No. There are no docks large enough for the *Wrath*, barring at Ilmarch, Valencia, and San Seras. We will have to offload via dropline or winches at Southmere and Ponsurno both."

Ermanno scratched at his beard. "We take Southmere alongside the Navy, yes? What word of their positions?"

"I have been in contact with the Admiralty, and kept tabs on their progress. They have an armada of fifty-four ships sailing towards Southmere, most with a full complement of the Third Regiment's marines. We will take Surmarch from two ends," said Siera.

"Like two men eating a pie," said Ermanno. "How exactly will we come in with the *Wrath*?"

Siera paused. "I will wait until the last moment to decide our exact order. If most of the mercenaries are clustered at the harbour and the fleet has arrived before us, then we will sail over the keep in the *Wrath* and assault the keep directly. If there are plenty of mercenaries around the front gates, then we might have to disembark and have the Second Battalion make a few neat holes with their greatbows for us to march through."

Adalberto tapped at the map before them, noting the short distance between Southmere's walls and its keep. "Yes, dropping down will be too dangerous if they see us coming. And if we sail over the soldiers at the walls, they can rush back to catch us at the keep... just the opposite of Surmarch, really."

Siera nodded curtly. "Correct, we cannot treat every scenario like the *Reimar's Vigilance*, much as I might want to."

"Wish we'd have the Noble Order with us. Well, not that we need them, of course," said Gretchen.

Siera shrugged. "The Noble Order are certainly competent, but they are trained to fight in small groups against abominations. We cannot expect them to maintain formations and fight well against masses. And if we need to breach the gap by foot, then it will be pikes and our large shields. The Noble Order has no such training or equipment.

"I swear I saw one of them with a rapier, earlier," said Ermanno.

"A rapier, for the battlefield?" said Gretchen, who uttered a short sharp laugh. "That's a dandy's weapon."

"Hear, hear," grumbled Ermanno. This isn't a duelling ground. How serious are those Noble Order types anyhow? I thought they were professionals."

Siera sighed. "They are… at hunting down necromancers and abominations. Also, more than just a few of them are mages, skilled at using magic in combat and such. And the people know them well, every second children's fable has them dashing around and putting dark mages and pagan priests to the sword and so on. They will do well patrolling Surmarch, along with the levies. After all, what good is retaking Surmarch if we have to do it twice?"

Adalberto nodded slowly. "Speaking of mages, I wish the Guard had more of those, like in Zarann. I hear they put mages in their elite battalions."

Gretchen shrugged. "If wishes were horses, beggars would ride. There's no replacing steel on the field, it always comes down to the point of your pike or your sword."

"Entirely so," said Siera. "Still hard to believe that all is truly in hand… Surmarch retaken, levies and the Noble Order taking care of settling everything here, and on to Southmere."

"Rebels haven't put up a good fight at all," said Adalberto with a smile.

"And there's the worry," said Ermanno. Adalberto stared at him.

"Heh, did you want a harder fight, Ermanno?" said Gretchen, smirking.

"No, he has a point. If they have fallen so easily, why rebel at all? Surely they would realise that it was hopeless."

"Well… between having sent out most of their troops for an ambush, and the *Wrath*, I don't think even a professional army would have been able to stop you here, Major," said Gretchen.

Siera rubbed her chin with her thumb. "Hmm. There is that. I suppose I cannot underestimate the effect of introducing a skyship into a conflict. Well, we depart in half an hour. Last readiness checks as you will."

Her lieutenants saluted to that.

While Siera conferred with her lieutenants in her cabin, Commodore Terciero held forth at his assistants.

"It was extreme, but… the crowd was getting ugly sir. I can understand why he did it, even if it is insane," said Igon Tapia.

Terciero glared at his assistant. "I cannot believe that Lieutenant Adalberto just… just whacked a greatarrow against his… his boot, for Sura's sakes. It could have blown the forecastle off the *Wrath* entirely. And Her Highness said there was nothing to be done for reprimanding him! Nothing!"

None of his assistants spoke. They had all learned that sometimes, Terciero just wanted to rant and brood.

Terciero turned to look out over the deck, as was his preference. The soft creaking of the ship and the stately mast always put him at ease.

He was about to open his mouth and continue complaining when a woman suddenly appeared on the deck.

"I – wait, who is that? How did she–"

As his assistants turned to look, she disappeared.

"Who is what, sir?" said Carmina Muraro.

"There – I… there was a woman, on the deck."

"Was it Major Siera? She does like to take in the air sometimes."

"No, she just – just appeared, and then was gone."

Terciero continued to peer around the deck, while behind him his assistants gave knowing looks to each other.

"Want me to take over for now, Sir?"

"Yes… yes. I'm going out on the deck," muttered Terciero.

Siera was reclining on her bunk, having intended to take a nap but was instead going over her decisions so far. Suddenly, someone appeared in her room, simply popping out of thin air.

"Aah!" she cried out, trying to reach for her sword and get out of bed at the same time.

The door burst open, and Clara ran into the room, sword drawn.

"You! Stay back from Her Highness!" she barked.

Lycea du Tilmost slowly turned to regard Clara, one brow raised.

"There is no need to yell, Viscount Mercer. I have only arrived to deliver an urgent message to Her Highness."

Siera by now had managed to stand, get her blade, and then put it back on her desk after realising that it was only Lycea, and not some shadowy assassin.

"Urgent message? Could this this not be sent by sorcery?" said Siera.

"His Noble Highness considered it to be too urgent. We were all in council when the news came, and he asked me to go as quickly as possible to your side."

Siera blinked. "Well, whatever has happened?"

Lycea's face was grave. "A full regiment of Sharan troops has almost made its way to the Casten. We fear that they might be in league with the rebels, and might march into Ponsurno to reinforce it. Should they do so, not only will we have a full war with Shardustur on our hands, but Ponsurno will probably be untouchable with the numbers you have at your disposal."

Siera blinked. "No... I knew it, dammit, I knew it!" she said.

"Knew what, Your Highness?" said Lycea.

Siera clenched her jaw. "I knew it had to be Shar. It had to be them, and even if it was not they would take advantage of the situation. They have just marched up, have they? Well, we will see about that. Tomasso, where is Tomasso? And my lieutenants, Clara, can you call for them?"

Clara leaned her head out of the room. Siera plugged her ears.

"ALL SENIOR STAFF TO THE MAJOR!" Clara roared. Clutching her hands to her ears, Lycea glared at Clara, who ignored her.

Tomasso appeared at a sprint.

"W– what's going on, Clara?" he said, short of breath.

"Tomasso, get up to Commodore Terciero and tell him we have a new destination: Ponsurno. Tell him to use all haste. Go!"

Tomasso saluted and bolted for the stairs, almost running

into Lieutenant Gretchen.

"Major, what's the alarm?" said Gretchen.

"Bad news. Shar is on the move. Here, here," said Siera as she moved over to her table, and quickly found a map of eastern Reimar. "Councillor, do you know exactly where the Sharans are encamped?"

Lycea nodded. "The last report put them in southern Casten, due east of Ponsurno."

Siera fumbled for a pencil, sketching in the assumed location of the Sharan force.

"They would still have a heavy march ahead of them if they are to reach Ponsurno. Assuming they haven't reached the border yet, we should be able to get to Ponsurno in time, although I do not know how we can retake it…"

"Well, Major…" said Gretchen.

"Major, you called?" said Adalberto as he and Ermanno arrived together.

"Clara, your voice is as terrifying as ever," said Ermanno with a grin.

Clara smirked.

"Bad news, Shar has marched a regiment to the Casten area, almost to the border."

Adalberto blanched. "What? But – can we even stop them?"

Ermanno scratched at his chin. "We have to try. General Andrayzn is halfway to Iln by now, and there's no one else. It's us or nothing."

"But what about the attack on Southmere? The Admiralty is already sailing," said Adalberto.

"I'll have a message sent to them to delay the attack. Southmere can wait, Ponsurno cannot. If the Sharans see that we hold Ponsurno, they might be dissuaded."

"Either way, I have been instructed to accompany you, Your Highness," said Lycea with a small bow.

"An odd question, Councillor, but do you have any experience with magic in battle?"

Lycea's face went momentarily blank.

"Councillor..?" said Siera, brows raised.

"Oh, my apologies Your Highness, I do not," said Lycea with a smile.

"I suppose not. We will need something clever to take Ponsurno. Ermanno, any ideas?"

Ermanno shrugged. "Have the Second Battalion knock a few holes in Ponsurno's walls, we march in. Ugly urban fighting... we've been lucky not to have too much of that so far. Noble Order might be useful, they probably do better at it than us, they like fighting in small groups. Either way, plenty of death. Street fighting means our formations going to shit and one ugly melee brawl."

Siera sighed, massaging her temples.

"Major, if I might..." said Gretchen.

Siera sighed.

"I do not suppose I have much of a choice. Very well, Gretchen. Your Battalion... will be using your idea."

Gretchen saluted.

"Idea, Your Highness?" said Lycea.

Siera paused for a moment. "Actually, Councillor, you would be much more useful at my brother's side. You should return to him."

Lycea frowned. "His Noble Majesty expressly asked that I assist you, Your Highness."

Siera shrugged. "And I am asking that you return to him. He will understand."

Lycea blanched, but after a brief moment bowed to Siera.

"Very well. I will relay your wishes to him," she said with a frown. "Before I depart, Your Highness, please take this ring."

Lycea had a silver ring which had a single, odd indentation on its surface. She eased it off her left index finger, and offered it to Siera.

"Why, councillor?" said Siera, not moving to take the ring.

Lycea smiled. "If you ever need my aid, or assistance, or anything at all, you can press your thumb into the indentation of this ring to summon me to your side."

Siera slowly reached out to take the ring, half expecting something to happen when she took it from Lycea, or when she put it on. Nothing did.

Siera shrugged. "Very well, and thank you."

With that, Lycea nodded as she drew a weird, ornate rod from one of the many sashes around her hips. It was silvery and pale, and had a variety of designs and indentations Siera didn't recognise. As Lycea thumbed a few of these marks, the rod began to split apart, revealing a glowing, brilliant core of some sharp blue crystal.

Adalberto squinted at it. "So–"

And with that, Lycea disappeared.

"Sura…" said Gretchen.

Siera shook her head. "Now there's a magical art that would make Reimar unstoppable. Alas that it is apparently difficult and unreliable."

"So, what's this plan that Gretchen has, anyhow?" said Ermanno.

"I did not want to say while Lycea was here, as I myself am… not proud of such a plan. And Lycea might pass along word of it to her husband, who would certainly not approve." Siera paused, then laughed bitterly, folding her arms. "But as I myself have said, we cannot afford tame justice at a time like this. So we cannot afford tame honour either. Gretchen and her troops will dress in civilian clothing and claim to be a new mercenary band looking for work. Once they get inside, they will try and take the gate by force as quietly as possible. If they succeed, we can at least get inside Ponsurno quietly."

Ermanno's face was blank. Adalberto appeared dumbfounded.

"Attack… without uniforms? But… that's the colours of the Guard. I mean…"

Siera looked down. "I know full well, Adalberto. The Guard's colours are the Guard's honour. It's despicable to attack like some… some pack of beggars with sticks. But I consider our alternatives to be worse. The Sharans might attack and take Ponsurno, they might be in league with the rebels, and they might be waiting for us to move to Southmere so they can plunder the countryside. I will not let any of these disasters befall Reimar."

Ermanno nodded slowly. "Ponsurno's keep will be harder to get to, but the town's long overgrown the original boundary between the keep's walls and the old city, hasn't it?"

Siera nodded, her eyes downcast. "It has, so at least we'll have some cover from archers and ballistae. We will not have any cover at all coming up the hillside to the city itself, from the outside. And is Terciero sure we can get to Ponsurno quickly enough, going past Emrish forest?"

"He says we won't have to skirt the forest at all." Siera winced. "I do hope he's right... I do not want to see what it would try to do to a skyship."

Adalberto looked from Ermanno to Siera. "Major, if I may, we can loose volleys from the *Wrath* to open a few holes in the walls. Then, after storming those gaps, we'll be inside Ponsurno. And no need for any underhanded methods."

Siera shook her head. "You would be right, if not for the Sharans. We won't be able to repair the defences before they realise the breaches are there, and that will offer them an easy attack.'"

Adalberto bit his lip. "They can't really be here to try to invade, they must just be a ploy. Even Shar doesn't have the gall to invade us."

Siera shook her head, still looking at the floor. "I cannot count on that. And it is hard to admit, but Reimar is weakened at the moment. Vulnerable. We cannot afford the risk."

Siera folded her arms, and sighed. "This small dishonour is an acceptable price to pay, to keep our own losses lower and take Ponsurno all the quicker. And ultimately, the responsibility falls on me. I cannot blame you for saying to all and sundry that you were forced to obey orders and had no choice. If my decision comes back to stalk us, then the blame lies entirely with me."

Adalberto looked down. Ermanno shrugged. Gretchen grinned.

"I won't let you down, Sir," she said.

'*It's the Third's time to shine*', she added to herself.

Chapter 17: Night Passage

27th Teurnot, late evening after dinner

Ermanno found his sergeants exactly where he expected them to be. Previously, they'd found the small liquor storage room, and had decided to sit about in there when they were playing cards. They had been lucky that he'd found them before Siera had thought to do a surprise inspection while the skyship was in the air, or they would have all had a few lashes.

That said, Ermanno remained amazed that none of them had got into the liquor, and so were breaking regulations by gambling on duty but not taking any alcohol for themselves. That said, they'd barely found the room before he'd found them.

Now they had congregated in a small room used for storing flour sacks next to the galley. The cooks gave him odd looks as he strode through the kitchen, but otherwise let him be.

Ermanno opened the storage room door. Inside, his sergeants had arranged two flour sacks as a makeshift table, so they could more easily play cards.

Giovanni Marino looked up, squinting. "Wha–"

"Knew it," muttered Pacifica Sastre.

Ermanno closed the door behind him, then looked around the room. "Hello all, what's the wager?"

Vincenzo di Vitis sighed. "How'd you know, lieutenant?"

Ermanno shrugged. "It's obvious when you think about it. Why are you all skulking in here, anyway? And where's Eugenio?"

The sergeants looked at each other.

Ermanno laughed. "He's not that bad, is he?"

Carmine snorted. "No, he *is* that goddamn bad. Every time, bitching and moaning about his luck."

Nico made to spit, but remembered he was onboard the *Wrath*. "Can't have a wager because if Eugie loses he'll piss

205

and gripe about how it's unfair, until we give it back to him just to shut him up. And if he wins he's crowing and preening in your face about it."

"Be more fun to play cards with Quintus," muttered Feliciano.

Ermanno shrugged. "Quintus isn't half as bad as he looks."

"So what, just regular terrifying and not truly terrifying?"

"Just his hands is enough for me," said Nico Labriola.

Ermanno and the other sergeants turned to stare at Nico, who scowled. "Eh, what?"

Feliciano Airaldi laughed softly. "What the– what do his hands have to do with it?"

Nico reddened. "W– well they're huge, right? I mean, just look next time you see him. The man's too big, and his hands are massive. It's strange. I just don't like it."

Ermanno shook his head. "Big hands. Now I've heard it all. I thought Carmine being scared of feathers because they look like arrow fletching was ridiculous, but this is better than a steak dinner. And enough of that – if you get caught in here the Major will break you in half. No cards while on duty and all that, and in-air is on duty. There's times she'll overlook it, and you know this isn't one of them."

Pacifica sighed. "'Specially after her old man was killed. Can't blame her."

Ermanno grimaced. "You're a fool if you think she's harder now than she used to be. It was there all along, if you looked for it. Now out with the lot of you."

It wasn't long until the *Sky's Wrath* darkened and quietened almost completely, its soldiers asleep and only Eneco Abaroa awake on the bridge, sipping maht tea to keep awake and alert, to ensure that all remained well with the ship.

Siera had tossed and turned for hours before falling into a restless sleep. Awaking what seemed to be hours before dawn, she grumbled and muttered to herself as she put her uniform on and slowly made her way to the galley.

Unsurprisingly, no one was around. Siera fumbled through a few pots and pans, but eventually got a pot of water on the hearthplate, which she tapped with its torch-rod to activate it.

As the water warmed, Siera muttered thanks to Sura.

Hearthplates were a godsend to any wooden vessel, being a stone plate inset with obsidian at certain places and marked with a few odd sigils and such. Siera didn't really care how they worked, as long as they worked as needed – a way to boil water and cook food without actual fire. And without actual fire, none of the risks a sailing ship or skyship used to run of fire-related accidents.

Siera winced as she remembered learning that they were slow to cool, when she was a child. She'd run into the kitchens to find a place to hide during a hide-and-seek game, and had accidentally touched a partially-cooled hearthplate.

Siera, lost in her thoughts, didn't realise that someone else had entered the galley.

"Is that you, sir?" said someone softly.

"Hmm? Who is there?" said Siera.

"Just me, Sir," said Quintus, coming into view through the gloom.

"What has you up at this hour, Quintus?" asked Siera.

"I'd ask you the same, Sir. But I was… just coming in to make some tea. Clara's snoring away and it's my shift, and I noticed that you weren't in your cabin either, so I figured I'd check here while I was at it."

Siera nodded. "Well, I've got the water going already, so… wait… Quintus, I have never seen you drink tea at all."

Quintus rubbed his hands together. "I uh… no, no, I drink it all the time. Tea's… nice."

Siera stared at him.

"For a man as skilled in so many ways as you are, you make a godawful liar, Quintus Castell."

Quintus started. "No, I… well… I'm not that bad. And I'm not lying much, I don't actually mind tea."

Siera grinned. "Let me guess. You woke up early so you could go back and wake a certain lieutenant with a nice mug of tea. Am I right?"

Siera couldn't know for sure in the darkness, but she was certain that Quintus' face was red. She sighed.

"I highly doubt anyone will look at you askance, Quintus. I do not speak to embarrass you, but why not be open about it?"

Quintus coughed. "It's not me, Sir. Gretchen… has her

preferences. And she says most of her troops already know, so word will spread anyway without her announcing anything."

Siera nodded slowly. "Hard enough when only one of a couple is serving, let alone two. Still, you cannot get anywhere by denying yourself. Besides, I see how she looks whenever you walk in. I do not really think that either of you can walk away at this point, although it is not my business to say one way or the other."

Quintus rubbed his hands together. "Heh, you're right about that, Sir. Still, no offence, but I never figured I'd speak with you about this."

Siera blinked. "Oh? How come?"

Quintus shifted from one leg to the other. "Well... I've been your bodyguard for years... I've never seen you... interested in anyone."

Siera snorted. "Fair enough. But it's different for me, and my brother the same. We will not choose who we want, nor who we marry, and despite our best intentions, even our smallest actions can carry a heavy weight at court. You do not have that burden. I have... spent a fair time of my life watching others, wanting to understand them, just like my father... understood people."

Siera sighed. "I suppose I sound pitiable. That said, if you and Gretchen are set on being together, I will support that however I can. I would have done so regardless, but... it really is the least I can do."

Quintus rubbed his knuckles on his chin. "Well, if you put it like that, thanks for the support, Sir. But... how do you mean? You don't owe me. If anything, I owe you."

Siera squinted at Quintus, only half able to make out his face in the low light of the galley.

"How would you owe me?"

Quintus laughed softly. "I suppose I owe all of you. You, your brother, your parents. Without the Guard, without the honour of serving as a whitecap, who'd I be? No one, that's who. I was a thug before I joined the Guard. They whipped me into shape, gave me something to strive for. If I hadn't joined, I'd be dead in some stupid street brawl, or turned to crime. Instead I'm in one of the most respected jobs in Reimar."

Quintus stretched and yawned. "You know, Major, I go back to see my parents when I have leave. My old man lost his hand in an accident, hasn't been able to work since, Stevedore's Guild pays him a pittance every month. But every time I went back, there were fewer of my old friends around. Five years ago... I think, five years ago I went back and the last of them were gone. Jail or dead. Every one of them. The ones who kept on with honest work had long since cut ties with the likes of me."

Siera was silent.

Quintus rubbed at his chin with his knuckles, his eyes unfocused. "I'm proud to have made something of myself. And it was your father who said that anyone could serve as a whitecap, not just nobles. He changed all that. He made it possible for me to serve with more honour than I'd ever dreamed of."

Siera nodded. "I see... although I suspect he passed that decree out of pragmatism more than anything else. More people are taking up trade than going into the Guard, these days."

Quintus shrugged. "Either way, Sir. Either way. But, why did you say that you owed me?"

Siera smiled, though she doubted Quintus could see it.

"I only realised the morning after... after the assassins came. I had not noticed at the time that one of them had struck me. It would have been you who ensured that they did not strike again. I... I might have been buried besides my father."

Quintus frowned. "You can't owe me for that, Sir! It's my duty to safeguard you. It's been my honour."

Siera smiled. "Still... if, for example, I can have you and Lieutenant Gretchen serving closely, then I will do so."

"Well... thanks, Sir," said Quintus.

A moment of silence settled in.

Siera coughed. "Well, water's almost done. I was going to go up on deck and just maybe see the sunrise."

Quintus was silent as Siera made her tea and left to go upstairs. In the dark, she couldn't see his lopsided smile either.

Gretchen slowly awoke, her cabin dark. For a moment

everything was still, half-drenched in sleep, her bed warm and her mind untroubled.

A soft knock came at her door.

Gretchen rubbed at her eyes, then stumbled out of bed, hastily grabbing at her uniform.

"'M coming. Just wait, dammit."

Gretchen squinted through the pre-dawn gloom, fumbling for the door handle, then swung the door open.

"Who–"

Even in the low light, there was no mistaking the outline of Quintus.

"Sorry to wake you, but you're usually up soon anyhow," he said.

"Well… come in, then," said Gretchen with a shrug. After Quintus has entered and closed the door behind him, she stripped off her uniform and got right back into bed.

"Join me?" she said with a smile.

Quintus' eyes strayed before he replied. "Huh… we don't have that much time."

Gretchen sighed. "Probably."

Quintus leaned forward, mug in hand. "Here, better to wake up warm with some tea."

Gretchen murmured her thanks as she took the mug from Quintus. "Wish I was captain, then I'd have my own aide to fetch me tea all the time. Not that you do a bad job. Just seems odd."

Quintus smirked. "Oh? How would it be done in the archipelago?"

Gretchen thought for a moment. "In Reimar, people are more concerned with gestures and their meanings. People fuss over all kinds of things. Not that I'm saying you're fussy, or anything. But in the archipelago things are… simpler, but also more formal. There's less room for confusion. You plainly state your interest, and then either you get a yes or a no."

Quintus frowned, then shrugged. "So, I should plainly be stating my interest then? More or less formal? Should I write a letter?"

Gretchen laughed. "Well, things are a bit less formal in some ways too. It could be me expressing my interest. In

Reimar, that seems to be the man's job."

Quintus nodded. "Huh. Odd difference. But I suppose you can write me a formal letter, if you like."

Gretchen rolled her eyes. "That's not what I mean. It's just... eh, never mind. We both know what we're about. No sending each other scarves, no empty chains around wrists. Just be honest."

Quintus chuckled. "I tried that, once, sending a girl I liked a scarf. She gave it to her brother."

Gretchen burst out laughing. "N– no insult but... hah, I can just see your face. Her goddamn brother, wearing your scarf..."

Quintus nodded. "So, you still worried about people talking behind your back?"

Gretchen sighed, her laughter quickly trailing off. "It's not that I'm worried. I just know that people will do it. I can hear the most obvious rumour now – 'foreigner tries social climbing by pursuing whitecap'."

Quintus smiled. It didn't reach his eyes. "Best not say it in my hearing."

Gretchen shrugged. "They won't, they'll say it in everyone else's hearing."

Quintus sucked his teeth. "Hmm, best not do that, either. There's a strong bond between whitecaps, we're like family. The wise wouldn't relish making us angry."

"Oh, enough," Gretchen said, trying to restrain her smile. "Just wish every gossip a rotten liver and be done with it."

Quintus scratched his head. "Well, either way. Doesn't matter. I won't have my life dictated to me by little people and cheap gossip."

Gretchen stretched, loath to leave her bunk. "Nor will I, but I have to be off to find my sergeants soon, so... we'll talk later. Oh, and what was all that stuff with the pickled eggs?"

Quintus squinted at Gretchen, "Eh?"

"You said something once about Tomasso and some pickled eggs or something, like it was a story."

"Oh, you didn't hear? When he was being trained in the First, his mother decided he wasn't getting enough food, so she sent him some pickled eggs. A crateful of the stupid things. Apparently he really likes them."

Gretchen snorted. "That it? Bit of an apron-clinger, but I thought it would be funny."

Quintus smirked. "He didn't want to get into any trouble for bringing in food, so he tried palming it off on everyone else. Lieutenant hears about Tomasso having a little something for himself, comes in for a spot inspection, but finds no pickled eggs in Tomasso's bed-chest. But almost everyone else in the company has pickled eggs in theirs."

Gretchen giggled, and Quintus grinned to himself. He loved that giggle.

"Well, best be off." Quintus nodded and made to stand and leave, but leaned in to kiss Gretchen's cheek before departing.

She said nothing as he left, but he had caught her smile out of the corner of his eye, and it was all he needed.

After breakfast, Gretchen met with her sergeants in the general cabin – two decks connected, that essentially formed just one large room full of hammocks and bunk beds, uniforms being hung out to air, and soldiers milling around. Although gambling was against regulations, games of chance for no wager were fine – and so regularly enjoyed. Bastard, sixes-and-sevens, and craps predominated.

"Good to see you're all gathered," said Gretchen as she found her sergeants gathered around a bunk, playing Bastard.

Giacinta Caivano looked up at Gretchen. "Figured we'd have a game in the meantime. You in, lieutenant?"

"No chance," said Gretchen with a laugh. "Who's winning?"

"I was," said Mario Corvi. "Until everyone realised I'd been putting down three cards at a time."

Paz Santiago laughed softly. "He's damn good at it too, but we realised his trick."

"Oh?" said Gretchen.

"Always plays with a fairly new pack of cards, so he can make them line up nicely. Older cards make it harder to do."

"How's Quintus, lieutenant?" said Erasmo Marino with a grin.

"Still taller than you," said Gretchen, matching him with a smile.

"Ho!" said Erasmo, using his fingers to mime tears.

"Haa, Erasmo, midget tears."

"Just asking, just asking," said Erasmo, putting his palms up.

Gretchen clicked her tongue. "Right, enough of that. Orders have come in about our next battle."

Celio Espinoza scratched his chin. "We suddenly changed to move to Ponsurno, right?"

Gretchen nodded. "Yes. Word is that Shar is nosing around, so we're retaking Ponsurno before they get any ideas."

Mario Corvi turned and flicked the ear of a nearby private who had tried to lean over his shoulder. "Are we dropping in, or storming the walls?"

"Neither," said Gretchen. "We're walking up to the front gate and asking nicely."

Scattered laughter bubbled around Gretchen, from her sergeants and the corporals and privates who had now gathered around.

Paz Santiago held up a hand for quiet. "No, but really, lieutenant, what's our order of battle?"

Gretchen smirked. "I'm serious," she said. "We're going up to the front gate in our civvies and bluffing our way in. So no talk while I'm trying to convince them. Once we're in, keep your wits about you. When things get ugly, we'll have to act fast. Anyone who feels like being a hero, well, this is the time for it."

A private piped up. "We're really going without our uniforms? But, when I was training in the First, they said–"

Before Gretchen could reply, Domenico Arnoni joined in the conversation. "Regimental colour on the flag flying high, and on your uniform, is the honour and pride of the Guard. And it's true. But put it this way: do you want to storm that wall with only a shield between you and a ballista bolt through the head, or change your pants for a bit while we go knock heads in?"

"We'll be trying for this at night, right sir?" said Mario Corvi.

Gretchen pointed at Mario. "Right, otherwise it will be obvious that we've all got the same Guard-issue weapons on us. Mercenaries, like most other Iberan armies as well, all have people who bring or buy their own gear. Make sure it's full gear – swords, shields, and pikes. Those who have been issued shortbows had best bring them along."

"Ugh, do we really need all of that? Pikes as well?" said Celio Espinoza.

"For what we're doing you'll want them, so no griping," said Gretchen.

"But – wait, won't they hear our accents?" said Paz Santiago.

Gretchen grinned. "Vhat akcents ahre you talking about?" she said, thickening her normally light Archipelagan lilt.

Giacinta stared at Gretchen. "Heh, lieutenant, you sound just like a pirate!"

Gretchen laughed. "I suppose I do, like that. So, change into civvies and meet on the deck in ten minutes. We'll have to march to Ponsurno, and across the country as well – can't risk taking a road. And we'll have to be there by nightfall."

Celio raised his hand. "Why not go there on the *Wrath*?"

Mario glared at him. "Are you stupid? They'll see us landing!"

"Oh, r–right." Celio let out a small laugh.

Chapter 18: First by Deceit

28th Teurnot, late evening

Commodore Terciero brought the *Wrath* over a small valley roughly two kilometres away from Ponsurno. Siera was certain that the distance and the gloom of late evening should keep any watchful eyes off the Third Battalion's drop.

Grumble as her soldiers might about having to march up the hillside to Ponsurno, Gretchen's good mood could not be brought down. Now, above any other time, she had her chance to shine.

The march to Ponsurno was a quiet one, a quarter moon providing the only heavenly light. Moving uphill as they were, and judging their footing by both the pale moonlight and the few scattered torches they carried with them, the Third Battalion made its way upwards.

Gretchen called for a halt a few hundred metres from the gate. This late at night, there was no traffic at all on the wide road to Ponsurno, which felt abandoned and ghostly.

Gretchen hastily assembled her sergeants. "Remember, one last time as a reminder to everyone: let me do the talking, and follow my cues. If we get any signal that we can enter, follow me in. Don't meet anyone's eyes and don't start any trouble until I say so. Now spread the word again, I don't want anyone forgetting."

As her sergeants sent the word to their corporals, and they to their privates, Gretchen mulled her plan. It all depended on what mercenary band she was dealing with, but she was going in blind on that score. Still, either way, she had to be just convincing enough.

The main entrance to Ponsurno was a large gate set into the thick stone walls, an iron portcullis set in front of two solid wooden doors. Gretchen knew that behind those doors was a short corridor through the breadth of the walls themselves, and all throughout that corridor lurked murder-holes through which defenders could loose arrows or drop stones at an attacker. She muttered a quick prayer that her ruse would work.

"Ho, the gate!" she called out, abruptly breaking the night's deep quiet.

A brief silence reigned.

"What? Who calls?" came the muffled reply from above the gate.

Gretchen craned her neck upwards, trying to gauge the number of guards looking down at her. The night sky was too dark to make out any silhouettes, and the guardhouse appeared dark as well. "We heard that there's plenty of contracts on offer." She shouted back.

"Oh, you want to sign up with du Quinones? Wait here, I'll get my captain."

Gretchen resisted the urge to fidget as she waited. Slowly, she looked over the walls. No particular details stood out in the gloom. There could be a Battalion of archers standing quietly and she wouldn't see them.

A new voice suddenly shouted down at Gretchen. "Hey, you out there. You want to sign up?"

"Yeah, we heard uh… du Quinones is hiring."

"Well too bad, we've got that contract and we're keeping it. Unless you're someone impressive, you can piss off."

Gretchen scowled. "Oh, we can impress," she shouted up to the gate.

"Really now? Who are you with?"

Gretchen's mind was blank for just a moment.

"We're the uh… the Band of Blood. Yeah, we're a new mercenary company."

"What…? Band of Blood? I haven't heard about you. Hah, you sure you're not just lost?"

Gretchen gritted her teeth. "No, no, we're hardened fighters. You should take us on!"

"Where are you from?"

Gretchen was sure he had a slight accent. "The Archland."

A brief pause came. Gretchen sorely hoped that this didn't turn out to be a band of Iltrayan mercenaries.

The same voice replied, this time in Archipelagan. *"Hey,*

you guys have come a long way. Come to make money off the rebels?"

Gretchen grinned. *"Yeah, we're late but we go where the money is good. So, here we are."*

"Huh... how many of you are there?"

"Two hundred, and we have our own weapons."

"Oh, weapons? That's good. Good. Hmm. Alright, I'll open the gate for you. But you'll have to prove yourselves to me in the morning before you can join, all new contracts but you can keep your uh... company name."

Gretchen grinned. "Sure, sure."

Celio Espinoza tapped Gretchen on the shoulder. "Lieutenant, are they believing you? What's happening?" he whispered.

"I'm not so sure... no." Gretchen said softly. "He only sounded interested when I said we all had weapons. They'll probably just try and steal our gear then throw us out, or kill us. But they're going to let us in, so get ready."

The portcullis rose as the gate slowly swung open, and Gretchen motioned for her troops to move forward. Gretchen herself walked at the front, never ordering her soldiers to do what she would not herself do.

The short walk through under the gatehouse felt like hours. A portcullis could be closed at either side of the gate, and the tunnel was more than long enough to sport dozens upon dozens of murder-holes in the ceiling and walls. Slits in the walls allowed for pikes to be shoved through at attackers.

Gretchen tried not to think about it.

When they finally emerged from the other side, Gretchen realised just how much of the town the walls' bulk hid. Immediately after she walked through there were buildings and streets clustered everywhere.

A lanky blond man, in much better armour than the other mercenaries milling around, walked up to Gretchen.

"So good to see others from the isles! Uh, how come you have Reimaran armour?"

Gretchen blinked. *"Oh, we – we stole it, of course. You heard about the... the Second Regiment's soldiers that were ambushed? Yeah, we stole it right off their warm bodies!"*

The mercenary captain laughed. *"Hah! That's practicality, right there. Berthold, captain of the Archland Corsairs, good to meet you. You know, I was going to refuse you, but I can't say no to a fellow Archipelagan. Especially not one blessed with such looks!"* he said with a wide smile.

Gretchen laughed. *"Uh, yeah. Gretchen... Gretchen Schmidt. Well, I–"*

Berthold pointed behind Gretchen. *"Hey, all of these have dark hair. You said you were all from the Archipelago, though."*

Gretchen blinked. *"Oh, well – we are, but we took on some Reimaran traitors."* Gretchen looked around, then leaned in to Berthold with a whisper. *"You know – arrow fodder."* Gretchen said. *"The main bulk of us comes in last, so if the traitors try anything, we can carve them up. They are traitors, after all..."*

Berthold nodded, a smile on his face. *"You were born to lead mercenaries, Gretchen Schmidt. We'll make a huge profit off of this Reimaran rebellion, you'll see."*

Gretchen looked around out of the corner of her eyes, seeing more and more of the third's troops getting through the gate. *"Er, what about Surmarch? The Reimarans just flew in and took over. Aren't you worried?"*

Berthold blinked. *"Flew in? I had heard that Surmarch had fallen, but I thought that was because the idiots tried to ambush the Royal Guard and missed them. How stupid! It's better to be behind some nice thick walls, not trying to be too clever. They got what they deserved."*

Gretchen was about to smile and nod when Berthold pointed behind her again. *"Hey, that's a lot of Reimarans. Where are the Archipelagans you had with you? Are you sure you want these traitors armed? They're making me nervous, we should disarm them."*

In one move, Gretchen stepped back and drew her sword as she cried out. "To arms! Attack!"

Berthold's eyes widened and he tried to draw his own sword, but Gretchen had lashed out and gutted him before he could do more than draw breath. As he fell she could see the surprise and fear in his eyes, but she turned away to see her soldiers falling onto the assembled mercenaries, few of whom even got their weapons out in time.

"Don't let any escape! Sergeant Santiago, chase those ones down!" Gretchen cried out.

"After them, there! Sprint!" shouted Paz.

All in all, it took one march and a little trickery to gain a foothold in Ponsurno.

"Hey, Paz, report," said Gretchen to Sergeant Santiago, who returned almost breathless.

"Some... ah... some of them... got away..." she panted.

Gretchen frowned. "Well. That's... well, that's no damn good at all."

Paz didn't meet her gaze. "Sorry... Sir we... weren't fast... enough."

Gretchen gripped Paz's shoulder, giving it a brief squeeze. "Yes, I understand, get some air in you before you collapse. We can't win them all, but we'll have to win defending this gate. Hmm."

Gretchen turned to her other sergeants as they finished getting their subordinates into formation.

"Right, here's what we're going to do. Any minute now we'll have dozens of mercenaries coming down those streets at us, probably from all sides. Thankfully the winding streets makes poor ground for archers."

"Aah, this is why you had us bring pikes, Lieutenant."

Gretchen grinned. "What, did you think I expected them to ride out against us, right out of the front gate, one on one? This isn't some fairy story. Mercenaries, even more than any soldier, love to hole up and play it safe. But they can't leave us holding the gate, so they'll come to us in short order. Have the troops present pikes and take formation at the mouth of each of the three roads that lead here. First and second squads, on me."

"What are we doing then, Lieutenant?" said Mario Corvi.

"Ambush," said Paz and Gretchen at the same time.

Paz shrugged as Gretchen stared at her.

"Is... is it that obvious?" said Gretchen.

Paz shrugged. "I have no idea how you intend to ambush them here, but you always do it, so I'm not really surprised anymore," she said with another shrug.

"Well, this time, we're going to try something novel. Those boots' enchantments are good for getting us up as well as across, so first we get onto that roof there –" said Gretchen, pointing at a nearby building that appeared to be communal storage, "– and once the mercenaries have come charging down the street we drop down from that building behind them."

"Err, what if more mercenaries just come in and trap us like we trapped them?"

Gretchen smiled. "Then leap back up onto the building. Watch out for any clever cocks with crossbows."

Gretchen turned to Eneko Abaroa. "I keep forgetting about you. Sorry. You've told the major that we're good to go, right?"

Eneko nodded. "Major du Tealdan has been informed. The *Wrath* is closing in as we speak, half a glass until arrival, Commodore Terciero said."

Gretchen nodded, scratching her chin with her thumb. "And we'll have to hold so that everyone else can drop down from the ship without being gutted as they land. Well, we have our orders. All in formation, pikes at front! Shortbows behind pikes and loose at will!"

The Third Battalion had assembled into formation in rapid order as Gretchen had directed. The Reimarans had scant time to contemplate their situation before a distant clattering of boots could be heard approaching them.

"Here they come, here they come! All bows, loose at will when you see them. When they hit the pikes, give them the tip and make them choke on it!"

For all that they were hired swords, the mercenaries pelted down the narrow streets into Gretchen's ambush roaring their battle cries and battle was joined.

The screams of the injured and dying soon filled the air as each side fought viciously, the Reimarans desperate to hold on to their slim gains in the city, the mercenaries eager to oust them. Gretchen herself was in the thick of things, batting aside enemy pikes and cutting down any foe that dared to push too close against the Reimaran line. And even as that line was pushed back, the soldiers of the Third Battalion fought like rabid dogs to keep it intact.

And as the Third Battalion kept the mercenaries' attention, the *Wrath* closed in above the city, quiet and ready. Down from the ship came the soldiers from the First Battalion, dropping into the main plaza of Ponsurno. From there, it was an easy matter to catch the mercenaries that had rushed to the gate between the beleaguered third and Ermanno's fresh soldiers.

And catching the mercenaries exposed in the streets, the Reimarans tore through them on both sides. No quarter was given, none was offered. Even after Surmarch, the soldiers of the Fourth Regiment wanted bloody revenge: Ponsurno was no different than Surmarch in that no offers of ransom for the Second Regiment's troops had been offered. In all likelihood, the Second Regiment's garrison in Ponsurno had been mercilessly put to death after the city was taken from within.

And as far as revenge went, the Reimarans got it.

After the battle wound down, Siera arranged for the Reimaran wounded to be tended to and any injured foe to be put out of their misery.

There were no *hors de combat* concerns for mere mercenaries.

Chapter 19: Then by Surrender

Hours yet before dawn, and Siera tallied the fallen.

The Fourth Regiment had lost forty-seven soldiers in the attack, which was far better than what they would have lost in a siege, but still a sting, considering how few troops she had to begin with. Siera had convened with Tomasso and her lieutenants on the *Wrath*'s bridge to strategise.

Ermanno had arrived right after breakfast, and seeing everyone else had already arrived, quickly chomped down a biscuit.

Gretchen looked over to Ermanno as he arrived, then turned back to Siera. "The battle at the gate put them in a sore spot, sir. Over two hundred or two hundred and fifty killed. Ugly work, but there can't be many more of them."

"That's a fair few dead mercenaries," said Siera. "They couldn't have had many more, and they will be sore pressed to defend the keep."

Ermanno shook his head. "It's Ponsurno's keep. You can hold it with two dead donkeys and a drunk baker," he said

"Why a baker?" said Gretchen.

"What's the baker going to do, hit you with a rolling pin?" said Ermanno.

Gretchen stared at him.

"Either way, things are well so far," said Siera. "We have a solid advantage, thanks to Gretchen. Even if the methods were… less than preferable, we won out handily."

"Imagine if all war were like that," said Adalberto. "You'd never guess what your opponent was doing, if everyone did things like that."

Quintus, standing at Siera's side, noted the slight creasing around Gretchen's eyes, and the way she looked slightly away from Adalberto as he said that. He said nothing.

"Well, we will not have to resort to anything like that

again, so stand easy," said Siera. "And as you mention defensibility, Ermanno, I have a report on that. Shortly after I dropped off the *Wrath*, a private came bearing a message to Tomasso from a small group who claimed to be servants at the keep. Turns out the mercenaries marched their main force out to attack the Third Regiment, but forgot to keep an eye on said servants. It seems those servants gathered their courage and fled – and so we now have a report from inside the keep: there are less than forty mercenaries remaining. And no sign of the traitors who hired them, unfortunately."

Ermanno's brows rose slowly, and Siera knew he'd been impressed. "Bold of them. Reckless, but bold. Bows?"

Siera glanced towards Tomasso, who cleared his throat. "Crossbows, Sir. Servants said they saw 'lots'."

Adalberto smirked. "And how many is 'lots'?"

Ermanno looked sidelong at Adalberto. "Doesn't matter, they'll hold that keep for a month. There's only one way in, drawbridge is up, and there's no nearby cover around besides."

Tomasso glanced from Ermanno to Adalberto. "I had the private who brought the message find the servants and bring them to me. When I questioned them further, they still weren't sure how many crossbows the mercenaries had. Probably enough for the mercenaries that remain inside the keep, though. Servants did say that there are plenty of provisions and stores in the keep."

Siera thought for a moment. "I think we can change their minds."

Adalberto looked over at Siera, and for a moment their eyes met.

Adalberto swallowed. "Major…"

Siera put up a hand to interrupt him. "The less we fight, the less of ours die. Believe me, I want to order every soldier we have to cut down not just traitors but their lackeys as well. But I cannot focus solely on revenge at the expense of the larger issue, that being that while rebels hold Reimar's cities, our nation is sorely weakened. They'll take a surrender, same deal as we gave that wretched band in Surmarch. That's what gave me the idea… although I really should have thought of it myself."

Ermanno nodded slowly, scratching at his beard. Gretchen betrayed no reaction. Adalberto looked from Siera to Ermanno. "As you order, so do I obey... but surely there's a cost to doing this sort of thing. People won't forget that we won Ponsurno through trickery, not valour," said Adalberto.

In a flash, Gretchen turned to face Adalberto and bared her teeth at him. "I was there, with my soldiers, fighting for our lives at that gate. Just because we used guile does not mean we did so without valour!" she snarled.

Adalberto blanched at her reaction. "I... well, that may be so, but–"

Ermanno clicked his tongue loudly. "You know what he means, Gretchen. Then again, Adalberto, you know what she means too," he said as he crossed his arms, not looking at either of them.

Siera's face was deliberately blank. "I do not wish to suggest that I do not care for my own officers' opinions, but the truth is that the less talk about this, the better. I made my choice and I gave the orders. It was my decision and it is my responsibility, and now it is quit. Let it remain done, with no further talk: an offer of peaceful conduct to the mercenaries for their surrender. Now, Southmere."

"Damn stupid name for a city," said Ermanno.

Siera looked up at Ermanno, her brow creasing. "What? Whatever does that have to do with anything? It is just a name, after all... I think it sounds fine."

Ermanno shrugged.

Siera resisted the urge to sigh. "Anyhow," she muttered. "Southmere should be easier than either Surmarch or Ponsurno have been, as we will have the Navy to assist us. Now, I want the First and Second Battalions coming in from the east, greatbows making some holes in the walls here, and here –" Siera tapped her finger against the map, "– and then the First and Second Battalions, along with the militia, pushing the rebels off the walls. They cannot hold the walls and the harbour both, so we can put pressure on both sides."

"Like two men eating a pie," said Ermanno.

Gretchen's brows furrowed. "You always say that. When have you ever seen two men eat a pie at the same time?"

"Wait, the same pie?" said Adalberto.

Ermanno glared at them. "You know what I mean. We come at them – both sides, they have to retreat to the fort, so we have them all in one place."

"Yes, pies or not, that is quite correct," said Siera. "Once the *Wrath* drops the First and Second Battalions, it will reposition to the navy's advance and help cover them.

"But myself and the Second Battalion will be off the ship," said Adalberto.

"Yes, so it will be the Third Battalion dropping onto any enemy ships they try to bring against us."

"That will put the *Wrath* in a precarious position if there are many enemy ships," said Terciero.

"There should be only a few," said Siera. "It is not as though the rebels have a fleet to back them up, after all. The few ships they bring – if any, really – we can drop down on and capture, allowing the Navy to sweep into the harbour and unload the Third Regiment's marines."

"And once we're in the city?" said Ermanno.

Siera licked her lips. "Honestly? I am hoping that the mercenaries surrender their masters and go peaceably. If not, well… we will co-ordinate a ground siege with the *Wrath* possibly attacking from the air."

Ermanno shook his head. "Daylight attack will get ugly, this isn't Surmarch," he said.

Siera sighed. "Yes, yes, I realise that. If it is plausible, then I will attempt it. If not, a more traditional siege will suit us. Holes in walls, take to the breach, and so on."

Adalberto sucked at his teeth. "Two wall charges in one day will be rough going. We should rest between engagements if possible."

"True," said Siera, rubbing her chin with her thumb. "Well, we can only lay plans for so far in advance. Once we have the city, we can decide on how to take the keep. Or we get lucky, and they focus on defending the city instead of the keep."

"They can't be that stupid," said Adalberto.

"One can but hope," said Siera. "We have benefitted from some enemy mistakes so far. As long as we avoid making any ourselves, I feel… no, I know, that we will have them in short order."

"I'd be easier if we had the levies going in first," said

Adalberto, who put up his hands as Siera turned to look at him. "I know, I know. We have to have someone holding Surmarch and Ponsurno while we retake the other cities. Just... well."

"I'd pay good money to see the Noble Order in action," said Gretchen with a half-smile.

"Better they remain guarding what we've retaken. The citizenry know and trust them, and if not for them, I'd have to have soldiers from the Fourth doing that job."

Ermanno sucked his teeth, then looked at Siera. "Things've gone well, so far. Not to pat your head, Siera, but you've gone lightning fast, all things considered."

Siera grinned. "Told you that skyship would pay itself off, pentuple."

"Penwhat?" said Ermanno.

"Paid back five times," said Adalberto.

"Huh," said Ermanno. "It's true, it has. You've bet well."

Siera smiled. "Damn right. You watch, every regiment will be sporting a ship after this."

"Third's already got dozens," said Ermanno with a straight face. Gretchen coughed to conceal a smirk.

Siera rolled her eyes. "You know what I mean, and those are not the Third's own ships. And if you were half as polite as you are clever you'd have friends from Jurien to Iln, Ermanno."

Ermanno shrugged.

Siera sighed, and massaged her temples for a moment. "Some of the levies and the Noble Order will be here in a mere few hours, and they will... make sure that Duke du Lucan's judges get their work done. Then, the judges and Duke du Donati's household guard will be in Southmere a day after us. And then we will have no need to spread ourselves thinly... San Seras will be ours again."

Her lieutenants saluted to that.

Hours later, after scant deliberation, the mercenaries holding Ponsurno's keep had given leery acceptance of Siera's offer of surrender. Under the close watch of the soldiers of the Royal Guard, the sell-swords departed Ponsurno without further incident.

Chapter 20: Southmere

1ˢᵗ Chem

Siera stood on the bridge with her lieutenants as Southmere Town slowly came into view.

A sailor stepped onto the bridge, saluting.

"Major, Commodore. Lookout's sighted mercenaries entering the town."

Siera scowled. "Entering? How many?"

"They said three hundred, maybe more."

"Godammit," muttered Siera.

"That's no patrol," said Gretchen, wincing. "Those are reinforcements."

"More mercenaries? Awful rats, like there's no end to them," said Adalberto.

"Rebels really have hired most of the goddamn continent's worth of sell-swords," said Ermanno.

Adalberto thumped his fist into his hand. "Major, we could quickly loose a volley on them as they enter the city. If the *Wrath* comes in low enough, we'll have perfect targets."

Siera grinned, and turned back to the sailor. "How close are they to the city gates?"

"Right on them, sir. Already entering by now, I'd rate."

Siera sighed.

Gretchen frowned, then looked sideways at Adalberto. "Even if they're behind walls, greatbows would solve that."

Siera frowned, and spoke before Adalberto could reply. "I will not stoop so low as to focus greatbows on soldiers. But if some should be in the way when we breach the walls, well…" Siera shrugged. "But come, quickly now, get your troops on deck. We have no time to waste, the Navy is about to commence their attack. Ermanno, make sure your soldiers are ready to drop. Adalberto, yours right behind his."

Ermanno nodded, and Adalberto saluted. Both hastened to obey.

The mercenary reinforcements had already marched through the city gates by the time Ermanno and Adalberto's Battalions had dropped down from the *Wrath* and formed up. The road to Southmere's Eastpost gate was broad and well-worn cobblestone, down which Ermanno's soldiers moved slowly, shields raised high. The mercenaries on the wall watched them with unease, their eyes more focused on the soldiers of the Second Battalion, who stood back well out of crossbow range. As the First Battalion had made its way almost to the front gate, with only three hundred metres to go, mercenary officers ordered the first volley, bolts whipping through the air to slam into Reimaran shields. Some soldiers were unlucky enough to have bolts impale their shields where their arms held them, and howled with pain. But the Reimaran's discipline held, and their advance did not slow.

"Godless horsefucking bolts, damn rings don't mean a thing," muttered Ermanno in the midst of his troops.

And as the mercenaries had switched their focus to the First Battalion, Adalberto grinned from his position well behind Ermanno's advance. As he raised his greatbow, eight of his troops matched his movements with their own.

"Southmere's Eastpost gate is thick oak, then a portcullis, then another great oak gate! Loose a half-breath after each other so we blast through them all!"

And with that, Adalberto released his draw.

The first greatarrows had been expensive failures, enchanted arrows used with ordinary bows that burst into splinters on impact or failed to go more than a few metres forward, one or two that simply exploded once nocked or drawn – overall, devices that would cause hardly any harm to an enemy at all. But once it was understood that a modified bow and arrow combination could achieve the desired effect, the full power of the magical weapon was realised.

Adalberto's aim was true, even from hundreds of metres away, his arrow slamming almost dead centre into the middle of the Southmere Eastpost's sturdy oak door.

With a sound akin to an angry mountain swinging at an offending tree, the door exploded inwards, one-third of a metre thick wood turning into so much ash and splinters. A spray of shattered masonry cracked out from the gate arch in accompaniment. Half a breath later, Adalberto's greatarchers loosed their own shots, which sailed straight through even the thick iron bars of the portcullis – but slammed into the door behind the portcullis, causing the iron to warp and even shatter in some places as the sheer force of the explosion tore segments of the gate apart.

As the greatarrows streaked above his head, Ermanno cried out to his troops "Advance! For Reimar, for the Major!"

The First Battalion's formerly slow pace was abandoned for a swift trot, shields at the ready.

The cries of the mercenaries guarding the gate had started long before the First Battalion set upon them.

On the *Wrath*, Siera resisted the urge to look back and see how Ermanno and Adalberto were faring.

Eneko Abaroa turned to Terciero. "Commodore, message from Admiral Ernesto du Firenze."

Terciero scratched at his beard. "Oh, has he started?"

Eneko nodded. "He reports that Archipelagan ships have been sighted closing in on Southmere's harbour, and requests that we move as quickly as possible."

"Eh, what? Archies?" said Terciero.

Siera winced. "Archipelagan mercenaries, with their ships too... really the worst time for it. Still, it is far from over. Reply to the Admiral – we will be there shortly to render aid. Commodore Terciero, change course away from the keep, take us over the harbour. I will be damned if I let the Navy take any excessive losses, not if I can stop it."

Terciero was still fiddling with his instruments as he replied, not looking up. "Yes sir, but I'll need to gain some height before we pass by the keep. I don't want those ballistae firing on us."

Siera rubbed her palms together. "Hmm. Better yet – quickly, Commodore, use that battle speed if you can."

Terciero pursed his lips. "Very well, Sir."

The *Wrath* creaked more urgently as the ship suddenly doubled its speed. Siera staggered as the floor under her lurched forward.

"Good – good Sura, that's fast," said Siera.

"Only for a short moment, we haven't much time," said Terciero.

"Sir, how do we know how much longer we can maintain it? Should I time it?" said an assistant, grabbing for an hourglass.

Terciero's mouth widened into a fat grin. "Hah, we'll know when it runs out! Good God, all of you, can you feel that thrum? Who in Sura's name thought of this enchantment, it's potent!"

Terciero continued grinning as the *Wrath* thundered forward. Siera could only imagine anyone trying to take aim at the ship as it whipped past them.

"Now imagine if this was our normal speed!" said Terciero as he fiddled with his odd instruments. "We'd storm through the sky!"

Siera felt tense as the ship creaked around her, even as it cleared its way past the keep and headed straight out to sea. Siera guessed that they were just clear of the harbour when the *Wrath* began to slow.

"Enchantment's out. Alas for that... well, let's take her closer," said Terciero.

One of the obsidian chunks, one with silver wire in an odd design around it, began to rattle on the table.

"The – oh for – get that, will you?" said Terciero to an assistant.

"Descent's too quick, Sir," she replied as she grabbed hold of it.

"It'll be fine, it'll be fine. The warnings go off too soon. It's those clowns at the Academy, they spend all their time fiddling with books and not ships!"

"Clowns?" said Siera.

"Oh, they mean well, but they don't really appreciate the ships they work on. It's all numbers and focus to them."

Siera raised her brows at that. "Didn't you graduate from the Luminary Academy, Commodore?

Terciero grinned. "Longest waste of my time that I ever had. Sky's where I belong."

Siera shook her head. "Either way, Lieutenant Ailbhe is getting ready to drop. I will tell her troops to move on deck, and return later."

Terciero nodded, appearing to focus on something other than the room around him. "Yes, of course. Just to starboard, like that."

Eneko Abaroa tapped Terciero's shoulder. "Sir? Lookouts report that some of the ships have large braziers on their decks lit."

"Eh? They want to fling fire, do they? Idiots," muttered Terciero.

Almost on cue, swatches of the deck of the *Wrath* suddenly sputtered with flame.

"Fire! Shit, fire on deck!"

"Lens that flame for me, Ms. Aldana," said Terciero calmly.

Pepita Aldana focused, drawing the flame into itself, even as it tried to ignite and intensify.

"I... I can't... there must be a few of them working toge– uh!"

The fire on the deck suddenly roiled and exploded, sending soldiers scrambling as it licked towards the masts.

"Take the wheel, Eneko," said Terciero, his face stony, stepping aside to grab a long, obsidian-capped staff before he exited the bridge.

Terciero strode out onto the deck, flame-warmed air pushing at him.

"Touch my deck, eh?" Terciero muttered.

The gems on the staff he held lit up with an eerie, flickering orange light.

"Fire on my ship, eh?" he said as he focused on the growing conflagration on the deck.

"No," he said as he forced it to draw in on itself, feeling the fire fight him, its will pushed at by others.

"Fucking."

The flame pushed in on itself, desperate for fuel, kept going by Terciero's will alone.

"Thank." Terciero walked over to the side of the ship, glaring down at the enemy ships below.

The flame seemed to suddenly flit around, a single intense orb of hungering fire, bright and quick as it flicked over the deck to the side.

"You!"

The bright, hungering orb leapt off the ship and flew through the air, sputtering and crackling as it went. It soared for a brief, short moment, then smacked into one of the many ships below.

The ship's rigging and large swathes of the sails simply evaporated as the concentrated core of flame bored into them. Terciero at last released his will, and the flame shot outwards in all directions, eagerly grasping and clawing its way across the deck towards any fuel it could find.

Siera had run back up to the bridge as she heard the commotion, but stopped when she saw Terciero peering over the side of the ship.

"Of all the times," muttered Siera to herself, then turned as she heard someone come up behind her.

"Ready to drop, sir," said Gretchen with a quick salute. On deck, Siera saw the Third Battalion's soldiers briskly take their positions, more than a few glancing at the burned sections of the deck.

Siera nodded curtly at Gretchen. "Drop as soon as I give the signal, we'll be over the first ship. Three squads for each ship. We will only engage those ships that have already initiated a boarding action. Sura be with you!"

Gretchen saluted. "Good as done, Major. Sergeant Caivano, have all squads check their lines, we're already closing in. Go!"

A sudden wind rocked the ship, bow to stern, some soldiers flailing to keep their balance as others fell sprawling across the deck.

Siera looked over to see Terciero still standing with that expression on his face. She shook her head and ran back to the bridge, fighting to keep her balance as she went.

"One of you give me a report," she said as soon as she entered.

"I – we – there must be a – a group of them, trying to capsize us."

Siera's mouth fell open. "C–capsize? An entire skyship? I... I was told that this was practically impossible!"

"Impossible for any but the greatest mages, but if they

work together, they can do it. Archie sorcerers... I would never have thought..." said Eneko as he ground his teeth, his eyes losing focus.

Siera realised that they all had that expression on their faces. A short moment passed while Siera felt she was just stuck in a room full of lifelike statues.

"God *fucking* dammit," Siera said as she clenched her fists, then turned to walk out.

If only she'd kept du Tilmost around...

Siera's eyes widened, and she fumbled at the ring that Lycea had given her, getting out back onto the deck as she did so.

"Finger in the indent? No, no... thumb?"

Siera stood on the deck as it heaved around her, like a ship in a massive sea-swell, her thumb jabbing into a groove in the silver ring that Lycea had given her.

Nothing happened.

Siera stared at the ring on her finger, feeling a complete fool. What had she expected to happen? For a fairy to come out?

On the deck behind her, soldiers tried to at least stand upright as the ship began to list to starboard. Siera realised that the inconceivable was here; the *Wrath* was tilting over.

Siera felt panic rise within her. "If you can get below deck, do so! All of you, off the deck!" Siera cried out, as she realised she should have called for everyone to move off the deck sooner.

A hand gripped Siera's shoulder, and she squeaked in surprise.

"W– who –ah – oh..." as she turned to see Lycea standing next to her, surprise on the councillor's face.

"What's happening, Your Highness? Why is the ship – oh, yes."

Lycea straightened, as though the deck were not pitching beneath her. "Take my hand, Your Highness. We cannot have you fall out of the sky. We will be safe back in Ilmarch in a mere moment."

Siera blinked. "What? No. I called upon your aid to stop the ship from falling at all."

Lycea's hand slowly fell to her side. "I suppose I can

remedy that." Lycea pulled her rod from her waist sash, and distractedly flicked at the gemstones at its sides. "I cannot tell if they are moving the ship itself, or the air currents... be right back, Your Highness."

And with that, Lycea flicked out the strange rod she'd used before, and was gone.

Siera resisted the urge to scream in frustration, instead gritting her teeth again.

A mere two hundred metres away, on the deck of an otherwise unremarkable Archipelagan ship, fourteen sorcerers worked in concert to bring the *Wrath* down. Combining both the literal and abstracts of sorcery, their concerted effort slowly yet surely tipping an entire skyship over.

They never noticed as Lycea appeared on deck. The sailors, though, did.

"Oi, hey!"

"Who's that?!"

"R–Remmy mage on deck, kill 'em!"

Lycea had long practiced her polite expressions to better move amongst her husband's social circles, the right smile here and there, faking interest all the while.

But the wild grin on her face now was all her own.

She let loose, once more, all her practiced mannerisms, all her control, just like the last time. For just this moment, she could stop being Lycea.

The powers of a warlock are completely different to that of a sorcerer. The sorcerer's focused, determined manipulation of the elements was more like clay sculpting or tapestry weaving than anything else.

But sorcerers used magic only through the screen of the elements. Warlocks needed no screens, no filters – only the true power of magic, the unbridled roiling energy of the astral itself.

That was probably why so many warlocks died young.

Lycea laughed as she let loose a bright, hissing energy. The sailors made no sound as they evaporated. She turned her attention to the small huddle of sorcerers, lost to their own determination, and simply blew them apart as well.

"More! More!" she screamed, horrible tearing and cracking noises coming from all around her as the ship's hull began to tear apart, the wood peeling and warping, in some places shattering into dust, in others exploding into a spray of splinters.

The Archipelagan pirates on deck scrambled amid the chaos, some simply leaping overboard.

"Oh god, oh god oh god!"

"Fucking kill her, fucking ki–"

Lycea giggled as she blew apart a small group of pirates who desperately tried to rush her, with a flick of her hand, as one would brush a cobweb from a window.

The ship she stood on began to list as it started rapidly taking on water.

Lycea laughed as she felt the potent, visceral flow of magic run through her, smiling and licking her lips. All around her, the ship bowed to her will and bled its form apart, everything coming away and moving to her whim. Like this, she could fly. Like this, she could turn mountains into rivers of molten slag and crack rivers into craters. The earth would flow and fall beneath her feet, even the sky would melt like butter in her hands, all around herself she could feel the ocean and its currents, moving and churning, and all the water and sky through the world flowed with a precise pattern, and if she just pushed a little, just here and there, she could...

Lycea was breathing hard as she fought to bring herself back to reality, sweat on her brow, her legs unsteady.

Slowly, she took stock of where she was.

The Archipelagan ship was devoid of life around her; it was as though no one had ever stepped onto its deck and the ship had sailed itself out to sea. The vessel was listing heavily, slowly sinking as it filled with seawater.

"T– time to go," Lycea said with a shiver, reminding herself of who she was supposed to be.

With a final flick of her wrist, she was gone.

Siera herself was below deck when the *Wrath* stopped heaving and listing to one side. Moments after that, she risked walking up to the bridge, arriving just as Terciero walked in.

"Crisis averted, Major," he said.

"What in the name of god happened, Terciero?" said Siera.

"Some loons tried to capsize us," Terciero muttered, massaging his head. "I never thought the Archipelagans would have sorcerers capable of working together so well... eh... I guess that we've underestimated them," he said with a shrug.

"Good to see you can shrug after we all almost died."

"Well, we didn't die, and – wait, is that Councillor du Tilmost?" he said, pointing out at the deck.

Lycea had just appeared on deck, looked around, and then started making her way to the bridge.

"I think she did it," said Siera with a sigh.

"Did what?" said Eneko.

"Good to see that you all held your composure while I was busy," said Terciero, smiling at his assistants.

At the back, Carmina saluted, but the others didn't notice. "Did what we could, Sir," she said.

Eneko rubbed at his face, his mouth twitching. "H–heh, we won't be brought down by some Archie hedge-mages."

"What were you doing out on the deck, Commodore?" asked Siera.

Terciero raised a brow. "Trying – well, succeeding – in stopping anyone from setting the ship on fire."

Siera felt an intense urge to simply punch Terciero in the face.

"You can stop a whole goddamn bonfire but you lose your humour over a cigarette, agh," said Siera under her breath.

Terciero blinked. "What, Major?"

"Never mind," said Siera, as Lycea walked in. "Ah, Councillor." Siera made a small bow. "Your aid was invaluable."

"Your immediate problem has been resolved, Your Highness," said Lycea, a serene smile on her face.

"My thanks to you, then, Councillor." Siera frowned. "I thought that you had said that you have no experience in using magic on the battlefield..."

Lycea shrugged.

Terciero looked from Siera to Lycea, his eyes narrowed.

"My crew would have kept the ship aright, regardless."

Siera glared at him. Lycea nodded. "But of course, Commodore. I merely rid the Major of a hindrance to her plans," said Lycea.

Siera pinched the bridge of her nose.

"Yes. Fine. Look." Siera sighed. "I have soldiers to organise. Councillor, might you wait here on the bridge? I will not be more than a moment."

Lycea bowed. "Of course, Your Highness."

Siera nodded, and turned to walk back down into the ship.

Without a concentrated effort from any enemy mages, the *Wrath* was able to drop soldiers ship by ship. The advantage that the Archipelagans had was whittled down until they were stymied, with some pirate vessels choosing to flee rather than risk a fight they might not win.

In doing so, they doomed those that did not flee to finding themselves captured in short order.

After the naval engagement, Siera met Gretchen on the bridge.

She nodded to Gretchen's salute. "All soldiers accounted for?"

"All including our six losses, sir."

Siera repressed a grin, her eyes lighting up. "Six...? Even if the *Wrath* was at risk from some... unexpected magical resistance, those are ridiculously good numbers."

Gretchen smirked. "Sailors aren't so good at stopping someone dropping out of the sky and kicking them in the head, Sir."

Siera raised a brow. "Sailors? Those were Archipelagan ships. Pirates, you mean."

Gretchen shrugged. "Sailor or pirate, got what was coming to them. And a few new ships for the Navy, even if they are a bit old."

Siera nodded curtly. "Patrol ships for Ilmarch, at least. And I hate to have the troops rush straight back into battle, but the Navy has to secure the sea approach before they can land any soldiers from the Third Regiment. As such, tend to any wounded and be ready to drop–" Siera grabbed a nearby hourglass off a shelf behind some of Terciero's implements "– after this glass has run, should be half an hour. We must have the harbour secured, there are quite a few empty ships that we might rue leaving unattended."

Gretchen saluted. "They're as good as yours, sir."

Twenty five minutes later, after leaving over a dozen of her troops on the *Wrath* due to injuries, Gretchen and the soldiers of the Third Battalion dropped again. This time, they found a largely deserted harbour.

Gretchen knew she should post guards at the docked ships to ensure they were not used for an escape, but either she dangerously split her forces in half or she consigned those few left to guard the ships to a grisly fate if an entire crew tried to get on board.

"Wish we could be sprinting along here, Lieutenant. We'd make better time."

Gretchen didn't turn to see who was complaining, she knew it was Erasmo.

"Those boots cost a fair teal to re-enchant, and the major trusts me not to use them unnecessarily. We're lucky our entire Battalion has the damn things, I'll not have the major's efforts in outfitting us with them put to waste. Besides… look ahead of us."

Gretchen and her Battalion had marched well into the harbour area, warehouses all around. As the Third Battalion closed on a large thoroughfare used to move freight next to the warehouses, Gretchen signalled a halt.

"Sir… there's no one here."

Gretchen squinted. "Exactly. Mercenaries were last seen trying to board ships, and when the Navy closed in, they fled. So where are they?"

"They must have cast off, got around the Navy somehow," said Erasmo. "If we'd been here sooner–"

Gretchen turned to glare at him. "I didn't realise that you had become lieutenant, as well as naval expert. You underestimate how much time it takes to ready a ship, Erasmo, let alone loot everything you can find as well. They are here, nearby… open ground, here, you have to cross this road to get out of the harbour. This is probably an ambush."

Silence met Gretchen's declaration. She could feel her sergeants' eyes on her.

"So… should we…" said Giacinta.

A voice cried out from across the wide road. "Ho, Reimarans! Put down your arms and we can all go quietly. We've got dozens of crossbows here, all sighted on you."

Both she and her troops had their blades in their hands before she had to issue an order, but a cold feeling spread through Gretchen's gut.

She swore she knew that voice.

Gretchen grimaced, then yelled her response. "Who dares impede the Royal Guard? A few mercenary backsides and your old gran's hunting bow won't stop us. If you think you can fight your way out, you're fools."

"There'll be no surrender, you… wait… who speaks, there?"

Gretchen squinted ahead of her. "Lieutenant Gretchen Ailbhe of the–"

Gretchen stopped suddenly as a face she knew all too well appeared from behind a half-open warehouse door.

"Never thought I'd see you again," said Luitger Ailbhe, her brother. "You wretch. You've got a pretty pack of whores and jokers with you there, but how about we settle things alone? Just step forward, without your troops."

For a moment, Gretchen's tongue failed her, but she forced herself to speak. "So I can walk into your craven crew's arrows?"

Luitger bared his teeth, eyes wide. "More of a chance than father got, you rancid bitch!"

Gretchen scowled. "It wasn't my hand that slew him, you fucking mistake!"

Luitger's eyes seemed as though they would keep bulging forever. "Mistake?! I proved a better heir than you ever could, traitor! Agh, doesn't matter! He died because of you! And I don't care about anything else, nothing! You and me, my dear, dear sister. Right here, right now!"

Gretchen grinned despite herself, her face feral and wild. A sudden memory surfaced in her mind of the only letter she'd received from her family, four years after she had left the isles. Not that she knew how they found out where she lived. Just a rambling screed of her various misdeeds, obviously written by Luitger while he was drunk out of his mind, writing to tell her that her mother had died. In it, he gloated that he'd faithfully been by her side as she slipped away, and that Gretchen had not.

Gretchen had wept, then burnt the damn thing.

Gretchen's troops' eyes darted around, taking stock of the warehouse doors on the opposite side of the street, catching sight of Archipelagan eyes and crossbow bolt tips at all too many windows.

Gretchen paid them no heed. "I got your letter, Luitger. Seems you were badgering mother about your inheritance even as she died."

Luitger spat, then raised his fist to Gretchen, thumb between his middle and ring fingers. "Better than not being there at all, you traitorous little dogshit. And I've made well while you fooled around with your Remmy friends. Lots of money in ferrying the rebel's mercenaries around to kill your lot."

"L–lieutenant…? What's going on? Should we attack?" asked one of Gretchen's sergeants, Mario Corvi.

Gretchen didn't look at Mario. "No. Leave this to me. If Luitger dies, his crew will flee. Stand ready with shortbows in case they try anything clever."

"Lieutenant, wh–" one of Gretchen's soldiers said as she stepped forward, blade drawn.

Gretchen bared her teeth to her brother, then yelled out. "Swords only, just you and me. You'd better not start crying about 'to first blood' or any fancy shit now, brother. It's to the death."

Luitger smiled, cold and thin. "I won't take anything else. Put up that sword you stole from our father and come at me, you glass-legged bitch."

Luitger drew his own claymore, a traditional Archipelagan ship captain's weapon. In the Archipelago, it was usually meant to distinguish a leader and afford reach over a crew armed with dirks or short hafted axes, although the claymore was somewhat impractical for use onboard a ship even with its advantages. But for the here and now, it was utterly deadly. The weight, the size, the reach – this could never be an elegant duel.

This was the grunting, heaving crash of first blood being last blood.

Gretchen took her first strides slow, sizing up her brother. He'd filled out since she'd last seen him, four years her junior but now as tall, yet bulkier. Gretchen dismissed his growing stomach as proof that he led by force and the family name, yet couldn't dismiss him as anything but dangerous.

She knew exactly who had taught him how to use that sword.

His stance was everything that their parents had both taught them, his blade hanging low, ready to gut her if she made any error.

Her brother's eyes narrowed as she slapped her right boot, and widened as she leapt at him, flying forward half a dozen metres to crash towards him at lightning speed, his block coming no slower.

Their clash was a quick flurry of steel broken only by the murmurs among his crew and her Battalion, their own pants and gasps of exertion overtaken by the slap of boots on cobblestone and their grunts as they each took a few flesh wounds. Gretchen was too slow to duck a side-swing that scraped right along a rib, Luitger was too slow to dodge aside from a thrust that took a chunk out of his thigh. But as fast as they were, this was never going to be a mere battle of blades alone.

Luitger's enraged eyes mirrored his snarl. "It was *you, you* caused his death. *You* chose to abandon us, traitor. And with mother dead, nothing stops me from avenging our family. Me!" he hissed between breaths.

Gretchen panted as she fought. "Look at you, pirates' get. Is this – is this it, is it all you have, Luitger? A half-assed outlaw's life, stealing from your betters?"

Luitger's face and neck were bright red. "You've no – room, no room to talk down to me, you Remmy-fucker! I bet they all dick you! How can you serve them? How can you–"

Gretchen saw her chance, and took it. Her left leg behind his right leg and her blade in his face meant he had to step back, and fell when he did so. His brief scream before she impaled him on the point of her claymore did not deter her.

He scrabbled blindly, his sword falling from his grasp as she ground her blade into the cobblestones through his stomach, as though trying to claw himself away from death, before falling limp.

Gretchen pulled her blade from her brother's corpse, and turned towards the still-silent warehouses where Luitger's crew stared wide-eyed at her.

Gretchen's breathing was heavy, and her eyes wild and blood-crazed. "Luitger's dead, you fucking garbage. Surrender and get the rope, or raise your swords and die to my blade."

Some fought. Some ran.
None escaped.

On the other side of the city, the First and Second Battalions had made good headway, but they could only push so far without encroaching on the keep. As such, after they had cleared the streets and swept through the city for stragglers, they waited for reinforcements, keeping their eyes warily on the keep all the while.

After the Third Regiment had helped secure over a dozen pirate vessels – new ships for the Admiralty – they assembled at the docks, where Siera had them march to trade places with the First and Second Battalions.

As the day began to fade into dusk, the Royal Guard mostly retired from the field, and lookouts were posted around the keep to watch for any counterattack while their fellows rested and tended to their wounds.

Chapter 21: Aftermath

1st Chem

The battle for Southmere would not be concluded so long as its keep was held, but Siera knew full well that tired soldiers capture no fortresses. As such, she placed sentries around the keep, which stood oddly silent with only the occasional mercenary peering over the walls to the roads and alleys below them.

Siera was confident that the mercenaries would not sally forth, and so for now, her troops rested while they could.

The Royal Guard scarce had to requisition a thing, so palpable was the citizenry's gratitude that bunks and food both were offered to weary soldiers left and right. Ermanno even broke a rare smile to see his troops walking into tavern and drinking houses next to the wright's district with weary faces, only to hear laughter and chatter a mere half an hour later. Even if in the middle of things, a break was exactly what they needed.

Ermanno found the First Battalion's fourth company where they had been billeted, at the Rounded Spoke Inn.

Ermanno nodded and exchanged a few embraces with passing soldiers, congratulations on every lip. Ermanno spied who he was looking for; the fourth company's sergeant, Vincenzo di Vitis. "Hey, Vincenzo, before you go, what about those four soft teals I lent you?"

Vincenzo had his eye on the barmaid even as his superior addressed him. "Eh? What teals?" said Vincenzo, then turning to Ermanno with a frown.

Ermanno leaned over to make sure none of his troops were too close by.

"Nothing. Look, I've heard a strange rumour, I want you to tell me if you've heard the same."

"Rumour? Lieutenant, what are you going on about, I

245

didn't borrow any teals, and wha–"

Ermanno clicked his tongue. "Pay attention. I hear someone's running a tontine. Now, I won't name any names, but whoever it is, is in trouble. If the Major finds out, she'll have your... well, someone's guts for garters." Ermanno rubbed his index finger and thumb together. "You see?"

Vincenzo stared. "I uh... yes sir. But... I, uh..."

Ermanno pursed his lips. "Idiot, just give them their money back."

Vincenzo nodded slowly, mouth slightly open. "Uh... I will. I mean uh, whoever it is, will? They will."

Ermanno shook his head as he stood to leave. "As you were, sergeant."

"Yessir."

Hours later, just past midnight, and Gretchen Ailbhe sat alone at a table in what had once been a well-decorated bar. During the chaos of the retaking some disturbance had occurred, and when she had come around to use the sizeable inn as accommodations for her troops, she couldn't even find an owner to persuade. A few bloodstains in the taproom and evident looting gave Gretchen an idea of what had taken place. Still, it made a decent barracks for a portion of the troops. Upstairs, even the last of the whoring had died down, and few were left awake.

A recent recruit from a few months ago, Mireia, who had previously served some time as a Gold Road caravan guard before joining the military, was sitting at another table. Gretchen roused herself, and went over.

"Mireia. How do you feel?" she asked as she seated herself.

Mireia looked up at Gretchen, and it was clear she'd been crying. Gretchen said nothing.

"I killed people today. I killed quite a few," she whispered.

Gretchen didn't meet her gaze. "I saw. You fought well."

Mireia turned to look at Gretchen, her eyes unfocused. "Was that really me? Can I kill that many people? Can I do something like that?"

Gretchen shifted, and looked at Mireia. "We all can, we all must. There's no winning this or any other war without killing."

Gretchen rose, and went over to the bar to pour a few drinks. As she put them onto a serving tray, one of her sergeants, Mario Corvi, came ambling into the taproom.

"Lieutenant! Good to see you following your true calling."

Gretchen turned to him, her face lost between a smirk and a glare. "I'll pack these all up your backside if you go around telling stories. Besides, it seems Mireia needs a few."

Mireia didn't look up.

"That bad, eh?" asked Mario softly.

"Seems so. Drag a chair up, Mr. Corvi."

Mireia still didn't look up as they both sat down at her table. "You don't need to comfort me. I'll be fine."

"Doubt that," said Gretchen. "Your face could melt Sura's own heart."

The front door clicked open, and they looked up to see a private, Ciro Carlevaro enter. "Oh, a midnight drink? I'm in," he said with a smile.

Gretchen nodded. "Mireia needs some comfort, so here, we drink," she said, indicating Ciro to get himself a chair.

"Is this an Archipelagan custom?" asked Mireia, her face morose.

Gretchen shrugged. "The Archipelago way is drink when you're sad, drink when you're happy, and drink in between just in case. But not so much in this case, I'd rather my soldiers didn't lose their heads because of some killing. Better to know your comrades are here for you than to just suffer alone." Gretchen tipped her drink to Mireia, and when she drank, they all drank.

"You never talk about the Archipelago, Lieutenant. Tell us a story?" said Ciro.

"Irrelevant as your commanding officer," said Gretchen. "Then again, all this officer stuff is a bit up its own arse for me. Don't mistake me, I like Reimar. But there are some things too Reimaran, if you see me." Gretchen mulled her thoughts for a moment. "In the Archipelago, there's no real appointed officers, or military. You earn your respect or you get nothing."

"Perhaps..." said Mario, shifting his feet.

Gretchen looked sideways at her sergeant. "Don't play the maiden with me, Mario. I've decided to make Reimar my home, and I won't have anyone guessing at me about it. Just how things are done in the Archland."

"Why Reimar, though?" asked Ciro, after a long sip.

Gretchen paused for a moment, then smirked. "Once, I was a silly young girl. I met a nice young sailor, who was Reimaran. When I went back to my parents, they refused to accept this. My father even went so far as so try to kill my lover, and so we fled. But my father caught up to us, and said that we'd shamed the family. We defended ourselves, us and the hired crew, but my father killed him and injured me. Because he'd hurt me, my mother killed him." Gretchen raised her mug, and drained the rest, ignoring the stares of those around her. "They never did like each other even after they'd been married for years. Guess it was just coming."

Ciro's eyes and mouth were both wide. "She… killed him? She just… killed her own husband?"

Gretchen nodded. "What would you do to protect your own child?" said Gretchen. "But Mattin loved Reimar, gods knows why. And so here I am. I can't – I won't return to the Archipelago, although I do miss it. But my home is here now, and I do well by it."

Ciro's eyes were misty. "You miss him still?"

"Sometimes," said Gretchen, looking at the bottom of her mug. "Sometimes. Ciro, do the honourable thing and get your lieutenant another drink."

Ciro threw a salute as he stood up.

Mario tapped his mug, indicating it was empty. Ciro half-turned and nodded. Mario turned back to Gretchen. "But, who are your parents, Lieutenant? You said your surname was common in the isles. Heh, for all I know it could be Salt-Sword himself! Wasn't he an Ailbhe too? And this man who was calling himself your brother today…"

Gretchen didn't look up, and spoke quietly. "Heinrich was an Ailbhe by name alone, he was born a Mac Niadh. But never you mind who they are. They don't matter anymore."

Mario looked as though he would say something, but shook his head.

Mireia turned her head to face her lieutenant. "Is it strange, taking orders from a Reimaran noble?"

Gretchen raised her brows. "Huh. Never thought about

it... no, not really. Not after everything else. Fighting's what I'm good at, it's in my blood. And fighting for the Major is purposeful work, she'll not spend anyone's life rashly." Gretchen took a long sip from her mug, draining it. "She dies, and the heart will fall out of this nation's arse."

Ciro had managed to roll a keg out to the table instead of bringing mugs over.

"Here we are, nice and well supplied. Logistics, after all, is most important." Ciro smiled.

"A wise tactical plan, Ciro. Let's take the vanguard and make sure our cups are full, you can't fight on an empty stomach."

"I'll have an empty head tomorrow morning," mumbled Mireia.

"But, what do you mean, Lieutenant?" said Mario as he filled his cup.

"I'm also a bit lost, don't get me wrong – here, let's raise a glass to the Major, right now," chimed in Ciro.

They all raised their cups.

"To the Major," said Mireia, smiling for once.

"To Her Highness!" said Ciro.

"To the Major–Captain," said Mario solemnly.

Gretchen raised her cup, but was silent for a moment until the others had finished.

"To Siera du Tealdan, best damned officer I've ever served under, and one day the best general I'll serve under. But to answer your question, what, you think people know Ramiros? You think people are sure about him? Think about it, for all that he's the older of the two, he's got a mixed reputation with all sorts, common or noble or rich or poor or whoever. Siera, though, brings home victories and protects the country with sword first. People respect that, it's obvious where she stands."

"Well... but, people love the king," said Mario.

"They do, and never think I mean any disrespect to His Noble Highness. But it's Siera they trust, she's who they know. Ramiros is an unknown, his mettle yet to be tested. Siera is proven, and if she dies, people will lose hope."

"The Captain won't die with us around, now that you can take home and eat for dinner," said Ciro.

"Major, and damn true. And once the war is over, we'll be heroes to boot," said Mario, leaning back in his chair.

Gretchen nodded slowly, but said nothing. A memory kept surfacing in her mind, unbidden, of Luitger when he was a baby. She'd been but a child herself, and had looked at her new baby brother with wonder, hoping only that he would be fun to play with when he grew a little older.

Sparse conversation continued, but they turned more often to their cups until one by one, they stumbled off to their beds.

Then only Gretchen remained, the fire low at her back, her mug empty. She snorted – she hated the sooty smell of an enclosed room with the fireplace burning for too long. She sighed then stood, kicked ash over the last sputtering flames, and left for her own bed.

Chapter 22: Trust

2nd Chem

Siera had called a meeting with her lieutenants in Southmere's Ombudsman's hall, a plain stone building that had seen over two hundred years of meetings, concords, and debates. Now it played host to her battle plans.

"What?" said Siera, her eyes widening. "No one in the keep? How did they get past our sentries?"

Gretchen grimaced. "We found a few servants, the ones who hid after the mercenaries murdered the others. There's tunnels under Southmere, for an emergency escape. Seems they found them and used that way to get out."

Siera's face was stony, her eyes downcast. "I... I had no idea... I wonder who built them. And how they have remained secret for so long, as well? Hmm."

"We keep getting surrenders or escaping mercenaries... I guess fate really does smile on you, Major," said Adalberto.

Gretchen snorted. "You can always rely on mercenaries – to have no backbone and run as soon as they can. Every time."

Siera smiled. "True, true indeed. Here I am worrying... things could have gone much worse. Instead we swept away rebels and mercenaries from three cities."

Adalberto snorted. "I'm still amazed they thought they could hold four cities, with mercenaries alone."

Siera looked down at her feet, then sighed. "I hate to say it... but I can understand their brashness. The Guard's not nearly at the strength it used to be, and after they took the Second Regiment by surprise... well. The First Regiment would never leave Ilmarch and the throne unguarded in a situation like this, and the other regiments are either small, or inexperienced. The Fourth's the only Regiment to have serious fighting experience aside from the Third, and you can hardly rely on marines alone."

Gretchen smirked. "They had a good assessment and a decent plan, but they underestimated you, Major."

Siera smiled softly. "They underestimated us all. Well, enough for now. The Noble Order and Duke du Donati's household guard will arrange the trials for Southmere, and we can retake San Seras. And then it will be done, just like that."

"A campaign of weeks indeed, Sir," said Adalberto with a wide smile.

Siera returned his smile, the concern in the back of her mind melting away.

Gretchen and Ermanno saluted, fists over their hearts, and turned to leave. Adalberto made no such move.

Siera raised her brows. "Something concerning you, Adalberto?"

Adalberto made a half-smile, and quickly looked over his shoulder to make sure his fellow lieutenants had left.

"Well, Major, there's a rumour going around. That Lieutenant Ailbhe ran into more than just common pirates at the docks, that she encountered a man calling himself her brother, one Luitger Ailbhe... son of Heinrich Ailbhe himself. Supposedly."

Siera's expression did not move. "I see. How widespread are these rumours?"

Adalberto blinked. "Hmm, quite widely, Sir. I myself try to maintain camaraderie with my subordinates, of course, but I hardly fraternise. And yet even I have heard them."

Siera looked down for a moment, then back at Adalberto. "There is clearly no substance to these rumours."

Adalberto furrowed his brows. "If you say that this is so, Sir, then it is so. However... well. I fear that if such a rumour spreads, belief will follow."

Siera resisted the urge to sigh, or massage her head. She could feel another headache building. "Be that as it may, I cannot arrest mere rumour and hearsay. As such, I will rely on my officers to stamp it out, as it deserves."

Adalberto saluted. Siera nodded.

Adalberto stepped outside the Ombudsman's hall, the sudden

change in brightness causing him to squint heavily. He turned to walk back to his billet, and never saw Gretchen behind him, her gaze heavy, her face flat. She spat after he had walked a dozen metres away, and turned to re-enter the hall.

Siera had herself almost exited the Ombudsman's hall, Tomasso beside her, and nearly walked into Gretchen.

"I– oh, Lieutenant. Er…" Siera stared at Gretchen, momentarily nonplussed.

Gretchen made a nervous smile, her mouth twitching. "If you have a moment to speak privately, Sir…"

Siera nodded slowly. "Very well… Tomasso, be so good as to make sure no one disturbs us."

Siera and Gretchen walked back a few metres inside the hall. As Gretchen turned to speak, Siera interrupted her.

"I know."

Gretchen scowled. "But–"

"Who do you think the troops will believe in the long run? Their commanding officer and a member of the royal family, or the words of a dead Archipelagan pirate?"

Gretchen bit her lip, glaring at the floor. "Next they'll be talking about me and Quintus, it'll never end."

Siera shrugged. "The more you and Quintus, the better."

Gretchen's head snapped up. "Eh? What?"

Siera nodded as she thumbed her chin. "No one will dare go against a whitecap. Even rumour and backbiting talk will be done more warily."

Gretchen clenched her teeth, then relaxed and closed her eyes. "Why can it never be simple? Just once."

Siera raised a brow at Gretchen. "The campaign has, overall, been simple. But I see your meaning, of course. However, see it this way: here you are, running about with your father's blade, and eyes, and hair. And it's taken all this time for any rumour to get going, and even then this one will be easily dispelled."

Gretchen sucked at her teeth as she mulled the thought over, staring at her feet again.

"And by God is that blade as bloodthirsty as ever," Siera muttered.

"Hmm? Blade?" said Gretchen, looking up.

Siera met Gretchen's gaze. "Honestly? I'm starting to think the sword is cursed, and as villainous as its former owner."

Gretchen blinked, taken aback. "It's... It's just a sword. I'll pass it along to my children, eventually. Been in the family for four generations."

"Either way, rumours will circulate then die down. Glare at anyone who suggests that you are Heinrich Ailbhe's daughter. Once the campaign is done, you'll have a nice fat ribbon to display, and any insinuations of disloyalty will look like the farce they are."

Gretchen nodded. "I'd told my troops that Luitger called me sister only because we're both from the Archland, so there's that too. Hmm. No, you're right, Major."

Gretchen saluted, then turned and left.

After she had left, Siera sighed.

"Four generations of Mac Niadh's, you mean. Hmph."

Chapter 23: To the Last

4th Chem

"Major, Commodore Terciero wants you on the bridge," said Tomasso.

Siera raised her brows. "Oh? Let us go and pay him a visit, then."

Siera and Tomasso made their way to the bridge.

"You requested my presence, Commodore?" said Siera as she stepped into the room.

Terciero threw a quick salute. "Yes, yes. It seems our arrival is not unanticipated. Here, look." Terciero offered Siera his eyeglass.

"What am I looking for?" said Siera as she extended it and put it to her eye.

"To the right of the keep, there."

Siera adjusted the eyeglass. "Where?"

"If you see the keep, then to the right and up in the air, just above that big – that big building with the large slate tiles."

"I – there… that is a skyship… not moving… do the rebels have a skyship?" said Siera.

Terciero made a moue of distaste. "It seems so. I wouldn't bet that they're friendly," said Terciero, popping the last piece of a strawberry tart into his mouth.

Siera adjusted the eyeglass as much as she could. "It seems they have more than a few people milling around on deck… I wonder… Tomasso, find Lieutenants Ailbhe, Gartzia, and du Gallo."

"Yes sir," said Tomasso, dashing away down stairs into the ship.

Siera stared off at the skyship hovering over San Seras.

"Knew it would come to this, just not so soon," she muttered.

Mere moments later, Siera was joined by her lieutenants.

"I was just making sure everyone had their bucklers, Sir," said Gretchen.

"Mine are ready as well, Sir. We're not there yet, are we?" said Ermanno.

Siera shook her head. "An unexpected turn of events." Siera offered the eyeglass to Ermanno. "It seems that they have a skyship."

"The rebels? How?" said Gretchen.

Ermanno scowled as he raised the eyeglass to take a look. "You need a solid crew for a skyship, how have the rebels acquired one?"

"San Seras has a ... history of disloyalty. It might be locals," said Siera.

"Oh, I remember that riot all too well," muttered Ermanno. "Fucking Archie sympathisers too, the lot of them."

Gretchen smirked. "And everyone knows, no blondie deserves sympathy."

"You know what I mean," said Ermanno as he passed the eyeglass to Gretchen.

"Well, we can't drop in at this rate," said Adalberto, watching as Gretchen peered through the eyeglass. "What's the plan, Major?"

Siera pursed her lips. "It is ship to ship, no doubt about it. Adalberto, I will need your Battalion on deck, forecastle and aftcastle both. We cannot truly draw alongside one another and attempt a boarding or the port and starboard yard-masts would be torn off and the ships badly damaged. Still, if they draw close enough, they might have some way to attempt a boarding."

"What, like naval combat? Firing at each other with bows? Major, that is..." said Adalberto.

Siera raised her brows. "What? There really is no other way to be rid of the rebel skyship. And there is little doubt that they mean to stand against us, otherwise they would be moving away from the city, or circling it. After all, there really is not a manual on skyship to skyship combat, unless we get to writing one right now. Have your Battalion on deck as quickly as you can."

"Yes... yes, Sir," said Adalberto, who saluted before

moving off to gather his troops.

"Major, a message," said Terciero.

"Oh?"

"From the crew of the *Cloud Chaser*. They say that while they yet stand, San Seras will not have you ah… dropping on top of them."

Siera scowled. "Reply to them that the wages of treason are death."

Terciero nodded, then after a moment replied. "They say that they stand true to the old duchy of San Seras, and recognise no Reimaran authority. They also said a variety of rude things about your father. I… won't bother repeating them."

Siera's eyes narrowed. "We will see how prettily they sing at the end of a rope. Commodore! Take us in. Would that we had that battle speed still, but we will do without."

"Over the city? They might use ballistae on us," said Ermanno.

Siera sucked at her teeth. "Try to get us just in range so the Second Battalion can attack, but stay away and above likely ballistae bolts. We can let loose with ours lower, and have the advantage. Not that they likely have any ballistae on the skyship."

Terciero nodded. "Don't worry about ballistae as much, even if they have them, I'm sure they can't tilt upwards enough to hit us. Never mind any in the city, they will also risk hitting the *Chaser*. It's their archers that will prove a nuisance."

Siera felt a sudden chill rest in her gut. "Terciero, what if they have greatbows?"

Terciero squinted. "I doubt they do, the process of making one is difficult. And I haven't heard anything about some being stolen from us. And even if they have the bows, the arrows are hard to make as well."

Siera nodded slowly. "I doubt they have any… alas that we ourselves are low on the arrows, otherwise we could decimate them. Still, the Second Regiment had some… well, nothing to be done about that." Siera stroked her chin with her thumb. "Commodore, if one were to focus on a skyship with a greatbow to disrupt its flight, where would be the best spot to strike?"

Terciero winced. "I don't even want to think about it... but, well, the enchantments are primarily focused on the obsidian slates, but those are inside the ship. Outside... the long silver lines that you see along the hull, for focusing. Hit those and the ship won't fly so well, might even start dropping."

Siera nodded. "Tomasso, relay this to Lieutenant du Gallo."

Tomasso saluted, and left.

"Eneko or Pepita, get me another pastry from the galley, would you?"

Eneko frowned. "Last time the cooks said they were out of strawberries, remember?"

"Dog peppers," muttered Terciero.

"Why not just have another kind?" said Siera.

"Eh, strawberry is the best. They're so wonderfully sweet. I can't have enough of them."

"Is that so," said Siera, her tone frigid.

Tomasso returned from the deck. "Lieutenant du Gallo says he'll keep that in mind, if things get dangerous."

"Good," said Siera. "Hopefully we can conserve our greatarrows for San Seras."

Slowly, the gravity-defying bulks of the *Sky's Wrath* and the *Cloud Chaser* squared up. The *Wrath* was built for combat, both forecastle and aftcastle prominent in its design. The *Chaser*, by comparison, was a fat merchant trader, wide and deep in the hull but flat on deck. In manoeuvability, the *Wrath* only slightly beat out the *Chaser*, but the latter offered scant protection on deck against arrows.

"If I'd wanted to fight like a sailor I'd have joined the Navy," muttered Adalberto to Cecilia Perez, as he peered over the crenellations on the forecastle.

Cecilia smirked. "At least we're built for it." she replied. "Those poor sons of bitches on the *Chaser* don't have a prayer."

"Brave, yet foolish... unless they know something we don't," said Adalberto. "Well, either way, we're drawing up close. Nock arrows, and loose a volley on my signal."

The ships drew closer. Adalberto could see a variety of different colours and outfits in the distance. "Looks like a militia of some kind, not even a proper army. I'll be amazed if they can even co-ordinate a volley."

Adalberto raised his own longbow. "Aftcastle will loose on their deck as we do, raise bows!"

"Raise bows!' repeated Cecilia.

"Bows up, arrows ready!" said Cristóbal du Alescio, the other sergeants echoing him.

"Loose!" barked Adalberto as he loosed his own shot.

The Reimarans loosed their volley as those on the *Chaser* did the same, and for a brief moment two flights of arrows arched into each other, making a dark cloud between the ships.

Then the arrows fell, and the screams began.

Without cover, those on the *Chaser* were pelted with arrows relentlessly. Dozens cried out in pain or died gurgling as the Reimaran volley laid into them. But the *Wrath* didn't offer perfect protection itself, and Adalberto winced as some of his own troops were hit by enemy arrows. He could practically feel an arrow shaft striking his own body...

Adalberto shook his head. "N– nock arrows again! Ready! Loose!" called out Adalberto too quickly. Only two thirds of his troops were ready, and the next volley was less effective.

For all that they were taking harsher losses, the fighters on the *Chaser* retained discipline enough to keep firing in strong volleys. Both sides kept taking losses as the shafts flew.

Adalberto forced himself to breathe deeply, and calm down.

"Nock arrows again, stand ready! Take aim... loose!" he called as he loosed his own shot, an orderly volley from the *Wrath* matching him this time.

Adalberto cried out as an ear-deafening crack seemed to come from all around them; something had hit the *Wrath* and caused the entire ship to shudder. Adalberto dropped his bow as he flailed, trying to keep upright.

"What was that?! What in the name of god – that was a greatarrow! They have a greatbow, how? Fiery fucking Sura, up, up all of you! Nock arrows again, give them another volley! Pick up your bows, up, nock arrows!"

But the damage had been done. The *Chaser* already had another volley coming down before Adalberto could call for his troops to do the same.

Arrows fell all around him as he loosed his own shot, before realising that few of his own troops had been ready to do the same.

Adalberto shivered. "Dammit, we'll have to use greatbows on them, we can't risk anoth–"

Adalberto toppled to the floor as the ship shuddered again, taking another greatarrow hit.

"Good god – Cecilia, give me my greatbow, I'll – I'll–"

Adalberto turned to his side to see Cecilia staring off into the sky. For a moment, Adalberto thought he'd somehow looked at her at just the right moment to see an arrow fly past her.

That's odd, he thought. *Everything seems so still. It's strange. I'll tell her after this, about how it just seemed to happen at just the right moment.*

Adalberto slowly realised that the arrow had struck her in the eye. Ever so slowly, she fell forward, almost drifting, and Adalberto fumbled with numb hands to catch her as she fell. A doctor, he thought to himself. She has to get to a doctor, or… or…

Adalberto realised he was sitting on the forecastle, Cecilia in his arms. He looked down and it hit him all at once, everything. There was no doctor on this earth who could save her now.

Cecilia was dead.

Adalberto shuddered as his tears began to fall, while all around him his troops simply let loose at will, making largely useless shots, and the *Chaser* continued to rain down arrows on the *Wrath* in close, accurate volleys.

Any moment now, Adalberto thought to himself, another greatarrow will fly right into us.

Adalberto looked down into his dead lover's face, and something in him broke.

He clenched his teeth as he felt a wild hate grow within him, something maddened and blind. His arms flailed at his side, finding his greatbow where Cecilia had dropped it, and the quiver that held just four enchanted arrows.

Adalberto bared his teeth as he heard Cristóbal yelling at him about a timed volley.

"Just fucking loose! Just kill them! Every single one of those whoreborn trash!" he screamed.

Adalberto stood on the *Wrath's* forecastle and drew a greatarrow. He could see the fighters on the *Chaser* preparing for another volley.

He felt no fear as he took quick aim, and loosed.

The greatarrow bolted forward, lifting quickly into the air, and flew fast and sure right into a cluster of those silver lines that Terciero has said helped the ship stay aloft.

Before it hit, Adalberto already had another greatarrow nocked.

The first arrow hit, and the *Chaser* shuddered. The second arrow that Adalberto loosed struck close to the main deck, blowing a wide hole in the side and sending the rebels on deck flying. Adalberto grinned widely as he saw some of them tossed over the sides of the ship, limbs flailing uselessly against the pull of the earth far below them.

His third arrow slammed into the hull at another cluster of silver markings. Adalberto felt a wild joy spring inside him as he saw that the *Chaser* was listing, and slowly losing height.

He grinned as he nocked his last arrow, aimed it at the central mast, and let loose.

It streaked in, fast and smooth, striking the mast halfway up. The section he hit seemed to just disintegrate in a spray of splinters and dust, the rigging snapping taut or ripping clean away as the mast toppled over onto the ship, crushing anyone it impacted, even as the *Chaser* began to fall faster towards the earth.

Ever more quickly, the *Cloud Chaser* fell away from the sky, its broad hull closing with San Seras.

On the *Wrath*'s bridge, chaos took root.

"That last hit took out too much of our hull focus!"

"Commodore, we're listing... I–I can't right it!"

"We're losing air here. We're falling!" cried Terciero.

"Can you not arrest our fall?" said Siera, trying not to panic, as the deck seemed to slowly shift beneath her, slipping this way and that.

The ship lurched anew, and Siera almost fell.

"No, you can't compensate by stressing the other enchantments! Dammit–" said Terciero, grabbing at some instrument that one of his subordinates was frantically trying to use.

Tomasso sat near the stairs down into the ship, where he'd fallen when the *Wrath* was first hit. Siera noted that he seemed loath to get up again.

"Godammit, what is Adalberto doing up there?" muttered Siera.

Quintus sprinted up the stairs and onto the bridge. "Sir, ship's swaying all over the place!"

Clara wasn't far behind. "Are we falling?!"

"I – yes, seems so," said Siera. "We can... well, I could ah..." Siera looked around her, as Terciero and his assistants scrabbled at a variety of implements and tools, apparently trying to right the ship.

Siera realised that it was Tomasso who had the right of it, not her. There was nothing she could do.

Siera stared at Quintus and Clara, as Gretchen raced up the stairs to the bridge, asking for orders.

"There's nothing," said Siera.

Gretchen stared at her.

"There's nothing at all, is there."

"The fucking thundering cunt of Sura there isn't! The fucking thundering cunt!" roared Terciero suddenly, as he reached out for that obsidian-tipped staff Siera had seen him using on the deck at Southmere.

"Igon get your fat fucking arse down to those midship plates and work from there! Focus or you won't be seeing that sweetheart of yours again! Eneko, stop fiddling with that amplifier, focus what's left on the hull! Even if it's damaged, it's all on the hull!" Terciero shouted.

Terciero didn't stop to see if his subordinates had heard him. He closed his eyes, holding the staff in both hands, and focused.

Sorcery is a patient art. As with all four of the great magical arts, either you were born with the talent or you weren't – but even being born with the talent isn't nearly enough for sorcerers. Sorcery offers nothing to the easily distracted, or the daydreamer. It demands constant focus and diligence, never letting a single stray thought interrupt one's attention on manipulating the elements.

And Terciero had distinguished himself even among his talented peers with a considerable single-mindedness in pursuit of magical control.

Sorcery also demands some of the element you are trying to work with. Terciero, however, had a whole skyful of air.

And he intended to use it.

It was two hundred metres below and closing that he focused his mind, at the limits of his ability to work at range. Skyship sorcerers were almost always skilled at using magic at a distance for this very reason. Terciero folded and heated, building an updraft as the *Wrath* began to fall faster and faster. Distantly, he could feel his assistants struggling to focus and buoy the *Wrath* in the air, all too many enchantments on the ship having dispersed and unwound after the materials that they flowed along had been destroyed or damaged.

Terciero felt nothing as the *Wrath* fell, closer and closer to the earth, as he still slowly built an updraft to cushion the ship at the last moment. All around him the low howl of air currents resisted him, wanting to rush out during any slip in his control. He bent the very winds to his control and he bent them well, every current in its place as he himself distantly felt the ever-faster falling, the quickening of the ship's descent. He could hear someone screaming, but he paid no mind.

His work was all.

The air fought him, resisting his attempts to condense it and shape it, heat it and pressure it, one hundred and sixty metres and closing as the *Wrath* dropped like a stone towards the earth, one hundred thirty and closer – a thickening haze of hot roiling air coming together at last – eighty metres and closer – still Terciero pushed on, condensing and funnelling, every last trick he had bent to this one solitary task, focusing and shaping – forty metres and the ship nigh sprinted towards the earth – and as the *Wrath* was set to crash into the ground, breaking, splintering and shattering apart with the certain violent death of all on board, Commodore Terciero du Valtiera stood as stern and proud as any of his distant royal ancestors, bending the air itself into a tight updraft funnel. That funnel suddenly unleashed and blew upwards around the skyship, roaring past it and buffeting the falling vessel, rapidly slowing it mere metres from the ground.

And for that brief second, the ship hung dead still in the air, seeming to defy gravity entirely.

With that effort expended, the ship fell those last few metres.

Soldiers and sailors alike were thrown about in the sudden impact, bodies living and dead tossed about like dolls and toys at the mercy of a wrathful child. The ship groaned as the keel took the brunt of the weight and simply shattered, even its magically reinforced length unable to withstand the sudden impact. All too many unfortunate souls fell to snapped necks or fatal head injuries as they were tossed to the floor and up against pillars and posts. Thanks to Terciero's last-ditch efforts, most managed to escape with only relatively minor injuries, though still scores more broke legs and arms in the shrieking crash.

If Terciero could have seen the *Sky's Wrath* slam into the earth, he would have wept. There was no other word to describe that action than death, the keel shattered asunder, the hull cracked and warped.
   Even though all those lives were saved, the *Wrath* was dead.

But most callous of all was Terciero's fate. He alone on the bridge did not reach out to support himself as the ship crashed, he alone on the bridge had nothing to brace himself against. And when the ship hit the ground, he slammed towards the floor and into the table in front of him at the same time, into that same table that held so many important instruments that he and his subordinates relied on to direct the ship, and smashed his throat and neck into pulp.

After the impact, the *Wrath* lay stricken on the torn earth outside San Seras, with only the cries of the injured carrying across the wind.

Chapter 24: To Toe the Brink of Ruin

4th Chem

Gretchen felt as though God had simply slammed her into the floor when the crash came. The entire ship seemed to groan and then crack as it came down, the sound of ripping wood booming all around her.

For a brief moment, Gretchen simply lay there, breathless and shaking, at the base of the stairs leading up to the *Wrath*'s bridge. A half-remembered sermon sprang to mind – a cantor speaking harshly of the certain suffering awaiting all those who defied Sura's holy words – and she realised that of all her life, now was the time that she felt the very fear of God that the cantor had spoken of: the sure and certain knowledge that you could be swatted like nothing more than a mere insect.

Slowly she tried to stand on the slanted floor – of course, the ship wouldn't land flat without a proper mooring – Gretchen muttered a prayer for her very life, even as she winced at the pain that shot all through her body.

"Who... who was injured, who else is okay? Report!" she called out.

Silence met her voice. Gretchen slowly made her way past her troops, trying to rouse any she could.

"Do... Domenico, that you?"

"I... ugh, I don't know who else survived, Lieutenant," replied Domenico Arnoni.

Gretchen shuddered. "Just... find whoever you can. Don't forget where we are – right outside San Seras. Sura... I'll bet every teal in the treasury that the rebels will be on us as soon as they can. Sura forgive us, Siera..."

Gretchen stumbled up the stairs to the bridge, coughing as she called out her commander's name.

Getting up to the bridge made her realise how little hope

she had left in her after the crash, because it fled.

Terciero had fallen into the table in front of him, his head bent back at an unnatural angle. Three of Terciero's sorcerers lay on the floor, one moving weakly, the other two having died despite trying to brace themselves before the ship fell; they had shared similar fates to their commodore.

Towards the rear of the bridge were two figures, Siera and Quintus. The whitecap had tried to shield Siera with his own body, but her head was leaning oddly against the cabin wall, and although Quintus was blinking and struggling to stand, Siera was not moving at all.

Slowly, chaos gave way to order as soldiers gathered and tried their best to recover. Gretchen moved through the ruined ship, doling out orders as she went. Although they outranked her, Quintus and Clara had never held command. And now, above all times, they wanted someone who knew what they were doing. Siera seemed to be alive, although a beating heart didn't guarantee that her mind would function after the impact.

Gretchen did her best not to think of what would happen if Siera simply never woke up.

Gretchen ordered the Major to be left on her bed in her cabin, with Tomasso to watch over her and report if she awoke.

And for everyone else, Gretchen slowly got soldiers and supplies off the ship and assembled onto the ground as best she could.

Ropes were hastily arranged to get those on board over the side of the ruined skyship. Gretchen rappelled the short distance over the side of the ship, and got a close-up view of the few troops that had so far got off the *Wrath* in one piece.

A mere hundred soldiers, from various Battalions – mostly the First and Third – were before her.

"Sir!" called out a nearby sergeant, who ran up to her.

"Uh... Pacifica, is it?" said Gretchen, recognising her as one of Ermanno's sergeants.

"Yes sir, Sergeant Pacifica Sastre. We caught sight of

movement from San Seras' gates, some mercenaries have marched out and are coming at us, and I can't find Sergeant du Cipriani."

"Never mind him, where is Lieutenant Gartzia?"

Pacifica swallowed hard. "He... he was shoving soldiers along into the sleeping quarters, telling them to hold on to whatever they could. He came to help me, but I tripped, and he pulled me on top of him. It was then that the ship crashed... he's dead, sir."

Gretchen winced, then reached out to squeeze Pacifica's shoulders. "He died as the noble man he was in life. Don't think about it now."

Pacifica's eyes widened. "Is... is the Major alright?"

Gretchen pulled away, and did not meet Pacifica's gaze.

"She's fine, just unconscious after the crash. When she wakes up, she'll have all this sorted out, you can be sure."

Pacifica nodded. "Of course. Sir, any orders?"

Gretchen stared ahead of her, a slow realisation coming over her. She was tempted to laugh at the bitter irony. For all she knew, her commanding officer might never get up, and at least one of her fellow officers was dead. She had long desired the high office of commanding a regiment, and she might have planned and desired it without end, but not like this.

Nothing like this.

Gretchen swallowed. "Right. Right... form up the troops who have made it up so far, and quickly now. To each their squad, or what's left of it. We need a formation to meet those mercenaries, First Battalion in front with... with pikes, if we can find enough. Second Battalion behind them, uh... loose arrows, or how you normally do it."

"Normally I think Lieutenant du Gallo gives the volley orders."

Gretchen swallowed. "Well, have Cecilia do it."

"Haven't seen her."

"Then the first sergeant you see from the Second Battalion gets to do it! Just go!" yelled Gretchen suddenly, taking a perverse pleasure in seeing Pacifica recoil slightly.

Pacifica saluted hastily and half-ran to find a sergeant from the Second Battalion.

Gretchen closed her eyes and massaged her temples, heartily wishing that Siera were here.

"Tired?" came Quintus' soft voice from behind her.

Gretchen turned to him. "If Siera's dead..." she said in a whisper.

Quintus's face was impassive. "If we don't win through we'll all be dead for sure, that you can take home and eat. What's the plan?"

Gretchen looked up, trying to think of how she could get any advantage for the Guard. Off in the distance, at steady pace, the Red Hart mercenary company formed up. Gretchen knew them by reputation as somewhat reliable mercenaries that held a good front line and knew well how to put their pikes to work, and grimaced as she saw that they had formed up and commenced their march – formation tight, polearms at the ready.

"Lieutenant Ailbhe, any order?" called Clara as she walked towards Gretchen.

"I... just a moment. There's got to be some way..."

"We toe the brink of ruin, here. We don't have many more moments," said Clara, her expression flat.

"Surprising, I hadn't realised," muttered Gretchen. "Just – just help anyone you can off the skyship... the soldiers will see a whitecap and think things better in hand than they are. And when the mercenaries get here, try and scout around the ship. They might try to get through a hole in the hull."

Clara stared at Gretchen. But Quintus saluted her, and Clara followed suit.

Gretchen looked at the bedraggled and bruised soldiers before her. More soldiers had emerged largely uninjured from the wreck, bringing the fighting force of the Fourth Regiment to a grand one hundred and fifty.

There were easily four times their number heading towards them.

Gretchen looked before her and saw despair, fear in every eye. She raised her voice to carry to every ear.

"Enough muttering. Close your mouths and open your ears."

Gretchen wasn't sure if some soldiers were staring or

glaring. She fought the urge to shake her head.

"By now you must have heard, Major du Tealdan cannot be roused. Lieutenants du Gallo and Gartzia are missing. As such, it falls to me to take command of what remains of the Fourth."

Gretchen took a deep breath.

"I don't care what you've heard and I don't care what you think. I'm your commanding officer, and if you don't like it, you can be hanged as a deserter. Your choice. I won't fight with a coward. Because I'll damn well tell you now, I will fight. It falls to all of us to fight, this hour over any other. I won't tell you pretty lies about glory and valour – marching on us is four times our number, and they didn't just fall out of the goddamn sky. But I tell you this: there will never be another hour like this hour."

"On that ship is your commanding officer, your wounded comrades. If the mercenaries win through, they'll loot it all and cut the throats of anyone who doesn't run. If the mercenaries win through it's all over, there's no one else to retake San Seras and finish the rebels off. If they win through, all of Reimar will suffer the price of our failure."

Gretchen saw a lot of uneasy looks shared between the soldiers before her.

"Maybe you're thinking, if you run, you can live. I tell you now, there's no life if you run. There's no life going back to your families in shame and confessing that when things turned bad, you ran like a mongrel, limping home like a dray-horse. The major has handed us some easy victories, and she's kept us well and done her best. Now things have gone to shit, and now the time has come to return the favour. When you joined the Guard you swore to defend Reimar no matter the cost."

Gretchen drew her sword.

"If there's a single one who wants to flee, then go. Get out of my sight. If I ever see you again, I'll kill you where you stand. Choose, right now."

No one moved. Whether through fear or respect, Gretchen could not tell.

Gretchen nodded. "Good. Now ready your pikes and your nerves, because today we die. But we do not die for nothing, we die for Reimar! We die for the Major! And I'll make damn sure that we die surrounded by a mound of filthy sell-sword corpses! Now, form up!"

When Gretchen looked anew at the soldiers before her, she saw steel in their eyes.

Gretchen quickly gathered the sergeants on the field.

"Here's what we're going to do." Gretchen quickly looked around, noting how the *Wrath* had fallen. She pointed off towards the cluster of mercenaries off in the distance. "They're going to fall on us like a pack of hungry dogs, even as everyone is trying to get out of the wreckage, or tend to the wounded. I want the First Battalion arranged in a triple line between the mercenaries and the deck of the wrath – don't worry as much about the hull, they can't get in as easily from that side. The Second Battalion will cover the First, and the Third will be up on the forecastle."

Mario Corvi's brows furrowed. "Eh? How come, Lieutenant?"

Gretchen glared at him. "That doesn't sound like 'Yes sir' to me!"

"Y– yes sir."

Gretchen paused, then sighed. "Third's up on the forecastle, ready to drop down as the mercenaries march into the first, keeping a double line. It's not much, but it's better than nothing."

Mario stared at Gretchen, then grinned. "Every time is ambush time with you, Lieutenant."

"Damn right. Sell-swords will never know what hit them. No easy meals on this battlefield, we'll teach them that. They can eat steel and die like beggars."

Gretchen felt none of the confidence she projected. To herself, she repeated a short prayer that Siera would recover any moment now.

Tomasso slowly peeked out around the doorway, looking down the corridor. Catching sight of movement, he quickly ducked back into the room.

Glancing over to Siera, he saw that she had not stirred at all, still looking for all the world as though she was sleeping peacefully on her bed.

"Hey, this looks like an officer's room!" called out an unknown voice.

"Good, grab anything valuable, and be quick!" came a reply.

Tomasso realised he was shaking as he slowly closed the door to Siera's room. No soldiers from the Fourth would be looting the ship; it had to be mercenaries.

Which meant that the fighting outside might have been lost.

Tomasso grimaced as the thought hit him, that everyone might have already been killed. He might well be the last of the whole regiment, standing here, surrounded by mercenaries looting a derelict skyship.

He wondered if they'd take the regimental standard as a trophy.

He wondered why he didn't care.

If everyone else was dead, the lieutenants as well, then what could he do?

He contemplated surrender. If he could talk his way out...

He looked over to Siera again. If the mercenaries got hold of her, they might kill her, but would probably ransom her. Still, there was no telling what the rebels would do when the moment came. Siera had cost them control of three cities, and sealed their rebellion's fate, even if it hadn't been doomed from the start. And Siera had executed every traitor so far... they might do the same to her, to send a message...

Tomasso tried not think what would happen if they did ransom her instead, and forced King Ramiros to grant San Seras its independence. People would hate Tomasso, and his parents... what would they think? They'd have to leave Reimar anyway, and do so knowing their son had pleaded for his life at the last, like a coward.

No.

He tightened his grip on his arming sword. Even if it meant his death here, he had to do what he could.

And abruptly, Tomasso both saw Siera twitch as she began to stir, and behind him hear the door handle click as it opened.

273

Tomasso turned and drew his blade, facing two surprised mercenaries with short swords.

"Hoi! There's one in here!" one of them cried out.

"Get back, dog!" shouted Tomasso, even as his hands shook.

The other mercenary was quicker on the uptake.

"Where're your friends, Remmy? All alone, are we? Hey, who's having a nap back there?"

"N–none of your concern!" said Tomasso.

"Heh, your hands are shaking, boy. Have you ever killed a man? Think you can take me?"

Tomasso heard more boots down the corridor outside. The two mercenaries in the door advanced into the room.

"Come on now, nice and quiet. Put that sword down and you can relax in a dungeon. Doesn't that sound better? Don't throw your life aw–"

"Get back!" said Tomasso as he swung out with his arming sword, aiming at the one to his right. That mercenary ducked back smoothly, as his companion didn't miss a beat and retaliated up and out with his shortsword, catching Tomasso along his torso.

"Ugh–"

"Come on then, boy! Do you want to die? Put that thing down before you cut yourself."

Tomasso shuddered as he tried not to think about the searing pain along his side, trying to keep his hands firm on his blade. His thoughts flickered between wanting to surrender and wishing he at least had a shield.

Suddenly, they both came at him, one from each side. No more time for errant thoughts, as Tomasso tried to duck sideways into the mercenary to his right and at least stab at them, but they were too fast for him, and then–

And then he was falling, hands numb, everything numb. Tomasso winced as his head smacked against the floor, and he struggled to get up, but for some reason he couldn't.

He gasped and shuddered as a sudden pain rocked through him, sharp and harsh.

The last thing that Tomasso Rossi ever saw was the mercenaries that had killed him turning to his commanding officer, looming over her, voices rough.

And then, only darkness.

If only he had lived a moment longer, he would have heard the screams.

Tearing down the corridor they came, ripping through the mercenaries in their way; Clara first, followed on her heels by Quintus. Scarcely did any of the mercenaries have a moment to realise someone was coming up behind them before they died, gurgling their last. Clara had cut down one and span to slash at another before the other dozen mercenary looters started to turn around. She quickly focused on the light coming from behind her through a broken window and blinded the mercenary in front of her, only to have Quintus barrel past her and kick the momentarily blinded mercenary out of his way, and cut down his friends.

"Move!" cried out one mercenary at the back as he managed to bring a crossbow to bear.

"Quintus!" bellowed Clara.

Quintus was flicking a single knife down the corridor even as Clara spoke, mercenaries trying to press themselves against the walls to get out of the way of the crossbow, inadvertently making way for Quintus's knife as well.

Quintus didn't wait to see if his throw had met its mark, immediately laying into the other mercenaries.

They didn't leave a single one alive.

Quintus and Clara burst into Siera's room, only to find Tomasso slumped on the floor, and Siera trying to sit up from her bed.

"What hap– ugh, what's–" said Siera, slowly sitting up.

"Your Highness!" said Clara as she ran over to her. Quintus turned around and checked the corridor again to see if any more mercenaries would try their luck.

"Your Highness, are you alright?" asked Clara.

Siera struggled to focus on her bodyguard. "I'm here, I'm here, I... what happened? Are we – where are we? Oh god, did the skyship–"

Siera suddenly sat up straight, and turned her head to Clara.

"Am I dead?" she said.

Clara blinked. "No... no, the ship crashed, but I think the Commodore was able to soften our landing somehow... almost everyone was alright."

Siera rubbed her palms against her eyes. "How is the ship?"

Clara sighed. "Wrecked."

Siera looked down. "I heard yelling," she said as she slowly stood up from her bed.

"Is–" Siera stopped as she saw Tomasso slumped on the floor. "Tomasso! Clara, quickly–"

Clara's face was blank. "Highness, he's dead," she said, as Siera tried to turn Tomasso over and rouse him.

"I – but... how?" she said as she looked up.

"When we crashed you were knocked unconscious. Rebels have sent their mercenaries out to attack while we're weak. The Fourth's been pushed back, and some mercenaries wanted to loot the ship. We had left Tomasso here to guard you and report if you woke up... so he was the only one here when the looters got in."

Siera bit her lip, and nodded. "I... I will see him buried with honour..."

"Sir, we should leave," said Clara, gently touching Siera's shoulder.

"Yes... yes, of course," Siera said as she stood. "How fares the battle?"

"The mercenaries have greater numbers and many of us are injured, but even being pushed back we still hold the line."

Siera winced as she started to walk. "Ugh, it's like every bone I have has been shaken around... how are my lieutenants?"

"Alive, last I knew," said Clara.

"I'll go on just ahead, Your Highness," said Quintus.

Carefully, they made their way out.

Despite sometimes seeing double and having sudden, excruciating spasms down her spine, Siera made her way out of the ship and into a pitched battle. The Fourth's soldiers had been pushed back and were half-wedged back against the aftcastle, which had partly come loose from the hull and was flat against the ground. Taking stock of the situation from amidst the second's archers, she realised that planning and tactics meant nothing, it was kill or be killed in bloody melee.

"You're no use by me, help out the First Battalion if you can!" Siera shouted at her bodyguards over the din of the melee. Reluctantly, they obeyed her.

Slowly the word made its way through the Reimaran soldiers: Siera was alive, up and about. Slowly, the rapidly fading morale of the Fourth Regiment came surging back.

If Siera lived, they could win. If there was one thing the Fourth's soldiers had come to believe in, it was the luck of their commander.

The turn of the tide never hinges on one sword stroke or pike thrust, not on a single bow or breastplate. Not even on Gretchen's largely successful close-range flanking by the Third Battalion's soldiers coming down from the forecastle. Always, the chance to turn things around and push back lay in the courage of every soldier of the Fourth. For Reimar, for their commander, for their families – for all of these things they fought, and for all of these things they fought harder and harder. As their numbers were whittled and their advantage was lost, the mercenaries slowly became more stagnated, pushing more and more weakly against the Reimaran lines as they tired.

And even though the tide doesn't turn on any one sword, it was Quintus that first took the chance offered.

Seeing that the men in the enemy front line were pressing less aggressively, Quintus took the chance to snatch up a fallen pike from a soldier near him and simply charge at the mercenaries. He screamed out a wordless cry and leapt forward, burying the pike in a hapless footman before him, and all around him his comrades realised that this was their hour indeed: that even if they toed the very brink of ruin, that so long as they fought, they might yet snatch a victory.

The Fourth Regiment began to push back, even though they had been pushed down to a mere hundred soldiers at the crush of things, with a few more clambering off the ruined skyship and into the thick of it, they began to push.

The Red Harts were slow to realise that they were being driven back, and slower to respond. Those at the front fell, and the ones behind them who had been expecting an easy battle now faced the desperate soldiers of the Fourth Regiment, along with Quintus and Clara – and the mercenaries knew full well what those white berets meant. Between Quintus' ducking and lunging as though he was fencing with a pike, and Clara using her quick spells to throw dirt in mercenary's eyes or trip them up, the whitecaps were worth more than five times their number each. And slowly yet surely, Reimaran momentum began to build. The more Red Harts that fell put an even great dampener on their morale, while lending a desperate hope to the Reimarans, who had nowhere to run to and nothing to lose. Even as soldiers died screaming and gurgling, pike-tips buried in their stomachs and faces cut apart, even as the melee churned all around them and the front lines were nothing but mud and gore, the Royal Guard fought like wolves who knew that they would never see a new day unless they gave everything they had.

None can say when the Red Hart's line at last broke, when they realised that they fought only madmen and devils instead of soldiers. But break it did, and as the first few mercenaries turned and cried out, trying to flee the front lines, the more of their fellows followed suit. And even as they began to flee in greater and greater numbers, behind them the Reimarans did not relent, coming ever onwards with blood-slicked pikes and feral yells.

It was in this way and at this hour that a Reimaran victory was torn bodily out of the iron jaws of defeat, with no heed to cost and pain, against four times their number and after barely surviving a crashing skyship; a victory scarcely rivalled in all Iberan history for its sheer desperation.

But for all that, a victory no less total.

Chapter 25: Under Her Gavel

4ᵗʰ Chem, afternoon

With Ermanno and a few sergeants dead, Siera was able to rally and form up her surviving soldiers more slowly than usual. Nonetheless, after salvaging what they could, they marched on San Seras.

The city gates, of course, had been barred. However, no one appeared to be manning the gate, so a hastily-made grapple was enough to get one volunteer from the Third Battalion over the wall and into the gatehouse.

Once the portcullis was raised, Siera found a city in shambles. The rebellion had gained a certain popularity in San Seras that it hadn't managed to maintain elsewhere, and Siera felt more of a conqueror than a liberator, with closed shutters all around her in every street that she marched her soldiers down.

Citizens cowered inside their homes, having been convinced by the rebels that once Siera took the city, everyone who had supported the rebellion would be hanged en masse. Merchants who had voiced support for the rebellion had fled, taking what goods and funds they had left with them, most of the mercenaries had been a step ahead of them, and the harbour was as bare as it had ever been.

Without support, the Navy had faced a hard battle to push the assortment of stolen Navy ships and Archipelagan pirates out of San Seras. Few ships that fled San Seras in the aftermath of the battle had been stopped.

Minor looting had begun to take hold as the city constables had holed up at the keep, sure that they would be the last holdouts of the city. With no one to enforce order, San Seras was sliding to chaos even as Siera arrived – some last few greedy pirates looting freely, some opportunistic citizens joining them, and even some mercenaries – mostly their officers, of course – seeking to pillage and then flee.

Alas for them, that their optimism was so great.

The looters that Siera caught, whether citizen, pirate, or mercenary, she had executed on the spot.

There was no talk of trials.

Siera fully expected to arrive at San Seras' keep and find it ready to hold out to the last, but as she turned into the main boulevard that led to the keep's inland entrance she was surprised to see the portcullis up and a dozen or so people waiting at the gate.

The regiment advanced, leery of an ambush, but none came. As Siera approached, she vaguely recognised Enio du Donati at the front, the other behind him being various constables.

He called out to Siera, shouting over the dozens of soldiers ahead of her.

"We stand unarmed, du Tealdan."

Siera motioned for her troops to move out of her way as she walked towards Enio, Quintus and Clara flanking her, their eyes darting here and there for any sign of an ambush.

"I more suspect that you have dozens of archers on the walls alongside you, ready to loose a volley as we approach, you murderous snake!" Siera shouted.

Enio shook his head as he yelled back. "I am no murderer, and there is no ambush. I will come with you peaceably, here." Enio walked forward, motioning to the nervous constables at his side to remain behind.

Slowly, Enio approached Siera. She resisted the urge to order her archers to shoot him where he stood. When he was a few dozen metres away from her, he stopped, and said loudly, "I ask that you give clemency to the people, and the constabulary, if you have any mercy in you."

Siera's face was stony. "Why should I bring mercy, Enio? All you and your lot have brought to Reimar is war and rebellion."

Enio shook his head. "It was you who brought war. True, we rebelled, but you could have dealt diplomatically."

Siera bared her teeth. "You had my father assassinated!"

Enio put up his hands. "No, not I! I can tell you who did, though."

Siera gritted her teeth. "Trying to pass along the blame, Enio? You are more of a coward that I realised."

Enio snorted. "I stand before a hostile force, unarmed and unguarded, and you call me a coward, du Tealdan? You are all talk, just like your father. But I have proof."

Siera's eyes narrowed. "Guard your tongue at least, Enio. I don't need to wait for any judges, I can have you put down like the mutt you are, right here and right now."

Enio glared at her. "I will not bow to threats. And it gives me no pleasure to barter, but barter I must. Let us talk in private."

Siera glared at Enio, then suddenly smiled. "Very well."

Siera ordered the Guard to search through the keep, ensuring no surprises were lying in wait. When they all reported back that there were no signs of any hostiles in the keep or its surrounds, Siera breathed a sigh of relief. She'd taken over the keep's dining hall as her temporary office, as the cooks and sailors of the *Wrath* who had survived had set up in the kitchens to feed the constant throughput of hungry soldiers.

Siera seated herself in one corner of the dining hall, her bodyguards and lieutenants with her.

"Even if it's cost this much, it appears that we have finally won," she said.

"Seems too easy, just taking over the keep like this," said Gretchen.

Adalberto said nothing. He'd been fairly quiet overall, not volunteering anything unless asked.

Siera turned to Enio du Donati, who had been shackled and seated opposite her. "So, where is this proof that you claim to have of my father's killer?"

Enio sat between Quintus and Clara, and for all that he should have looked like a rat stuck between two feral dogs, he retained a considerable composure and bearing, even with his hands tied behind his back.

"I do not have them on me, for to hand them over would deny me any ability to bargain. And bargain I must, for so long as I live I can dream for San Seras' independence. I can do nothing while dead."

Siera drew her sword, and laid it on the table.

"Here is how this will work, Enio. You tell me what I want to hear, and–"

Enio shook his head as she spoke. "I cannot trust to a deal with you. I insist on making such an agreement with your brother."

Siera paused as he spoke, then nodded at Quintus.

Quintus turned slightly to his left and grabbed Enio by the neck before slamming his head into the table.

Enio cried out in pain, his nose twisted.

"When Her Highness talks, you don't," said Clara from Enio's left.

Siera waited for a moment as Enio ground his teeth, unable to hold his face, his breathing heavy.

"My brother is not here, and I have a writ to act with his full approval in all matters. You deal with me, or you do not deal at all."

Siera tapped her sword hilt. "If I do not like what I hear, then I am going to let them hurt you. And Enio," Siera said softly as she reached forward and grabbed at Enio's hair, forcing him to look up at her, "they will hurt you very, very badly. The others that I have questioned have given very poor answers; apparently they were the juniors to a senior council of three people – yourself among them. From the bodies of the trash that attacked us after the *Wrath* fell, I take it that one of you went down fighting and was killed. Rumour has it that someone central to the rebels has taken their own life, I'm thinking that was Francisco du Covas. That leaves you as the most senior of all the rebel garbage running around. You see, we are all convinced that you ordered my father's murder. If you do not prove otherwise, we are going to do more than just hurt you. We will take you back to Ilmarch and drag you through the street, and I have a panel of judges who will let the crowd do to you what they want while the judges swear up and down that justice was served. You might not make it alive to your own hanging."

Enio scowled, his face bloody. "Is this your high Reimaran talk? Low threats, mob violence?"

Siera smiled. "That is unless you really make me angry, Enio. Then I will do to you what I want. And what I want is far, far worse than what the mob wants. So tell me, who had my father murdered?" she let go of his hair and leaned forward, her eyes bright.

Enio breathed heavily. "I have an ally, and you might well want to disbelieve what I am saying, but this is a single individual who has provided me with considerable information about the operations of the military."

"In the Admiralty," said Siera, her voice flat.

Enio's eyes went wide. "You... you knew? But then..."

Siera shook her head. "We do not know who. But General Andrayzn and I have our suspicions."

Enio snorted. "For all that does you. I have kept my correspondences with this individual, including the letter that they sent me wherein they confess that they have hired assassins to kill your father."

"Hired who?"

Enio gave a wan smile. "The Jackals."

Siera's eyes widened.

"Can't be," said Clara and Quintus both.

"How not?" said Gretchen.

Quintus scowled. "The Jackals are a ridiculously expensive group of famous killers, with their own strict rules and hierarchy. No one knows where they are based, or if they're even in Iber at all. Although..."

"Oh?" said Siera.

Enio smirked. "Yes, you see it now. The Jackals knew that they would not win a fight against the whitecaps, or at least did not like their chances. They arranged for the actual attackers to be street thugs, and themselves only organised the intrusion and placement. From there, it was all the work of cheap gutter-trash. The Jackals did the organising, and my man on the inside, well, he provided them with the funds and initiative. Funds he took from us without permission, I will add."

"A man, eh?" said Siera.

Enio bit his lip. "Plenty of men in the Admiralty."

"I only said I suspected the Admiralty, but thank you for confirming it," said Siera with a smile that didn't reach her eyes.

Enio shrugged. "He has likely already started running, now that San Seras has fallen. He knows that sooner or later someone will come after him. You will have to move soon to catch him."

Siera nodded slowly. "I cannot let you live after what you have done."

Enio sighed. "Then you will never find your father's true killer. Will not a life in prison assuage your blood thirst?"

Siera was silent for a moment. "I suppose it will have to do. Very well. If you tell me all that I want to know, and show me proof that someone else arranged the assassination, I will spare you the rope, and the mob. You can rot in jail instead."

Siera could feel Gretchen and Adalberto's eyes on her. "Where do you have your proof?"

Enio glared at her. "Your word? Swear on your father's name, du Tealdan."

Siera's mouth twitched, and Quintus's left hand drifted towards Enio's head.

Siera's face twitched as she swallowed. "Fine. Fine, then. I swear on the name of my father, Abarron du Tealdan, Sura grant him eternal rest, that if you give me the name of your informant and the proof that they acted alone in arranging my fathers' death then I will let you live out your days in jail."

Enio paused, then sighed. "I have your word, for whatever a du Tealdan's word is worth. Very well, the letters are hidden in the solar. Underneath the second cabinet on your right as you enter there is a panel hidden among the floorboards. Press against it to unlock it, the letters are in a small box underneath that panel."

Siera turned to Gretchen. "Send someone to get it. Wait, send a squad. There might be an ambush."

Gretchen nodded, then stood to give the order.

Siera turned back to Enio. "Now then little Enio, when did you decide to love Shar's money?"

Enio looked at Siera, frowning, then laughed. "You have been fooled, du Tealdan. Shar never funded our efforts. No, they wanted too many guarantees, and then when they had their hundredth border dispute they decided to keep their money instead."

Siera scowled. "I do not care. Who funded you, then?"

Enio's smirked slightly. "Arndustur."

"But then why did Shar try and attack?" said Quintus, his hand still hovering above Enio's neck.

"Rank opportunism," muttered Siera.

"Quite correct," said Enio. "We never planned for Shar to get involved. And my informant told me that you and the Admiralty were working together to attack Southmere, so we marched reinforcements there."

"And the Archipelagans? How did you get their allegiance?"

Enio sagged. "I am not proud of the bargain we made, but it was necessary. We promised them free trade through the Helion, and the use of both San Seras and Southmere as naval bases for any captain that sent ships to the rebellion's aid. They planned to raid Arnagol and Iltraya, as well as up and down the west coast of Reimar."

Siera's fists clenched. "We could have had Archipelagan pirates raiding Ilmarch because of you, you despicable filth," she snarled

Enio sneered. "Oh, and yourself, Major? How exactly did you convince the church to loan you the Noble Order of Eneco? Did you pay that price with your hand, perhaps? Or maybe with your mouth?"

Clara tapped Quintus' hand, which he removed from behind Enio's head. Siera barely realised what Clara was doing, so quickly did she move, as Clara put Enio in a headlock and smashed her fist into his face.

He howled.

Clara's voice was steady. "Now, many people think that Quintus is the one to fear, out of the pair of us. But it's really, really me."

Clara had a dagger in her hand before she finished speaking. She tightened her grip on Enio's head, keeping him still as she brought the dagger up to his left eye.

"Now, pain makes people behave for a short time. But fear? Fear keeps them good for much longer. Next time you talk sideways about Her Highness, I'm going to take a chunk right out of your eye."

For all that Siera wanted to see Enio beaten and bloody, Clara's threat made her wince. There was something utterly cruel about hurting the softness of the eye, about placing something so razor sharp and unrelenting right in front of something so weak and yet so vital to one's body and life.

Clara slowly moved the knife slightly closer as Enio tried to squirm away.

"Say 'Yes Sir', boy."

Enio tried to struggle more.

"Say it, boy. Say 'Yes Sir'."

"Yes, Sir," came Enio's muffled reply.

"Not to me, you stupid cunt, say it to Her Highness. Say it!"

Enio turned to glare at Siera. The hate she saw in his eyes was pure and unbridled.

"Yes, Sir," he spat

Siera realised that there was a small part of her that relished what had just happened. There was something stark and powerful about holding someone so close to pain and maiming, and having them obey.

She tried to push such thoughts out of her head as Clara relaxed her hold on Enio and withdrew her knife.

Siera let out a breath she hadn't realised she'd been holding in. "Arn's money, Archipelagan ships in return for raiding privileges… and every mercenary you could get your hands on. How did you intend to keep things under control once the money ran out?"

Enio coughed to clear his throat. "I only offered the others a chance to hold their own estates, how they controlled them was their problem. In truth, I expected Surmarch and Southmere to fall to Reimar once again. Surmarch always was more Reimaran than anything else. Well, so is Ponsurno, but they had a better chance of holding out. And San Seras… We have many citizens who remember the days when we were free of Reimaran rule, and desire to be so again. We here in San Seras believed that we could bargain our independence once Reimar had had enough of war."

Siera frowned. "You always planned to abandon your

fellow rebels, eh? Then why send aid to Southmere?"

Enio scowled. "That was Federica du Jasso and Francisco du Covas's work. We three together formed the triumvirate of San Seras, some of the most powerful landowners in the region. Well, after the land of Reimar-loving diehards had been redistributed to more appropriate owners, of course. And as we three were the ones dealing with Arn and securing the rebellion's viability, we were thus the de facto powers of the rebellion itself. But Federica and Francisco, they got cold feet and thought we could spare the mercenaries to send aid to Southmere, and they were scared after you took Surmarch so quickly. They wanted to have a buffer against attack. Then, after the mercenaries had been sent out, we heard that you had taken Ponsurno. It was then that I knew we were undone, but they thought – goddamn fools – they thought that the extra troops would stop you from taking Southmere. They should have realised that the Reimaran Navy would be too strong to beat at Southmere, but would be worn down when they came at San Seras."

Enio sighed, then continued.

"You timed your assault on Southmere well with the Navy, but failed to do so here in San Seras when we were able to get the *Cloud Chaser* up and going against you. It gave me no pleasure to see those ships sunk."

Siera looked up to see a squad of soldiers headed her way.

"Sir, we found these, right where you said." They offered the letters to Gretchen, who pointed at Siera.

"Oh, right. Here you are, Sir," their leader said as Siera took the letters.

One by one, she read the documents, and the story was complete.

The ones that weren't written and signed by Enio were signed by another's name, and the last and final letter laid out the plan to murder her father, even as Enio protested it in simple and bare language.

There, in plain ink it was written, and Siera knew that name.

Rear Admiral Alejandro du Salamanca.

"There it is," said Siera. "Good God... even after he was allowed to serve in the Navy, despite his heritage... he turned on Reimar."

"Of course he would," said Enio. "Your family took everything from his family and treated him like garbage."

Siera scowled. "My family took nothing, but it was my family that let him serve and make a name for himself, even despite his family having fought against Reimar. My own father said that he should be allowed to serve, the same man that du Salamanca murdered! And now I sit here and listen to you makes excuses for him, traitor?!"

Enio glared at Siera. "I do not care how often you say it. I am not a traitor to San Seras, and I never swore any fealty to Reimar."

Suddenly, Siera laughed, and held up her hand to stop Quintus as he reached for Enio. "Neither did I when I was a mere child, but when you take on a position of rank in the kingdom, you have already accepted the hierarchy as it stands. And besides, no amount of legal wrangling and arguments will save you. Enjoy your cell, for you will damn well never leave it."

Enio shrugged. "If I must languish in a Reimaran jail, then at least I can do so knowing that I did all I could to try for freedom for my home."

Siera sneered. "What freedom? You started a pointless rebellion that cost hundreds or even thousands of lives, for freedom? What did Reimar deny you?"

Enio's face betrayed little. "Choice. The choice to be led by our own, and pay taxes to no foreign overlords, no matter how graceful. The chance to have pride in our own ways, not to be told that we are nothing more than uncultured and uncouth because our traditions are different to those of Reimar."

Siera clicked her tongue. "Overlords! Horse peppers! You think your own family originally controlled San Sera province, or even San Seras?"

Enio sneered. "I don't need to justify my family's position to you." Enio turned his head away from Siera.

Siera shrugged. "Then nor do I need to justify my own family's position to you. And it is quite clear that you wanted more power for you and your allies. You wanted to rule. Greed pushed you more than any so-called patriotism."

Enio did not reply.

Siera motioned to Quintus, who stood to lead Enio away. "Right now I would dearly love to have you hanged anyway, but I will not break my word, on my father's own name, and stoop to your level. You worthless, worthless garbage, Enio. Would that you had been thrown in a trash heap when you were born. Well... enough of you. There is much to be done about Alejandro. Toma– ah... Adalberto, send someone to find one of Terciero's assistants. I must send word."

Enio said nothing as he was hauled to his feet, and led away.

Epilogue: Every Due Paid in Full

8th Chem, morning, the day after Siera's return to Ilmarch

On the 7th day of Chem, Mariska Rossi had got the day off work, as had everyone else, to see Princess Siera in her triumphant return come sailing back after defeating the rebels. Mariska and her husband had waited and waited, and many soldiers had walked out of the docks, but Tomasso hadn't been there. It was now a full day since Siera had returned. They had waited for news, and still Tomasso had sent no word.

At least he could have written a letter, she thought to herself.

Mariska put down her knitting, and sighed. She had so wanted to finish before Tomasso had come home, but perhaps she could finish before his leave was up.

A knock at the door had her looking over at Emilio, her husband, with a smile on her face. He was right behind her as she trotted to the front door and flung it open.

But it wasn't Tomasso. A brown-haired woman stood at the front door, with a man in a white cap standing behind her.

"Hello?" said Mariska.

Siera coughed. "Mr. and Mrs. Rossi?"

"Yes, that's correct. Oh, are you...?" said Emilio

"Oh, it is! Y–your Highness, please, come in!" said Mariska. "But, where is Tomasso? Is he still at the barracks?" she continued, nonplussed.

Siera had a speech prepared; she had practiced it in her head as she rode a carriage over. But now, in the moment, she could remember nothing.

She looked over at Emilio, and realised that he already knew. His gaze was hollow, his lips fluttered helplessly.

Mariska was still looking at Siera, but as her husband let out a cry of anguish, she turned to him, and realised as well.

"No... No please, not my son... Please, Your Highness,

291

where is my son?" she shrieked.

Siera stood helplessly as they wailed, the medal in her pocket forgotten.

"I… I'm so sorry… Tomasso, he…"

Siera realised they couldn't hear her. Wherever their thoughts were, there was no room for 'sorry' and other platitudes.

Half an hour had passed since Siera had arrived, and although Tomasso's parents were still beside themselves, they were able to carry on a conversation. Mariska, Emilio, and Siera were seated around a small table in the kitchen, the only table in the house.

"Please, Your Highness… tell us h– how our son died…" said Emilio, his eyes slightly bloodshot.

Siera swallowed. "It is no exaggeration to say that without your son's courage, I might not be alive today."

Siera looked down to collect her thoughts before continuing.

"It was in San Seras, after an air battle with the rebels. The *Sky's Wrath* had crashed, and mercenaries were attacking us as we tried to get free of the wreckage. While my troops fought, I myself had been knocked unconscious in the crash. Tomasso watched over me as the battle raged. Some mercenaries got aboard the ship, and he… he died protecting me, just before my guards could arrive."

Mariska burst into tears again, but Emilio simply closed his eyes.

"At least… at least I can grieve… knowing that he died with honour," he said.

"I don't want honour! I want my son! Tomasso…" said Mariska between sobs.

Siera swallowed. "It is a cold comfort, but I must also tell you that your son's heroism has not gone unrecognised. My brother has declared that Tomasso has fulfilled every obligation to the Royal Guard and more. He died as a citizen, and as such, you may remain in Reimar as citizens yourselves."

Mariska gave no sign of hearing. Emilio nodded, his eyes closed.

Siera pulled out the Medal of the Crown and Shield, and placed it on the table in front of her. She folded her hands on the table. "The Crown and Shield is only awarded to those who have given their lives in service to the realm and in defence of a member of the royal family. It also grants a small stipend."

Siera blinked rapidly, feeling a few hot tears try and escape. She composed herself quickly before continuing.

"I... I know a medal is just a lump of metal, and money is cold comfort. I know... I know that nothing I can say will take away your pain. Please... just know that your son died as bravely as any. He and all his comrades slain in this war died as heroes. It might not be much, but all those who fought with them salute their memory. I– I'm so sorry..."

Siera stood quickly, bowed, and left. Emilio half-stood to bow as she left, but then slumped back into his chair.

"Why did we come to this country, Mari? Our only child is dead. Oh God, my boy. No, God, no. Oh Sura, Tomasso..." Emilio pushed his face into his hands as his tears began to fall again. "Please God, please God take him into your arms... Please take my boy into your embrace, please God..."

Outside, Siera stepped back into her carriage, Quintus stepping in after her. Neither spoke on the ride back to the palace.

8th Chem, Afternoon

Great haste had been made to honour as many of the Reimaran fallen as was feasible. The military paid for a full cremation for all of its fallen if possible, not just cheap burials, and it was traditional to hold a ceremonial cremation at the end of a campaign to honour all those who were lost.

General Andrayzn, Siera, and each regimental captain – as well as their lieutenants – were all there, in full dress uniform. It was traditional for the First Regiment to stand to and present arms as the Suranic Church's cantors led an oration for the fallen, then lit the pyre.

The lead cantor returned to the pulpit after overseeing the lighting of the pyre, her face grave.

"We consign those who have given their lives for their country into Sura's grace. In her light, we find redemption."

Siera stood with the front rank of those observing the proceedings, her face impassive. If there was any emotion that stirred in her, it was relief.

As the first flames licked the base of the pyre, the sweetly-scented wood smoke filled the air, and Siera felt empty inside.

"In her light, we find solace."

Andrayzn had already watched his fallen soldiers cremated in the field, but felt a solemn satisfaction at this particular ritual. A large pyre to remember the fallen felt appropriate. He made as though to scratch his cheek, and brushed a stray tear from his face.

"In her light, we find hope."

Gretchen glanced to her right, and was surprised to see Adalberto standing impassively, his cheeks glistening with tears. In the midst of one of the pyres, a garnet lay among the flames.

9th Chem

Siera looked around her office. The cluttered heaps of gifts and letters actually made it feel welcoming for once.

A knock came at her door. Siera blinked, then realised Tomasso wouldn't be getting it for her. Standing, she walked over to open it herself.

"Captain du Vives!" she said as she saw that it was her old commanding officer. "Sir, it's – it's a pleasure. Do come in."

Dante shook his head. "I did not come by for a social call, and I will not be long."

Siera shrugged, still smiling. "Oh, still, do come in. I have been wanting to talk to you."

Dante regarded Siera with an odd look, and Siera couldn't place his mood. She was about to say something when he sighed and nodded, motioning her inside.

"Anything to drink, Sir?"

Dante shook his head. "I'm not your captain any more, Siera. And for that I am grateful," said Dante, who stood with his hands on the back of a chair in front of Siera's desk.

Siera paused. "I know, old habit. I am... not certain why this makes you grateful... Will you not sit?" said Siera with a half-smile.

Dante did not meet her gaze. "You have disgraced yourself, Siera du Tealdan. And you have disgraced me as your former mentor and commander," he said, not looking up at her.

"I... w– what?" said Siera.

"I was impressed at your determination at acquiring and employing that skyship. I was not impressed to hear that you brought some... some rabid hanging judges with you to each city the rebels had taken. You brought military justice before civil justice."

Siera scowled. "Hear me, du Vives, when I say that although I admire your commitment to honour, I could not have–"

Dante flicked his fingers at her. "Excuses. You chose

expediency over the harder road. You chose to do what is easy, not what it right."

Siera very slowly clenched her fists and rested them on her desk. "Interrupt me again and I will throw you out on your ear. Myself."

Dante laughed softly. "Is that so? You cannot bear to be reprimanded? And how did you convince the Noble Order to fight with you?"

Siera glared at Dante. "Would you have done otherwise?"

Dante looked right back at her. "I would have kept my honour, Siera. I would have held my head high."

"You would have kept pride over victory, you mean. I did what I had to, took what measures I had to. And I would do it again to ensure any and all victory for Reimar."

"You have not been victorious. The root of this lies in Reimar's aggressions, and you have continued that – in the eyes of all too many in San Seras and other cities, you are just another conqueror."

Siera made a curt laugh. "Yes, life was wonderful when the old city-states ruled the region around the Helion. Constant fighting, cities being bled white, coffers perennially empty, surrounded by hungrier and larger nations who wanted to control the Helion. Reimar won with guile and bloodshed both, I will not deny it, but–"

"Excuses," muttered Dante.

"Are what you make for yourself!" barked Siera. "Your guilt drove you to resign. You care nothing for any so-called sovereign rights or what Reimar has done to bring both peace and prosperity to those provinces. You berate me out of your own stubborn guilt."

Dante laughed softly. "Do I? You never told me what you did to secure the Noble Order for yourself."

"None of your concern, du Vives. It is not a price you had to pay."

"Were I captain still, I would not have paid it."

"Because you could not bow your head to do so. I did what you could not do, and if you were still captain we might have lost against the rebels."

Dante scowled. "I would have found a way. A way that honoured what Reimar stands for. And what has Andrayzn said to you, hmm?" a smirk crept onto Dante's lips.

Siera gaze was stony. "He trusted me when I said that no dishonour had been brought upon the Guard."

Dante's face fell flat. "Even Andrayzn, then... and what about the dishonour to Reimar?" Dante said softly.

Siera scowled. "Death before dishonour, eh Dante? Then go and fall on your sword. Reimar has no need of those who will not claim victory at any price."

Dante flicked his right hand's fingers at Siera. "Your brother has no need, perhaps. Reimar is more than just you or your sibling. Your father–"

Siera bared her teeth, her eyes wide. "My father put Reimar first and himself second! You can keep your cheap opinions about what my father would have done where you spawned them from; namely, up your backside! And how easy is it for you to talk of honour, you old goat? Who took your illegitimate daughter in as a page? I did! I could have taken her on campaign against the rebellion – I chose to leave her behind! I could have used militia as arrow-food, I could have used Reimar's wealth to build a thousand greatarrows and level cities with them!" Siera breathed heavily as Dante looked at her, his face impassive. "So what if I hanged traitors before the mob, so what that I did not patiently siege cities like an old shepherd?! And so what that I made a deal with du Nascimbeni and got the Noble Order's assistance?! No one cares what you would have done, fool. You were asked to put your hands to a dirty task and cut down criminals – mere rioters and looters – oh and then you did your duty willingly – yet then afterwards had the temerity to cry about it! I have not shamed Reimar, I have given all I have for Reimar!"

Dante stared at her, his gaze pitying. "You will say it for months, maybe years. But in due time, what you have done will come back to lurk in your mind. You will feel the guilt of your actions weigh upon you, you will know well what you have done."

Siera's left hand tapped at her sword pommel. "Yes indeed. Yes, I too will stand and be judged after my final hour, Dante. I too will stand and be counted, for all the good and ill that I have done, and old man, note this: it will not be by you. You will not stand in judgement over me, and I daresay, you will be judged for your own arrogance. You too, are far from stainless. Very far. You too will stand before Riest, Dante."

Dante shook his head. "Tell yourself what you like. You will not listen and you will not hear. I came in vain."

Siera's gaze was stony. "Then go in vain, you old goat, just like when you resigned. Be resigned to your vain acts. Get out and do not return."

After Dante had left, a brief silence reigned. Siera sighed, pinching the bridge of her nose.

12th Chem

Ramiros leaned back in his chair, in the royal council chambers after congratulations had been passed around by all, some more enthusiastically than others.

"Rebellion crushed, war over. And all in all, Reimar has her cities back and a mere pauper's peace with Iln," muttered Ramiros.

"To pursue Iln into their own lands would be ruinous," said Andrayzn. "We suffered far fewer losses than when we previously fought against them."

"By using trickery and deceit, General Andrayzn," said Zaballa du Arista. "By your own admission, trickery."

Andrayzn looked up at Zaballa, his face stony. "Admission? The only admission you will get from me is that I would dearly haul your viper's tongue from your head."

Zaballa's eyes flashed, and she started to rebut him, but Andrayzn talked over her, his eyes narrowed.

"And no matter your insistence, you would have done no better. I will not lose soldiers to satisfy your ego, du Arista."

Zaballa sputtered, looked as though she would continue.

"Oh, give it up, Zaballa, for God's sake! Or the sake of my ears," said Modesto du Greco suddenly, his mouth in a moue of distaste.

"She has a point, though," said Silvio du Firenze. "Certain actions undertaken by the military have been... disreputable. Of course, not the actions undertaken by Duke du Tilmost. I mean, who cares if you trick Ilnians in battle? Certain other actions, though... they defame the Guard."

Ramiros coughed. "Are you calling my sister disreputable, Duke du Firenze?"

Silence took sudden root in the council chambers.

Silvio du Firenze scratched at his chin. "No, of course not, Your Noble Highness. Still, I–"

Silvio du Donati make an odd slapping noise with his lips, and turned to glare at Silvio du Firenze. "Yes, yes – and you are clearly pleased with the progress that the military has made. Are you not?" said Silvio du Donati. "Rebels defeated, Iln at bay once more. Good." He clapped his hands once, the sudden echo bouncing around the chamber. "You want to cry about the King's sister? Your head should rot for that. That woman is nigh a saint. Where would we be without her?"

"Yes, well... as you like it," said Silvio du Firenze, throwing his hands up in the air.

Nicodemo coughed. "Well, also, Mordeno has sent a letter, begging for forgiveness after refusing to help us," said Nicodemo.

Gaspar du Covas' eyes widened slightly at that. "Do they actually say that in the letter? That they refused to help us, do they admit it?" he said.

"Not literally, no," said Nicodemo. "But they claim that they now realise the error of their ways and note down... dozens of what amount to weak excuses."

Ramiros let out a short laugh, baring his teeth. "I don't care how much they beg. They turned on us when we needed them, they should suffer the price. They should do without Helion trade."

Modesto du Greco sniffed. "The better price of their disloyalty is that they can do without any form of military alliance from us. Nations like Altren and Mordeno have survived in large part due to siding with a larger nation against an aggressor. They will see how much they like being alone against Shar or Arn," he said.

"And they will enjoy no special rates through the Helion now either, let them pay full price," said Gaspar du Covas with a small smile.

Ramiros gritted his teeth. "If it is the Council's stubborn insistence that we forgive and forget, then I will abide by the Council's whim."

"Such churlish petulance is unbecoming of a king," said Zaballa du Arista.

"And such naked greed is unbecoming a duke," snapped Ramiros.

"It is scarce greed and more pragmatism that pushes me to such a course of action," said Gaspar du Covas, still smiling. "And my family has not endured these hundreds of years to merely be called greedy."

Ramiros' mouth twitched. "I meant no insult to you, Duke du Covas."

Gaspar shrugged, still smiling. "None is taken. In the matter of the Helion, the only thing of importance is that Reimar controls it."

Ramiros nodded. "Quite. Well, if the Council has no objections, I have a matter I must attend to."

Nicodemo smiled weakly. "Something drawing you away from our august presences, Your Noble Highness?"

Ramiros chuckled. "Well, if you must know, they've been going at Alejandro Salamanca for a day now. They must have some results."

Andrayzn frowned, looking askance at Ramiros. "Who is 'they'?"

Ramiros did not meet Andrayzn's gaze. "Just a few people I trust to have no sympathy for Salamanca's pleas for mercy. I will have answers out of him come death or disaster."

The End

From the author:

Reimar's future is uncertain. Whether or not the nation's leaders continue to choose expediency over values is yet to be seen. Although the kingdom has survived a dark and fractious hour, the future still holds no guarantees.

Reimar's future is uncovered in the sequel, *The Iberan War*.

Thank you for reading.

Acknowledgements

My personal thanks to those who took their time to give advice and commentary. Without you, this book would be half of what it is.

Aradna S.
Sofia
Jacob B.
Chris R.

Appendix:

Selected information on Reimar has been included in this appendix. Even with an appendix, one book is not enough to contain all details about the cultures and people of Brisia. You can visit *The Fourth World* website at jrivalland.com for more information on the setting of *Reimar Breaking*.

Timeline

0 C.E.: Sura creates humanity. Human groups, polities, tribes, and nations spread out across many worlds and regions; the world of Brisia (and its continent, Iber) included.

562 C.E.: Arn Empire formed, the pre-eminent political and military power of its time.

566 C.E.: The Arn Empire crushes Jurien in a series of wars over four years that see the country reduced to a mere city-state.

571 C.E.: Reimar founded under King Tomasso du Valtiera. Royal Army formed.

725 C.E.: Reimaran Teal designed and minted.

840 C.E.: Capital of Reimar moved from Valencia to Ilmarch under Queen Hirune du Messina.

961 C.E.: Iberan Helion discovered to be portal between worlds. Commerce soon proves immensely profitable. Conflict ensues over the coming decades concerning ownership of the Helion.

972 C.E.: Reimaran Royal Army dissolved. Reimaran Royal Guard formed as a professional standing army.

1149 C.E.: King Sendoa du Messina the Third incorporates the territory of Guerda (Guerda Province, Capital: Southmere Town). After dying of liver failure three months later, he is succeeded by his heir, King Eneco du Messina the Second, who plans and executes a war in 1151 C.E. to gain the provinces of Gavar, San Seras, and Espinoza. Reimar now controls the Helion.

1233 C.E.: Abarron du Tealdan born.

1252 C.E.: Abarron du Tealdan and Fede du Acquino marry.

1253 C.E.: Ramiros du Tealdan born.

1254 C.E.: Siera du Tealdan born.

1279 C.E.: Current time.

Dates

Reimar uses the common Suranic calendar endorsed by the Suranic Church (S.G. – Suranic Genesis). S.G. can be substituted for C.E. (common era). Reimar also notes years by R.G. (Reimaran Genesis), this of course is specific to Reimar and begins in 571 C.E.

Every month has thirty days, except every three years when Newarn has an extra day. The months are, from the beginning of the year to the end: Imbril, Hara, Jurom, Murmet, Joien, Iriken, Cestis, Teurnot, Chem, Norem, Ohfust, Newarn. Teurnot, Chem, and Norem are the autumn months.

Languages

Arinholer: the most common language in Iber. Usually the de facto language of most human nations.

Old Reimaran: the lingua franca of northern and some parts of central Reimar.

Espinozan: the lingua franca of southern Reimar. Less pervasive than it once was.

Vig: a dead language, said to be the first ever used by humans. Now spoken by very few, it primarily remains in use for ceremonies by the Suranic Churches, as well as by scholars of the origins of humanity, and those who want to add gravitas to their words.

Altrenese: the most common language in Altren, with Arinholer a distant second (except amongst the nobility, who are almost all bilingual).

Currency

The *Teal* is the currency of Reimar, named for a member of the du Tealdan family who served as the Royal Exchequer at the time, and who was responsible for designing the first coins. The gold Teal is mainly used as a marker by trading companies and Reimaran nobles, and is capitalised. The silver teal is not capitalised, to denote its common-use status by the majority of the populace. Still in circulation are the variety of lesser coins dating from before the introduction of the Teal, referred to as copper bits. Although silver teals have actual silver in them, gold Teals contain no gold.

Religion

Religion in Reimar is primarily concerned with worship of two entities known as Sura and Riest. Sura is the god that created humanity, and Riest a divine being that was sent by Sura to educate humanity. As such, many things that Riest proposed (such as a feudal hierarchy) are widely viewed as divine mandates.

The Suranic Church is the primary religious institution of Reimar. It enjoys significant patronage from both the monarchy and the Dukes, and serves to reinforce the status quo of the feudal order in claiming that this is right and proper under God. Only recently has the Suranic Church changed their stance on religious artwork, into allowing it under certain conditions.

The Riestan Church differs from the Suranic Church in that they focus primarily on Sura's agent Riest, and Riest's personal appearance in the world in human form. The Riestan push for religious art displaying the human form (sometimes nude) differs greatly from traditional Suranic approaches. Overall, the two churches remain very similar in dogma and hierarchy.

The Church of the Second Dawn espouses a bizarre and convoluted creed that somehow holds Sura equal to the other gods but of some superiority as well. They have pushed for non-human races to be expelled from human lands, even as rare as any non-humans in Reimar are.

The Whitechapel Cult is a heresy condemned by mainstream Suranism, and claims that Riest was human and not divine, only divinely appointed. They also claim that Sura was human once but became divine through achieving spiritual perfection; that the various mortal races are equal; and that those who oppose Sura are not reincarnated but instead sent to a realm of flies and maggots to rot forever. Although not illegal, followers of the Whitechapel Sect are so routinely condemned by the mainstream faith that they risk severe persecution, and hence worship in secret.

Appendix

Government
Reimar: [Rayi-Mar]

Reimar is a monarchy. However, the monarch's power is not absolute – although monarchs pass and rescind laws by decree, a council of the realm's dukes must endorse or veto said decrees. A simple majority can veto any decree, however if the monarch feels the matter is important they can override this veto. A greater majority (two thirds) council veto can overturn this royal veto and reinstate the original council veto (this is likely to create considerable friction, though). A two third council veto, however, cannot be overridden.

Each of Reimar's Dukes or Duchesses has an automatic and permanent position on the council. Certain notable experts and guild representatives have also been offered positions at different times, however they cannot vote on all matters, only those falling into their speciality. The Ducal councillors can also vote to expel a non-Ducal councillor, but a Ducal councillor cannot be expelled.

The monarch also appoints Dukes to certain high offices, often as a part of trading favours and politicking. Whether a given Duke is any good at their supposed job depends on the individual (often the actual work is left to other family members, subordinates, courtiers, etc.).

The Royal Guard:

Reimar is rich enough to afford a standing army. The First Regiment trains all new recruits, and places them in the other regiments (as the First Regiment only accepts veterans from the other regiments). Each regiment of the guard has its own particular duty. The First Regiment is stationed in the capital to train recruits or be dispatched as needed, the Second Regiment is stationed throughout Reimar and guards various important locations, the Third Regiment is comprised mainly of marines who work with the Royal Navy, the Fourth Regiment is used as an internal security regiment to bolster the Second and First, the Fifth is the engineer corps, the Seventh is a regiment comprised of mercenary troops with retired Reimaran officers, and the Eighth is a foreign service regiment that guards various embassies and concerns abroad for the state. There is no sixth regiment.

Titles and Peerage:
Reimar has an odd incarnation of the feudal system. Previously, the largest of the various territories in northern and central Reimar were palatine dukedoms, and although some conflicts occurred, they were largely agreeable to one another. However, when the Arn Empire was formed, it established a non-hereditary system of rulership; with the dukes of the empire electing the emperor. The other nations of Iber felt threatened by this new military powerhouse (for good reason, as the Arn Empire proceeded to quickly knock over Jurien, its neighbour to the south), and also felt that the established order of things had been upset by the emergence of a powerful nonhereditary feudal ruler. As such, the nation of Altren decided on a monarchy. The most prominent (and de facto king anyway) duke was chosen to be the king of Altren, to better bring the entire region against a military invasion if needs be.

In Reimar (as in Arnagol and Nordem), however, no duke or duchess would accede to any other becoming king or queen over them, as they were all at a similar level of wealth and land ownership. Therefore, it was decided that the ruler would initially be chosen by vote, but thereafter the title would be hereditary. However, only the firstborn child could inherit the position of king or queen, ensuring that no single dynasty could rule forever. Thus, they gained some of the authority that the Arn Empire offered its dukes, and gained the stability that a monarchy offered.

So in Reimar, the monarch is not a powerful landowner as the dukes are, in that although they come from a ducal lineage they must pass up their ducal title to another in the family in order to accept the royal title (so a monarch cannot also be an elector). However, the royal family in Reimar receives a sizeable stipend for expenses, and housing in the royal palace in Reimar. The costs to maintain the palace, host court, fund the military, receive foreign dignitaries, and fund public works all come out of the royal treasury, not the royal family's pocket. The monarch requires the council's permission to decide on a budget, but performs all international diplomacy as they see fit (which can cause friction if the monarch decrees a treaty that offers financial aid to another nation). Most internal Reimaran politics is thus the same as any nation: the prominent landowners, with their wealth inherited through dynasties, decide the majority of affairs for the entire nation.

Your Noble Majesty: the King or Queen. The monarchy of Reimar is an hereditary title carrying with it the authority to make propose decrees, preside over the royal council, propose and co-authorise the kingdom's budget, sign treaties, arrange the kingdom's military, and declare war or peace.

Your Highness: a Prince or Princess. Although of a high rank, this title carries little authority, as in Reimar princes and princesses rarely own any land of their own, and rarely do they hold lower titles either.

Your Grace: a Duke or Duchess. A Duke or Duchess bears a heritable title that confers with it significant land ownership as well as the right to sit on the royal council. Reimar's Dukes and Duchesses are among the foremost political and economic figures of importance in the realm. A considerable debate exists as to whether Dukes or Duchesses should be addressed as 'Your Worthiness' or 'Your Grace' in Reimar, and different generations have adopted different preferences. Currently, the preference is for Dukes or Duchesses to be referred to as 'Your Grace'.

Your Worthiness: a Marquess/ Marchioness. Dukes do not own all their territory directly, although they own a great deal of their own land they also oversee the lands of their feudal vassals. A marquess or marchioness is the foremost of these vassals, themselves wealthy and privileged peers of the realm.   A considerable debate exists as to whether Marquesses should be addressed as 'Your Worthiness' or 'Your Grace' in Reimar, and different generations have adopted different preferences. Currently, the preference is 'Your Worthiness', and using 'Your Grace' is seen as gross impropriety. Normally in Reimar, 'Marquess' is used for men and 'Marchioness' for women, however in more recent times the distinction is often ignored.

Your Lordship/Ladyship: a Baron or Baroness. A baron or baroness does not necessarily own land, but the vast majority of barons and baronesses are landowners underneath the various marquesses and marchionesses. However, saying 'my lord' is appropriate for speaking to any lord, not simply to a baron.

Sir: a Count or Countess. A noble title given for exceptional service; if the service was military then the title is hereditary. Confers no land, but does grant a small stipend. Those families with this title are often found in a military or advisory role to higher ranking nobles.

Viscount, a Lord or Lady: Viscounts are a recent addition to the peerage of Reimar, being a title that has been used for less than two hundred years. It denotes an unlanded noble who has no obligation to any feudal lord who then swears fealty to the reigning monarch of Reimar. The title can also be awarded by the reigning monarch to anyone who has rendered especially meritorious service. Oddly enough, the title of Viscount is considered gender neutral.

Page: pages are usually younger members of noble houses (major or minor) who are sent to serve with other noble families, to both build ties and to give them an idea of how to conduct themselves outside of their own family, even when young (ages 8 to 14 is common). Pages are higher ranked than servants (who are, after all, commoners), and are often used in official events, parties, or anything that requires a servant but will impress more if so-and-so's second cousin is doing it instead.

Military Equipment

Skyship:
Enchanted vessels capable of flight, although the enchantments are primarily there to keep the ship aloft and skyships rely on sails to propel them. Skyship design has diverged significantly from seaborne ship design, although the basic shape remains the same, as seaborne ship design was the foundation for skyship design.

Greatbows:
Greatbows are large, enchanted longbows used by infantry, that loose explosive arrows. Primarily used as siege weapons. The bows themselves are a metre tall, thickly built, and enchanted to trigger any arrows they launch. Normal arrows are warped by the force a greatbow exerts, but greatarrows are metre-long iron shafts with fist-sized obsidian heads. There is a danger that any force exerted on the arrowhead can trigger it to detonate prematurely. As such, safety precautions for greatarrow storage are paramount.

Hanging:
Throughout the campaign against the secessionists, there is a strong usage of the threat of hanging. In Reimar, the common penalty for lesser crimes is the stockade or the local community forcing a wayward individual to atone through a service of some kind. For more serious crimes, such as theft or arson, lengthy prison sentences with manual labour are the order of the day. For murder or rape, though, there is only execution, usually by the rope. Nobles, however, can generally expect the 'less dishonourable' death by decapitation, which is seen as more reasonable than hanging in Reimaran society – the noose is for hardened, lower-class criminals, and the nobility do so love their differentiating privileges. That said, for treason, hanging is almost always used – as it's seen as the 'worst' way to die. A drop (which might make for a clean death by one's neck snapping) is not used for hanging in Reimar, rather the accused is hoisted up and strangled.

Locations
Gold Road:
The Gold Road is a longstanding nickname for the road that runs from Ilmarch to the Helion, the official name being King Eneco the Second Highway. Few use the official name.

The Helion:
A massive freestanding structure built by an unknown people, there is only one known Helion on Iber. Others exist on various different worlds. The Iberan Helion is currently claimed by Reimar, and the vast amount of trade that comes through it has made an already wealthy nation fabulously rich. The Helion has seen a steady buildup of various structures (mostly customs and excise buildings, inns, pubs, and warehouses) catering to merchants and travellers, and there is effectively a small unnamed town around it.

The Helion's operation is utterly beyond the understanding of any mages that have inspected it to date. A Helion requires either a trained sorcerer to set it to a specific destination, or a warlock. Significant trial and error is required to work out even a single destination, although it has been noted that warlocks seem to have an easier time of both working this out as well as activating the device.

Miscellaneous
Nita/Nitia:
A nita is a small lighter, often used by smokers, invented over a decade ago and in the last few years come into immense popularity for its convenience. Reimaran sorcerer-artificers often make them as an easy form of income, and there isn't a tobacconist in Reimar that fails to stock a few of them.

Slang:
Horse/Dog peppers: slang for faeces.
To be at ashes: to be at war.
Keep your knife at/to someone/something: to keep your attention or suspicion on someone.

Pies, tarts, and other baked goods:
Many baked goods have particular meanings in different
contexts in Reimar. Strawberries are held to be sexually
suggestive, so strawberry pies or tarts are seen as crude in
most contexts. Apple pies are seen as provincial and boorish.

Gestures:
Flicking one's fingers: a dismissive gesture, whether
dismissing a concern or a person depends on the context.
Rubbing one's index finger and thumb: a subtle gesture
indicating that the speaker wants to emphasize what they are
saying, and that listeners should pay attention.
Wiggling one's little finger: meant to indicate that the
gesturer has caught someone like a fish on a hook, "I have
you" or "I got you".
Clicking one's tongue: tongue clicking is associated with
commanding horses, so to click your tongue at someone is to
say that they are behaving so poorly as to deserve to be
trained like a horse. Somewhat insulting.

Card Games:
Bastard: Each player gets an equal share of the overall
number of cards, and plays one card per round onto a central
pile. Cards must be placed on the pile in order. Lying about
having the correct card or putting down multiple cards is the
usual way to play cheat, where the only failing is getting
caught – which means you take up all the cards in the pile.
The goal of the game is to cheat, and "Bastard!" is what you
yell out when you catch someone cheating.

Romance:
In Reimar, it is customary for a couple to announce their
engagement by hanging their prospective wedding rings on
short chains off their left wrists to symbolise their impending
marriage. One can also announce a desire for a relationship
by hanging an empty chain (no ring) off the left wrist.

Elsewhen Press

an independent publisher specialising in Speculative Fiction

Visit the Elsewhen Press website at elsewhen.co.uk for the latest information on all of our titles, authors and events; to read our blog; find out where to buy our books and ebooks; or to place an order.

THE FIRST BOOK IN THE
INVERSE SHADOWS UNIVERSE

SUFFICIENTLY
ADVANCED
TECHNOLOGY

CHRISTOPHER NUTTALL

For the post-singularity Confederation, manipulating the quantum foam – the ability to alter the base code of the universe itself and achieve transcendence – is the holy grail of science. But it seems an impossible dream until their scouts encounter Darius, a lost colony world whose inhabitants have apparently discarded the technology that brought them to the planet in order to adopt a virtually feudal culture. On Darius, the ruling elite exhibits abilities that defy the accepted laws of physics. They can manipulate the quantum foam!

Desperate to understand what is happening on Darius, the Confederation dispatches a stealth team to infiltrate the planet's society and discover the truth behind their strange abilities. But they will soon realise that the people on Darius are not all the simple folk that they seem – and they are sitting on a secret that threatens the entire universe ...

Christopher Nuttall has been planning sci-fi books since he learnt to read. Born and raised in Edinburgh, Chris created an alternate history website and eventually graduated to writing full-sized novels. Studying history independently allowed him to develop worlds that hung together and provided a base for storytelling. After graduating from university, Chris started writing full-time. As an indie author he has self-published a number of novels, but this is his fourth fantasy to be published by Elsewhen Press. *Sufficiently Advanced Technology* is his fourth novel to be published by Elsewhen Press, and the first in the Inverse Shadows universe. Chris is currently living in Edinburgh with his wife, muse, and critic Aisha and their son.

ISBN: 9781908168344 (epub, kindle)
ISBN: 9781908168245 (336pp, paperback)

Visit bit.ly/SAT-Nuttall

SAILOR TO A SIREN
ZOË SUMRA

A space opera novel with significant nods to the gangland thriller genre.

"If you like your space opera fast and violent, this book is for you"
– Jaine Fenn

When Connor and Logan Cardwain, a gangster's lieutenants, steal a shipment of high-grade narcotics on the orders of their boss, Connor dreams of diverting the profits and setting up in business for himself. His plans encounter a hurdle in the form of Éloise Falavière, Logan's former girlfriend, who has been hired by an interplanetary police force's vice squad.

Logan wants a family; Éloise wants to stop the drugs shipment from being sent to her home planet; Connor wants to gain independence without angering his boss. All of their plans are derailed, though, when they discover that the shipment was hiding a much deadlier secret – the prototype of a tiny superweapon powerful enough to destabilise galactic peace.

Crime lords, corrupt officials and interstellar magicians soon begin pursuing them, and Connor, Logan and Éloise realise they have to identify and confront the superweapon's smuggler in order to survive. But, when one by one their friends begin to betray them, their self-imposed mission transforms from difficult to near-impossible.

Sailor to a Siren is a great debut from Zoë Sumra and establishes her as a name to watch in epic space opera. These are stories that Zoë has been thinking about, preparing and crafting for many years; stories that deserve to be told, from a story-teller who deserves to be heard.

Zoë was born in London, but spent her later childhood living in Lancashire, where she started writing novels at the age of twelve due to extreme boredom. After completing the obligatory epic fantasy trilogy in her teens, she spent four years at the University of St Andrews, where she learnt to fence both foil and sabre and cemented her passion for space opera. She now lives in London with her husband and their daughter, and a collection of swords. When she's not writing or fencing, Zoë works as a print controller for an advertising company.

ISBN: 9781908168771 (epub, kindle)
ISBN: 9781908168672 (288pp paperback)

Visit bit.ly/SailorSiren

GLASS SHORE
STEFAN JACKSON

What if 'Think Differently' was more than a campaign slogan? What if it was part of a mind control network geared towards advanced sciences, creating a vibrant, creative and competitive workforce? This is the world of *Glass Shore*, a dynamic existence featuring fierce vehicles, cruel weapons and serious body augmentation.

Manhattan, 2076. The fabled city of gold realised; a city of dazzling buildings and beautiful people; a city celebrated for converting an obsolete subway system into an adult playground. Manhattanite Nikki's life changes forever when she finds the files labelled 'Project Blue Book appendix 63-A'. The report contains a disc related to the Glass Shore, the horrendous nuclear event at Puget Sound in 2062. Disclosure of these files is not an option, so powerful people want Nikki dead. To protect her Nikki hires Apollo, her long-time friend and lover, who is magnificent at his job. He is also a clothes whore with an honest enthusiasm for life.

Nikki and Apollo are the hottest couple in Manhattan. Betrayed by friends at every turn, set upon by bounty hunters and other elements of security, law enforcement and civil protection, they utilise the best hotels, the sexy Underground and the glorious city of Manhattan as their shield.

Stefan Jackson was born in North Carolina beside the calm eddies of the Trent and Neuse rivers, but spent the latter part of his childhood in southern California. In 1994 he moved to Brooklyn looking for a change, drawn to the energetic confluence of the Hudson and East rivers of the Big Bright City. There he met a lovely woman who became his wife, and they have an enchanting daughter. And a cat.

He now lives in Queens, where he writes stories, plays drums, coaches pee-wee girl's basketball, works the cubicle life, cooks breakfast, rides the F line, laughs and rests his head in the land of jazz.

Stefan says "Cheers to the first fifty years. Hoping the next fifty are just as kind."

ISBN: 9781908168580 (epub, kindle)
ISBN: 9781908168481 (288pp paperback)

Visit bit.ly/GlassShore

TimeStorm
Steve Harrison

In 1795 a convict ship leaves England for New South Wales in Australia. Nearing its destination, it encounters a savage storm but, miraculously, the battered ship stays afloat and limps into Sydney Harbour. The convicts rebel, overpower the crew and make their escape, destroying the ship in the process. Fleeing the sinking vessel with only the clothes on their backs, the survivors struggle ashore.

Among the escaped convicts, seething resentments fuel an appetite for brutal revenge against their former captors, while the crew attempts to track down and kill or recapture the escapees. However, it soon becomes apparent that both convicts and crew have more to concern them than shipwreck and a ruthless fight for survival; they have arrived in Sydney in 2017.

TimeStorm is a thrilling epic adventure story of revenge, survival and honour. In the literary footsteps of Hornblower, comes Lieutenant Christopher 'Kit' Blaney, an old-fashioned hero, a man of honour, duty and principle. But dragged into the 21st century... literally.

A great fan of the grand seafaring adventure fiction of CS Forester, Patrick O'Brien and Alexander Kent and modern action thriller writers like Lee Child, Steve Harrison combines several genres in his fast-paced debut novel as a group of desperate men from the 1700s clash in modern-day Sydney.

Steve Harrison was born in Yorkshire, England, grew up in Lancashire, migrated to New Zealand and eventually settled in Sydney, Australia, where he lives with his wife and daughter.

As he juggled careers in shipping, insurance, online gardening and the postal service, Steve wrote short stories, sports articles and a long running newspaper humour column called *HARRISCOPE: a mix of ancient wisdom and modern nonsense*. In recent years he has written a number of unproduced feature screenplays, although being unproduced was not the intention, and developed projects with producers in the US and UK. His script, *Sox*, was nominated for an Australian Writers' Guild 'Awgie' Award and he has written and produced three short films under his *Pronunciation Fillums* partnership. TimeStorm was Highly Commended in the Fellowship of Australian Writers (FAW) National Literary Awards for 2013.

ISBN: 9781908168542 (epub, kindle)
ISBN: 9781908168443 (368pp paperback)

Visit bit.ly/TimeStorm

About the author

A sharp dislike of anything to do with the outside has greatly complemented Jonathan Rivalland's intense desire to write novels and stories. Having finished his first book he is eagerly moving forward on to the other dozen or so titles that all deserve their turn (ability to complete them all in a standard lifetime notwithstanding). After incidentally being from South Africa, graduating university with majors in History and Psychology, moving to South Korea to teach ESL (and staying for four years), he moved to the US, where he primarily spends his time either writing or thinking about writing.

Reimar Breaking is both the beginning of a series (*The Iberan War*) as well as the first of a variety of titles, set in the same universe (*The Fourth World*), concerning an array of characters, locations, and events. None of these have any reliable completion dates because the author is vigorously allergic to deadlines.